LEGEND UNBOUND

MOLLY C. GROSS

AVALOON

ENERGY "MAGIC" RELEASED FROM
TWO
UNIVERSES COLLIDING
(THE BEGINNING OF LIFE)

THE PROTOGENOI
1ST GENERATION

CELESTIALS
2ND GENERATION

INCANTERS
3RD GENERATION

SEPARATION INTO VESTIGIUM
AND HAVCIRE

HUMANS
ABSOLUTELY NO MAGIC

*Distinguished by amount of energy absorbed from initial collision

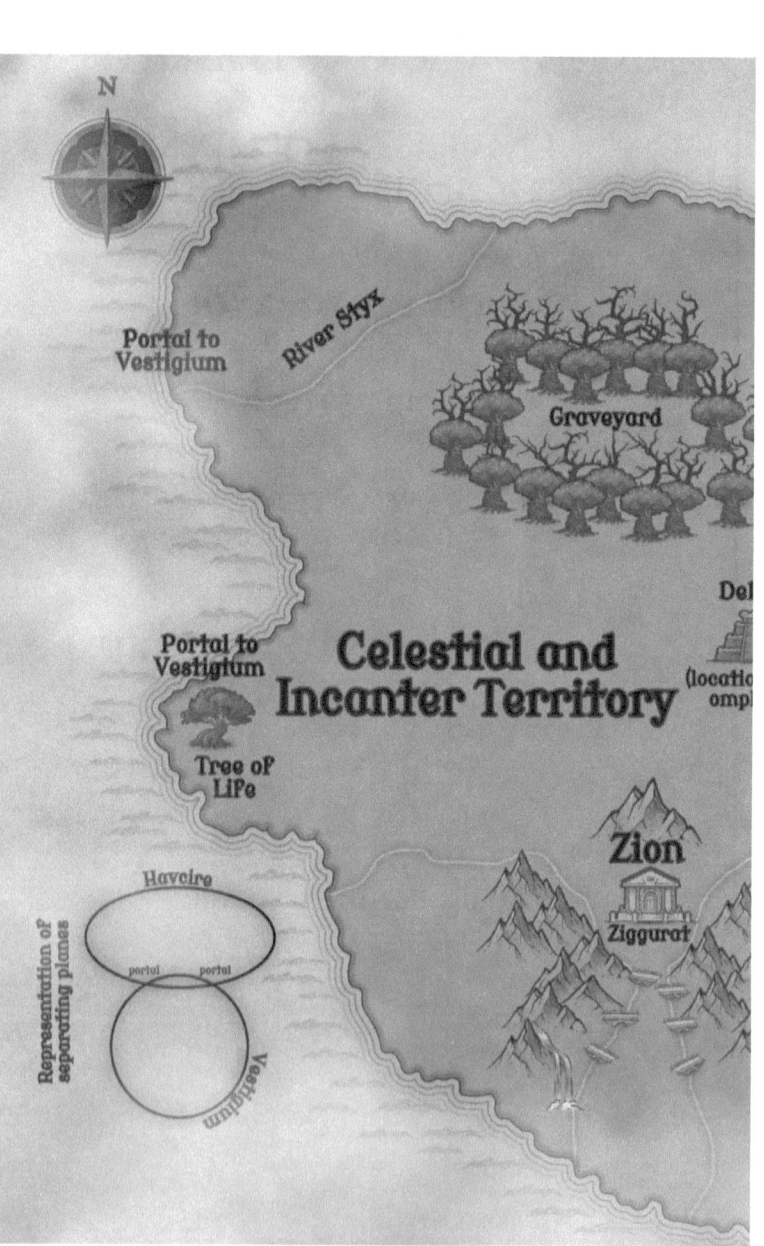

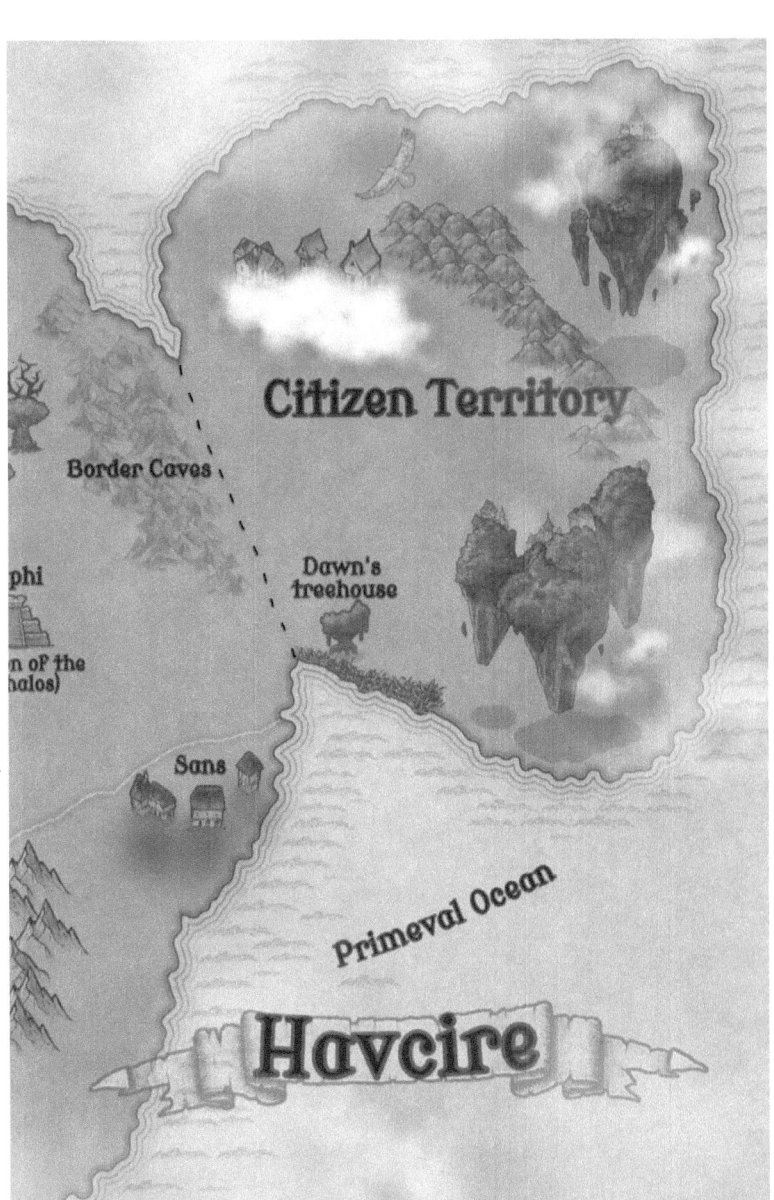

LONG AGO...

Before the world split and myth was born from history erased, there was a legend. It was a story told in excited, hushed tones amongst the Celestials and Incanters during the time of the Protogenoi's cruel rule. There was little reprieve to be had, for the Protogenoi controlled every aspect of the people's lives.

With a word, Dabar could change reality. With a twist of her wrist, Magister could make it so time moved to her will. With a look, Void could bring death to an immortal. With a thought, Maze could make a puppet of one's body with their mind. With all the disorder, Chaos thrived.

The legend I speak of told of a sixth Protogenoi kept hidden. Like the other Protogenoi, he had great power. However, from early on, he lived in secret beside the Celestials and Incanters, disguised as one of them. He was charged with keeping an eye on the people and was to report back to the Protogenoi if there was ever talk of rebellion.

The sixth Protogenoi saw what it was like to live in the world the other Protogenoi crafted and grew sympathetic to the Celestials and Incanters. When the first sparks of rebellion ignited, he not only failed to report to the other Protogenoi, but he fanned the flame. And when the war waged, he took up arms against his fellow Protogenoi.

The Protogenoi had called him by the name Nephil. Fallen. Pretending to be less than, a Celestial or Incanter, was like falling, or so they believed. In the end, the Protogenoi realized with bitterness that he had lived up to the name, choosing to fall and place himself side by side with the Celestials and Incanters so that they could rise together against the other Protogenoi.

The truth of this legend was never validated. Perhaps, like many stories, it was fabricated to inspire hope in hard times. A selfless hero of great power who would come to everyone's rescue, risking everything he had to help those less powerful, who cared so little for said power that he gave it up in the end to better live out life hidden among those he saw as just as worthy of living as any Protogenoi.

There is no sixth Protogenoi. Nephil was merely a symbol to bring the people to action.

Or, maybe, I personally can attest that every word was true.

CHAPTER ONE

The yoga instructor's voice fills the room, stemming from Gene's computer atop her desk. The instructor sounds like she's seconds away from sleep, each word coming out like a sigh, meant to bring serenity to those listening.

It is quite relaxing, or it would be if my arms weren't still sore from the drills Minerva forced me through yesterday. If I'm told to get into Downward Dog one more time, I'm going to find Ms. Serene Voice and break every single one of her limbs so she can never do Downward Dog again.

Or, I'll just collapse.

Why is it that seventy percent of every yoga video involves Downward Dog when there are loads of other poses? I like the ones where I get to rest my head on the floor. Any way works. My forehead can be on the floor, the back of my head, side. I'm not picky.

"And now we flow into Downward Dog," her voice says, and there she's done it.

I attempt it even though my whole body protests, and my right elbow gives up under my weight.

"I'm gonna skip ahead, if that's alright," I tell my parents.

"Haley!" Harry shouts.

This can't be stopped. I fall slowly, sloth-speed, but the floor is coming for me all the same. My body isn't even able to manage falling fast, my muscles too tired to rip off the proverbial bandaid. As I lay down, their protests rise above the yoga instructor's calming voice.

"No, do not pull the Shavasana move," Gene warns.

"Don't do it."

"It's inevitable," I manage on an exhale.

And... I'm on the floor.

I turn my head to the side, where their yoga mats are laid out, and shoot them a sheepish smile. Gene, next to me, drops her head down, her brown hair falling forward into her face. She shakes it in exaggerated mock disapproval of my failure.

"Fine," Harry relents, rolling his eyes at me. "If you're going to just lay there, then tell us more about how your first semester at your new school was."

"Okay," I agree, automatically.

Let's see, what can I tell them? I look around Gene's office as I think. It makes for a pretty good makeshift yoga studio. There's nice, natural light coming in from the large window behind us, and there's plenty of space between her heavy-looking, wood desk and the window for our mats.

It's become tradition for me to visit from my new prestigious "boarding school" once a month for lunch and sometimes yoga also to help with digestion, or so Gene and Harry claim it does, as does the title of the YouTube video.

Ironically, now that I live out of the house, I actually see Gene and Harry more often.

It didn't seem right to kill off Haley Dawson of this most recent life of mine, Life Twenty-Seven. For one, I'm still alive, despite Chaos's best efforts. Thanks, bio-magic mom. I neither miss you nor love you. Respectfully, do not RIP.

Two, Gene and Harry would have been the only ones to notice or care about my death, and I couldn't do that to them. They were busy and mostly absent parents, but they are good and nice people.

With Max's manipulations out of the equation, they opened up their own law practice, Dawson and Dawson. They're still extremely busy, but they make their own hours now. Since their schedule is more flexible, I make sure to visit once a month. After all, everyone has to make time to eat.

As for me, they believe I got a scholarship to this boarding school in Manhattan. I am not living in Manhattan. I also am not at a boarding school. So, back to the question at hand. What can I tell them?

"First semester was good."

I push myself up into a seated position.

"Your arms are all muscle," Gene says, as they switch to a new pose and, along with it, a new topic, thankfully saving me from having to come up with anything more to say about school. "How do you not kick both our butts at yoga?"

I glance down at my arms, as if they've only just now appeared as part of my body, considering them. They have toned up nicely since I took up training with Minerva again. Despite the almost constant soreness, I was the one who suggested she train with me. Not only is it necessary because of whenever these Protogenoi decide to show their faces, but it is also an efficient method to clear my head, and there's a lot my head needs clearing of these days.

"I didn't realize yoga was something to kick butt at," I tell Gene, and then shrug nonchalantly. "My arms are tired from..." holding them up in the air for hours on end practicing to use my magical power? "...tennis," I finish, remembering I had mentioned I'd started playing. Apparently, it's required to take part in an extracurricular activity at my new school.

I try to keep what I tell Harry and Gene as close to the truth as possible, but it's not exactly possible, which is not ideal. Who hates liars? Me! What am I? A liar. Boo.

Since Chaos left us with her cryptic warning and we found the rest of the prophecy essentially confirming that cryptic warning, about five months have passed with no sign of the other Protogenoi. That's been five months of revamping the Subject

System, overseeing the new Subject System, and researching this unknown threat.

Lada has actually taken on much of the research, which she never fails to complain about.

Anyway, it's meant five visits with Harry and Gene where I had to search my mind for truths that wouldn't reveal the fact that I am living in a hidden, magical world rather than at a boarding school.

"I told you about Sin, didn't I?" I ask, finally thinking of a somewhat safe subject, something real I can share with them.

Shifting into the Warrior Two pose, Gene faces me with a smile.

"You did," she says.

"Sin," Harry says, as if feeling out the word. "Sin? Sin." He says the name the last time with recognition.

"Her *friend*, Harry."

"Yes, Gene, I remember now."

"Why do you say it like that?" I ask. "He *is* my friend. He helped me adjust to the school."

Actually, to accepting myself as a Protogenoi. It was weird, even after everything, to get over that fact. Sure, I am also very much human, but my powers make me a Protogenoi, as in the group of people known for their crazy and cruel rule of Havcire back in archaic times. It's not a great association.

I remember one of the first things Sin said to me: "No one ever really knows who or what they are. If you don't, you're far from being alone. Humans as a whole don't know that their ancestors were capable of magic, and that's part of their history as a people."

So, maybe acceptance is a bit of a stretch. But, I accept that I'm just as confused as the majority of people, and I'm good with that.

Sure, I spent multiple lives with a different identity in each one, only to be told by Max that no matter what environment I was born into, I had strong tendencies to be exactly the same person. I may have been trapped in a rigged psychological experiment, but at least I was confident in who I was then.

Is it strange that now, for the first time, when I know the truth of exactly what I am, I can't make sense of who I am? Nope. Apparently, according to Sin, that's normal.

I am normal. Yay.

It doesn't make me at all uneasy that the source of the magic that flows through my veins comes from the same group of beings who all were equally horrible and terrorized the whole rest of the population. That's just a tiny bit of me. I can figure out how that bit meshes with all the other bits of me as I go. But, for now, confusion is completely normal, and I am good.

"An odd name," Harry says, as he did the last time I brought Sin up. I try to hide my smile at the repeating topic. "Where's it from?"

"It was the name of the ancient Babylonian god of the moon," I answer, *honestly*.

"Oh, right," Harry says, "the one associated with justice. Does he want to go into law?"

Actually, he currently has a job, and it involves overseeing a fairly unruly group.

The Council has him keeping an eye on Phoenix, Dex, Lada, and me. The rest aren't so happy about it, but I'm just glad the spying is taking place out in the open this time. Plus, I trust Sin. He didn't waste any time opening up to me about the fact that he was the reason I was practically invisible during my twenty-seventh life here.

Sin agreed to help Max with his experiments, me being one of those experiments. Sin has a certain power over people's emotions. He can't control minds, but he can interpret and influence emotions.

Apparently, indifference is what my fellow classmates felt whenever they crossed my path. It wasn't so much that they didn't notice me as much as they just didn't care. I was just below the threshold that would have allowed for the acknowledgment of my existence, thanks to Sin.

My point is, though, he didn't have to admit to any of that, but he did.

"Not really," I answer Harry. "By the way, how did that case of yours turn out? The one with the cyberbullying?" I ask, bringing the conversation away from me and my life.

"We got her off," Gene responds, proudly. "Some hours of community service but that was all. The expert witness worked wonders, supporting our defense that the diary entries were cathartic and not a real threat. After all, it was the other girl that released them publicly, not our defendant."

The virtual yoga instructor announces that we should make our way into Shavasana. I uncross my legs and lie back down with a loud sigh.

"What a relief," I say, spreading my arms out to my side.

"Yes, you really worked hard," Gene says sarcastically, as she and Harry lie down on their respective mats.

"*You're needed in the lab.*"

Sin's all-business voice speaks inside my head.

Oh yeah, he's also telepathic. It's a handy little ability that allows us all to communicate. He does this thing where it's like creating an open channel between the five of us, as we are rarely in the same place - Lada researching, Dex playing guardian angel for Subjects, me directing from Max's lab (usually), and Phoenix... who knows where.

Phoenix is supposed to be the one who checks in with the Council about our progress, which I believe he is doing presently.

"*Good morning to you, too, Sin.*"

Knowing whatever I'm needed for must be of some urgency, I don't waste any time getting up, springing off my hands behind my head to jump up to my feet.

When I turn to say goodbye to Gene and Harry, I'm met with stunned expressions. Oops. Minerva never should have taught me how to do a kip-up. I knew I'd get carried away with it.

"Where'd you learn to do that?" Harry asks.

"*It's afternoon, Dawn.*"

I work to keep my expression neutral from Sin's dry response and focus on thinking up an explanation for Gene and Harry.

"I watch the karate team practice sometimes at school. I picked up a few things."

They look skeptical for a moment more before...

"That's cool, honey," Gene says with a smile, accepting that as a reasonable explanation. "Maybe you should look into joining."

"I don't know. Tennis keeps me busy." And the lie just slips right on out. "I'm gonna get going and let you guys get back to work. I'll see you soon," I say, bending down to give them both quick hugs.

They say their goodbyes, and I keep a smile on my face as I wave goodbye, but my mind is already elsewhere as I walk out of Gene's office and out to the parking lot outside the building.

"*Am I connected to Phoenix?*"

"*Always,*" I hear Phoenix's voice respond in my head and can practically see the wink that accompanies it. "*By the heartstrings.*"

"*I forgot to tell you I cut those a while back?*"

My intact heartstrings work to prove me wrong. Hearing his voice alone causes a twinge in my chest.

"*They replenish each life so you should be good again,*" his response comes, which I actually laugh at, but only because he's not here to catch me.

I miss him, and it's pathetic.

We've both been busy lately. It's been rare that we've spent time alone since the day we faced Chaos and he showed me the previously hidden part of the prophecy. Still, I see him a good amount. Maybe not as much as the others. But, he's been around whenever any of us needed him, helping Lada with research and Dex and me with the Subject System.

From what I've heard, he's done a good job reporting to the Council. Actually, it's more accurately what I haven't heard, which is the good sign. The Council hasn't complained much about him over the past months.

Maybe it's not missing him that I feel, but just some odd guilt for being the reason there's been distance between us, even when he is near. I made it pretty clear I still don't trust him.

And then there was Sin, who Phoenix noticed I did openly trust. Except, I have reason to trust Sin and plenty of reason to be wary of Phoenix.

Also, keeping Phoenix held to the vow I had him make to me back before we got our memories returned has added to some of the strain. "I promise to honestly inform you about every little thing from now on."

If I really wanted to show him that I was ready to begin trusting him, I'd release him from the vow. Maybe I will. Maybe.

But, if it's really guilt I feel over creating the distance between us, then why do I *want* to be with him? I shouldn't want to be around anyone as much as I want to be with him. Which is why, I need to be creating some distance.

Maybe it's growing pains? I simply need to adjust to not having Phoenix around.

"*Think of Max's lab. Ready?*" Phoenix asks.

Can't exactly make that adjustment when he's literally in my head.

I do what he says. I think of the lab. It's much more crowded than it used to be, with the added number of computers and desks. It looks more like the headquarters of a government agency than a scientist's lab these days. In fact, the only thing that looks exactly the same anymore is the tub in the center of the large room.

Real glad that's still there.

We basically commandeered Max's lab. He still uses it, but he sticks to his one desk and computer to record the data from his Subjects. He was quick to agree to the arrangement, having held onto his guilt over aiding Chaos for so long.

At this point, however, it's pretty clear that the well of guilt that motivated him to be helpful has run dry. He no longer hides the fact that he doesn't appreciate us in his space.

"*Ready.*"

The world blurs, seeming to speed by even though I'm standing in place. The cars in the lot blend into one, colors flashing and combining. The trees become indistinguishable from the street lamps and the ground indistinguishable from the sky. I shut my eyes. There's a second where I can no longer breathe but I barely notice it anymore. The ground is gone, and then it's solid, back under my feet.

I open my eyes to find Max's lab.

CHAPTER TWO

Turns out, another fun thing about Phoenix's powers is that he can teleport people from one place to another without actually being with them, just as he does with objects. However, it only works if the person imagines where it is they're going beforehand. Phoenix needs to be thinking of the same place at the same time, or else things could get messy.

So far, it's been working pretty well for us. No casualties yet. I don't even experience side effects from the teleportation anymore.

When I questioned why he hadn't shared before that he was capable of such a thing, I got some vague answer about it simply never having come up. It seems quite impossible to me that after the length of time I've known him, there wasn't one moment where it would have been relevant to mention such an aspect of his power.

But, what do I know? Apparently, nothing from Phoenix unless I question him directly on a subject. Although, to be fair, that's not exactly true. I remember times, back when I was a Citizen, that Phoenix treated me like a partner in crime and did tell me everything. I traveled all throughout Havcire because of him, whereas most Citizens stay in their designated areas.

While Minerva was the one to teach me about Havcire, its people and history, Phoenix told me about Vest so I'd know about the world from which I came, even if I'd only had the chance to live there for days. He told me the truth, or at least what we all had believed was the truth, about how I'd died, even when the others, Barnabas, Lucifer, and Minerva, thought I shouldn't hear it.

He *was* honest with me, and I handled the truth. My own mother had killed me, but I was my own person. It didn't matter what I'd thought my mother had done. I didn't even remember her, so how much of an impact could she really have possibly had on who I was?

None, I had thought, and it was Phoenix who also helped me feel confident in that. I remember how my doubts had spurred him into telling me how I got my name.

Dawn, the name I've carried with me life after life, wasn't given to me by my mother. In a rare occurrence, the Council members agreed on something. They named me because they decided, when I showed up in Havcire, that it would be a beginning rather than an end for me, that my life would start there. Phoenix insisted that meant that it would be in my power to always choose how I wanted to live, who I wanted to be.

But, that was all before I went through Max's experiment and learned from him that I am heavily influenced by my DNA, my nature. So, good thing I was wrong about my biological mother having a mental break and killing me. It was just the Protogenoi who took over her body that killed me.

Point is, it never came up that Phoenix could teleport a whole person, actually multiple people, without even being near them. He's like a *Star Trek* transporter, beaming people up here and there.

I look around, quickly scanning the computer monitors that run the length of every wall of the lab now, each one containing information on a different Subject. I find the one that stands out. It helps that it's bordered in alarming red.

Besides fixing the Subject System so that negative actions were no longer given much more weight than positive actions, as Chaos had unfairly arranged for the system to function, I also had to set up certain guidelines for the Experimenters to follow.

The new rule that seems to cause the most problems these days is: "No manipulation made in the lives of Subjects can result in the endangerment of a human."

It's not that the Experimenters mean for their tweaks to cause harm. It's more that they just amazingly, absolutely suck at foreseeing such consequences. Hence, the need for our ongoing role in keeping an eye on the Subjects.

Guardian angels, as Dex likes to call us.

"Yoga, again?" Sin asks, as I come to stand beside him, in front of the screen with the flashing, red border.

He's eyeing my outfit.

I tighten my high ponytail self-consciously, as I look down at my neon blue tank top and black leggings. It's not like we have a dress code.

I thought when Dex dropped the facade of Poindexter and we learned that he much prefers graphic tees to suits, we'd all happily adopt the casual work environment. But, turns out, Sin shares Poindexter's sense of style.

Sin swipes the red bordered screen to view more information about the problem Subject.

"I'm not the one who looks like an FBI agent and makes my minions dress the same as me."

Sin wears a blue button-down shirt, that brings out the light blue in his gray eyes, and black dress pants, which the shirt is neatly tucked into.

I glance over to the opposite wall where another Celestial stands keeping an eye on the rest of the monitors. He wears almost an identical outfit to Sin but his shirt is white, unsurprisingly the color most common of Celestials.

Briefly, I imagine the two of them approaching a Subject on Vest and flashing their badges before announcing stone-faced that they're FBI and there to inform the Subject about a whole new world. And then, they break out into the song from *Aladdin*. Once that beautiful song is complete, they pull out the flashy memory wiping things from *Men In Black* and erase the Subject's memory, and it's a gosh darn shame no one is there to remember the one of a kind performance.

"It's called being professional," Sin responds.

Despite the clear implication that I am the opposite of professional, Sin's voice, per usual, remains monotone without any hint of disapproval. The Celestial's incapable of judgment, I swear, which is ironic considering his namesake is associated with justice. The correct way to describe Sin would be a fair judge, with not a single judgy bone in his body.

Then again, sometimes I think the reason for his lack of emoting has more to do with the fact that he feels *too* much, seeing as his power involves being able to sense other's emotions. It must get confusing to have other emotions, as well as your own, swimming around in your brain. And, I suspect it's easier to just numb all of the above sometimes, hence the monotone.

The screen above our heads (well, above my shortass head) reads the name of the Subject: Daniel Hill. It also provides the name of the Experimenter: Ian Jeffreys. And, the title of the experiment: Dreamcatcher.

"At the initial alert, we sent Dex down to watch over Daniel. Ian's experiment aims to discover why people dream by testing what happens to people when they are unable to experience their dreams."

How logical. I was wondering recently why exactly we need food and water so I decided to do an experiment where I didn't allow my friend to have food or water for days. Guess what happened? I found out we need food and water to survive.

"He uses specially spelled dreamcatchers to not only capture and record bad dreams, but all dreams, and then he observes how his Subjects act. Daniel has been showing a lack of impulse control and problem solving skills," Sin explains.

"Shocking," I say, sarcastically.

I'm starting to think I need to personally review every single experiment. I could have guessed this one wouldn't hold up to our new Subject System code of ethics.

"How is everyone doing today?"

Dex's voice echoes within my head.

"Please tell me someone's dying so I can get a break from this research," Lada responds in a matter of seconds.

I've noticed when Dex is in the picture, she's never far behind, despite not being what I would classify exactly as a team player. Then again, none of us really are. Except Dex.

"Tact, Lada, ever heard of it?" Phoenix chimes in. *"Although, I wouldn't mind an excuse to get out of this Council meeting. And hi, Dex. How are you?"*

"See, Sin. Dex knows how to kindly start an invasive telepathic conversation."

"Well, since you ask," Dex continues, *"I know I'm great at secretly watching the Subjects here on Vest since Bishop went AWOL, but I'm pretty useless without someone to siphon a power from so I could use*

some assistance in preventing a couple of humans from dying right about now."

Sin crosses his arms against his broad chest and gives me a look that says everything.

"So, he could have led with that," I admit.

Sin doesn't bother to reply, just stares at me expectantly. He's a Celestial of few words, but he really does know how to get a message across.

It's my job to get things done at the end of the day. I'm the one who agreed to take control of the Subject System. The rest just agreed to help, some of their reasoning more clear than others but, whatever that reasoning was, it's not their job to make sure this new Subject System is successful. It's mine.

"Phoenix, get me to Dex."

Not a second after the order is given, Phoenix and Lada are in the lab, standing behind Sin and me.

Although he just came from a meeting with the Council, Phoenix is nowhere near as professional looking as Sin. He's dressed in a plain white, v-neck t-shirt that shows off his muscled arms, not to mention a hint of his just as muscled chest with that v, and a pair of faded jeans. His brown, wavy hair is mussed from the teleportation, sweeping down over his dark eyebrow, masking the scar I know is there.

I take a step back before I can think about it, which of course he clocks, his eyes following the movement even if they don't show any reaction to it.

Seriously, what's wrong with me? Throw me in front of some big bad monster, and I'll run toward it. Have Phoenix pop up in front of me, and I'll stumble back, afraid some other, stronger force might push me toward him.

It doesn't matter how long I've known him, my body still reacts like it's got a mind of its own every time I find myself near him. Maybe if I just— No. I can't consider that.

But, maybe if I just did... then things wouldn't be this tense? I could move on? Move on to what, though? What if I don't want to move anywhere?

Despite the trip through space, Lada looks flawless, not a piece of golden hair out of place. Even her straight bangs are perfectly aligned across her forehead. She looks relaxed, most likely just happy to be away from the loads of books that take up most her time these days.

Sin adjusts the display on the red-bordered screen so that it shows a map of the world, a red dot highlighting Daniel's location.

Phoenix observes the map quickly and nods his head succinctly. I look to see for myself where it is we're headed but Sin clears his throat loudly. It has the same effect as Barnabas's booming voice. It makes you want to drop whatever you were doing to listen up.

"It's not necessary for you all to go," he says.

Lada places her hand on top of Phoenix's shoulder, smiling all the while, making it clear that she will be going.

Phoenix stares down Sin.

I open my mouth to suggest that I can advise on the situation from here but Phoenix reaches out and grabs my hand, that one touch sending a traitorous thrill through me. He pulls me toward him and Lada. Instead of words, a startled gasp escapes my mouth.

"The more the merrier," Phoenix says, and then we're gone.

It's not the first time I've felt like the rope in a game of tug of war. I have to admit that I did want to come along and make sure in person that everything was handled. Regardless, the thing between Phoenix and Sin has less to do with me and more to do with their conflicting personalities in general. I'm just the "boss" who needs them to work with each other.

Still, I can't help but think about how Gene called Sin my friend, with that weird emphasis on the word. That means very little, though. Gene, in her motherly way, is always looking for romance in my life where there is none.

My feet have barely touched solid ground again before Sin's voice is back in my head.

"Daniel, the Subject, mentally unraveled this morning when he had to choose an outfit for the day. The lack of dreams has severely compromised his reasoning."

Phoenix brought us right to Dex, who stands about two feet to my right. From the looks of the others, they're also listening to the briefing we didn't get the chance to have in person because of *someone* being in such a rush to leave.

"*His response to this frustration was to destroy his bedroom, which included the spelled dreamcatcher in there.*"

"For safety reasons, we're supposed to be briefed before we're on location," I tell Phoenix pointedly.

"I'll keep you safe. That is, if you let me near you."

My gaze snaps to his, which looks back at me in challenge. As if I need safekeeping. Also, I thought we had an unspoken agreement not to speak about this. He actually looks irritated with me, like me taking that step back was the last straw to break whatever truce it was we had going on.

It was working, as in we were able to work together. He was giving me my space so I could figure things out, and I was keeping my space.

"I'd let you sweep me off my feet and carry me around like a damsel for a day if you'd learn to follow a single rule."

"Don't tempt me," he fires back.

"To actually do your job correctly?"

"To get to carry you around," he says, and we're back to his senseless flirting, the type that doesn't need to mean anything because it's nothing special. It's just how he is. It means he won't push me to talk about anything that could mean something.

"What about when the damsel needs to take care of business?" he goes on, lips quirking into a smile. "Do I get to carry her to the bathroom, as well? All the way to the toilet?"

"You can't let go the whole day."

"Sounds lovely. I'll never let go, Rose."

Lada pushes away from us and outright groans. "You two make me miserable. I'm trying to vacation here."

"*Attention, please,*" Sin says, realizing he lost us at some point.

I notice where it is that we are. Even focused on Sin, I hear the familiar sounds of the place. There's the creaking of metal on metal, the cacophony of numerous voices talking simultaneously, and the intermittent screams.

We stand on a small bridge, the large green Hulk rollercoaster looping around high above our heads. Crowds of people part around us automatically, paying us no attention as they focus on what ride they're headed to next.

With all the commotion, it's difficult to tell if there's anything out of the ordinary or any real danger here. It, oddly, doesn't seem like that long ago that I was here. It was only my last life, Life Twenty-Six, that I lived in Florida. It was fairly normal for my family to take trips to Universal.

This visit is, without question, very different from any of those other visits. For one, we didn't have to pay for admission. But, I don't imagine we'll be hopping on any rides.

"The broken dreamcatcher released Daniel's most recently recorded dreams. He's at your current location with, according to Dex—"

"According to me," Dex continues, *"the dreams have not returned to Daniel, but he's transmitting them to random people he comes into contact with here, and it's starting to cause some major issues."*

Before I can question what exactly that means, as if summoned by Dex's comment, there's a large, out of the ordinary, crashing sound.

Reflexively, I step further away from the origin of the sound, bumping into Phoenix. There goes my fought for personal space. He doesn't react, focused on something else. He points. Rather than the usual metallic sounds of the rollercoasters, this sounded more like a crunch, which explains the completely flattened garbage bin Phoenix is indicating.

A entirely different kind of screaming begins as the people near the previously whole garbage bin rush to back away. And, rightfully so, as a huge, red spider stands before them, one leg still on top of the crushed garbage.

CHAPTER THREE

When I say huge, I mean this spider is at least two stories high. Its legs spread out to cover twenty feet of space, some of which is currently occupied by startled looking people. Except, they don't look up at the body of the spider above them or run away. Instead, they look around frantically in confusion.

They can't see it.

"Run!" a young girl shouts, pausing in her own attempt to escape to look back at the other people still in close proximity to the spider.

She, unlike the rest, has somewhere to direct her fear. Her eyes focus right in on the spider.

"What is going on?" Dex asks no one in particular.

"I thought you were supposed to know," Lada responds.

"I did my briefing duties. I gave you the whole forest. I'm just asking for the tree, the tree being the reason that garbage can got crushed like Big Mario stomped on it."

"I got the forest metaphor, and I'd happily give you a tree if I didn't just come from my head buried in a book full of more completely useless information, but Big Mario?"

"Oh, Lada," Dex says, sounding completely devastated, and yet excited at the same time. "I haven't yet introduced you to the Vest world of video gaming, but we will get there."

I spare a glance back at them, fearing we're getting a little sidetracked. What else is new? I peel my eyes away from the spider, which remains still, at least for the moment. I fear it'll take on a sudden burst of unnatural speed and race right at me on those numerous legs.

"Daniel must have infected her with one of his dreams, and only she can see what it is," Phoenix says, watching the young girl as she continues to attempt to warn everyone else about the spider, her blonde hair whipping around her violently as she turns from person to person.

Every single one of them is tense, ready to make a run for it, knowing there is a danger. And yet, they don't listen to her, not willing to trust a stranger in the haze of their own fear.

"Except, I can see it, too," I tell them, and turn to get a better look at the spider. It doesn't resemble just any spider blown up to a monstrous size. It's not fully solid, the red I mistook for its coloring actually something else entirely. Its whole body is made up of energy, sparking with a very familiar, red power.

Of course.

"It's made from chaotic energy," I explain.

If the human brain is full of chaotic actions and reactions and dreams are powered by the mind, then any product of those dreams would be chaos.

"What's going on then? What does she see?" Lada asks, looking worriedly after the girl.

"Nothing. I mean, I can see a gigantic spider with one foot on top of the smashed garbage, but it's just standing there," I answer, watching the spider wearily.

"Why is it that monsters in dreams just stop sometimes? Have you noticed that, too?" Dex asks, sounding genuinely curious, while following my gaze to focus inquisitively on something he can't see.

"It wants her sense of hopelessness to build, to see that all those people she's trying to warn won't come around, and they also won't be of any help to her, either. She's on her own," Phoenix answers, and I turn around to face him, lifting my eyebrows skeptically.

He's not looking at me, though. He watches the girl slowly back away from the spider. She's no longer screaming at the other people to run, but she's also not running herself.

"When did you become such the dream expert?" I ask him.

"It's just what I would do." The seriousness has gone from his expression. He turns back to face me with a nonchalant shrug.

"What? If you were a giant, nightmarish spider?"

"Exactly."

"Right, naturally."

"Why is no one listening to me?"

The girl's frustrated and panicked words travel to us even though she says them in a hushed voice, a benefit of supernatural hearing.

Like a spell broken, the spider reawakens, focusing in on the girl. It lifts one of its legs to close the distance between itself and the girl, as the leg opposite the one that crashed into the trash threatens to come down on an oblivious bystander.

I reach my arms out above my head, palms up, as if the spider's ginormous leg were about to come down right on me rather than a distance away on a stranger, and push up. My own chaotic, golden energy pulses upwards from my palms and appears across the distance, manifesting as a shield above the bystander's head, preventing the spider's leg from coming down.

The guy keeps running, too busy running to notice the crackling golden shield that sprung up right above his head. He gets out of harm's way, saving me from expending energy on keeping that shield in place.

The spider stumbles for a moment, its leg unexpectedly meeting resistance, having tripped on the now disappeared barrier. But, it merely regains its balance and continues on, and there are plenty of other people in its path if it is to catch up to the girl, who has sped up her retreat.

I run toward the spider, creating more small shields as I go whenever a person comes in danger of being crushed under the weight of one of the spider's legs. It works, but the spider still stumbles along, stepping around my shields and, therefore, the people, as it gains on the girl it continues to haunt.

"If the dreams manifest as chaotic energy, then Dawn can absorb it, erasing the figments." Sin's voice is back in our heads, consulting from safety, where I also could have stayed as he'd suggested.

The spider is nearly to the girl now. Between the running and the need to continue making barriers to shield the surrounding people, my breath is struggling to come out evenly. I know if the spider makes it to the girl, I won't be able to hold the shield for forever. We will need a better solution than playing defense.

Still, I can't agree to Sin's plan.

"That's not my energy to take. These dreams belong to Daniel. I don't steal."

Chaos stole.

Sin's response comes fast.

"Even if it means saving these people's lives?"

"Dawn can return the energy to Daniel if we find him, a transfer rather than absorbing it herself," Phoenix suggests.

I feel a second of gratitude for the solution before I realize, at this speed, I'm not going to make it to the girl on time.

I could put up another shield from a distance, like I've been doing to protect the others, but the spider is after her. It won't just move once it has her right beneath it. It will fight. I need to be with her, at her side, to combat whatever the spider does when it realizes something is directly in its way of getting to its target.

Screw it. There was little chance we were going to make it through this without revealing ourselves. We'll just have to cover our tracks after the fact.

The spider is two steps away from being on top of the girl, and I push myself forward with my full speed, blurring past the people around me.

The girl, realizing she won't make it, crouches down and throws her arms up above her head in an attempt to provide herself with some defense as the spider's leg bears down on her.

I throw myself down, ducking under the leg, and slide to a stop beside the girl, my arms coming up to form the shield a second before we both meet the same fate as the garbage can. The girl stops mid-scream to stare at me with wide, green eyes that threaten to spill tears. She looks to be about Daniel's age, sixteen, the age I still appear as, as well. It's possible that she's a friend he came here with. It would make sense that his dreams would latch onto those closest to him. That is, if it spreads like a contagion.

The girl shifts between frantically looking at the spider's leg and my shield of golden energy that keeps us from being crushed.

Her panic and confusion are completely understandable. The spider is not letting up on her, its leg continuing to try to force the shield. My shield.

"*Help!*" I shout internally, but force a smile onto my face as I face the girl, keeping my arms, which are beginning to shake from the strain, up above my head.

"What's your name?" I ask her.

I'm not great with friendly conversation under non-stressful situations. I don't know what I think I'm doing right now. Panicking, probably. Trying to distract her from the life-threatening circumstances.

Maybe I should have tried to keep this shield up from a distance rather than run full speed into social interaction.

She looks almost more surprised that I've spoken to her than by the fact that there's an outrageously large spider attacking her at the moment. I think it's actually the shock that has her choking out the answer to my question.

"Emily," she says, at about the same time Phoenix teleports to my side, earning a short scream, practically a squeak, from Emily.

"Hi, Emily," he says, all comforting and charming, the casual smile on his face looking like a sin.

Despite the life threat, Emily is totally checking him out.

I want to roll my eyes at him.

"No need to worry," he assures her. "Dawn here may look small but she could keep this shield up all day. Look at this strong, wittle muscle."

I'm not sure whether it's the baby voice or the fact that Phoenix pinches my bicep that is actually straining to keep this shield up right now that makes me want to transform said shield into a hammer and just lightly bonk him on the head with it.

I want to sag my whole body and look at him in a way that says, "Are you fucking for real right now?" But, then this shield would come down and that'd be the last thing I did.

I want to kiss him. Nope. Not that last one. I'm under duress here.

Emily seems to relax at the mere words uttered from his mouth, even managing a smile. Of course, what's a gigantic spider when suddenly a cute guy appears by your side to save the day? Forget the fact that it's my body about to give up on me from the effort of keeping this shield up as this monstrous spider continues to slam not one, but two of its legs down on it.

Honestly, I get it, Emily. No judgment here.

"Get us out of here," I tell Phoenix, grinding the words out through the exertion.

Phoenix grabs onto both our arms, and I'm able to drop the shield as we disappear from existence, only to pop up on the other side of the bridge we'd been standing on before.

Emily doesn't take her first teleportation so smoothly. I lunge quick to pull her hair back from her face, as she leans over to throw up.

I don't see Dex and Lada, and I've no idea where it is they've gone to. The spider, on the other hand, is in the same spot on the other side of the bridge. It's too big to use the bridge so the only way for it to get across to us is through the water.

Question is, does this spider like water?

"Dawn, is it possible to share a little mental map of this place with us?"

"I'm a little busy, Dex."

"Hold up," Lada says, halting Dex by grabbing onto his arm. He stops, staring down at that point of contact like Lada's hand was coated in liquid nitrogen and she's got him frozen in place forever.

"I heard him again," Lada goes on, focusing on something out of sight.

Dex mentally slaps himself and refocuses, lightly pulling his arm out of Lada's grip, but staying in place otherwise. She shows no sign of noticing or caring one way or another.

Lada looks off to the side of the main path she and Dex stand on. A few people walk by them, heading back in the direction of the spider.

"Hey!" Dex calls out to them.

They stop and look back at him expectantly, but Dex doesn't miss a beat. He points in the opposite direction, motioning them onward.

"We just came from that way. That part of the park is temporarily closed," he explains.

After some mumbled thanks and exclamations of disappointment, the group moves on in the direction Dex indicated.

"Oh no," Lada says.

She's staring at the sign above the line for the ride closest to them. It reads "Jurassic Park River Adventure."

"Probably best to avoid alarming, uninformative statements like 'oh no' when we're on a mission that's already a mess," Dex says, turning his attention back to her. "What is it? The guy you heard?"

Lada grimaces and starts making her way through the line for the ride, which is empty. Dex follows, as she takes shortcuts through the line, hopping over and ducking under logs of wood that make the line for the ride longer and more winding than they have the time for.

"Yeah, he's in trouble. More importantly, this is a water ride. I really hope we don't have to get wet," Lada answers in a whine, managing somehow to make it sound not irritating.

"Shoot," Dex says, as he vaults over another wooden log. "I knew I was forgetting something when we left. The ponchos."

Lada laughs, smiling back at Dex, as she approaches the boy working the front of the line. As she turns away from Dex, she seems to shine even brighter than usual, immediately capturing the full attention of the boy manning the rafts for the ride. He returns her smile, a blush spreading across his freckled cheeks.

"Excuse us," Lada says, the full force of her persuasion power clear in the singsong quality of her voice, "we need to pass by here."

"Enjoy the ride," the boy says easily, as he watches Dex and Lada clearly not get in the raft lined up and, instead, walk directly through the gate that says the area beyond is for staff only.

Dex and Lada run along the narrow, stoned passageway that runs alongside the "river," where the automated dinosaurs bathe. They come across a grassy area, where others are planted in the ground, their heads moving to make them look alive to those passing in the rafts. Or, well, alive enough for the suspension of belief needed for such a ride.

They spot the raft filled with people further ahead, heading towards the large incline.

"I'm just trying to get to class!" a man's voice shouts from ahead.

He attempts to stand up from his seat and succeeds partially, until his wife next to him pulls him back down.

"That's not Daniel," Dex says, looking at the man still frantically moving about in his seat on the raft, attempting to escape.

The man looks to be in his fifties, with mostly gray hair that's thinning on the back of his head. As he turns around in Dex and Lada's direction, stress is written clearly across his features.

"No, but he's experiencing one of Daniel's dreams," Lada responds.

They run after the raft, which becomes more difficult as the pathway on either side of the water becomes narrower and steeper.

"And that's why."

Lada points to the boy sitting right behind the man, and, like Lada, Dex recognizes him as Daniel from the monitor he studied in Max's lab before coming here. That is, before the raft enters a tunnel that is shrouded in darkness.

"I can't be here! I'm going to be late!" the man shouts, and again attempts to stand up in the raft.

This time, he falls back into his seat from the motion of the raft tilting upwards, but it's not long until he's back up and seems to be shimmying his way out of the restraints meant to keep the riders secure for the coming drop.

"Anxiety over school tardiness is no joke. I've had this dream before," Dex says, rushing after Lada into the dark tunnel after the raft.

Lada is squirt in the chest by a fake raptor shooting water from its mouth, aimed for the people passing in the raft, but she gets the blunt of it. Lada lets out a grunt of frustration, seemingly holding back a growl at the automated raptor. Still, she holds herself back from taking a moment to pause and sneer at it, as she wishes to do.

"What—" Lada begins to ask Dex, but then spots the drop up ahead and the large, automaton T-rex that stands over it.

The man is fully standing in the raft as it slows in its ascent right before the fall, enough to build that suspense for what's to come. Except, that man's biggest concern is not the drop coming.

He's attempting to climb his way over to the side, which involves climbing over people.

His wife's screams of caution and the protests of the others in the raft do nothing to wake him from the dream. They're nearing the edge.

"We need to get on that raft now!"

"Okay," Dex says, grabbing onto Lada's arm as he reaches her side. "Jump!" he shouts, pulling her along with him.

They land on the edge of the raft, Lada perfectly balanced on the slippery surface. Dex slips and falls forward into the raft, hitting the man attempting to leap off on the way down. Dex and the man fall across the laps of the other passengers in the row, earning further exclamations of protest, but everyone is quickly distracted when the raft tips forward.

Dex braces himself against the walls of the raft to keep himself in place and to keep the man trapped inside the raft beneath him. Lada crouches down on the floor in the row behind them, right by Daniel, as the raft plunges forward.

CHAPTER FOUR

A ccording to the Ojibwe legend, the dreamcatcher was a gift to a woman who saved a spider from being killed by her grandson. The dreamcatcher was meant to trap bad dreams. Watching this nightmarish spider coming for Emily right now and paying no attention to those in its path, I can't help but think this is what we get for allowing an Experimenter to corrupt a gift for such purposes, to drive Subjects practically insane.

"*We've got Daniel,*" Lada says.

"*Good, because it turns out spiders are not afraid of a little water,*" I reply, watching the spider make its way across the water to us. "*At least, not according to Daniel's imagination.*"

On the bright side, there are no people in the water for it to crush along the way. It offers a nice reprieve from having to form shields.

"*I'm close enough to sense Phoenix's power.*"

"*Opposite side of the bridge,*" Phoenix informs Dex before he has to ask.

Dex shows up with Lada by his side, an unconscious Daniel in her arms.

"Before you say anything," Lada says, "there wasn't enough time to explain everything to him, nor was it worth the explanation."

I assume Lada convinced Daniel that now was a good time for a nap.

Despite their success at finding him, Lada looks positively peeved, which probably has a lot to do with the fact that she and Dex are soaking wet. She sets Daniel down on the ground. Emily rushes to his side, grabbing his face in her hands to check for any apparent damage. I guess I was right. They do know each other.

Okay, time to see if this will work. As I turn my focus back to the spider crackling with the familiar red energy, Phoenix, Dex, and Lada place themselves at my back, another barrier between Emily and Daniel and the spider.

Alarmed, the rest of the people around us watch as the water splashes up with each step the spider takes. One person goes so far as to step closer to the water, as if inspecting it for hidden jets. They get a small tsunami to the face.

It's easy sensing the dream energy. It's hectic, still eager to escape, as if it believes the dreamcatcher will come back for it and reel it back in. But, it's also lost, unsure of where exactly to escape to. I just have to show it the way.

Daniel, conveniently already asleep, courtesy of Lada, has the same type of energy flowing through his mind. Something within me feels naturally drawn to the energy. That part instinctively wants to pull it in, let it join with my own chaotic energy, like calling to like. But, it's a tug on my end and that's all. The foreign energy of the dream isn't drawn to me in the same way I am to it.

It's not mine; and although some part of me that I don't understand wants it, it's not dominant. At least, it isn't yet. I can fight that desire. I don't *need* it like Chaos did. I have my own pool of chaos within to power me. My humanity. I don't need to steal.

Rather than absorbing that energy, I direct it. I give it something it will want to unite with. I pull from Daniel's mind the energy that is a match for what forms the spider, imagining it trailing out, creating a thin path to the stray energy, like breadcrumbs to follow.

The spider stops walking only a couple feet away from me and only one step away from exiting the water. Its body leans forward toward the thread of energy stemming from Daniel. It recognizes it as the same. They connect.

The spider loses its form. The water fills the space where its legs had been, the surface flattening out again. Like air leaving a balloon, the energy deflates, streaming back towards Daniel along the path I created.

From further away, more energy joins that which belonged to the spider, following its lead back to Daniel. It must be from another dream that had escaped and attached itself elsewhere.

Soon, the only thing left visible of the energy is the homing beacon of a path I'd created myself. I relinquish my hold on it, and it, too, returns to Daniel, who still sleeps, finally dreaming freely, no dreamcatcher snatching them away.

Good or bad, we all need to face our dreams and nightmares. That doesn't stop me from being grateful that, these days, I wake up not remembering what I dreamt.

The water show over, voices rise around us. Many of the people have turned back to stare inquisitively at the crushed garbage can, thankfully the only real casualty of this disaster.

"Hey, Sin. Clean up on aisle ten please," I say.

Daniel is starting to come to. Lada, Dex, and Phoenix seemingly have put together that the threat is gone, despite never having been able to see it. They relax, dispersing the barrier they formed with their own bodies to protect Daniel and Emily.

"This one's up to Lada. I can't make all these people indifferent about something they've already experienced, not permanently."

Sin's response comes back to all of us. Lada, despite being soaked from head to toe, pulls her shoulders back and manages to look like she's glistening beautifully rather than like a drowned rat, as I would look in her position.

A barely audible, self-righteous humph comes from Phoenix's direction.

"What?" I ask, as I turn around to face him, even though I know I'd be better off ignoring whatever this is.

"Nothing," he claims, acting overly innocent. "It's just, I guess Sin can't fix everything."

It's my own fault for acknowledging.

Dex makes the wise decision, cracking a smile before physically excusing himself from this conversation by walking over to check on Daniel and Emily, which is actually a good use of time.

Lada moves back to the center of the bridge, where we'd first arrived, preparing to address the masses.

"We're a team. He doesn't need to 'fix' everything," I point out.

I should just roll my eyes and turn my attention elsewhere. I'm very talented at knowing what I *should* be doing.

This stupid thing between Phoenix and Sin is so... stupid. No one said they had to like each other, only work together, but they are such a pain in any capacity together. Sin lives for balance and order, and Phoenix is a freaking broken seesaw dangling off the roof of a building.

"Some of us pull more weight, is all," he says, with a shrug.

"Really?" I challenge. "What have you done today that was so vital to the group?"

"Dawn, this isn't about me," he says, with mock offense.

"Of course not," I say, heavy sarcasm taking over my tone. "It never is. You're so selfless."

"I'm talking about you, of course. You just saved everyone, while Sin sits pretty in the lab."

"You can stay behind next time, too," I offer, sounding over-eager for him to take me up on that offer.

"Don't be silly. Then who would whisk you away from danger?"

"Still you. From afar. Did you forget you finally shared with us that you could teleport people without being with them?"

He tsks at me.

"You're missing the point."

"That you're jealous of Sin?" I question, half joking. Because, as much as their personalities don't spell easy companionship, Phoenix's attitude makes little sense. He doesn't let anyone rile him normally.

"Yes," he admits, but he's moving on before I can question if he meant that. "*I* want to be here," he says, taking a step up, closer to me. "He doesn't."

His eyes search my own, challenging me, missing nothing. He doesn't touch or even breathe on me, but I can feel him all the same across that small distance.

Define "here," is what I want to say. "Here," as in helping Subjects? "Here," as in at Islands of Adventure because he always wanted to have that human experience? Or, "here," as in with me?

After all the time I've known him, I have no idea how to answer that question myself. I have no idea how he feels because he's never once told me. He's rarely told me the truth at all.

But, it doesn't matter. I don't need any more confusion in my life. I don't *need* him, despite the fact that, in one way or another, it feels as if he's always been there for me, which is exactly why I need to prove to myself that I'm perfectly good. Without him.

Not that my confusion over Phoenix even matters. It's a non-issue. If he truly felt anything for me, he would have done something by now. We've known each other for more lifetimes than anyone ever lives.

I step back, regaining that distance and, in doing so, failing the challenge set up for me.

I focus on Lada, pretending that my attention was naturally drawn away, rather than that I just needed something to focus on other than him.

Lada effortlessly leaps up onto one of the narrow rails of the bridge, balancing there. She faces the crowd of people on the elevated surface, the world her stage. Or, at least, this amusement park.

They're all looking at her before she's even opened her mouth. In fact, I'm not sure it's completely necessary for her to say anything. At this point, they may have all chosen to forget about the events of the last few minutes in favor of focusing solely on Lada.

"Hello, everyone," she begins, her voice carrying with that singsong quality even though she manages to sound like she isn't screaming. I imagine every single person here believes she just talked to them individually. "Thank you for being part of the test for our new, immersive special effects. These exciting features will be implemented in our rides here in the near future. Have a lovely rest of your day and enjoy."

Yes, because making everyone think their lives are in danger is definitely the Islands of Adventure way. What's more exciting than almost dying?

It doesn't matter how believable or not Lada's improvised explanation is. Her power does the rest of the work, persuading everyone to believe it.

With a smile, she jumps down from the bridge's railing, her feet barely making any sound as she lands. The crowd returns to normal, moving on with their lives. Even Emily seems unbothered, even though she was the one who actually saw the spider. Not to mention, traveled through space. Daniel now stands by her side, looking tired but otherwise unaffected.

"What happened?" he asks Emily.

As Emily breaks out into a detailed explanation about the "crazy immersive experience" that Daniel somehow fell asleep during, we make our getaway.

"Phoenix," Sin says, *"the Council is requesting your return."*

"They're so needy," Phoenix responds, but he's teleporting us back to Havcire a second later, which is good because I have an Experimenter that needs dealing with.

CHAPTER FIVE

"**D**r. Jeffreys," I begin, addressing Daniel's Experimenter.

In his life on Vest, Ian Jeffreys was a neuroscientist with a special interest in the unconscious mind. Although he lived a full life to the age of ninety-seven on Vest, he appears to be in his late thirties here in Havcire, with a full head of sandy blonde hair. The age people choose to stay at in Havcire always says something about them, how they want to be seen.

If he merely wanted to keep a young appearance, he'd have gone for his twenties, but this man doesn't want to chance being mistaken for a kid who lacks experience. He values, to some extent at least, his own authority. He didn't want to go any older, though. He prioritizes being seen as youthful over traits like maturity and wisdom.

Not wanting to make an enemy out of him before we even get to the topic in need of discussion, I address him formally with the title he earned in Vest.

Even to me, this situation is a little odd, considering I *do* look like a kid. One of the drawbacks of still technically being alive from my life as a Subject is that I can't alter my age, not that it would help a whole lot.

By age sixteen, I reach my peak height anyway. I wouldn't look much different ten years older. I'd still be just a few inches over five feet, while Ian is over six feet tall.

But, this isn't my first time addressing an Experimenter like I am their superior. After all, I am in charge of the Subject System now. So, I stand in front of him, still in my yoga attire, looking a little worse for wear from my confrontation with a nightmare spider, and continue on.

"I thought every scientist knew that correlation doesn't prove causation. Just because your Subjects act a certain way when they are unable to dream does not mean that the lack of dreaming caused that behavior. Is it not possible that lack of quality rest, or some other variable, was the cause?"

"I suppose," Ian manages, looking deep in thought, truly considering this.

That's good at least.

"You need to find a new way to conduct your experiment, as you no longer will be allowed to prevent your Subjects from experiencing their dreams. The consequences are too risky. The dreamcatchers will be re-spelled to record their dreams for your observation, if you so desire, but not to steal them," I tell him.

He leans back against his desk, as if he needs its support and looks almost ashamed. I'm tempted to say something to reassure him that his experiment can still work, that this was just a mistake, a mistake that almost cost lives. But, we learn from mistakes.

"The purpose of allowing Experimenters to conduct experiments is to provide the opportunity to still have an impact on Vest, to help make life better there. Today, your experiment came close to being the reason why those same people we are trying to help nearly died," I say, the words coming out before I've consciously decided against playing the role of cheerleader.

There are too many experiments to deal with. I can't afford to address one problem only to have to go back to it later because I failed to get the point across the first time around. He needs to understand now.

Ian nods his head, his eyes on the floor, as if he can't bring himself to look at me, but I need a clear confirmation that he understands and will follow through, so I wait.

I get that no one, except probably a psychopath, likes hearing that their actions put others in danger. I'm not exactly a huge fan of this part of the job. I wish I could correct through motivation rather than the threat of another mistake meaning something as bad as lives at stake. But, I don't know every Experimenter personally. How can I trust that anything other than the most serious threat will get the job done correctly? Threat's a little harsh. I'm not threatening. I'm... warning.

I could get to know the Experimenters I oversee. It wouldn't take much time. I'm generally good at getting people quickly, with very little to go on. I should get to know them so these types of conversations can be more effective. I'll do that.

Ian's lab is much smaller than Max's. I don't think he has as many Subjects under his watch. The lab, though, greatly resembles Max's before we took over and redecorated.

There's the tub in the center for transporting the Subjects back to Vest, and there's a single computer on the desk covered with papers, which Ian still leans on. Nodding his head once more, he looks up from the floor.

"I will do my best to redesign my experiment, and none of my Subjects will be deprived of their dreams anymore," he says, giving me the confirmation I needed.

"Good. Any updates regarding what you intend to change about your experiment, let me know," I tell him, before turning to leave, but his voice stops me.

"I messed up," he confesses, sounding a lot like he's looking for me, or anyone, to reassure him of the opposite. "Conducting these experiments from Havcire, it can be hard not to become detached to what happens on Vest," he admits.

The smile I attempt on my face feels bitter when I turn back to him. Once again, though, he's not looking at me so I give up forcing it.

I know exactly how easy it is for an Experimenter to become detached from what they cause on Vest. I was a victim of it, after all.

"I was a Citizen before I was made into a Subject," I tell him, even though I know that by now everyone knows my story, which is ironic considering how long it took for me to figure it out. "There's nothing preventing an Experimenter from becoming a Subject if the situation calls for it, so do your best to remember that Havcire and Vest are not as separate as you've come to think."

Threats it is. Getting to know the Experimenters is for another day.

Worse, this threat isn't even true. I don't have the authority to punish an Experimenter by making them into a Subject. When it was done to me as a Citizen, it wasn't even legal. Not even the Council approved of it.

Even worse, his admission was admirable. It showed he truly understood not only what had gone wrong but why, meaning he was already more likely not to make the same mistake again than many others in his place.

And still, I couldn't help myself.

I agreed to oversee the new Subject System because I wanted to ensure someone was looking out for the Subjects, but it's the Experimenters I have to interact with primarily, and maybe it wasn't the best idea to have me work closely with those I associate with trapping me in yesterday's version of this system.

I recognize most Experimenters have good intentions, wanting to keep working in their afterlife and help those on Vest. I'm working on not being bitter over what's over and done, even if what's over and done will always have a lasting impact on me. I am working on it.

I don't wait to see if my words sink in. I turn away and walk out of the glass doors into the Ziggurat hallway, where I find Lada waiting for me.

The light shimmers around her as she makes herself visible again. To think I once eavesdropped on her and Phoenix when she's the master of eavesdropping with her handy ability to bend light.

"Damn," she says, holding out the word as she walks in step beside me.

It's a little eerie. Although she's walking right next to me, it's only my footsteps I hear against the marble floor. I thought with my Protogenoi abilities finally manifesting I'd also develop the insane agility the Celestials have. However, I've come to realize that none of the Celestials can quite match Lada's graceful stealth.

"Yes, Lada?" I ask, with an overly sweet smile when she doesn't continue on.

"That," she says, incredulously indicating my smile with a circling finger in front of my face, as if she hopes to capture the image of it and then show it back to me like a human mirror. Actually, maybe she could do that. "How can you be like this 24/7 and then go talk to an Experimenter and suddenly become absolutely savage?"

Answer is, I've got anger issues. Again, working on it.

She's narrowing her eyes at me, as if my face might shapeshift into another human being all together.

I laugh, and I'm not positive if it's because of her perplexed reaction in general or because of her slang use of savage. Or, at least, I hope it's the more modern meaning of the word she's using. Was I *that* bad with Ian? I mean, yeah. But...

"What exactly am I like 24/7? Sunshine and rainbows?" I ask, focusing on that instead.

"Maybe not rainbows, but you are sunshiny. Except when it comes to Phoenix. He seems to make you more thunderstormy with a rainbow aftermath," Lada says, smiling, seemingly happy with herself for her nonsensical evaluation of me.

"Hm," I feign deep in thought.

"Hm?"

"It's just that I'm realizing you've only seen Dawn on a Mission, Dawn Your Ally, and Dawn Your Friend."

"I didn't realize there were so many of you."

I raise an eyebrow at that irony. We both know there have been a whole lot of me. Lots and lots of lives, but that's not what we're talking about.

"My point is," I continue with said point, "I'm not generally a people person. You've just had the delightful opportunity of being one of the few people I personally like, or you've been around me when I have to pretend to be a people person, like Dawn on a Mission, for example."

"You do a lot of saving people for someone who claims they don't like people," Lada points out.

"Well, I am a good person."

"Sunshiny, with a chance of thunderstorms when Phoenix is about, which I believe you're avoiding the subject of."

"Whatever. Do you really think I was that bad with the Experimenter?"

Ugh. Guilt. I feel it.

Lada rolls her eyes at me.

"You made sure he got the message," she says. "Now, stop looking so pitiful. He survived the confrontation. Barely."

Lada laughs, but I force down any reaction, not wanting to give her the satisfaction of eliciting any more of a reaction from me. But, her laugh is contagious, and a smile threatens my face as we round the corner into the hallway lined with portals.

I planned on taking a portal back to my house, my *tree*house. But, as Lada's laughter quiets, we hear voices coming from inside the Council room, and I remember Phoenix was meeting with the Council.

CHAPTER SIX

L ada and I pause and look at each other for not more than one second before coming to a silent agreement.

We walk up closer to the doors, me trying to mirror Lada's silent footsteps, and press our ears against the heavy, wooden doors.

To a normal human, the doors would be soundproof. This close to them, though, we can just make out the voices coming from inside with our enhanced hearing. Of course, standing this close to a door would look suspicious from a mile away, so I keep an eye out for anyone who might be passing by.

"Any news from Lada about the Protogenoi?" Barnabas asks.

"She's been working with an Incanter to try and locate them but they haven't had much luck," Phoenix reports.

I didn't know about the Incanter, so I look to Lada in question. She mouths "Gatlin," before turning her attention fully back to the conversation on the opposite side of the doors.

Makes sense. Gatlin does always seem open to helping, even if he likes that fact to remain on the down low. I think he doesn't want it getting out that he's got a helping soul, or else he'd be receiving an overwhelming amount of visitors at his intentionally isolated house.

Phoenix is more than willing to help keep that secret. At least this particular one is being kept out of loyalty to a friend.

"Other than that," Phoenix continues, "all she has to work with are accounts from back when the Protogenoi ruled. Since we all were there at the time, there isn't much useful information to come across, at least that we don't already know. Although, she does have a theory. Lada believes they'll be out for revenge, especially against the three of you and—"

Phoenix stops abruptly, cutting himself off, or at least it sounds that way. One of the Council members could have stopped him with a gesture, but I doubt a mere hand held up would stop Phoenix from going on.

Perhaps he's finally gotten lost within his maze of secrets and stumbled upon one that creeped up on him, disguising itself as a known truth. But, he caught himself too late. It's perfectly clear that he was going to say *something*.

"And?" Barnabas prompts, confirming for me that he did stop on his own accord.

Even from outside the room, I can hear Phoenix's sigh as he gives in and finishes the sentence he started.

"And the sixth Protogenoi."

A moment passes where the only sound coming from behind the doors is the slow tapping of a foot against the floor. I can just assume it's Lucifer behind the noise. He always was the more fidgety one of the group. In this moment, where it seems even breathing has quieted, he still manages to fill the silence with some action.

I, it seems, am the only one solely confused by what's been said because my response would have been a simple, inquiring, "What?"

I've never heard of any sixth Protogenoi. Unsurprisingly, I'm in the dark.

Lucifer lets out a short laugh.

"A children's story?" he asks, clearly skeptical.

"No," Minerva speaks up, "a legend many of our people believe in."

"Once, they believed in it. And, after all this time, it's never been proven true," Lucifer refutes.

"This is why I was attempting to move on past that part of the theory," Phoenix points out.

"We are not here to dispute the validity of a legend," Barnabas cuts in, and I take notice of the fact that he refers to it as a legend, as Minerva did, rather than a mere story.

Legends are thought to be based in some element of truth, unlike myth, which is generally accepted as fantasy, a story created only to explain the unexplainable. Then again, I am surrounded by myths.

"We can all agree that Lada is right, that the Protogenoi will want revenge, against who specifically is of little importance right now," Barnabas continues. "The Protogenoi were not in their right minds at the beginning of time, and it is unlikely that they've become more sane over the years, so we can't pretend to understand the full extent of their motives. We must, however, stop them before whatever they are planning is put into action, for we know their power has no limits."

"Only loopholes," Phoenix says. My hand comes up to rest flat against the door, as I lean closer at the sound of Phoenix's voice again. "What they neglect is the only power we have against them."

I drop my hand back to my side.

I need to get ahold of myself. I'm just drawn to Phoenix because I believe he has all the answers, and I want those answers. That's all. I want to know what he knows. I don't want to be blindsided by anything. Except, just because he withholds tons of information doesn't mean he has all the information.

It's genius, really. You act all knowing and get a reputation as a liar, and people will assume you must know everything, that you're just keeping it all to yourself.

So, now I'm going with he either really does know everything or he's a genius. Thank god he can't read my mind because apparently even when I'm looking for fault, I end up complimenting him. His ego simply couldn't handle that.

"We can't depend on a mistake on their part," Minerva argues.

"Ensure Lada's focus is on finding the Protogenoi before they attack, and you continue to research a way to take them down without another full out war," Barnabas orders.

"Will do."

I hear Phoenix head toward the doors, towards us. Lada and I retreat back ourselves, but Barnabas's voice stops us all.

"One last thing," he says. "How's Dawn?"

His voice is different, less business. It's a personal question and a reminder that this council helped raise me, something we all remember now. It warms me, truly, but also, more primarily, worries me that he feels the need to ask Phoenix about my well-being. Is he concerned? Should he be?

I look down at myself. I'm fine.

It'd be smart for Lada and I to leave. We don't want to be caught eavesdropping when Phoenix does make his way out of the Council Room, but I can't not hear the part where I'm the topic of conversation.

"You mean besides being extremely busy with the Subject System?" Phoenix asks.

"Yes," Barnabas responds.

I have to force myself to stay quiet even though it sounds to me like my heartbeat just got significantly louder. It needs to hush. We're hiding here.

It's not like I've done anything I'm not supposed to, not really. Still, I'm also not sure the Council would be especially happy with what I've been up to in the little free time I've had. Then again, what is the harm in finding those from my past lives?

It's not only my parents from this most recent life that I've kept in contact with. I've located those I was close with in other lives, who have since passed on from their mortal lives and live now in Havcire. The only one I haven't yet had the nerve to find is my real birth mother.

While the Council may be fine with it technically, again there's the issue of whether this is really a question of my well-being. It's healthy and normal to want to connect with those from your life. Well, lives.

Maybe that's not what Barnabas is asking at all. He really could just be asking how I am, generally, a harmless, mostly useless question because it *is* so general.

Regardless, they shouldn't question Phoenix about me. Ask me about me.

"It's not my job to keep tabs on Dawn's life," Phoenix responds, sounding bored, as if it would be extremely boring to spend time paying attention to everything I do. "I'm sure she would be happy to talk to you about herself if you asked."

Despite making everything he says sound half like an insult directed at me, I can't help but be grateful.

Still, he doesn't care what I'm up to?

It's fine. Whatever. This is what I want, to hear what Phoenix really thinks about me. The truth. And, if the truth is he doesn't think about me at all... then great. In fact, go on, Phoenix. Tell them how you really feel.

"Come on," Lada whispers, nodding her head towards the portal that leads back to my home.

The portal back to my home in Havcire lies on the wall right above the lone, marble bench, the one I used to slump down on to await my meetings with the Council in between every life. To think that I was clueless all those times about the fact that that part of my forgotten life as a Citizen, the home I lived in for years, was right above my head.

We land in front of the treehouse, on the strip of grass that leads like a red carpet to the ocean at one end and the trees of the forest at the other end.

"Welcome home, Dawn," a friendly, male voice says the moment my feet touch the ground.

The voice comes from Peter, as in my car from my life as a Subject. I had Phoenix teleport him to Havcire a while back and, more recently, had him enchanted to speak.

Thank you, Gatlin.

The Jeep Wrangler is parked under an orange, curtained canopy that hangs between two trees of the forest. It's a pretty nice setup for a car, if I am to say so myself.

"Hello, Lada," he says, earning a wide-eyed gaze from the Celestial, which she turns on me.

"Tell me your car did not just speak to me."

"It's nice to meet you," Peter continues, as I do my best to hold back a laugh.

Lada shakes her head unfathomably.

"Hi, Peter," I tell him, ignoring Lada. I'm pretty sure it's clear that my car is, in fact, speaking to her. "Are you going to respond?" I ask her. "It seems rude not to."

"Sometimes I question—"

"My sanity," I finish for her. "Yes, I know."

"No no. No, that's not it. *My* sanity for calling you my friend."

"Please, I'm so very likable."

"She is," Peter says, helpfully chiming in.

I point to him, as if that's all the proof she needs. From the car's non-existent mouth to Lada's ears.

Who wouldn't want a talking car?

I felt he already had a personality. He should be able to express himself.

I walk over to the canopy covering Peter. I keep a bucket of soapy water and another one of clean water beside him, along with a few wash cloths. I dip one into the soapy water and begin cleaning the car, even though there's barely a speck of dirt to be seen, probably because I do this practically every day. Wax on, wax off.

"I swear I secretly loathe you," Lada says, as she leans against the front of the car, a smile on her face.

It's ridiculous how often I wash this car. Scratch that, I'm ridiculous, but it makes me feel normal. Not that normal is so amazing, but it is a comfort. I think Lada understands at least that much, so she doesn't comment on the fact that I'm cleaning a perfectly clean car.

"So, what's this legend about a sixth Protogenoi?" I finally get to ask.

Because five weren't enough.

She turns around to face me, resting her forearms on Peter's hood.

"It probably is just that. A legend, which is definitely what Phoenix believes," she says, and pauses.

I wait for her to continue, rather than asking her to explain again. She's clearly thinking over it herself.

"There were rumors about a sixth Protogenoi," she continues, "who was sent to spy on the Celestials and Incanters, posing as a Celestial himself, so that he could inform the other Protogenoi of any talk of rebellion. But, instead of reporting back to the Protogenoi, he sympathized with us and fought against the Protogenoi in the Firstlast War."

Absentmindedly, Lada picks up the wash cloth in the clean water bucket and begins spreading it across where I left the soap behind. She drags the cloth across the hood of the car in circles as her mind wanders.

"At the time, I heard the rumors myself, everyone did, whether or not they were true. The existence of the sixth Protogenoi became a legend, which portrayed him as having a large role in our victory over the other Protogenoi. People went so far as to claim we wouldn't have won without him fighting, disguised as one of us, at our side."

It feels strange to me that the Celestials and Incanters would take away from their own victory by spreading a story of a Protogenoi who was essential for their win. Then again, there is always another way to look at something. Maybe it wasn't about the credit after the fact, but the motivation before.

Maybe they needed to believe they had a chance of winning against the Protogenoi in order to have the courage to go into battle in the first place. And, the idea that a powerful Protogenoi was fighting on their side? That could have been enough to make them step out onto that battlefield.

"So, if he were real, this sixth Protogenoi, the other Protogenoi would view his actions as a betrayal."

My voice brings Lada back to the present. She realizes what she's doing, makes a face at the wet cloth in her hand, and drops it back into the bucket. As she dries off her hand, directing the light of the sun onto it so the heat evaporates the offending water there, something else occurs to me.

"He'd also be a real threat to the Protogenoi," I say, thinking maybe the answer to defeating them lies in the past with one person, a most likely imaginary person, but still.

"Yeah, if he were real," Lada says, echoing my thoughts. "Even so, if he were interested in helping, he would have made himself known to us by now."

I pick up the cloth Lada discarded, as I move onto rinsing.

"How do you know this fake person is a he?" I ask her.

"Always was, according to the legend," she says with a shrug.

"Hey."

The voice comes suddenly from behind me.

Even though part of me recognizes the voice automatically, the other part, that is completely startled, jumps around and whips the wet cloth I'm holding at the source.

Dex laughs at my reaction, instinctively catching the cloth against his chest, where it soaks his dark blue t-shirt.

"Hi, Dex," Peter says, greeting him.

"Hey, Peter," Dex says, not missing a beat.

"Of course he's fine with talking to a car," Lada comments.

"You're even worse than Phoenix," I tell him, once I've recovered.

"If I'd known I was going to be attacked by a wet rag, I would have chosen to make my entrance differently," he says, tossing the wet rag back to me. "Speaking of Phoenix, have you decided to take the training wheels off yet?"

If Dex was able to teleport here, then that means that he had to have been with Phoenix.

"Did he put you up to this?" I ask.

"Does that seem like something he'd do?" Dex says, answering my question with a question.

But, no, it's not something Phoenix would do. He's not big into sending others to fight his battles for him. He's pretty confrontational, being the messenger for the Celestials and all.

Also, apparently, he doesn't care about what I do at all so couldn't be Phoenix who this question is stemming from.

Rather than answering Dex, I turn back to Peter, only to realize there's no more surface area left to clean. I drop the wash cloth back into the bucket with a sigh and face Dex with an eyebrow raised.

"Training wheels? Is that how you're referring to the vow these days?"

"You're using it to teach him to be honest with you. So, yes. Are you ready to see if he can ride on his own?"

Both eyebrows go up. "Ride what, exactly? Am I the bike?"

"Best to leave the metaphor behind, Dex," Lada says. "It's not a bad idea, though. Trust needs to go both ways, and it's not a good sign if you don't ever trust him enough to be honest with you of his own volition."

"Okay, tell me how you all really feel."

It's one thing, and a normal thing, for Dex to offer arguments in support of Phoenix. Ever since Dex came clean about who he really is, he's owned it and his opinions. He completely left any fabricated personality traits that belonged to Poindexter behind.

For one, there is nothing uptight about him. Additionally, the biggest difference is that he has no lack of social skills. He can charm pretty much anyone, something he has in common with Phoenix. Except, Dex manages it in a cute, awkward sort of way, by being so authentically himself, whereas Phoenix does it in the way that you know he's being completely insincere and, at the same time, he still manages to win you over regardless. It also involves a lot of shameless flirting.

Not the point.

Point is, Dex, even when he was pretending to be Poindexter clearly took a liking to Phoenix. And now, it's one of the things that have stayed consistent about him. Still rah-rah Phoenix.

Lada is the one who surprises me. Usually, she doesn't get involved unless I really force her to share her opinion with me. Sure, there are the side comments she can't help but mutter around Phoenix and I when our... situation gets on her nerves. But, for a god of love, she seems to want nothing to do with us. If you ask me, that's got to be a sign.

Who's next? I wonder if Peter has an opinion in favor of Phoenix, as well.

"Doesn't someone have to play devil's advocate?" I ask, practically pleading for anyone to plead my case.

Although, the truth is, I *was* planning on releasing Phoenix from the vow.

"I love that role," Phoenix says, appearing in front of Lada. "What's the argument?"

A beautifully wicked smile plays on Lada's lips as she turns her attention to Phoenix.

"Real simple," she says. "You need to argue against—"

"What are you doing here?" I ask, the words rushing out to cut off Lada.

"No fun," Lada says, pouting, even though I'm fairly certain she spoke extra slow before in order to give me the chance to stop her.

Phoenix shifts his seafoam eyes between Lada and me but clearly decides to let it go.

His focus lands on me.

"I have to bring you to check on your border shields. Council's orders."

Great. Alone time. With Phoenix.

CHAPTER SEVEN

There are only two remaining portals.

All it would take for the two worlds to separate completely, for the two remaining portals to disappear, would be a complete cessation of interaction between Vest and Havcire, as was initially intended after the Firstlast War. But, Chaos prevented that by beginning the Subject System and, in a twisted way, I'm continuing what she started. But, for very different reasons.

The location of one of the portals is the legendary Tree of Life, also known by some as The Tree of the Knowledge of Good and Evil, which infamously led to Adam and Eve's downfall.

What type of message does that send? One of the two remaining locations from which people can travel between Havcire and Vest is the mythological tree associated with humanity's fall from grace. It seems like a message in of itself that maybe the two worlds shouldn't be connected anymore.

But, I've never been one to really heed warnings, especially those that stem from a religious text littered with misogyny and other not so up-to-date beliefs. Call it blasphemy, but the thing could use a rewrite.

Plus, I'm not willing to believe Havcire and Vest should remain entirely separate, seeing as I'm alive, which makes Vest where I technically belong but Havcire is my home. Not to mention, my work-base is here in Havcire and that work often requires me to travel to Vest.

The tree itself is a physical tether, anchoring Vest to Havcire. While the very top of its trunk and the crown is located in Havcire, the roots are planted in Vestigium.

Phoenix used to take me here during my life as a Citizen. We'd lie beneath the branches and leaves as he'd eat an apple, as if mocking the old stories. It was just an ordinary apple, not one from the tree itself. That, he wouldn't do, as eating an apple from the tree does, in fact, give you knowledge. It gives you a truth, the one you are most reluctant to face. And, no, taking from the tree does not really condemn the seeker of the knowledge.

It's weird remembering parts of my past lives now. Ever since I used my power, my own power and not the chaos which I'd stolen from others, the vivid flashes of my past lives have stopped, as if using my power was the glue needed to finally meld all my lives together.

On the one hand, not having memory attacks is good. On the other hand, there are relatively few memories left that I can recall in great detail, which is normal.

I learned briefly about memory, multiple times in fact, in psychology classes I took over the course of my later lives. I think about it often, how we recall most of our past like stories. We remember the event happened and know how to recite what happened to others, but we don't actually remember living it anymore, what it felt like to be in that moment. Except, with flashbulb memories, which, for some reason, stay with us longer and more vividly.

Phoenix sat with me here once and created an illusion of a phoenix flying through the branches of the tree, leaving a trail of fire behind it. I can still see it in my mind as if it happened yesterday.

I remember listening to him that day as he told me something that held all my interest. Maybe he even voluntarily opened up to me and explained why he had chosen to name himself after the nonexistent bird that flew above our heads, as he was forced to admit during Gatlin's tests. Whatever it was he said, I can't remember for sure, and it bothers me.

But, I'm not here to walk down a very long memory lane.

The tree looks the same as always. The trunk is huge, with a circumference of over twenty meters. Making up the entire trunk, instead of regular grooves, there are overlapping circles and ovals, the spaces in between the shapes empty, exposing the hollow center of the tree. Although they appear to create one large, random design, each circle and oval is paired, representing Havcire and Vest.

Every representation overlaps with the ones surrounding it; but, if separated, they would simply each be one oval surrounding one circle, with two points of intersection. The two remaining portals. It's not exactly geographically accurate to say the least.

The trunk extends up only about three feet before the green canopy takes over, which makes being under the tree feel like being in a tent made of branches and leaves, completely closed off from the rest of the world. However, we can't go under the tree now, no one can, because my gold shield of energy surrounds it in a dome.

Phoenix reaches out toward the golden barrier. Before he can make contact, it reacts to him, sending out a spark to his extended hand. He doesn't jerk away, so I assume that the contact doesn't hurt him at all. Confirming he isn't a threat, the spark retreats back into the dome, becoming part of the whole again.

"Well done," he says. "It's still standing, just like all the other times the Council sent us to check on it."

The Council is a little overly vigilant when it comes to checking on the portals. Then again, I understand.

We've had little success uncovering the location or plans of the Protogenoi, but Lada did come up with the idea to have me shield the portals. Apparently, Protogenoi powers can't directly reverse each other. As my chaotic power is Protogenoi in origin, my shields should hold back the Protogenoi, no matter how powerful their magic. Theoretically, only I should be able to take my shields down.

At least the Protogenoi are trapped on this side. Since we assume their goal, like Chaos, is to rule both worlds, having no access to Vest should prove to be a problem for them. Plus, it keeps Vest safe from them for now.

Still, the shields I created don't need refueling or babysitting. The golden energy is an extension of myself. As long as I live, the shields guarding the two portals will remain powered. Actually, when I think about it like that, maybe its me that needs the checking up on and not my shields.

"One more to go," Phoenix says, holding out his hand to me, ready to move onto checking the other portal.

This is how it's been recently with him. The absolute bare minimum. He's all sarcastic and willing to interact with me when everyone else is around, but when it's just the two of us, he treats whatever it is we have to do together like ripping off a bandaid. He barely even looks at me.

It's fine. I mean, it hurts. I can't help that it hurts, and I miss him.

I wanted to get to know Phoenix, really know him now that I know our history, so that I could know whether or not I could trust the Phoenix that exists now, not whoever he was in the past. That's hard to do when he treats me like this.

But, there is something I can do, something everyone apparently thinks I should do, which could possibly, maybe be why he gives me the cold shoulder when it's just the two of us.

"Wait a minute. There's something I wanted to discuss with you," I tell him.

We could talk at the other portal, but Styx still guards the river even though my shield makes the job redundant.

"Yes?" he asks, genuinely curious.

Under his no longer uncaring gaze, I can't figure out how I'm supposed to start. Should I have rehearsed this? I'm just releasing him from a vow. That's all I have to say. I am releasing you from the vow. That's it. It's the right thing to do, and I should have done it a while ago. And, no, I was not swayed to this decision because of two traitorous friends. I came to this decision on my own.

"You're like a yo-yo."

"What?" he asks, taken aback. So am I.

"Yeah," I confirm, sounding confident. No. What am I saying? "A yo-yo, always bouncing away in different directions until the string gets so tangled up you're unsure about what's even happened."

I've committed.

"I'm glad that after all these months, this is the stimulating conversation I've waited to have with you," Phoenix says, looking entirely amused.

"After all these months?" I question, hoping we can move on from my disastrous yo-yo analogy.

"You've been avoiding me."

He says this as though it's a fact, one that doesn't bother him in the slightest. I'm surprised he doesn't shrug carelessly along with the statement. Why even bring it up if he doesn't care?

"I've been busy. You're the one who's been distant."

"Distant?" he asks with a scoff. "You don't trust me enough to release me from the vow. I'd say that's what's creating distance," he says, taking a step closer to me as the last word leaves his mouth, as if mocking any efforts I've made to create that distance. Which I have not!

I really have been busy. I've tried to talk with him when I've had the chance... I am pretty sure I have. He's the one who's always closed off when it's just us two.

Yeah, the vow's been kind of a barrier between us, of my own making. I've already acknowledged this, though. To myself.

I should've opened with the vow and not the damn yo-yo.

It's not like I've even made use of the vow. I haven't asked him any direct questions putting him a position where he'd have no choice but to answer honestly. It's merely a safety net knowing it's there because without it... I don't know.

I'm not good enough at reminding myself of all the times in the past he's deceived me, and I'm not good enough at reminding myself to care about all those times. Maybe I just don't want him to think that I trust him enough to let go of the vow. That idea alone is scary. But, that is the point Lada made. Trust goes both ways. I have to show a little trust.

He just had to be dramatic and step into my personal space. It's especially hard to give him my trust when simply his close proximity makes me feel like I'm teetering off a cliff.

"What do you think I wanted to talk about?" I ask, dragging myself out of my own thoughts before I can change my mind and allowing frustration to be the emotion that rules me in the moment. If he'd just let me go through with my yo-yo analogy, I'd have already gotten to the point of... "I am releasing you from your vow."

They're just words but they come out with a supernatural force.

Though there's no flashy lights or colorful smoke, I see them strike Phoenix like an Incanter's spell. Surprise crosses his features for a split second, so quickly that I may be convinced I imagined it there.

"That's not really how a yo-yo works. The goal really is to control it so it comes back to your hand," Phoenix explains, deadpan.

"Well, I'm not an expert yo-yo er."

"You shouldn't have done that," he says, his tone shifting in that split second, the warning rumbling low in his throat, and he actually has the nerve to look pissed at me for doing exactly what it was that he wanted me to do.

I want to flip him off and call him out for being insufferable, but I want even more not to show how his contradictory, confusing self effects me.

He hasn't backed away from me, leaving us standing only a foot apart. At my short height, my eyes are level with the dip of his v-neck shirt. I drag my eyes away from him, looking off to the side. I take a step back and simply hold out my hand, ready to be teleported out of here.

"Time to go."

"Thank you," he says, voice soft.

I drop my hand and look up at him. His eyes are sincere.

"May I just say," he continues, a small smile now teasing his lips, "you never asked the right questions."

I push that chest I was just avoiding admiring. He barely budges.

"Bastard."

Damn rollercoaster of a man— Celestial. Whatever.

"Hey now, that's uncalled for. I didn't say I wouldn't still answer truthfully if you asked."

I open my mouth to hit him with a question to test exactly that, but he holds out a hand to stall me. "Sometimes, though, no matter what you say, you don't want the truth but I'll give it to you anyway, Dawn Rayburn. Always."

Rayburn.

That last name drops like a stone in my gut.

He knows I know exactly why he used my last name, the name I only recently found out about. It's the name that belonged to my birth parents. The fact that I know it now is evidence of the fact that I found them in Havcire. Or, at least, I located them. I have not actually gone to meet them, which is Phoenix's point. I'm not yet ready to know them, not yet ready to know that last bit of my past.

Per usual, Phoenix sees too much and shows nothing.

I glare at him. I'm not backing down. There's nothing wrong with pacing oneself when confronting lifetimes of history. It is totally a separate matter from Phoenix and his tendency to thrive on deception and secrecy.

I'm going to ask him a question, a hard one, and we will see if he can answer honestly. I am not letting him off easily. I'm going to think of a good question, really. Any second now.

Why am I so intent on testing him again?

Phoenix has always been there for me, even if he's very secretive. He's saved my life countless times. He grew up with me, kind of. And then, even when he didn't remember me, he still found me as a Subject and offered me reprieves from Max's experiment. He continued my research into the Subject System. He found me again and gave me something to fight for even when he didn't remember I was a necessary part of his plan.

Is it possible Phoenix maybe does just like having me around? Does he actually like me and not just put up with me? I would like if that were true. I'd like it even more if he'd just be open for once and tell me how he feels instead of driving me crazy.

"Your eyes look like mint."

What? Did I just say that?

I was supposed to ask him a question, something about... to test something... Why can't I think?

Phoenix smiles sweetly. Now I really can't think. The smile drops, though, and he looks really sad suddenly. I realize I've never seen such open emotion on his face, nothing that's ever looked this raw and unguarded.

"I'm sorry. You don't have to rush into meeting your parents," he says.

Not sad, he looks repentant. He lifts up a piece of my hair, one of the curly strands that always comes loose from my ponytail, and twirls it around his finger. It unfurls, falling back against my face. As it falls, Phoenix's eyes focus.

"Something's wrong."

I know something's not right, but wrong seems a little harsh. Phoenix grabs my face between his hands, and my pulse flutters at the feel of him but he's looking down into my eyes with concern.

"Hi," I say, unsure what the problem is. "Oh, I forgive you."

"Someone just tried searching my mind."

Sin's voice rings through my head. It feels like my brain itself is plunged suddenly into ice water, my thoughts scrambling and clearing fast. Not fast enough.

Phoenix drops his hands from my face and glances away from me. He looks lost in thought, and then his voice is in my head also, responding to Sin.

"*It's them, the Protogenoi. They're looking for something or someone. We have to—*"

Alarmed, his gaze finds me again. He reaches out for me.

"*Dawn,*" he says, as if I'm the very answer he hoped not to find.

He never gets to me.

CHAPTER EIGHT

They're coming.

I can hear their footsteps pounding the ground behind me in between the loud bursts of air escaping my mouth. It's so dark I can barely see the ground right below me. The trees in my path spring into view when just a couple feet in front of me, looking like pillars of shadow, at which point I only have time to take one jerky step to the side to avoid running face first into the trunks.

My legs feel pins and needles from pounding against the ground repeatedly. There are trees everywhere, and it's really slowing me down to have to sidestep to avoid them every few feet. It frustratingly makes me feel like I'm running in slow motion when I want to be at a full sprint.

I don't know where I'm going. It's not a location I'm aiming for, but something else. If I can just make it a little while longer, it will come to me. Already, it's as though I can feel it burning in my hand, the promise of a rejuvenating heat rather than a punishing burn.

I stop. The trees are gone. Before me, there is a deeper, darker shadow than those that I have run past so far.

A chasm. It extends out to either side of me as far as I can see, which isn't very far, but I feel it's continuous. I could easily jump over it. It's only about six feet across.

They're almost here. The burning intensifies, takes over my right palm to the point that I have to force down a scream. It has me itching to hold tight to something.

I jump, not over, but into the chasm. This is the end. No more running.

I'm falling down, head first, further into the ground, as if I expect an ocean at the bottom of it all to dive into. The dark walls rush by me, and then I'm no longer diving, but falling in the opposite direction, being dragged back up toward the surface.

I reach out to catch myself along the walls, trying to slow the progress. I'm more scared of resurfacing, of finding what waits for me up there, than I was of diving to certain death. My hands feel wet as they scratch along the walls, trying to find purchase.

And then, even through the sting of my cut hands, I feel the burning, stronger than before. Above my head, a flash catches my eye.

It's a sword, the blade engulfed in flames. I reach out to grab the hilt, my body screaming to make contact. If only I could get to it, it could stop my fall to the surface, stop those who wait for me there. Bring an end to everything.

Before my hand can close around it, my feet hit water.

My toes squish around in my soaked socks and shoes.

That's not right.

Also confirmation that something's wrong is the world shaking around me. Strong hands grip my upper arms and shake me awake.

"I'm up," I manage.

Groggily, I sit upright, rubbing my eyes. My feet splash in water when I drop my legs off the side of the bed, expecting to find the floor.

For the past few days, I've woken up confused as to where I was. It's that short-lived disorientation that you're vulnerable to whenever you sleep in any place other than your own home, those few seconds of "where am I" and "what am I doing here."

Where am I?

Hiding out in Sans, the Incanter town nearest the Ziggurat. More specifically, I'm squatting in this Incanter's house. The owner is out, probably hunting for any resources they can acquire, which isn't an easy task and is why I thought I could steal a few good hours of sleep here.

What am I doing here?

I am Havcire's most wanted, who anyone would be happy to kill, as it would mean a great reward from the Protogenoi.

I killed one of their own, Chaos.

Of course, no one except the Protogenoi know her death is the reason for why I'm wanted dead, as advertising the fact that a Protogenoi was killed by a Celestial would be providing evidence that the Protogenoi *can* be killed. I'd scream that fact from the rooftops if I could get to a rooftop without being killed myself.

Why are my feet soaked, and why does the water appear to be rising?

Now, that I don't know, which could very much prove to be a problem.

The house is shaped like a sphere. There are three levels to it, with one staircase in the center leading from one to the other. We're camped out on the bottom level, as the entrance to the house is on the middle floor. We figured if the owner returned, this way, we wouldn't be spotted immediately and might have a chance to escape unseen.

But, the house isn't built on the ground. It's one of the levitating houses, a twenty-foot-high spiral staircase the only way up to the entrance. So, how is it that the floor is so clearly flooding, water flowing down the center stairs at a rapid pace?

"You're up, but I don't see you moving," Sin says.

He stands by the staircase. The house is looking increasingly more like a fish bowl as I sit here doing nothing. The water has reached my knees. Past time to move.

I slosh my way through the room to reach Sin at the stairs, which resemble a waterfall. I walk right past him and climb the stairs ahead of him, knowing he won't go anywhere until I do.

Sin is determined to keep me alive, not that he approves of my past actions. He knows why the Protogenoi are after me and highly disapproves of my killing Chaos, as "to stand up against the Protogenoi is unnecessarily reckless and idiotic."

He may even think I should be killed for my crime, not that he would admit this. But, regardless, he won't let anything happen to me without a fair trial, which the Protogenoi will never offer. Consequently, his determination to stick to his values means he may be stuck with me for a long, long time. Justice has never been easy to come by in this world.

The water is coming from the outside, trickling in through the bottom of the front door. I open the door and get a wave of salt water in the face.

What the hell?

Outside the house, everything below this level is flooded, the water taking up the whole twenty feet of area, completely submerging the grounded houses below. Correction, the previously grounded houses. Now, they are bobbing in the water around us, spelled to remain upright and afloat. Good thing someone was alert enough when this all began to do damage control.

Another wave comes in. I let it hit, not wanting to use my power to redirect it, for fear it might just send the water into someone else's house. Sin shuts the door behind us to minimize the damage to our squatter house, and I lift my hands in a feeble attempt to block my face.

"I've always wanted to live on the ocean, but this wasn't what I had in mind," I say, spitting out some of the salt water that still managed to get into my mouth.

The town of Sans is right on the coast, but tsunamis have never been a fear for the people. Natural disasters can be managed easily without them ever causing real damage. There *is* plenty to fear in Havcire, and there is nothing natural about this.

"Come on."

I turn to find Sin jumping off the porch of the house and into the water surrounding us. He's left his boots discarded on the porch.

"We have to swim?" I ask.

"Did you have a better idea?" he replies, treading water.

For a second, I consider breaking the door off the house and using it as a raft of some sort. I'm not sure if it would hold us both... deja vu.

Doesn't matter. I discard that idea. Two of us floating above the water on a raft would be more noticeable than being hidden partially by the water as we swim our way through.

It's my fault this town has been flooded. I face the truth, connecting the obvious dots. Not acknowledging that wouldn't make it any less true. It would just make me an asshole unwilling to face consequences.

They did it to try and draw me out of hiding. They destroyed numerous homes to force me out into the open. Getting caught now just because I despise swimming would not only be letting them win, but it would also make what they've done to this town a success from their point of view.

It's the least I can do. Not get caught.

I grimace, pulling off my own shoes. It's going to be hard acquiring another pair of good shoes, but the boots will weigh me down if I try to hold onto them.

We swim past and under houses, trying to stay under as much as our bodies allow us to, remaining out of sight. As we move around the side of a house, one shaped interestingly like a triangle, the wide base offering good coverage, I spot the Incanter who's at work spelling the houses to keep them above sea level.

No wonder he was able to take action so quickly. He knew this was going to happen.

His gray hair and navy eyes make him look part of the storm as he levitates among the houses, directing logs of wood beneath them so they can float on the risen ocean without the use of a spell.

I've never seen Gatlin in person, but everyone has seen him portrayed alongside the Protogenoi as their prize Incanter. The

Protogenoi rarely show themselves in person to the rest of us, choosing instead to project their image up across all of Havcire. It's a spell Gatlin performs, making the sky itself a stage for them to address us like the lowly subjects we are.

Gatlin gets certain benefits being their on-call Incanter but I'm not sure I believe Gatlin is as content with the arrangement as many assume, and I'm positive the Protogenoi would not want him here helping the other Incanters save their homes.

Still, I wouldn't bet my life on a mere suspicion that Gatlin doesn't work for the Protogenoi willingly. He may have snuck out here to protect this town from as much collateral damage as possible, but there's little chance he would directly go against the Protogenoi and let me go if he spotted me.

"Watch out," I tell Sin, grabbing onto his arm beneath the water.

Thankfully, he reacts quickly and stops moving forward. Just in front of him, in the water where his foot would have passed by, is a change in color. It's subtle, but missing the subtle things in this world means death.

While the rest of the ocean water is a dark blue, this small section is turquoise. It could mean nothing, a change in depth only. Or, it could be one of the many traps set up randomly throughout all of Havcire by Void.

The traps hold traces of his power. If set off, it means immediate death for the victim. Just another one of the Protogenoi's attempts to make life more interesting. They're hard to notice but I've become conditioned to take notice of many of the telltale signs.

It takes a moment, but Sin sees what I see. He lets out a relieved sigh before pulling me along, around the trap's trigger.

It isn't long after that we reach the edge of the town, where the Protogenoi didn't even bother to make the tsunami appear natural.

With Dabar's complete control over reality, his power is practically limitless. He can make anything out of anything, or anything out of nothing. Here, he's made it so that the flooding ends abruptly at the town's border, meaning there's a twenty foot wall of water rising straight up from the ground, of which we are at the top.

To be honest, I'm surprised he didn't just let the flood move onto the adjacent Celestial city. However, it is the city where the Ziggurat is located so, most likely, he wanted to protect his own precious home.

We don't bother diving down to swim closer to the ground. We jump from the top of the wall of water, landing on the rocky ground below. I forget I'm barefoot, though, so ow. Why couldn't there be a nice, soft meadow outside of Sans?

I walk on, across the rocky terrain that separates Sans from Zion, the Celestial city, home to the Ziggurat and the Protogenoi. My destination.

We're so close. We could have pushed through last night and made it to Zion, but Sin thought it was best we were rested before we arrived, so we got that rest, at the expense of a whole town.

I don't stop, and I don't look at my feet, which I can feel being torn up by the hard ground. I'll heal quickly and probably have stones to pull out of healed over skin as an activity to take up my time later.

"This is unwise."

"That's not news, Sin."

"Because I have told you before, but it is especially unwise now that it is clear that they knew where you were hiding. They'll know where you're going."

I keep walking, and he keeps pace beside me, showing no discomfort over the fact that he, too, is walking barefoot. I, on the other hand, am alternating between limping on one side then the other. Sure, I look like I'm struggling, but I am moving along quickly.

"That's not true," I say, with a smile. "They'll expect that I'm running, getting far away from Zion."

"Right," Sin says. "Instead, your plan is to walk right into the most dangerous city in order to compete in the annual Ascension Contest, in which people die all the time for the small chance that they'll be the victor that gets to live a privileged life in the Ziggurat for a single year up until the next contest."

My smile doesn't drop. I nod my head to confirm. Yup, that's the plan.

"And," Sin continues, "the reason you want to do this is because, once entered in the Ascension, it is illegal to attempt to kill the contestants. That is, unless it is part of the competition. If you can't be killed the second you show your face, you'll have the opportunity to announce to all of Havcire that the Protogenoi are not invincible."

"I knew you were paying attention."

Sin reciting my plan back to me, despite his best efforts, is not going to convince me that it is a bad plan and that I shouldn't follow through with it. Because, I already know it is. It's just the only plan I've got.

Sin grabs my arm, stopping me, and I groan because I know it's going to be all the more difficult to get started walking again, but I'll do it.

I meet his gray eyes, and the doubt that I've fought not to feel creeps in. It might be the only plan I've got, but it's going to get me killed.

I'm going to die. Even if I get the message out. Even if it makes people realize the Protogenoi can be killed. Even if that convinces them to rise up against them after all this time. Even if my plan plays out exactly as I intend, they will kill me.

Stepping into Zion means never leaving again. I feel like I've barely lived. How can any of us call this living with the Protogenoi in control, when we need to spend every second trying to survive? I'm not ready to die.

"Stop!" I yell, yanking my arm out from his grasp.

Immediately, the negative thoughts disappear. There's still an echo of the feelings left over, but that's all it is.

"I merely brought to the surface your own emotions," Sin says, calmly, but the blue flecks in his eyes look unsettled among the gray. "I'm trying to keep you alive. I thought you knew that much by now."

I'm angry, but I don't let any more of that show. Sin is the one ally I've got. So, maybe I'm angry he got in my head and maybe I am scared, but it doesn't change anything.

"I appreciate you trying to keep me alive, really. I recommend staying out of my head."

"All right," Sin agrees, "but it won't do you good to ignore that fear. It will attack you when you most need it to stay buried."

"So I'll play hide and seek with it when I have some down time."

Over the past few weeks, if I've noticed anything about Sin, it's that he never backs down. Even if I hint with all I've got that I don't want to talk about something, he doesn't shut up until he's said what he wants to say. And, he does it in such a way that it's clear he's not trying to force any sort of opinion on you but simply feels the responsibility to speak his own mind. And, it's normally a pretty hard to argue with point he is making.

Most of the time, it's surprisingly insightful what he has to say, which can be a good thing, and it is something I have come to admire. I guess it's not so surprising, as he does have the power to feel and influence other people's emotions. He expresses what he already knows you feel, at least at some level. It's hard to deny your own truth. But, also not impossible.

He is usually good at respecting privacy. Usually.

As the ground inclines, the rocks roll beneath my feet, and I listen to them tumble down the hill behind me. This ground used to be a road, which Incanters would use to travel to Zion and Celestials would use to travel to Sans and beyond, but the Protogenoi like to keep us all separated.

There have been no roads outside of towns and cities for a long time now. Instead, rocky, mountainous terrain, or rivers functioning as moats, divide people from each other. Anything Dabar can imagine and put into words can be made reality.

At the peak of the hill, the city comes into view. I've never been, but there's no mistaking it for another place.

It's hidden by the hills. Two rivers run through the city, bordering either side. Multiple small bridges, just large enough to fit two people across at a time, are built over the rivers to allow entry into the city.

It's beautiful, but it's all for show. The majority of the buildings are made of wood with gold woven in to both strengthen the structures and add to the picturesque scene. From afar, the gold is what catches the eye, the sun reflecting off its surface.

The whole place, however, is designed to draw your eye to the Ziggurat, which is at the end of the valley, where the rivers diverge to form a delta in which the Ziggurat sits in the center. The buildings in the rest of the city look to be bowing down to the Ziggurat, which rises above them all, reaching four stories high, while the rest barely pass as one stories.

The Ziggurat, from the outside, looks to be made fully of white marble. Although it lacks the flashy gold adorning the rest of the city, it doesn't need it to look worthy of royalty, which is what the Protogenoi are, or at least proclaim themselves to be.

Structurally, there is nothing fancy about the Ziggurat. In fact, it is oddly simple, with its rectangular shape, but the arches that form the entrances are more than enough to make up for that.

"Welcome to Zion," Sin says.

I'd describe his tone as unenthusiastic, but I've also never heard him sound particularly enthusiastic.

"Hardly," I reply.

Everyone knows the real Zion is beneath the surface.

CHAPTER NINE

The cobblestone streets are full of Ghosts. They wander aimlessly, sometimes seeming to peer into the shops' windows, but there's no desire or interest in their expressions, their apparent interest mere coincidence. Any emotion or thought has been taken from them by Maze.

The Protogenoi is powerful. He can get into anyone's mind and control every thought and, therefore, every action. Ironically, he struggles to control his own mind, which is why he prefers these days to escape into the minds of others. But, if he inhabits a mind for too long, which he tends to do because it is the only place he can achieve any semblance of peace anymore, what he leaves behind is a mere shell.

I'm not even positive it's intentional, whether Maze goes in and wrecks havoc in the minds of his hosts, or whether the mind of an Incanter or Celestial simply can't contain Maze for long without dying. One way or another, he's not blind to the impact he has as he leaves one mind to go to the next.

I don't know how the Ghosts survive. In Havcire, even to get food, you need to pay a steep price, one that no Ghost would be able to manage, at least not on their own.

For clothes, food, or anything of value, one has to go to one of the three Corporates. For as long as I can remember, they have held a monopoly on all resources.

I look into a storefront window where jewelry is on display. There are no doors leading into the store, and there's no one manning the store. The jewelry isn't really even inside. The truth is, I'm looking at a mirror, spelled to show a place in Havcire far from where I stand, for there is no way to access any of the items displayed at any of these "stores" without going through one of the Corporates.

The stores are merely advertisements, meant to entice people to sell their souls for a nice piece of jewelry, when what almost everyone needs is their next meal to survive another day. That's the way the Protogenoi want it. If everyone is focused on simply surviving, no one can stop long enough to question why we allow them to stay in power, if there is an alternative.

The Protogenoi gave the Corporates everything they have. They chose three Celestials to have everything so that the rest of the population would never have enough. And, they chose to hand that power over to the worst Celestials.

Ignoring the jewelry, I focus instead on my reflection staring back at me through the window. Finally, my clothes have dried, but the oversized hood of my black coat is stiff around my face. It no longer hides my amber eyes, the edges curving, some parts of the hood fanning out away from my face. It still does a decent job of hiding my identity from those who would want to kill me for the award, but I let my hair down before entering the city to better shield the sides of my face as well.

My pants are a bright purple, which was actually Sin's idea to help me pass more convincingly as an Incanter. The Protogenoi tend to be less suspicious of Incanters, thinking them less of a threat to their power. Additionally, no one would suspect that someone being hunted would don such a bright color.

I frown down at my bare feet. I miss my boots. Hopefully Sin will be back soon with some good news on that front.

A flash in the window's reflection catches my attention, and I turn around in time to see someone disappear through a portal.

Damn it. Dabar is always changing the location of the portals. Considering they're invisible, too, there's no way to keep track of where they are and avoid them. Once through, they all transport you to the same place. The Labyrinth, and most never make it out.

"Each store leads to a Corporate."

Sin begins speaking without preamble, having just appeared by my side.

He's back from his information gathering quest. And, apparently, that's all it was, as he's unfortunately not carrying a new pair of boots for me.

Sin doesn't ever waste any time with unnecessary greetings or a simple, "Glad to see you weren't killed in my short time away." After all, the whole reason I couldn't go along with him was because the people he needed to speak to would be inclined to murder me. That pretty much describes everyone these days.

"Wait, where'd you even come from?" I ask.

Sin glances up briefly at the top of the store.

"Anyone who is not a Ghost doesn't risk walking on these streets, which are full of Dabar's portals. They walk across the roofs."

"Wow, thanks. That's great to know, especially since I've been walking down here for quite a while now." Sometimes I really wonder how I've made it this far.

"I thought you'd notice the movement up on the roofs," Sin says, worry for my death that didn't happen starting to dawn on his face.

He looks up at the rooftops. So do I. Except, from my height, I can't actually see over the tops of the roofs. The most I can see is the golden borders of the triangular roofs. The slopes of the roofs aren't too extreme. It wouldn't be easy necessarily to walk across them, but it also could be worse.

Sin looks back down at me, emphasis on the "down" in this moment because, yeah, I am significantly shorter than he is. Sure, I thought I'd heard something coming from above the shops, but I simply am not tall enough to have found the source of the noise.

Note to self, next time I take notice of an unexplained sound, check it out and maybe avoid some close calls with death.

"The roofs I'm not tall enough to see, got it. So, how do these stores lead to the Corporates? There aren't even doors."

In response, Sin sticks his hand out to the side and right through the display window of the shop nearest us. It disappears through the glass and reappears when he pulls it back out.

"The windows portal you to where the items you see through the window really are, the Corporates."

Of course. Makes sense. The Corporates like to ensure that everyone has easy access to them. If you can't get to the Corporates, the Corporates can't take the little you have in exchange for an iota of their abundant resources.

"All right."

I bend my knees and jump, grasping onto the edge of the roof above me, and pull myself up. A hand touches me underneath my thigh, and I still. Not a second later, the touch is gone.

"Sorry, thought I'd help," Sin's voice comes from below.

It's the first time I've ever heard any real, well anything in his voice. Discomfort. Usually, Sin's tone ranges from indifference to minor curiosity.

I pull myself up and over onto the top of the roof in one quick motion and look back over the edge.

"I got it."

Sin clears his throat.

"I see that."

I reflexively pull on my hood to make sure it still shields my face.

It's not like I haven't noticed that Sin is attractive, with the way his gray eyes brightly contrast with the darker tones of his skin, they look nearly luminescent. And, super plus that he's one of the only people not looking to kill me.

Have I been tempted to ask him to carry me in his strong arms and rest my head upon his broad shoulders after days on end of walking and more days ahead of the same? Yes, I have been. But, I have not. For one, because I still have my dignity. And, two, because I don't want to give him the wrong idea.

I like Sin, but I'm not looking to jump into some relationship with the only person in this world not set on murdering me. If it went wrong, I could have absolutely no one in this world anymore who isn't looking to kill me. Not worth the risk.

Surviving is priority number one. There's no time to stop and smell the roses, whether the roses in question is Sin or some tulip who's yet to come along. I am misusing this expression. Actually, I don't know where it is I've even heard the expression before.

I shake my head, a physical attempt at clearing it, and adjust my hood once again.

From up here, I can see other Celestials roaming the city, not just the Ghosts below. There still aren't many, maybe four others as far as I can see. Zion is far from a bustling city.

It doesn't look like the Celestials are here for shopping. Rather, they run and leap across the roofs of the stores, as if all they want is to stretch their legs in the open air. It's likely, considering the stories I've heard about Zion's underground. Not much light and fresh air down there. And, with the other alternative being running in the streets that are riddled with portals to the Labyrinth, this does seem like the best choice.

"So," I say, once Sin's joined me on the roof, "let's find the storefront then that has a nice pair of boots. Not to mention, food and something to get me through the Ascension."

"Hold up. There's another option."

"You're not convincing me not to enter the Ascension Contest."

"That's not where I was going. Although, you shouldn't."

I glare at Sin, but my heart's not in it. I just have to make sure he knows there's no way he'll talk me out of entering the contest, and I need him to not even consider doing anything to take the choice out of my hands. I don't think that's something he'd do, but I can't take the chance.

"I overheard another way to come across resources in Zion," Sin continues. "There's a Celestial who sees the Corporates on a daily basis to gather resources, and he redistributes the resources himself."

Going to see the Corporates daily is unheard of. Everyone goes only when absolutely necessary. Anything more would be insanity.

"What's his price?" I ask, skeptical.

"If what I heard is true, nothing."

"We're to believe he's a Celestial Robin Hood?"

"A what?"

"You know, takes from the rich and gives to the poor," I say, but even as I explain, the words leaving my mouth, I can't help but wonder where I first heard them from... again.

"Then yes, that would be an accurate description."

"Well, it's worth checking out. Where can we find him?" I ask.

"He favors Hadur's."

"So he's a masochist." I state this as a fact.

Hadur is a Corporate who makes Havcirians fight each other to receive payment in the form of resources. That is, the winners get what they came for, while the losers are just lucky to get out alive.

"I guess that depends on how good a fighter he is."

I'm in the very city where the Protogenoi reside, and I plan to show up on their doorstep in the hope that I can enter the Ascension before they can strike me dead. I may die in the contest itself before I get the chance to let Havcire know the Protogenoi are not invincible.

But, despite all that, a smile comes to my face. I can't help it. I'm kind of excited to meet this masochistic Robin Hood.

Again, where do I know that name from?

CHAPTER TEN

T he entrance to Zion's underground is through either of the two rivers that border the city.

Once again, my clothes are all wet. The only source of light when we enter is that which seeps through the water of the river above us. The river forms the ceiling, suspended magically in the air, just as the water that flooded Sans defied gravity to create a wall.

Despite the lack of natural light down here, it is pretty warm, which I'm grateful for considering the chills that threaten me as a result of my soaked clothing. Perhaps all the body heat from those moving through the tunnels keeps the cold away.

The presence of so many people about naturally makes me nervous. Someone could recognize me, but my hood is in its place and everyone seems too busy trying to get to wherever it is they're in a rush to get to. And, it is, as I mentioned, dark. All in all, a good place to slip by unnoticed.

A take a breath and keep my head down, becoming a part of the flow of people.

The tunnel is as wide as the river, about ten feet. Everyone is walking in the same direction, to an area further down that glows bright with a warm, orange light. It is also in that direction that all the noise is coming from, cheers and jeers blending to create a cacophony.

It becomes blazingly clear where the heat is coming from as we reach the arch that leads into Hadur's crowded arena.

The walls are lined with fire, which Hadur must be controlling to ensure no one burns. They let off a dry heat, making the air feel too thin. Between that and all the people stuffed in here, it's not exactly a place of comfort.

The entrance is a pointed arch, through which the ground suddenly drops off. Down below is the round room, with its walls of fire rising up above. Essentially, it's a pit.

The ground is about three stories down. There is a metal ladder against the wall, but one touch of it reveals that's not the best option. It burns nearly as hot as the surrounding fire. The other three entrances, identical to this one, are spread out evenly around the periphery.

I want to observe the area more from this vantage point, but we've reached the literal end of the road, the location everyone was heading toward. I feel the press of anxious bodies behind me. Though I don't think they'd go so far as to push us down to get in faster, I would rather not chance it.

I jump down, bending my knees to brace against the fall, and land on the stone ground below. The voices rise around me. A moment ago, there was only the small arch through which sound could escape, but now I'm submerged in the commotion.

An Incanter couldn't make that jump. They would have had to find a spell to use for the descent or risk the torturous ladder. Even as a Celestial, it's not a particularly easy jump to land. Although my legs hold strong, the soles of my feet suffer again. Wow, do I miss shoes.

The full audience watches the fight that takes place in the center of the room in a square cage. It's just four walls and a ceiling made of linked metal. Nothing fancy. The ground is the same hard stone as the rest of the room. I don't know why that looks odd. Did I expect the ground in the fighting cage to be nice and cushioned for the fighters? It's also bloodstained.

One of the new members of the audience, who jumped in behind me, checks my shoulder as he walks around me in the narrow aisle to find a seat. The jolt is enough to remind me that, while everyone is busy watching this fight and couldn't care less about me right now, I am still essentially standing in a burning tomb full of people who could all turn on me at any second if they recognized my face.

Again, I tug on the hood, making sure it's still secure. One day, I might actually not have to wear this anymore and find myself reaching for a phantom hood.

The seats on which the audience watches the fight look no more comfortable than the cage. I'm not even sure they were designed as seats, as they are made from the stone of the rest of the underground.

The stone juts out around the cage like rocks along a rough shoreline, and people climb up onto them for a better view of the fight. At their backs, the fire along the wall rages, but no one seems to care about that or show any concern that Hadur, wherever he is, might let it loose on them.

I guess the threat of being burned pales in comparison to the constant threats that lie above the surface, created by the Protogenoi.

I let Sin lead me through the crowd and boulders of stone so I can keep my head down. Having little to look at other than the ground, I try to make out the cacophony of shouts.

"Finish him" is the most popular, but apparently the message isn't getting through because the fight continues on. Whoever has the upper hand, which it is clear someone does, they're choosing to draw out the fight.

Or, an alternate possibility, maybe the loser is refusing to stay down.

In Hadur's fights, the loser doesn't always have to die. It depends on (1) the winner's desire to kill and (2) the loser's willingness to take the loss. The latter can just easily result in death as the former.

I'm fairly close to the cage now, and I chance a glance up. It's only enough to make out the feet and legs of those fighting.

One of the fighters, the one who wears shorts, is dragging his left leg, favoring his right. His body shifts as he throws what I assume to be a punch at his opponent, who is wearing jeans.

Jean Guy, light on his feet, steps to the side, and I hear no impact made. He evaded the hit, but he also doesn't shift his weight to retaliate. Instead, he keeps moving, walking around the edge of the cage, his gait seemingly relaxed.

Is he cruelly playing with Shorts Guy, or is he simply reluctant to harm him further?

"I need to ask around about this benefactor," Sin shouts over the voices around us.

I nod, pulling my attention away from the fight.

"I will, too."

I start to walk off in the opposite direction from Sin to cover more area, but he grabs my arm, stopping me.

"No, you can't be recognized."

I yank my arm down, the one he grabbed, so he's pulled down toward me, and I can see him without looking up and risking exposing myself.

"I know how to be careful, and we'll find him faster if we're both looking."

"Fine," Sin relents and releases my arm.

I walk along the edge of the cage to keep track of who I've asked and the area I've yet to cover. People barely pay me any attention, even when I approach them.

The second I spare to peer up at the person I've asked about the location of the Celestial reveals that I'm being fully ignored in favor of the events taking place in the fighting cage, so I take a moment to scan the area around me for anyone who seems even slightly likely to be of some help.

My attention falls on a male with long, silver hair who isn't even pretending to feign interest in the fight. He sits in what could be called the front row, if anything about these seating arrangements was organized at all. Yet, he doesn't even watch the fight, seeming to find the ground significantly more interesting. Whatever his reasoning, it works for me.

"Hi, if you could spare a moment," I start.

"All I have are moments," the male says, his deep voice easy to hear over the shouting of the crowd, "very boring moments. The name's Barnabas."

I can't see his face, but he reaches out a hand for me to shake, so I do, hoping it doesn't seem too odd that I can't look him in the eye. Maybe Sin was right, and I should have just waited for him to make the rounds.

Too late now. If anyone gets suspicious, I'll just slink on away before suspicion can turn into confident accusation.

I smile, hoping Barnabas can at least see that. Smiles put people at ease, most people.

"Nice to meet you," I say. "Do you know where I could find a Celestial named Phoenix?"

A fist connecting with a jaw sounds out from behind me as Barnabas laughs and says, "Behind you."

I mumble a thanks, but I'm already turning around to the cage, where the guy in the jeans hits the wall of the cage nearest me, the metal links screeching from the impact. His fingers wrap through the links as he holds on to stay standing, and he's staring right at me.

He looks completely unaffected by the fight, except for a single drop of blood dripping from the split in his lip, presumably from the punch he just took to the face. It appears to be the only injury he's sustained from the entirety of the fight.

Despite the split lip, his mouth forms a crooked smile as he looks at me, his green eyes sparking with intrigue.

At the sight of that smile, I have the sudden, strong desire to slap it right off his face. And, at the same time, to grab the rough metal links of the cage, pull myself up, and carefully brush my thumb across his lip to rid him of that drop of blood.

"I heard you and your friend asking for me," he says, snapping me back to reality. "I'll just be a second."

He winks and then turns away just in time to face his opponent who'd been attempting to attack while his back was turned.

It's only then that I realize I forgot to hide my face from him.

I look up to fully witness the fight, my face only visible to the two fighters. I figure the one who hasn't already seen me is too preoccupied to notice anyways.

Shorts Guy stops his advance when he sees Phoenix's back is no longer turned to him. Instead, he lifts his arms up in front of him. I think he's surrendering, but then the air between them ripples as waves stem out from his hands. Shorts Guy is telekinetic.

Before there can be any impact, Phoenix is gone. He reappears directly behind Shorts Guy and knocks him out with one elbow to the temple.

It's a clean and easy end to the fight. Most of the crowd is cheering, but I hear a few who make their desire for a more bloody ending known.

The fire along the walls pulses with the end of the fight, expanding to cover even the metal ladders. I wouldn't want to be heading up or down one of those at a fight's resolution.

Hadur, the cause of the extra lively fire, walks into the cage to stand beside Phoenix. He's as big as Barnabas behind me and looks to be about the same age. Although, age is superficial for us.

His face seems drained of the strength the rest of his body shows, as if the fire extending from his hands up to his shoulders is taking the oxygen from his own chest, which is bare, probably because the fire would burn away any material.

His eyes, too close together, narrow at Phoenix for barely a second before his thin lips stretch into a smile directed at the crowd. He grabs Phoenix's hand in his burning one and raises them both in the air above their heads. Phoenix doesn't show any sign that the fire hurts, but it must.

"Our champion! Once again," Hadur announces in a loud and grating voice. His eyes move through the crowd, as their cheering increases with his words.

I quickly lower my head again. Assuming Phoenix doesn't turn me in within the next few seconds, I need to prevent others, especially those like Hadur, from discovering me.

Hadur goes on explaining the benefits of fighting down here, as if we don't all already know. It's either fight here with the chance of dying in the process, or risk paying the equally high price of the other Corporates. Although, depending on one's perspective, the other Corporates might be considered to ask for an even higher price than your life.

Of course, there's always the option of stealing from other Celestials and Incanters who have gone through the effort of paying for the resources. I'm not proud of the fact that I've taken that route before. Now, however, it seems there's a fourth option. I hope the fourth option isn't still having his arm slowly burned off as Hadur rambles on.

Across, through the metal links of the cage, I spot Sin's bare feet and peek up enough just to confirm it is him standing on the opposite side. When I do, I notice Phoenix is no longer inside the cage. Already, Hadur is leading the next two fighters in.

"Hey, Killer," Phoenix says from behind me, close enough that I can feel his breath on the back of my neck.

I'm not certain whether the shivers that run through my body are a result of his physical presence behind me or because of what he's just called me. He knows exactly who I am and has made some accurate assumptions about why it is the Protogenoi want me.

I am positive it is him, already recognizing his deep but flippant voice from the few words he spoke to me from inside the cage. His tone sends a clear message that he doesn't take anything too seriously, that he's unfazed, or at least wants you to think as much.

I send a quick *I got this* glance to Sin before turning to face Phoenix. I suspect Sin will still set out to reach us, but I didn't want to turn my back to him without some reassurance first. He's put in a lot of effort to ensure I stay alive. It's the least I can do.

Although it's clear there's no point in hiding my identity from Phoenix at this point, I still have to keep my head lowered beneath my hood for those around us.

"I prefer the name Dawn," I tell him, keeping my voice below the roar of the crowd.

"And I prefer not to be caught associating with a known fugitive. Come on," he says, and begins walking away. He doesn't bother to stop and check if I'm following. Either he assumes I will or doesn't care whether or not I do. "Your bodyguard may follow if he'd like."

The way he adds on that last bit is much more of a message than an allowance. Nothing gets past him, so don't bother trying anything.

Sin joins me at my side not long after as Phoenix leads us through the jutting stone that functions as seats. We reach the wall covered in fire in all places, except where an especially large boulder sticks out from it. No one sits or stands on top of it, probably because it's too close to the fire to seem like a safe bet.

Phoenix stops and gestures toward the boulder, as if he believes it to be one of the archways leading in and out of the room.

"You may enter."

Sin doesn't miss a beat. "That's a rock."

"Is it?" Phoenix counters.

With a wave of his hand, the boulder disappears to reveal a small tunnel leading out of the room.

"It's not a rock," I tell Sin, who gives me an uncharacteristic glare, which almost has me breaking out into a grin. It's fun to get Sin to show some emotion.

Sin goes to enter through the now open wall, but Phoenix holds out a hand in the universal sign for stop. Sin does no such thing, and Phoenix doesn't move, leading to his hand coming to rest flat against Sin's chest.

Sin does not look happy at the fact that Phoenix is touching him. It's not apparent in his facial expression, but his whole body appears tensed to attack. Phoenix merely offers a small smile as he lowers his hand.

"I need to speak with her alone. I promise I won't kill her. Unless she tries to kill me. Plus, this is the only way in or out of this tunnel, so I also won't be able to take her to you know whom without coming back through here."

"I saw you teleport," Sin points out, unconvinced.

"Myself. I can't take someone else with me."

Sin looks skeptical. He doesn't pull his gray eyes away from Phoenix for even a second, and there's no doubt in me that Sin doesn't believe him. And yet...

"I'll be here."

I feel my eyebrows pull up, displaying my surprise. That is, if my face were visible beneath this hood.

Well, if that's settled. I reach out and squeeze Sin's forearm lightly. I'll be back. After all, people call me Killer, as of one moment ago. I can take care of myself.

CHAPTER ELEVEN

I nearly walk into Phoenix's back. He's stopped suddenly. The tunnel is so narrow that I have to remain behind him, and his body blocks basically my entire view of what's ahead of him. But, I can tell from the light that now sneaks in around Phoenix that the tunnel must open up into a larger space soon.

He turns to look at me.

"I could teleport you."

He says it so matter-of-fact. I stop the instinctive step back I was about to take.

As in, he could teleport me straight to one of the Protogenoi, straight to my death, which is exactly what he claimed to Sin he couldn't do.

"And I *could* kill you," I shoot right back.

"I've no doubt." He smiles, like the idea of me killing him is something he welcomes.

"Why tell me now that you can?"

He thinks about it.

"I'm not sure. I wanted to," he answers, looking genuinely confused by that fact.

And then he's walking forward again. And, I'm following.

The single room the tunnel leads us to is crowded but organized. It's nearly as large as Hadur's club but less threatening considering the lack of fire on the walls. In fact, half of the area looks like a farmers' market, with resources displayed out for anyone to peruse.

The other half, I couldn't say, as it's concealed by a white curtain that hangs from the stone ceiling by hooks, creating a wall that essentially divides the room in two. I'm not curious at all as to what could be behind it.

It's also lighter in here, not shadowed like Hadur's club or just plain dark like the tunnel we walked through to arrive here. In the center of the room's stone ceiling hangs a chandelier. It's the only place where the curtain dips at all. The chandelier looks to be made of copper, the arms shaped like long feathers. The feathers are spread out in a variety of directions, casting white light across the entire room.

The resources are set up on shelves that begin right at the arched entrance to the room. They create a narrow pathway through which to enter the room and then split off into two separate directions like a street's intersection. One path ends abruptly, offering an exit from the shelves.

Because the shelves are low, I can see everything, where the path that continues on leads. The rest of the shelves are organized in the form of a squared spiral. You have to walk past every resource displayed in order to get to the center ones.

The necessities - food, water, and clothing - are located at the beginning of the spiral, while other, more flashy items are located in the center. So, the truly most valuable items then are on the exterior. The most expensive items are in the center.

He's either organized this place with the goal of keeping those expensive items secure, or he's trying to encourage whoever enters here to take what it is they truly need and not get sidetracked by the items in the middle.

"Ascension will begin at next light," Phoenix says, as he makes his way through the resources.

I can't even imagine what he's had to do in order to have this many resources to spare. Wait, next light? I don't have to hide my shock despite it being clear on my face. Out of habit, my head is still ducked, my hood pulled up. I follow Phoenix's feet and keep my eyes on the resources on the lower shelves.

I knew the Ascension Contest had to be coming up soon, but no one really knows exactly when. It's just one other thing the Protogenoi use against us. Except, apparently Phoenix knows.

Sure, Ascension is supposed to offer an opportunity for the winner to live like royalty in the Ziggurat for a year, but it's hard to enter a contest you don't know is happening until it's already begun.

Magister, with her control over time, makes it almost impossible to keep track at all of what hour of the day it is. One moment, it will be mid-night and the next mid-day. In fact, light and dark is the only way to tell the passage of time at all. Usually, each last a minimum of three hours and a maximum of eighteen.

Being in the underground of Zion, I'm not even sure whether it's gotten dark yet. Either way, next light is not much time.

"Why are you telling me about Ascension?" I ask, playing dumb.

Phoenix reaches out and grabs a pair of black boots, knee high, off the shelf to our right. His hands, which make me think he'd be a beautiful piano player, have the dried blood of his opponent still on them. Those hands shove the boots at my chest, and I grab onto them, the boots, not his hands, even though I appear to have an odd fascination with them. Or, him in general.

Who wouldn't? He knows things no one should. He has all these resources that come at high prices, and he just gives them away to people. He's obviously a highly skilled fighter. Plus, I mean, I'm not going to lie, he looks like *that*. But, that's barely the leading cause of my interest. I hardly got a good look at him in the dark lighting of Hadur's anyway. Just his eyes.

"Because," he says, and I can hear the smile in his voice, "you want to compete. Why else would a fugitive stroll into Zion?"

"To hide in plain sight?"

He continues walking on, and I rush to pull the boots on and follow.

"You could have less than three hours before the contest starts, and you're going to want to accept my help. So, I would just start telling me the truth."

I can't help the scoff that escapes me.

"Why should I? It seems you already know everything." For example, that it must have turned dark outside while I was down here. "How do you know it's dark?"

"I asked my question first."

"Technically, you didn't ask a question."

Phoenix stops walking through the spiral and points to something off to the side. I follow and find what I'd neglected when I entered.

Against the wall to my left, a dim light reflects off a mirror and up onto the ceiling above. That mirror is reflecting the light that shines off another mirror further up the wall. The mirrors go up higher than I can see, reflecting the one beam of light all the way down to us. The mirrors probably, I'd guess, start at one of the rivers above. When it's light outside, they must catch the yellower, brighter shine of the sun. The current dimmer, blue light means darkness.

So, in conclusion, it is dark out presently. Got it.

And, that makes that the second answer he's given me without anything in return.

"Alright, what is your question?" I relent.

"Are you going to accept my help to win the Ascension?"

"Why would you want to help?" I ask.

"Why do you want to compete?"

"To get out in the open long enough without being targeted to announce that I killed Chaos."

Why did I just admit that?

Maybe, because it seems as though he already knows the answers to all the questions he's asking. It's as if he asks only so I'm aware we're already on the same page. Or, rather, that he's been on the same page as I am. He's on his second read of this book.

What exactly do I know about him? He supposedly is a Celestial that provides resources illegally to others. Illegally, because he doesn't ask for any payment of his own. It's suspicious because it's so... nice.

"Exactly, Killer. I want that for you, too."

Killer. He wasn't merely making assumptions earlier about the crime the Protogenoi have made me enemy number one for. He knew from the start exactly what I did. He knew *who* I killed.

"How do you know so much?" I ask outright. "The Protogenoi made sure no one knew what I was being hunted for."

"I have connections."

Phoenix keeps walking among the shelves.

"Why do you want me to tell everyone what I did?"

"For the same reason you do."

"And how do you know my reasoning?"

"Must you question everything?"

"Must you be so cryptic?"

He stops walking near another shelf with clothes folded neatly on top.

"There's one I can answer. Yes." He picks a tight pair of black pants off one pile and a fitted, long-sleeve black shirt off another and holds them out to me. "Here."

"I already have clothes," I tell him, glancing down at myself.

"They're stiff and dirty. Plus, the whole point will be to reveal yourself as you. You won't be needing that hood, and you might as well dress the part of intimidating assassin, make the claim more believable for the masses. By the way, no one else knows about this tunnel or room."

"Is this your way of giving me a heads up that you're about to murder me and no one will ever find the body?"

His smile comes easy.

"I just meant you can lower your hood in here."

"Oh."

I do and take the clothes from Phoenix's hands, which briefly brush against my own, sending a surprisingly enticing warmth through my chilled body. I pull the clothes close, breaking the contact, and look up at him for the first time since I forgot myself outside Hadur's fighting cage.

Unlike in Hadur's club, which was full of dark shadows cast by the walls of fire, Phoenix's face is clear.

The cut on his full lower lip is gone, already healed, smooth. Although he didn't seem to be working too hard in the fight, a thin sheen of sweat coats his skin, making his dark brown, wavy hair stick to his forehead in some places. His white shirt, too, is damp, especially over his abdomen, where it clings to his skin, showing off the hard, toned stomach beneath.

I force my eyes away and back to his face, but he's staring right back at me when I look up, and I feel my face heat.

"Do I know you?" he asks, staring into my eyes, as if the answer to something that's slipped his mind is hidden in their depths. It's too much, and thankfully I find something else to focus on.

His hair mostly covers it, but there's a scar across his right eyebrow. It looks especially pale against his dark hair and tan skin.

One of the few things I thought I knew about him was that he was a Celestial. Incanters can scar but Celestials...

"What are you?" I ask, eyeing the scar still.

"You know what I am." For the first time, Phoenix sounds somewhat perplexed.

"No." I reach up and brush his hair to the side, more clearly revealing the scar. He shifts under my touch but doesn't pull away.

I drag a finger across the scar, from about an inch above his eyebrow to a little below, across his eyelid. I can feel his eyes stay on me as my focus stays on that scar, my palm resting on his cheek, my other fingers trailing lightly along his temple, weaving between the hair there on their own accord.

"Celestials can't scar," I state.

When he responds, his voice sounds tight.

"Protogenoi can't be killed. And yet..."

Touché. I drop my hand and back away, not because I'm dropping the topic, but because it's probably a good idea right about now to take a physical step back and stop touching the stranger.

"Explain this one thing *fully*, and I'll accept your help."

"Wow, what an offer." The carefree, sarcastic tone is back.

I stare back, refusing to say anything more until he does what I suggested. Sure, I could use his help and maybe even want it. But, he seems motivated enough to help me for whatever reason, so it might just work, and the explanation might just reveal something about his true intentions, especially seeing how guarded he appears to be about this topic.

Not sure when it became my mission to learn about Phoenix. Well, my mission second to winning the Ascension.

"Okay, fine," he relents.

I mask my surprise.

Rather than pulling his hair back down to hide the scar again, he threads the strands through his fingers, pushing it even more back from his forehead to clearly reveal the scar.

"Dabar made me mortal for seven light phases and seven dark phases. He didn't like that I had a way of avoiding his portals to the Labyrinth and Void's death traps with my teleportation. It was during that time, when I was mortal, that I got injured. It healed slowly, scarring before he turned me back. That's the story. The end."

"An Incanter could heal the scar," I suggest stupidly, as he must know that.

"It helps remind me."

Of revenge? Maybe he's so eager to help me because he hates Dabar on a personal level.

"No, of mortality."

"What?" I ask, confused, and not at Phoenix's response, but at the fact that he responded at all. I didn't say that out loud.

"You—" Phoenix pauses. "I thought I'd heard you earlier also, but—"

"*Dawn?*" Sin's voice questions.

"*Dawn? The Protogenoi's most wanted is in my head? How interesting,*" another male's voice muses. This one, I don't recognize.

"*Sin, what's going on?*" I ask, and turn my attention back to Phoenix at the same time. "Can you hear them also?"

He simply nods.

"*I don't know what this is,*" another voice, female this time, drawls, "*but it better not last.*"

CHAPTER TWELVE

"Can you fix it?" I ask Sin.

"What, you don't want to have four voices inside your head at all times?"

"Five," I correct Phoenix. "Mine, too."

He leads us back through the hidden tunnel.

He gave Sin permission to follow us in. Either he'd made the decision to let Sin in because of our conversation or because Sin had already managed to intrude in on his mind.

"Actually, I'm not sure fixing it is a good idea until we've figured out why it is," Sin says.

"So, you can fix it."

"Yes," Sin answers, simply.

Phoenix is ahead of us. We left his storage room not long ago and are following him to I don't know where, but I do know it's in the direction away from Hadur's club.

"You trust him now?" Sin asks, lowering his voice, although I'm sure Phoenix could hear if he were listening.

"I barely trust you," I say back in a hushed tone, "but I'm willing to work with the both of you."

"*I'm* trying to save your life."

The sound of dripping water reaches me from further down the tunnel in the direction we're heading. The way in and out of Zion's underground is through water, so I'm holding the clothes Phoenix gave me in a water-proof bag, which he also gave me, free of charge.

"He claims to want the same thing I do," I tell Sin.

Free of charge. For now. The price could still drop at any moment.

"If you trust no one, you risk trusting the untrustworthy the same amount as the trustworthy," Sin says.

"I think you're gonna have to check the logic of that one. Also, I'm losing your point. Do you *want* me to trust Phoenix?"

"I want you to trust me."

"Well, that's exactly what someone would want me to do if they weren't trustworthy, wouldn't they?"

"I'm not justifying that with an answer. You know I am trustworthy."

"That is an answer."

This time, he actually doesn't answer, shooting me some side eye and leaving it at that.

"Technically, since Phoenix wants what I want, and you just want to keep me alive, he is more trustworthy than you because you can always count on people to do what they themselves want to do."

That is, if I am to believe Phoenix when he says that he, too, wants me to be able to reveal to Havcire that I killed Chaos.

"You're saying it's not important to you that you stay alive?"

Gasp! And, I do gasp out loud.

"Of course I value my own life. How dare you suggest that I do not," I insist, flabbergasted, but then shrug, adding, "but it is primarily important to me that everyone learns the truth about the Protogenoi so they can fight back. I just am optimistic achieving that won't entail me dying."

"So we do want the same thing," Sin concludes, as final evidence that I should trust him.

"Eh," I respond, half-heartedly disagreeing.

I *do* trust. I trust that Sin's values are strong, and they are motivating him to keep me alive. As for Phoenix, I have a strong desire to trust him. My gut tells me I can, which is frightening because it's not exactly fool proof reasoning. Maybe I'm just desperate to believe there is someone doing good for others, including for myself, for no nefarious reason.

No, that can't be it because even the thought of someone behaving in such a selfless way is suspicious to me. It's not desperation. I trust myself. I'm low on people I can ally with, seeing as most wouldn't hesitate to turn me into the Protogenoi. So, I'm not going to turn my back on this opportunity. I choose to trust my gut on this one because my gut is, after all, pretty selective.

But, all that doesn't mean I can't still keep a close eye on Phoenix and be cautious. And, it also doesn't mean I'm about to openly admit to Sin that I trust Phoenix for no explicit reason.

Phoenix stops walking ahead of us, and I see the source of the dripping sound. It's not the river we entered through like I expected, but a smaller, round body of water up above. Blue, dim light shines through the water and reflects off the stone walls around us, creating luminescent ripples.

The tunnel comes to a dead end. The perfect trap, which is something I am simply acknowledging, not something that I actually believe Phoenix has just led me and Sin into.

"I'll go first," Sin says. No doubt he wants to scout out the area above before I reach it.

"Where is this?" I ask Phoenix, but Sin answers before he gets the chance.

"The fountain in the center of Zion."

I guess I didn't get far enough into the city to see it. But, if there's a fountain that functions as an entrance right into Phoenix's "secret" tunnel, then how secret could it be?

"No one else knows it leads down here like the rivers do," Phoenix answers my unspoken question, as if reading my mind.

He lifts his hand up to the water above and drags a finger through it. It disperses around his finger, but not a single drop drips down. The continuous dripping must sound from above, probably from the fountain itself, because nothing appears to disturb whatever magic keeps the water down here suspended.

Phoenix lowers his hand and nods at Sin, who jumps into the air. His arms go into the water up to just above his elbows. He grabs onto the water itself and pulls himself the rest of the way up and into it. It seems only to take a small push against the water to get himself fully submerged in it, but maybe he just makes the action seem effortless.

"Go on," Phoenix says, gesturing up to the fountain.

I hesitate.

"There's no trap waiting for you up there."

I look at him in question because that was not the cause of my hesitation. Embarrassingly enough, something else was occupying my mind.

"I could teleport you at any point straight into a trap," he goes on. "No point in going about it this way."

"Was that meant to be comforting?"

"Just the truth. Why? Did it come across as comforting?" he asks, mock curious.

"Well, I hadn't been concerned about a trap. But now..."

"So then what's the hold up, Killer?"

"It's Dawn."

"Not yet, thankfully."

I frown. "I meant my name."

The amusement in his eyes makes it clear he knew what I meant. He gestures from me to the water above. The question still stands.

"It's just, it's pretty high up. I'm short." And I don't want to make a fool of myself in front of him. That's apparently important to me that I not do that.

The image of me jumping up and down, arms reaching for the water above, and failing to get enough of my arms submerged to pull myself up as Phoenix watches me struggle plays on repeat in my head.

For barely a second, Phoenix looks confused.

Then, he's moving closer to me, and it occurs to me that Sin going up first meant leaving me alone down here with Phoenix.

He places his hands on my waist. Heat stirs within me at his touch, my stomach tightening, which I'm positive he can feel against his palms. His fingers flex against my back as if in response, despite nothing on his face indicating that he feels anything at all.

"You're saying you need a lift?" he asks, so innocent it might actually just be an innocent question, and I'm just delusional here, overreacting to every single thing he does.

"No, I'm sure I can manage."

I thank whatever gracious higher power there is that my autopilot mode is stubborn.

"That's what I thought. Because, no matter how short you are, a Celestial should be able to make this jump," Phoenix says.

Of course he's right. How is it that I can just forget something like that? I can easily make this jump.

I push Phoenix's hands off me in as defiant of a manner as I can muster, ignoring the brush of his knuckles on my palms as I do.

He backs up, an annoyingly knowing smile on his face, which feels doubly annoying because of his seemingly all-knowing nature I've gotten to know in this short amount of time I've been acquainted with him.

Suddenly, my initial reaction to seeing him and that smile makes so much sense, as in the fact that I both wanted to slap it off his face and fix his little lip boo boo. I'll just take that as evidence that my gut was right about him initially and is still right about trusting him.

"Hello?"

The unfamiliar, male voice is back.

Phoenix barely shows any sign of hearing him, but I notice an almost imperceptible tilt of his head, as if he thinks he can shake the voice out of his ear like some stray water.

"Hi," I reply automatically, before I can think better of it.

It's probably not best to speak so openly, even if it is telepathically, to other Havcirians. I'm still being hunted, at least until I can enter the Ascension and get that temporary immunity. What if I give up my location accidentally and one of these two other people in my head comes looking?

I jump up, done putting it off, and land like Sin had, with my arms mostly submerged in the water. Sin didn't just make it seem easy. The second my hands are in the water, a different gravity takes over, pulling me up rather than down, like the world has flipped.

It felt the opposite coming down into the underground through the rivers, but it wasn't as noticeable then. When we entered, the water held us up as we floated. But, the second my feet broke through the bottom on the other side, I started to fall, the water no longer having any hold on me.

Exiting works in the reverse. All it takes to fully enter the water now is a slight push of my arms against it, and I swim up to the opposite surface.

"Hi," the voice continues in my head, sounding unusually happy. Most are not that upbeat in this world. Understandably. *"Just wanted to make sure I hadn't hallucinated the voices in my head."*

"Great, you're all still here." The female's voice is back, fully sarcastic. *"Can someone explain why this is happening?"*

I breathe in a gulp of air as I surface. It's dark, like really dark. Of course, it's night right now. But, other than the blue light that seems to stem from the water itself, I can't see anything around me. I reach out an arm to swim forward with caution, but I hit something cold and hard.

"I'm a telepath," I hear Sin's voice half explain in my head. He's actually more of an empath, with a telepathic ability.

Where is Sin?

"I'm capable of opening others' minds to each other so a group can communicate telepathically. Except, it doesn't happen accidentally, and I don't remember ever putting this into effect. I don't even know who two of you are."

Finally, my eyes adjust better to the lighting, and I can make out shapes rather than just shades of darkness.

What I hit was thick metal. It surrounds me, forming a curved wall in front of me. I look up and realize it's attached to a figure, a person's back, like a cape. It must be part of the fountain's design, part of the statue in its center.

"How's that possible?" the female asks.

"It shouldn't be," Sin answers. *"Even if I somehow managed to pull this off instinctively, I'm only capable of doing this with people I know."*

Sin already explained this all to me and Phoenix earlier, but it still is confusing to hear. It probably is smart to not close up the connection just yet. According to Sin, this can't be random. So, keeping the connection will help us figure out faster who these people are and, therefore, why this is happening. Few things in life are coincidental.

Although, it means I'll have to watch the thoughts I project from now on. I have gotten better at that, though, having to travel with Sin.

I feel under for where the metal cape ends. It only extends on for a few inches below the water. I push the bag of clothes I brought with me under it and make to follow, but the water laps lightly against my back. I turn around at the movement to find Phoenix, who breaks through the surface of the water.

His hair sends small droplets of water flying when he shakes it out of his face. I hold onto the bottom of the statue's cape with my fingers so I don't have to work as hard to tread water.

Putting aside the issue or non-issue of trust, seeing as I really don't need to trust anyone to work with them, knowing more about Phoenix couldn't hurt. Call it curiosity, seeing as I was interested in his motivations before even meeting him.

He swims up to my side and grabs onto the statue, as well.

"Are you coming?" he asks. "Or do you like being in Void's cold embrace?"

"Void?"

He points up to the face of the statue in answer.

I know it's a statue, but even for a statue it looks lifeless, emotionless. Just like Void. And, even though it's just a statue, I freeze. My heart jumps and then feels like it overcompensates, slowing back down too fast.

I rush to take my hands off the cape, not to touch anything associated with Void. I forget I'm in water like a dumbass and slip down under, which brings back my senses, thankfully. But, not before hands are reaching down to pull me back up.

I cough and grasp back onto the statue's cape.

"Whoah," Phoenix says, his hands releasing my arms once I've proven I can once again stay above water without assistance. "I'll take that as a vote to get out of here."

"Wait," I tell him, groaning mentally at myself.

I had a conversation I wanted to have, and then I let myself freak out over an inanimate object. It's not really Void that frightens me so much, as his traps. To be walking around one day and then suddenly have it all be over. Dying is something I think I could manage, but having no warning at all that it's coming? Having it be so random and unfair? I mean, I guess that is how death generally is.

But, there are too many things I need to get done before I die, and death by one of Void's traps would be too fast. There would be no chance to fight it. And, it's permanent.

Also, can I please stop getting myself into situations that end with Phoenix's hands on me?

He's watching me patiently, expectantly but patiently, his green eyes somehow alight in this dim place. He'd asked earlier, "Do I know you?" Does he? Something, maybe everything, seems familiar about him, familiarly puzzling at least.

Focus.

"Why would you want to remind yourself of mortality?"

"Back to my scar?" he asks.

"Yes, it's fascinating," I deadpan, even though it's true.

Phoenix's response is a deep hum of agreement I can feel. "Because it's on my beautiful face."

"Your beautiful, supposed to be scar impervious face, yes."

"So you think I'm pretty?" he says, ridiculously batting his equally ridiculous dark and long eyelashes.

"If I say so, will you answer my question?"

He doesn't make me say it.

"Death is the absence of life," he says.

If it weren't for the smile teasing his lips, I'd think he were already taking lessons from Sin, who's always saying things like that but with his perpetual stoicism.

He reaches up and brushes a piece of wet hair off my cheek, making me forget the chill of the water. He doesn't even seem to realize he's done it. When his hand drops back down, his expression is serious.

"They give each other meaning," he continues. "If something lives, it can die. Even immortals, but you know that. Right, Killer?"

I bristle at the nickname I've apparently adopted.

"I'm not a killer."

"Then why'd you kill Chaos?"

Before I can answer, there's a voice in both our heads again.

"I was with a customer," the male voice says. *"Did I miss something?"*

Phoenix's easy smile is back. He ducks beneath the water and swims out from under the statue.

I try to refocus, think about the implications, if any, of his answer, but there are literal voices in my head.

"How do you miss something going on in your own head?" Phoenix asks.

"Easily," the reply comes; and I have to admit, I totally understand unidentified male voice.

I take a breath and swim under the metal cape.

CHAPTER
THIRTEEN

Torches light the darkness out here, illuminating the fountain's design in orange, making the statue itself appear on fire. It depicts all five Protogenoi, or the five that were.

Next to Void's caped figure is Maze. He appears to sit right on top of the water, one of his legs bent and pulled up against his chest and the other dangling into the water. His hands frame his head, clearly indicating the source of his power.

Beside Maze, Chaos stands in a crouch, the metal hair of her statue falling around her furious face.

Completing the circle is Magister. Her arms are spread out like she's performing, but they're designed to look like the hands of a clock, for with Magister, there is no time that matters other than the one she creates.

Standing above them all, in the center of the circle they form, is Dabar. One hand of Dabar's is lifted up in the air, and water from the fountain shoots out of it, arcing out in four separate directions to envelope the statues of the five Protogenoi. Rather than the water coming down in streams, however, it gushes out of his hand and then disperses into small droplets that drip down into the pool below. The dripping sound I'd heard from underground. The water falls slowly enough that I can make out each individual drop.

I grab my bag of clothes that floats in the water near me and pull myself out of the fountain to join Sin and Phoenix already standing on the street.

"*You get customers?*" the female asks.

"*Yes. You don't know who I am?*"

I wring out my wet hair and watch Sin regret his decision not to close up this telepathic connection after all.

"*That's precisely what we just established,*" Sin responds.

I work hard to hold back the smile threatening my face. I'm a fairly no nonsense type of person, so Sin and I have been getting along swimmingly. Unlike Sin, however, I can appreciate some good nonsense... even if I haven't got the time for any.

I pull up my hood again, which is weighted down once again by water. I don't see anyone out here, but better safe than sorry. It won't be much longer now until I won't have to disguise myself. I know the rules of Ascension should keep me safe from outright assassination, but the idea of revealing myself still leaves me feeling uneasy.

Sure, there's a general respect for tradition and rules amongst Havcirians, but am I absolutely positive that Havcirian culture will win out over the promise of a great reward for killing me? No, it probably will not. At least, not with everyone.

It's still dark outside, but that means very little. It could be light in a second, and then I'd be at risk of being late for Ascension, so I'm quick to follow Phoenix when he starts leading us again. This time, in the direction of the Ziggurat.

Although Sin had said the fountain was in the center of Zion, it definitely seems nearer the Ziggurat to me, or maybe that's just my reluctance to approach the Ziggurat influencing my perception of the distance.

I've never seen the arena where the Ascension Contest takes place. I assume it must be not too far from us now, seeing as the city doesn't extend past the Ziggurat. I find I'm wrong when Phoenix leads us right up to the marble walls of the Ziggurat and beyond.

We walk along the side of the enormous building, where a loggia trails all the way to the back of the Ziggurat. My soft steps get even quieter, and I struggle to keep up with Phoenix and Sin with how carefully I'm stepping.

I'm creeping around right outside where the Protogenoi dwell. And yeah, I'm a bit freaked out. I'm not afraid. I'm anxious. I almost wish the Protogenoi would just step out on this path in front of me. Safety be damned so I can be done with the suspense.

Very few have ever seen the Protogenoi in person, as they normally choose to project their likeness throughout Havcire rather than show themselves. It's what makes them seem invincible and bigger than life. What we imagine of the unknown is often more daunting than the reality. It also doesn't help that, in this case, they really are the most powerful beings in existence.

Directly next to where we walk, is one of the rivers bordering the city. Here, it much resembles a moat. On the other side of the river, the mountains almost immediately jut out of the ground. To say the Ziggurat is naturally fortified would be an understatement.

The loggia is made of the same white marble as the rest of the Ziggurat, but the arches that make up the roof and the columns that support them are intricately designed.

To be so close to the home of the Protogenoi, it feels like they should be able to sense us trespassing.

"*I'm Dex,*" the male says, cheerily, making me jump. "*Nice to meet all of you.*"

"*Dex? As in the Informer?*" the female asks.

I stop walking at this news. I catch Sin also falter, but Phoenix looks like he expected nothing else.

Did he already know? Perhaps he's just used to being surprised, numb to it. If you expect everyone to have a secret, then you're not as surprised when one is revealed.

The Informer is famous for knowing things, as the title suggests. I've heard that he, Dex, has maps that depict where every single one of Void's traps are. He also has tricks for getting out of the Labyrinth, the place the portals take you. Those are the two things most high in demand that he deals with, but I've always assumed that's not all he knows.

"Maybe this isn't a disaster. I could use your help," she continues. *"Lada, by the way."*

"Always happy to be of service," Dex replies.

My surprise only increases tenfold. Lada, the last winner of Ascension.

"If you're going to stop here," Phoenix says, reminding me that I have yet to continue on, "You might as well take the opportunity to change." He points at the bag of clothes I've tucked into my coat.

I pull the surprisingly soft, and thankfully dry, clothes out of the plastic bag and then pause, having instinctively just been following Phoenix's suggestion. I'm a bit distracted by the added number of voices in my head.

I look around self-consciously. I don't see anyone else.

"No one's around here," Phoenix assures me. "No one else knows to use this path."

First, the tunnel. Now this.

"Then how do you?" I ask.

"I've used it before."

Evasion. I let him know I think as much by holding his gaze a moment longer. I won't let him think I accept that as an actual answer because it's not.

Phoenix smiles. He leans in closer to me, and I can sense Sin stiffen.

"Stop looking at me like that, Killer," Phoenix whispers, close enough that his lips accidentally brush my ear. "You're making me want to spill all my secrets."

"Here," Phoenix says, suddenly distanced from me, the black boots he'd promised to hold onto for me earlier tossed at me.

I catch them. They're still dry somehow, even though I didn't see him pull them out of another water-proof bag. In fact, I have no idea where he's been keeping them since we left the room in the underground tunnels.

"Thanks."

Before I can tell him and Sin to turn around, Sin's already looping his arm around Phoenix's shoulders to turn him in the opposite direction.

I smile. I'd thank Sin telepathically but it's no longer a private channel. The rest would hear.

"You won the last Ascension," I say instead, to Lada, as I pull off my wet clothes.

"Supposedly."

I shake my head, although no one can see. Can anyone answer a question clearly around here?

The new clothes feel snug but comfortable, like a second skin. The shirt and pants are made of the same, stretchy material. The pants are thicker, though, while the shirt is thin enough to see my pale skin even underneath the black material. It's enough to block the chill of the air, but still breathable.

The boots, however, are the most impressive. They slide on easily, fitting my feet well but my legs loosely. As I straighten out to look down at the whole outfit, they tighten to fit my legs perfectly.

I can't help but move around a bit, twisting my body to test out the feel of the new clothes. I jump a couple feet into the air, and the rubber soles barely make a sound when I land back on the marble ground. Is it possible for a sound to sound silent? If so, that's how these boots sound when I move.

I do a little dance, caught up in the shoes and how impressively quiet they are, tapping my feet on the marble and sliding across, impressed even more when they don't squeak against the floor but also allow me to easily grip the surface so I can come to a stop.

No more worrying about my footsteps being too loud.

"Ready?" Phoenix asks, sounding amused, but when I look over to where he and Sin stand, his back is still turned to me.

"What does that mean?" Sin questions Lada, when she fails to elaborate.

I jog up to them.

Sin glances over and gives me an approving nod. Yes, that outfit will be good to die in, is what I imagine he's thinking.

Phoenix, on the other hand, starts walking again without even a glance in my direction. I catch up with a few small, quick steps to match his longer strides and place my old, wet clothes into his arms. He keeps walking but looks down at them with an eyebrow raised.

"What do you want me to do with these?" he asks.

I smile.

"I figured you could store them in the same place you kept the boots."

"Right," he says, smiles kindly, and then drops the clothes onto the ground at his feet, stepping over them.

Fine. I guess I don't need them anymore anyways. The mystery of the hidden boots will go unsolved for now.

I frown back at the hooded coat as we walk away. It does feel wrong leaving it behind. It's kept me alive. But, maybe someone else will find it and be able to put it to good use... find it on this path that, according to Phoenix, no one else uses.

"It means," Lada says, *"I think I may know how this all happened. Roughly. I, too, have evidence of something I did that I no longer remember doing."*

"Yes, that's not cryptic at all," Phoenix says.

"Pot and kettle," comes to mind.

"I have no idea what that means," Lada says, as Sin questions seriously, *"Is that meant to be a metaphor?"*

"No, it's an expression meaning—" I attempt to explain, but Phoenix takes over.

"She thinks I've no right calling Lada cryptic—"

"Because he himself is cryptic." And Dex is the one to finish.

The strangers in my head are finishing my sentences now.

I look at Phoenix, with no attempt to hide the confusion on my face. *"Exactly. Except, I can't recall where I ever heard that expression before."*

Phoenix shakes his head. Neither can he. And...

"Nope," Dex's cheery voice shares, *"Me neither."*

"Well, when I find out more, I'll be sure to share," Lada offers, in a way that makes it sounds like she plans to do the exact opposite.

So, we know nothing. Even Lada, who claims to know something, sounds like all she really knows is that there is something she doesn't know. More importantly, we've reached the arena.

"You want to ask the supposed last winner of Ascension for any tips?" Phoenix asks me.

"If Lada's coming to me for help, I can update you all on what it is she's looking into," Dex volunteers.

"Maybe I can do without your help," Lada fires back.

"Too late. You already admitted you need me."

I'd always thought the Ziggurat was backed by mountains, and for good reason. From Zion, it looks like it is. With the size of the Ziggurat, it's impossible to see the base of the mountain behind it.

Now, standing behind the Ziggurat, reveals that there's an entrance to a huge structure. It only appears like a normal mountain from afar.

This couldn't have been accomplished without magic, probably a Celestial with some form of control over earth.

The mountain has been completely hollowed out. There is one large, round archway that functions as the entrance in the center. Roots twist along the perimeter of the arch, as if the entrance was made forcefully, a big punch to the side of the mountain that opened it up, and the roots and vines clung to the surface that was left behind.

The sun appears in the sky without an ascent, immediately above our heads, and the world seems to awaken with it. Kaelis, their cloud bodies lit by the sun's rays, sweep down from the sky, people riding on their backs, arriving.

Although the Protogenoi don't make it clear when exactly Ascension will take place, people manage to show. Maybe they all have "connections," as Phoenix claims he does.

There are excited shouts as the people land in front of us, too busy rushing into the arena to pay us, me, any attention. Others stream in from the sides of the arena, having come on foot from outside of Zion.

I peer up at the top of the mountain turned arena, squinting against the sun. It's at least triple the height of the Ziggurat. My neck can't even crane up enough to see the top from this angle.

"Any advice on how to win Ascension?" I ask Lada, even though I'm not positive Phoenix was serious when he suggested asking for tips.

I've given away where I am with that one question. But, a large part of me doubts that they'll come rushing to assassinate me for the Protogenoi before Ascension begins. There wouldn't be much time to accomplish that anyway. If they want to try, though, I guess now's their chance. They'll have to compete with all the others already here.

"Why would the Protogenoi's most wanted be competing?" Lada asks.

"I have my reasons."

"For a group that can literally hear each other's thoughts, you are all surprisingly secretive," Dex says.

"Now or never," Phoenix says.

Sin moves to stand in front of me. He'll be almost as effective as my discarded hood, helping to keep my face hidden, at least until I can enter the arena and officially make it known that I intend to be a competitor.

I step out from under the loggia, no longer shaded by its roof. Phoenix follows my lead for once, remaining a step behind me. Watching my back, maybe?

I though we'd have the cover of darkness to make it inside the arena, but it's just a short distance to the entrance. I can make it.

Maybe I was too quick to leave the coat behind.

"Alright," Lada speaks up, *"just try to survive."*

"Sage advice," I think back.

Something rushes past me, whistling through the air. It skims my cheek, and I feel a warm trickle down my face. Blood.

Turning, I find a sword now lodged in a column of the Ziggurat.

CHAPTER FOURTEEN

The sword vibrates from the impact.

Damn. To damage the home of the Protogenoi just to try to kill me? I know it was the Protogenoi who put out the award for my death, but I still don't think they'd be very happy with someone embedding a sword in the Ziggurat.

"Dawn, duck!" Sin shouts.

Right.

The sword moves within the marble, attempting to dislodge itself. I kneel to the ground the second before it succeeds.

It flies back over my head and Sin's, who's crouched down in front of me. He drags me back up with him as he stands and readies to make a run for the arena's entrance, but between us and the entrance are three others, including the male who threw the sword. It returns to his palm with a resounding thunk.

Phoenix didn't bother to evade, being neither the target of the attack nor in the crossfire. I look at him, expecting to see some measure of alarm on his face.

Nope. He's calm, focused, looking totally unbothered, seemingly distracted by whatever it is going on in his own head at the moment. Because, apparently, an attempt on my life isn't worthy of note, despite his desire for me to survive long enough to reveal the truth about the Protogenoi. Rather, he stares ahead, looking straight through the three Celestials targeting me and to the entrance of the arena.

The sword twirls in the air beside the Celestial who threw it, though he no longer holds it in his grasp. His hand closest to the sword turns around and around in a lazy motion. He can't be telekinetic because no two Celestials have the same power, and he isn't the same from the fighting cage.

He must be able to control the metal in the sword, which limits him somewhat. But, his exact methods aren't particularly important when the sword spins through the air again and heads right for Sin's back.

I push Sin out of the way. Why can't they just let me enter this arena?

Everyone else seems past caring, more interested in the promise of competing in Ascension than hunting me down anymore. But, no, not these three.

I reach for my power, pulling on my own frustration, and it appears before me in a slash of gold. Like an extension of my hand, it swipes at the sword as it comes near and throws it off far to the side, out of sight. Maybe it will be too far for the Celestial to summon again. His ability could have a limited reach.

It doesn't matter. He whips out a fully metal mace.

I think I preferred the sword. Is it too late to bring the sword back?

His two buddies don't instill much confidence in me now either. The male on the left has engulfed himself in a cyclone that picks up rocks and dirt from the ground around him. He shows no sign of being affected by the hurtling rocks, but I have a feeling it wouldn't be so safe for anyone else.

Somehow, the female in the middle seems the most frightening, even though she bears no weapon. She stands between them and stares straight ahead at me with narrowed eyes, and I fear she may be able to split me in two with a glare.

The mace comes flying at the same time the cyclone attacks. I throw up a barrier of golden energy around Sin, Phoenix, and me. If I could just hold it up around us until we can get through the entrance, it'd be okay.

The mace hits the barrier, which holds strong, but the Celestial that controls it keeps at it, pounding the mace against my gold shield with an unyielding determination.

The Celestial in the cyclone doesn't fare as well. The energy infects him once he makes contact, spreading through his veins like his own blood. It won't kill him because that's not my intention, but it weakens him, bringing him to the ground and keeping him there.

"Come on," I tell Sin and Phoenix.

The mace is still banging against my barrier, but after metal guy and frightening glare lady saw what happened to cyclone guy when he approached, I think they'll be keeping their distance.

It's not hard keeping up the barrier. It's like holding my arms up in the air. It doesn't take a lot of effort, but it does get tiring after too long.

I start with a few hesitant steps, making sure Sin and Phoenix are following and the barrier is holding around all three of us, but I quickly hasten into a run. A few feet away from metal guy, he steps aside, letting his mace continue the fight for him.

A sharp pain pierces my chest and brings me to my knees. For a second, I think the sword must have come back and gotten through somehow. Reflexively, I clutch at my chest and find nothing there but my pounding heart. It feels like it's expanding past where it's able. I try to look around for the cause and find the remaining Celestial standing in our way with a cruel smile on her face. Her eyes are still trained on me.

She's going to explode my heart right inside my chest. I gasp for air through the pain.

My shield comes down, and the metal guy sees his opening. He raises the mace again and lets it fly.

Sin steps in front of me.

"Enough," I hear Phoenix say, exasperated, as if reluctantly giving in to some request I missed anyone making.

He reaches out to grab Sin as I feel him squeeze my shoulder at the same moment. I'm surprised I can feel anything at this point other than the intense tightening in my chest.

The pressure around my heart releases. The frightening, death glare, heart killing lady is gone, and so is the metal guy.

So is everything. My breath feels vacuumed out of me, but then the air is back and so are my surroundings, but I'm somewhere else.

He really can teleport other people.

I'm standing inside the arena, Sin in the same position in front of me and Phoenix still at my side. He lowers his hand from my shoulder, grabs a torch from the large pile at the entrance to the arena, shoves it in front of me, and places two rocks in my hands.

"Light it. Now."

I do what he says. I scrape the two rocks together, hard. The spark that forms catches on the torch Phoenix holds and sets it aflame. He passes it to me with what I think is an exhalation of relief. Then, picks up another torch and lights his own.

We're officially in the contest.

I look behind us, out of the arena to where my attackers still stand. Their eyes are on the flame. They can no longer make a move against me. Unless, of course, it's part of the contest. Turning back around, I realize they're not the only ones staring. The knowledge of my identity and presence seems to have finally spread to everyone here, both the competitors who stand in the circular center of the arena and the spectators who sit in the seats that rise up all around the mountain walls of the arena.

They all stare in silence, as if waiting for me to make an announcement confirming that I am who they already know I am. I could announce the truth of what I did now, but my plan is to wait to get the opportunity to announce it to everyone in Havcire. That plan requires me to win the contest, which may or may not be even possible. But, if I blurted it out now, would it be enough? Or, would the Protogenoi ensure it never made it out of this arena?

I know the answer to that.

I hold myself up taller, but I keep my mouth shut, turning to face Phoenix instead. The second I turn away, the usual noises resume, ending the tense silence.

"What was that?"

Phoenix is scanning the arena, as is Sin, but he stops to listen for Phoenix's answer. Except, all Phoenix responds with is a genuinely clueless, "What?"

"I believe she means the fact that you claimed you couldn't teleport anyone or anything but yourself," Sin supplies.

"Actually, no," I respond, as apologetically to Sin as possible.

Oops. Did I forget to mention to Sin that I already knew that because I thought he might overreact to the fact that Phoenix initially lied about it? Yes, I did forget to do that. Intentionally.

"Right," Phoenix says to Sin, not drawing his watchful gaze away from those surrounding us. "I had lied to you about that. But, aren't you glad I can teleport others now?"

Sin's glare is answer enough.

"*I* meant, what took you so long to teleport us away?" I ask, clarifying my actual question.

Now, Phoenix looks at me.

"That's a poor way to thank me for saving your life. But, you're welcome anyway."

Phoenix makes his way away from the entrance, toward the center of the arena.

Sin and I share a look, which questions what we both signed up for in teaming up with Phoenix. Then, Sin's face tells me that we will be discussing later the fact that I omitted the teleportation detail from him. And, my face responds with an unconvincing, placating, "Of course we will."

We manage this telepathic communication all very well without actually resorting to telepathy as that would turn it, against our will, into a group chat.

Then, we follow Phoenix.

A large portion of the area in the middle of the arena is closed off. There's a cylindrical barrier keeping everyone out of the very center. Attempting to look through it to what's on the other side is a lot like looking through badly cracked glass. I can make out that there is some structure on the other side, but the picture as a whole is distorted.

Some of the other competitors continue to stare at me, but most appear to be actively avoiding me.

"They're afraid of you," Sin says, seeing me looking around.

"They're the ones that want to kill *me*," I tell him, unconvinced.

But, Sin can sense emotions, so if he's saying they're afraid, they must be, no matter how ridiculous that is.

Or, is it? All they know is that, for some reason, the Protogenoi really want me dead. The Protogenoi don't care about us, beyond making our world generally impossible to live in. They definitely don't take the time to devote attention to a specific person.

If I were any other Celestial or an Incanter, I would wonder what motivated the Protogenoi to target me. What could possibly be bad enough to make the Protogenoi care to do so? Maybe what I've done is nearly as big a mystery as the legendary sixth Protogenoi.

Except, unlike the sixth Protogenoi, I know for a fact that I exist and that what I've done is real. If it were all just a story, I wouldn't be in this situation.

"The difference is, they can't kill you now, and it's that forced idleness that has them stopping and recognizing their fear," Sin explains further.

"Well, they won't have to be idle for long."

"I think you're real scary," Phoenix chimes in facetiously, as he digs his torch into the sandy ground so it stays upright on its own.

"You say that as a jest, but you mean it," Sin says, staring at Phoenix as he does when reading someone's emotions, like he's piecing together a puzzle.

"That's an irksome ability of yours," Phoenix says, his frivolous smile fallen.

"You mean that, too," Sin replies.

I have to work to keep my mouth from falling open when Sin actually cracks a small smile. I'm not sure what's more shocking, the fact that Phoenix is reportedly scared of me or that Sin is smiling, even if it is a very teeny tiny one.

Why would Phoenix be afraid of me? I didn't get the sense that he actually thinks I go around killing as a hobby, despite his habit of calling me Killer.

I stick the torch that saved my life into the ground beside Phoenix's and look around. The seating arrangement for the spectators is... interesting. They sit on ledges of rock that jut out from the walls of the hollowed out mountain. Stairs of matching rock lead up to the different ledges, while in some other places, ladders provide access. The ledges vary in size. The people sit on them with their legs dangling off the edge.

Because the only opening is the entrance, little natural light filters in. Each ledge provides the light for the arena, the undersides lit up with a bright, white light. The lighting and the surrounding rock gives the place a cold feeling, but the center of the arena, filled with sand and the competitors' torches, adds heat.

The flames of all the competitors' torches, including my own, suddenly shoot high into the air with a hiss. As they come back down, a hush follows, and an image appears reflected on the cylindrical wall. I recognize his image from the fountain before his voice fills the arena.

"Welcome to the Ascension Contest," Dabar says, his head the only part of him visible up on the wall.

For someone who controls reality, he looks far from real. Despite this present manifestation, I actually felt like he was nearer, more of a threat when I looked up at the imposing statue of the Protogenoi in the fountain. Something about this artificial projection feels detached.

His face looks drained of color, especially in contrast with his vibrant, purple eyes, which appear to look at everyone simultaneously. His ash blonde eyebrows have unnaturally steep arches that frame his eyes, making them look even sharper.

Whether he's always looked this unnatural is a question I guess only the other Protogenoi could answer. Either way, it's reality now.

I've always found it odd that Dabar looks not much older than me, but I guess when it's clear to the whole world just how much power you have, it's unnecessary to attempt to display that power and authority through something as trivial as age.

"The first challenge is hidden up until the moment of commencement to ensure no one has the advantage of studying its layout. Myself and the other Protogenoi believe in a fair contest."

I hear Phoenix scoff at my side. I expect to find him focusing on Dabar with an expression of hate or, at the very least, major dislike. Instead, it's amusement I find. Sure, there's definitely some dislike there, but it's overshadowed by his amusement. When he catches me looking, I quickly turn my attention back to Dabar.

I should really stop expecting to know what I'll find when it comes to Phoenix. He's unpredictable in a way I should be wary of, but it only keeps increasing my interest in him. Still, that gut of mine isn't shouting any warnings at me when it comes to him, and Sin wasn't wrong. I don't normally trust very easily because I'm decent at reading people, and the truth just is that most people are not trustworthy.

"We want the winner of Ascension to rightfully earn their time living as royalty in the Ziggurat," Dabar continues. "The goal of this challenge is to reach the highest platform. The first five to do so will move onto the next round, while the rest will be eliminated. I wish you all good fortune, and may reality favor you."

With a sudden loud shattering, the cylindrical wall falls, Dabar's face cracking apart with it and then disappearing entirely. As the broken shards of the wall fall to the sandy ground below, they burst into bits of sand themselves and sprinkle down to join the rest.

Before all the sand has even touched the floor, everyone's rushing to the challenge now on display.

CHAPTER FIFTEEN

Someone attempts to run right through me. I catch myself before I can hit the ground. But, when I look back up, regaining my balance, I've lost Sin and Phoenix.

I could search for Phoenix, seeing as he did agree to help, but there's no time. Half the competitors that had crowded the arena's center are already up on the course. Only the first five to reach the top will move on.

I rush forward with the rest of the crowd toward the towering challenge, but a gut wrenching scream stops me dead.

The course is shaped like a cone, the highest platform a point in the air, which I can't even make out from the ground. But, just about five levels up, a competitor clutches his stomach, where a spear has impaled him. He tumbles backward off the small platform on which he stands and plummets to the ground, where he lands. The sand does little to cushion his fall and his already punctured abdomen doesn't fare very well.

I look away, back up to where he fell from. Standing on the opposite side of the course is another competitor, whose hand is still on a thick rope that he's pulled out from the inside of the cone. A wicked smile spreads on his face as he glances down at the fallen competitor, before continuing on up the course.

I scan the rest of the cone-shaped course, attempting to ignore the others rushing ahead of me and my own little voice in my head screaming at me to get a move on.

There are ropes, much like the one already pulled, throughout. Traps that can be set off by the competitors themselves, if they want to stop and take the time to sabotage. The cone is hollow, and I can see inside it where it opens up between the platforms. The interior is cluttered, probably with other dangerous weapons ready to be released, so I can't see through all the way to the opposite side.

The platforms attached around the perimeter of the cone vary in shape and size. I watch as other competitors attempt to jump and climb the distance between different platforms. Climbing seems like the safer option for me.

Okay, enough observing.

Watch out for the center of the cone, climb when possible between platforms, and keep an eye out for Phoenix if possible.

Very few competitors are still left on the ground. Actually, except for those that have already been up and fallen, it's just me down here. Some of them, however, have managed to survive the fall and pull themselves up to give it another go. They pay me no attention, more focused on making up for lost time than ensuring someone else at the bottom doesn't get ahead of them.

I have no choice but to jump up to the first platform. It encircles the entire cone about six feet up, several inches taller than me.

I run and leap.

My hands close around the edge of the cold, metal platform. Using the momentum of the jump, I pull, getting my elbows up and over the edge and swing my leg around to bring myself the rest of the way.

There isn't much room up here, the platform being only about three feet wide, so I turn around to face the cone, hugging it and keeping an eye out for any movement within, but I need to risk looking away and up to search for the next platform.

I need to pick up the pace.

The platform above, to my right, is too high for me to jump up onto, but it has bars sticking out from the bottom. I jump and grab onto the first bar, climbing from one to the next underneath the platform.

When I reach the last bar, I swing my legs back and forth to gather momentum and leap to the next platform, landing steadily on my feet. This platform is much shorter than the last two but wider. On the wall of the cone right next to me is a rope, a trigger. I don't pull it, but I use the groove it comes out of as a foothold to give me a boost up to the next platform.

I hear the snap of a string. I crouch down, not wasting any time looking for the source, and an arrow whizzes through the air above me, where I had stood a moment ago. With no target to hit, it flies through the air and thunks into the sand below.

Someone released it from inside the cone. That someone clings to the interior of the cone and stares at me through the small empty space left by the arrow. I recognize those narrowed eyes, the same ones that had attempted to explode my heart earlier. I don't wait for her to incapacitate me again.

I send a bolt of golden energy through the hole in the cone. It hits her right between the eyes before she can blink and sends her falling backwards, through the center, hitting the hidden weapons within on her way down.

My power. Why hadn't I thought to use it?

I reach for it now. I have to pull on it. Other Celestials can just summon their power without any thought. It's a part of them, instinctual. But, for some reason, I have to coax mine out, tame and mold it into what I need it to be.

A bell rings. The first competitor has reached the top.

Enough dawdling.

A long, golden rope, sparks of energy shooting off it, flows from my hand. I spin the end around and around, building up its momentum, and whip it up. It loops and tightens around a platform five levels up from where I am. I pull on the end still in my grip, testing its sturdiness, and begin the climb.

I pass by platform after platform that I avoid having to even step on, pulling myself up my self-made rope, the energy that makes the rope gripping me right back. I pass by other competitors on the platforms.

One competitor, an Incanter with an extremely uneven jaw, reaches for my rope in an attempt to break it. I almost warn him against it, but there are only five winners of this challenge.

The second he touches my rope, the golden energy attacks him, sending him tumbling down.

I don't check to see if he's survived the fall... but I may be living up to that nickname.

I reach the end of the line and pull myself up on top of the platform. I must be ten levels above the ground, at least halfway to the top. The bell rings again, signaling the second to make it, and then it rings again.

Only two spots left.

Metal slides against metal. I duck, dropping to my stomach on the platform. Above me, large blades slide out from the center of the cone. The blade that came out through my side swings back through, scissoring with the blade that exited out the opposite side before coming out the other end.

I peer down and spot multiple sets of the blades, maybe even one per level. That's comforting. It's not just me facing off against the deadly pendulum blades, but every competitor below and above me. It'll slow us all down in our race to the top.

As the blades swing out, they leave the inside of the cone empty, and I can finally see clearly through to the opposite side.

Phoenix lies flat on his stomach across from me on a platform one level above mine. He spots me.

"Dawn," I hear him say, *"sit up, with your knees bent in front of you."*

I do as he says, but I wait until the blade recedes back into the cone. I assume he wasn't giving me instructions just to get me cut in half. There I go again, making assumptions regarding his trustworthiness.

The second I'm up, Phoenix appears kneeling at my side. He reaches one arm under my bent knees and the other behind my back, pulling me in tight to his chest. The blade is coming back.

"Hold on."

I wrap my arms around his neck, and we're gone. Again, the world seems to squeeze around me, taking my breath with it, as we teleport.

We stop, and that moment of stillness is enough for me to notice that we're not on solid ground.

The sky surrounds us.

"Sorry," he apologizes, not really sounding sorry at all.

"Phoenix," I warn, unable to hide the panic also in my voice.

And then he's pushing me away from him.

Oh no. No no no. I reach back out for him, but he's already teleported away. From somewhere below, I hear the chime of the bell again.

One spot left.

As if gravity's taken sudden notice of my presence, the stillness leaves, and I'm falling.

The force of the wind against my face as I fall from the sky makes my eyes water, making it difficult to spot exactly where I am in relation to the course and the ground below.

I thought the worst thing about plummeting from the sky would be the nauseating stomach drop but, no, it's the disorientation.

I force my arms out in front of me and my legs back behind me so I stop tumbling crazily through the air. Breathe, I remind myself, and force a long exhale out of my mouth, which is so much harder to do than it should be. I try to focus my blurry eyes.

The top platform! It's right below me, and I'm about to splat onto it. Something tells me that won't count as a win for this challenge. I flatten my hands out to face the platform, as if they'll be able to break my fall.

My golden energy explodes out of me, responding with no thought, fueled by my panic.

I hit what feels like a net, surprised my neck doesn't just snap, as I bounce back up into the air, the net-like thing springing me back up. I twist in the air and land a second time, this time the landing less jolting as I fall on my backside.

I settle, the bounces losing momentum. I open my eyes, which at some point I must have squeezed shut.

The net that felt like a net is in fact a net, stitched together completely by threads of my golden power. There are no poles or beams supporting it. It merely floats steadily in the air above the top platform, like its own, added platform to the course.

I let the energy go, let it flow back into me, and the net disappears. I drop the last few feet onto the platform below. The second my feet touch, the final, fifth bell rings out.

I made it.

Correction, *we* made it. Phoenix stands among the other three winners of the first Ascension challenge.

CHAPTER SIXTEEN

I study the tattoo on the inside of my left wrist. It appeared there after I completed the first challenge, marking me as a final five in Ascension, and it also is what will keep me alive between now and the next challenge.

The tattoo is of three triangles. The one in the middle is raised higher above the other two, its bottom points overlapping with the sides of the others. Sloping lines connect the top points of all three triangles to each other.

Sin and I followed Phoenix back to his hidden tunnel and room after the challenge, as in after he dropped me from the middle of the sky to fall to my death. It was actually Sin who insisted staying with Phoenix was the best course of action.

Phoenix had an explanation for everything.

First, I asked why he had dropped me from a height I definitely could have died from. Well, of course, because he knew I'd be "fine."

Second, I questioned, why didn't he just teleport me down to the platform with him? Because, he couldn't be seen so obviously helping me win.

"It's not against the rules to form alliances," I'd pointed out.

"We'll have an advantage later if the remaining contestants don't know of our alliance."

"Fine, then why did you wait so long to pull your teleportation trick?" I asked, moving on to find a hole in his reasoning elsewhere.

I was already following Phoenix back to his home base while I was doing this questioning. So, as skeptical of him my relentless questioning may have made me seem, I clearly still didn't mistrust him enough to insist we part ways.

Phoenix had an explanation for everything, and I completely, wholeheartedly bought into it all. And yet, I still had to go through the paces and ask the questions. Because, although I was positive, for some reason, that Phoenix in fact wasn't trying to kill me when he dropped me from the sky, I wanted to hear his justification.

He *should* want me dead. Everyone wants me dead, except Sin. But, he doesn't. And, I believe him when he says he doesn't want to kill me. Two equally unusual occurrences.

Regardless, I have to ask because I need to be cautious, and I know that under any other circumstances I would be highly suspicious of someone who'd done the things Phoenix has.

"I couldn't find you on the course at the beginning, and I can't teleport to an unknown location."

That explanation, I admitted, made sense.

There was one more tactic to try. Using Sin. I thought he'd support getting the truth out of Phoenix. After all, Sin fully believes in always being honest, even brutally so. However, he'd remained characteristically silent throughout my interrogation.

"Sin, this doesn't concern you at all? You've spent all this time trying to make sure I don't get dead."

Sin had spared me a reassuring glance but hadn't even looked at Phoenix before saying, "His emotions are far from conducive to murdering you."

"Alright," Phoenix said, "that's enough of that."

"And yours, Dawn—" Sin continued, but I wasn't any more a fan of hearing about my own emotions than Phoenix was of his.

I'm fully self aware. I didn't need Sin's brutal honesty broadcasting the fact that I embarrassingly, implicitly trust the stranger walking ahead of us. Or, any minor intrusive thoughts I may have had about him either.

"Okay," I'd cut in, before Sin could go on. "We'll stay in Phoenix's lair for now."

"My lair?" he asked.

"What else would you call that place?" I questioned.

"Home?" Phoenix answered. "Well, my lair is invitation only."

I'd indicated the path we were traveling.

"I thought we were already on our way there, no?"

"*I* am on my way there," Phoenix had said, making Sin and I both realize that we had made some assumptions.

We managed to get an actual invite, albeit reluctantly.

It's dark outside again, and Sin sleeps on a large, cushioned chair in the part of Phoenix's lair with all his resources. Sin had offered to let me rest on the chair, but I didn't feel like sleeping and dreaming again. At this point, I can't remember the last time I slept without dreaming of being hunted and coming across the elusive sword on fire.

Phoenix disappeared behind the curtain concealing the other side of the room. There was no need for him to tell us we weren't welcome on that side.

Maybe he's asleep, as well.

With that thought, I get up from my spot on the floor and make my way over to the white curtain. I raise a hand to brush it aside, but it pulls back and Phoenix walks through, blocking me from entering. The curtain drops back into place behind him but not before I get a glimpse of the other side.

There's a bed in the center and piles of books cover the floor, leaving only a path large enough for someone to navigate around the area. On the wall opposite the curtain, there's a painting. It looks like two large wings, but one of the wings is obviously broken, bent at an unnatural angle.

My curiosity overshadows the fact that Phoenix has made it clear I'm not welcome to enter. I try to move forward and get a better look, but he's directly in my way. And, rather than step aside when he sees clearly the direction I'm headed in, he does nothing.

I stupidly bump right into his chest, which doesn't budge him one bit. Instead, I'm the one forced to take a step back. I don't know why I thought walking forward confidently would initiate some instinct of Phoenix's to be polite and move out of my way.

When he realizes I have no intention of turning away from the curtain and what it hides, he wordlessly grabs my shoulders and physically turns me in the opposite direction so that my back is to the curtain.

I sigh and take an exaggerated step forward, a "look at me walking away, giving up" step. Another one, and then...

I spin and rush the curtain again, only to stop myself a second before bumping into Phoenix yet again, as he has not moved an inch. And then, he's outright laughing at me.

I glare up at him.

"Ugh! Just let me see!"

"Hush. You'll wake Sin," he says, all fake considerate.

"Good idea. I'll wake him up and tell him how you're hiding a perfectly comfortable bed behind that curtain, and we'll see what he does to you. He takes his beauty rest very seriously."

Phoenix shakes his head in disbelief.

"Why do you want to see what's behind here so badly?"

"Because you're just so mysterious, and I want to know more about you," I say, in the most sarcastic, flirty voice I can muster.

I reach up and place my hand flat against Phoenix's chest, sliding it up and around to the back of his neck, stepping closer. The hair on his nape brushes through my fingers. His eyes lose their flicker of amusement and latch onto mine, and I forget for a second what it is I'm doing. Creating a distraction.

And then I'm diving.

The curtains have the place where they meet in the center, but that's not the only opening. On my knees, I lift the curtain up, exposing space between its bottom and the floor. I throw the material over myself so I'm on the other side and crawl forward, but one of my legs is dragged out from beneath me at the same time the curtain is thrown back over my head, obstructing my view.

I kick my trapped leg to free myself, my foot making contact. A pained grunt quickly follows.

I'm crawling forward again, quick. A weight presses down on my back. My arms and legs go out from under me, and I'm flattened to the floor, unable to move forward, or anywhere really.

I have to bring my arms into a push up position to get my chest off the floor enough to even take in a breath of air. I'm freakin' anchored to the floor.

I turn my head.

Phoenix sits on me. He's actually sitting on me, his arms behind him on the floor, propping him up. He looks like he's lounging.

"How is everyone?"

Just dandy.

Dex's pleasant voice fills my head, all of our heads. I hear Sin jerk awake. Hear, because I can't turn around all the way to actually see him.

"Get off me." I try to say the words with power, which doesn't work, but at least they come out irritated.

"Admit defeat," Phoenix responds, and I can hear the smile in his voice.

"No."

"Then, no."

"*We survived the first challenge,*" I tell Dex.

"Of course we did," Phoenix says.

"*That's great news.*" It's nice he sounds like he means that.

"This is ridiculous. Get off."

"It's not like it's comfortable for me. Your back is bony."

"You look comfortable enough."

"It's bony in all the right places."

"Sin!" I call, like an annoying child, tattle telling.

"Don't involve me," is all I get in response, which Phoenix snickers at.

Haha, yeah. Very funny.

I'm finding it hard not to imagine how comfortable or not I might be if Phoenix had me pinned in another way.

"I..." I gasp for air, "can't..." another gasp, "breathe." Another one, for good measure.

"Nice try. You can breathe fine."

I resist the urge to kick my feet and hit my hands against the floor in a tantrum.

Alright, he asked for it.

All it takes is a flick of my wrist, gold energy summoned to my hand. I let it go and SLAP!

Phoenix falls off my back, and I immediately flip myself over. Now I'm the one lounging on the floor. He's holding the side of his face, which has a red mark on it already. He looks at me, flabbergasted.

"Did you just slap me?"

"I didn't touch you," I answer, innocently. Then, smile.

"*So,*" Dex continues, "*Lada is looking for Styx it turns out, and we could use your help.*"

"*Actually, Dex thinks we could use your help,*" Lada corrects.

"*What can we do? We don't know where she is. I don't know who she is,*" I respond, and then look around at Phoenix and Sin. "Right?" I ask. Sin nods in confirmation.

"She's a Celestial. I know about her but not where she is," Phoenix says.

"*We already know where she is,*" Lada says, haughtily.

"*We know because of me,*" Dex clarifies. "*But, it's more a matter of getting to her.*"

"*Where?*" Sin asks.

"*Whiro's,*" Dex answers.

"*Whiro's House of Death?*" I ask.

"That would be the one. So, you're out, right?" Lada sounds hopeful for once at this prospect.

"I practically live there," Phoenix replies, and I can attest to the fact that he looks just as confident as he sounds in our heads.

I turn around to glance again at the curtain that hides the rest of the room, the part of the room that has the comfy bed. I face Phoenix and point back at the curtain and what's beyond.

"No, you live there, where there's a..." I cup my mouth conspiratorially and stage whisper the next part, "comfy bed."

"Did you just say there's a comfy bed behind that curtain, and I've been sleeping on this lumpy couch?" Sin asks, as enraged as Sin ever gets.

"We're in," Phoenix answers for us all, signing us up for the field trip to Whiro's House of Death.

This won't be fun, but if Lada thinks the answer to why we can hear each other lies with Styx for some reason, it's worth looking into. Plus, what else are we going to do with ourselves until the next challenge? Rest? I think not.

CHAPTER SEVENTEEN

Most go to Whiro's because he's a Corporate, because they have no other choice and need access to resources.

Whiro is the lord of darkness, the embodiment of evil, not the type of guy one elects to visit. He gains strength from evil acts, which is why the payment he asks for in return for resources is the performance of an evil act. Naturally.

The first to show up at his House of Death must stay trapped there until another arrives and can be used to pay the price of the resources. That second person, the one to be tortured by whatever act Whiro conjures up for the first arrival to perform, then must stay trapped there until the next person arrives and the next evil act can be done unto the new arrival. And so on and so forth.

As a result, every Celestial and Incanter you may come across when in Whiro's House of Death is a potential threat, someone looking to use you to pay their price. But, they're not the only ones you have to look out for.

The place itself is a threat. To be trapped there until the next person arrives is to be confined with the personifications of ones own fears and doubts. It's because of this that even those desperate, especially those who know better, try to avoid going to Whiro and elect to pay the price of the other Corporates.

However, if one hasn't enough fight to win at Hadur's and has nothing to offer Lamashtu, there's no other option but Whiro. Until now, I've avoided it.

I've avoided the deep, dark hole in the ground, which I now stare into, blind as to what lies at the bottom.

There are many entrances to Whiro's throughout Havcire, but this is the one Dex and Lada chose, having been the closest to it. It also happens to be the one that is located right outside an exit from the Labyrinth. Just imagine someone having miraculously survived the Labyrinth and managed to find their way out only to fall right into Whiro's.

All of Havcire is designed to ensure we can never rise up. We can barely keep our feet on the ground.

"Why are you afraid of me?" I ask Phoenix.

He laughs, which is fair. Sin went off to scout the area, seeing as we don't actually know Dex or Lada, and meeting them here could be a trap. My question is completely out of blue. That is, if you're not inside my racing head.

"It's a serious question," I press. "We are about to enter a place where fears are used against you."

"So you want to help me face my fear," he says, looking me up and down, as if him being afraid of me must be a joke, "before it can haunt me down there?"

I shrug, faking nonchalance. Because, the truth is, I really do want to know the answer, regardless of what lies ahead of us.

"One of them, yeah, sure. You're welcome."

I understand the general population, those who don't know me or even know what I did, other than the fact that it was bad enough for the Protogenoi to want me dead one way or another... I understand those people being afraid of me.

I don't love that. It's not like I'm some fictional, power-crazed villain who gets off on people fearing me, like their fear gives me some superiority over them. But, it is what it is.

Phoenix, on the other hand, he *knows* what I did to get me here. I wouldn't say he knows me, but he knows me about as well as anyone around here. So, why?

"That is very kind of you, Killer, but I'm not afraid of you."

"Not according to Sin."

"Who wouldn't be afraid of you? You were able to kill a Protogenoi."

"Which one is it? Are you or are you not afraid of me?"

"Not."

I roll my eyes, turning away from him and the huge hole in front of us. Whatever. I was just looking to generously help out before we both have to jump into that dark hole, but if he can't own up to his own fears, fine.

"Forget it."

I shoulder check him as I walk past, but he stalls me, his hand gripping my arm before I can get by him.

"Giving up so easily?" he taunts, a smile lifting his lips.

"No," I huff.

He steps around me so I'm facing him again, and my stubborn self keeps me from walking away or even taking a single step back even though I can feel him across the small, tense distance that separates us.

"I'm not afraid of *you*."

"So you claim."

"I'm afraid of what you are," he clarifies, "to me."

I open my mouth to ask what that means, but I can't get any words to come out.

Why do I wish more than anything that I genuinely mean something to this Celestial who I met only days ago? I'd put my life in his hands even after he let me fall from a height that could have killed me. I trust him instinctively, despite barely knowing him, despite rarely trusting anyone.

His seafoam green eyes are unwavering, pools of the clearest ocean water that I could watch forever. It's because of that that I force myself to look away.

"You're afraid of strangers, then?" I suggest.

"I've been alone in my fight against the Protogenoi for what feels like my whole life, and it's felt pointless more times than I care to admit," he confesses.

I look back at him, struck by the actual pain I hear in his voice. The idea of fighting a fight you suspect is impossible to win but going on regardless and doing it alone, it resonates with me.

He reaches up and tucks a stray piece of hair behind my ear, where his fingers brush against the shell of my ear, a stirring warmth echoing through the rest of my body.

He goes to lower his hand, but I catch it before I know what I'm doing. He lets his hand fall to my neck instead, his fingers threading through my hair there that hangs down from my ponytail.

"You've given me the first real glance of a future where maybe there are no more Protogenoi ruling, where we succeed. I'm afraid of losing that hope," Phoenix admits.

"So you really don't want to kill me?" I ask.

Phoenix tugs on the back of my neck, and my feet easily comply, closing the distance between us, steadying myself against him with a hand to his chest.

A gasp escapes me as I practically end up straddling his leg. I hold still, resisting the tempting urge to give into the friction.

"Not at all, Killer," he says, voice low as he leans in.

Next thing I know, he's fully lifting me off him and placing me to stand a distance away.

"Wasn't sure you were going to show," he says, looking off, past the hole that leads down to Whiro's.

I wipe the confusion I feel off my face and follow his gaze to find who I can only assume is Dex and Lada approaching us. The arches of Lada's brows rise even higher into the blonde fringe of her bangs.

"This was all my idea. Of course I was coming," she says.

They're still a distance away, hopefully far enough away to not have seen the exact position me and Phoenix had just found ourselves in, but we can hear each other well enough without needing to raise our voices.

Dex matches how I imagined the person who's been talking in my head, but he doesn't match how I've always imagined the famous Informer. Although, they are one and the same.

He looks about the same age as I am, which isn't surprising. What doesn't match the image of the Informer I'd always envisioned is his casual, laid-back style. His short, black hair sticks up in every direction, and he's wearing a t-shirt with a large smiley face design in its center. I assumed the Celestial known for knowing everything would look more, I don't know, tidy?

Sin walks up, joining us.

"You took your time," Phoenix jibes.

"Well, we can't all teleport."

"Actually..." Dex begins, and then he's no longer standing a few feet in front of us, but right in between Phoenix and me, in all that space Phoenix assured was between us. Dex is there now. "Now I can," he continues with a shrug.

Even Sin looks surprised, which is hard to pull off.

Dex turns to face me and holds out his hand.

"Nice to meet you in person, Dawn."

In a not so subtle way, I give Dex an awkward wave with my left hand, flashing that tattoo on my wrist that identifies me as one of the Ascension competitors, as in off limits for killing outside of the contest.

Then, I shake the hand he's offered, which all seems too normal, especially considering people have been trying to kill me and not make my acquaintance for so long now.

"How did you teleport?" Sin asks, stopping Dex from continuing his formal introductions. He lowers his hand, which he'd extended out to Phoenix next and turns his attention to Sin.

"Oh, my power is borrowing other Celestials' powers. I can do it as long as I'm physically close enough," he explains.

Lada and her long legs take one step and then she's in my face, searching it for some answer.

She looks me up and down, curious but not judgmental.

"You do look more formidable than I would expect from someone your size."

"Is there a question there?" I ask her.

She gives me a little more breathing room.

"Yes. What exactly did you do to the Protogenoi?"

"I killed Chaos."

Sin lets out one of his grunts I've come to learn means he's dissatisfied.

What? I'm not the one trying to keep it a secret. It's quite the opposite of what I'm attempting to do as a matter of fact.

Lada's naturally narrow eyes widen.

"Well then, I'm your biggest fan," Dex proclaims.

"But, how?" Lada asks.

"Good question," Phoenix says, and it's only then that I realize he never asked it himself.

"Easy," Dex replies. "I hate Protogenoi. Everyone does. She killed one. Ergo, fan."

Lada nearly smiles, but she hides it quick, not even glancing at Dex. She sighs and roll her eyes, which are still trained on me. "Do you see what I've had to deal with?"

She just looks so theatrically done. I can't help it. A laugh escapes.

Lada joins in. Surrounded by basically all strangers, somehow the tension is gone. Things feel normal for maybe the first time ever. It's like we all give each other permission to just take a breath for one moment.

"Oh," Dex says, letting the word trail on. "You were referring to the Chaos killing thing."

From the way Dex is smiling, too, I'm positive he was well aware of Lada's meaning from the start.

Lada shakes her head, sobering.

"I'm already here for answers. That one can wait. Shall we?" Lada asks, gesturing to the hole in the ground.

Dex nods and walks up to the entrance, but Phoenix holds up his arm, gesturing for him to wait.

"Actually, I should teleport us all in. If we enter in normally, we'll be sent directly to Whiro and forced to pay the price for resources we're not here for," Phoenix explains.

Sin nods his agreement.

"I do prefer to avoid torture," Lada says, with an elegant shrug.

"Sounds good to me," Dex says. He pivots away from the hole to face us again, but his foot slips against the dirt floor.

"Dex!" I shout, and try to grab for him but he's already out of reach, falling backwards into the entrance in the ground.

A thud from behind me draws my attention, and I turn to find Dex lying on the ground on his stomach. He spits some dirt out of his mouth, having face planted, and looks up at us, a sheepish smile on his face.

A breath of relief escapes me for this person I met a moment ago. Dex pulls himself up onto his knees.

"Seriously?" Phoenix asks.

"How do you survive on a daily basis?" Sin questions him.

Dex gets up off the ground, brushing the dirt from his knees, and looks at the two of them indignantly.

"I am capable. I just saved myself, and teleportation is not so easy when you're plummeting."

"He's right about that," Phoenix says. "It takes practice and skill."

"Okay, practice and skill our way down there." I hold my hand out to Phoenix and look to the rest to do the same.

We only have so much time before the next Ascension challenge. It got dark again while we were in Phoenix's lair, and there's always one light period in between challenges. If we want to ensure that we get back in time for the challenge, we'll have to be done at Whiro's by at most three hours into the next dark period.

"Please," I add.

Phoenix grabs my hand and the rest follow, forming a circle.

"Wait," Sin says. He stands on my other side, between me and Dex. He narrows his eyes at Phoenix, a look with which I am familiar. "Why are you afraid?"

Wasn't expecting that to come up again so soon. Startled by the familiar topic, I look between Sin and Phoenix, wondering if Sin did overhear our conversation. But, that's not why he's brought this up. He just now sensed Phoenix's fear.

Phoenix, for once, doesn't look mad at having his emotions read. He doesn't try to deny it either.

"You're not?" he asks of us all. "None of you have ever been to Whiro's before, have you?" Phoenix continues. "We'll be able to avoid Whiro, but you all need to be prepared for the place itself.

The cave is enchanted to manifest what you most fear, so it's best to enter already acknowledging that fear."

I try to think of what it is I most fear so I'm better prepared for what I'm about to see, but my mind is coming up blank. I'm deeply afraid that I don't know what it is I fear.

"How's the fear level now?" Phoenix asks Sin.

I look around our circle.

Dex nervously nibbles on his lower lip, his eyes lowered but darting back and forth, as if searching inside his own head. Lada's eyes are steel. They're focused behind me at the hole in the ground, as if she thinks she can stare down the fear the place will pull out from her.

Phoenix awaits Sin's answer. If I didn't know for a fact that he was afraid, no one could have convinced me of it. Sin holds Phoenix's stare as he reevaluates and then answers.

"We're ready."

Phoenix's grip tightens on my hand.

CHAPTER EIGHTEEN

I'm in darkness, but the floor beneath my feet is solid so I focus on that. Phoenix and Sin are gone from what I can tell, their hands no longer in my own. I reach out to test where I am and find a cold, stone wall only a few inches to my right. The whole place has a cold feeling, and I get the sense that I'm completely shut in by the stone walls, with no entrance or exit.

"Who are you?" a monotone voice asks, neither male or female, completely void of anything that could distinguish it.

I try to locate the direction from which it comes, but the words echo around me.

It repeats, again and again. I try to warm up, rubbing my hands over my arms even though they're already covered by my long-sleeved shirt. I admit that another reason for the action is to try and keep myself occupied in some way so I don't respond to the disembodied voice that is getting increasingly more insistent. Each word feels like it's physically pushing in on my head, pushing against my consciousness.

The cave lights up, the walls containing some sort of yellow, luminescent vein that casts a sickly glow on everything.

I startle. Someone stands directly in front of me, the pale skin of her lower face, the only part of her visible, reflecting that yellow light. The rest of her body is covered in a cloak and hood.

"Who are you?"

I'm the one to ask this time around.

Was she there the whole time, and I just couldn't see? The thought is frightening but that is the whole point of this isn't it?

I force myself to take a deep breath. I don't bother backing up because I see now that I'm in a corner of the room, a room with no opening, as I'd suspected.

Her mouth lifts into a tight-lipped smile.

"Who are you?" she asks back, but this time the voice changes on the last word. The monotone, anonymous voice is gone, replaced by a voice that sounds too familiar.

It's my voice.

The hood falls down, and I'm left staring at myself. The feeling in my head has increased. It feels now as though my brain has fallen asleep and has pins and needles. The other version of me standing in front of me stares back at me with that smile, but otherwise emotionless. I'm tempted to reach out and check that there isn't a funhouse mirror between us.

"I am Dawn," she says, "but you are *not*."

She speaks so aggressively that I find my back bumping against the wall of the cave behind me even though, as I'd known, there's nowhere to go.

"That's not true," I say, shaking my head, disagreeing, but also trying to rid myself of the incessant pins and needles.

"Who are you?" she asks again.

"Dawn."

"Are you sure?"

I look at her. She looks just like me, and she's standing right in front of me, just as I am her. She can't be real. I know who I am. Everyone knows who I am. I killed Chaos, and I did that because—

How did I kill a Protogenoi? How can I not remember?

I'm slipping away. The piercing in my head is the only thing reminding me that I am present. My hands are numb. Everything is numb.

"Who else would I be?" I ask her.

"*It's not real!*"

I hear Phoenix's voice shout in my head, and the pins and needles poking at me scatter as I recognize them for what they are. These caves manifest fears, the power of which I can sense along with my own. The chaotic energy was screaming at me to let it in.

"*What* else, you mean," she answers. "You are a product of manipulation, while I am what you were meant to be."

Her eyes glow red as she leans toward me, somehow towering over me.

Those eyes are Chaos's.

"I don't care who you are," I tell her, "but you're not me."

I push against her shoulders, and she disappears in a burst of smoke. I don't take a second to hesitate. I walk right through the smoke that was whatever my fear conjured and towards the opposite wall of the cave. There was smoke, but no mirrors.

I pull from within, and my golden energy flows out of me in four separate streams. As the streams make contact with the wall, it disappears like the other me had. I was never really trapped.

I can't feel and interpret emotions like Sin can, but I can feel the chaotic energy of the infecting fear. I seek it out, tracking it back to Phoenix, Dex, Lada, and Sin. I don't have to look far. After all, we teleported in together. We were never as far from each other as I would have thought only a moment ago.

We still stand in a circle, as we had when we teleported in, but we've spread out. I can see what their fears have manifested, as real as my own appeared to me.

Sin's feet are melded into the stone floor, and he struggles to escape.

Dex is drowning in a mound of papers, seemingly unable to find the one thing he is actually looking for.

Lada holds a large trophy, but it's weighing her down. She tries to let go of it but it appears right back in her grasp.

Phoenix stands before a manifestation of Dabar, who holds a lit match.

I shouldn't look at their fears. But, then again, I can't understand their meaning anyway. I barely understood my own.

Still, it's private.

I focus back on the streams of golden energy I released and make them latch onto each of their wrists like pieces of rope. I pull, tethering them to me and back to reality. I don't want to look again at what their fears have manifested, but I have to ensure it's working. It only takes a glance, though.

When I look back, they're all focused now on the tether as it tightens around their wrists.

Sin breaks free from the floor. Dex pushes the mound of papers aside, the sheets swirling in the air before dispersing into smoke. Lada throws the trophy onto the floor, where it crashes, before also turning to smoke. Phoenix takes the match from Dabar and blows out the flame, smoke unfurling in Dabar's face before he, too, blows away.

I unclench my fists, opening up my palms, and the energy flows back to me, releasing everyone else. It gets dimmer in the caves without the golden source of light, but the luminescent cave walls keep us from being completely in the dark again.

"As enjoyable as that was," Dex says, being the first to find his voice as he stands up from the cave floor, "does anyone mind if we just find Styx and get out of here as soon as possible?"

"This way," Lada says.

She's already walking off into another area of the cave, toward a narrow tunnel. The ground slopes downward in that direction.

I look to Sin, who nods before following her himself. Sin is a skilled fighter, but the thing that really makes him a good, albeit reluctant bodyguard, is the fact that he can sense when someone's out to deceive. Lada, apparently, has no intention to betray us, at least not currently.

The decline becomes increasingly more steep, to the point that the ground morphs into stairs. They start off wide but narrow as we descend.

We reach a point where the path diverges. The two paths on either side of the main one are level. I expect Lada to lead us down one or the other; but instead, she continues to face forward in the direction that we've been headed.

The center path doesn't continue on in that direction, though. It ends in a sheer drop. She looks back at us in the single-file line we've been forced to walk in.

"You can teleport us back out of here, right?" she asks Phoenix.

Dex leans against the cave wall to allow her to more easily address the question to Phoenix, who stands behind him. Sin made sure I walked in front of him so that he could watch our backs, so I ended up walking behind Phoenix, who's remained quiet, like the rest of us, throughout the trek.

I have a feeling our fears remain on our minds, despite them literally going up in smoke.

Phoenix doesn't hesitate to speak now, though.

"Of course," he assures her.

"Good."

And then she's jumping off the edge.

CHAPTER NINETEEN

I rush forward past Phoenix, but Dex's upheld arm stops me from diving headfirst after Lada. I try to push him aside. I can no longer even see her.

"Wait," Dex tells me, "look."

He lowers his arm so I can move forward enough to look over the edge. When I do, I see that it's not a complete drop down as I'd thought.

There's a drop for a few feet, but then the path picks up again. This time, however, the stone floor forms what could only be described as a slide down to who knows where. It's too far down and too dark to see where it leads exactly, but it does lead somewhere, presumably.

I guess it's a good thing then that I didn't unnecessarily jump in head first. Although, now that I actually think about it, it's probably a dumb idea in any situation. I'd only be lying to myself if I imagined there wouldn't be another time ever again that I dive without thinking. So, reminder to self that next time I feel the urge to dive into a situation, try leading with the feet.

"*Come on. Styx already doesn't like me.*"

Lada's voice in my head further confirms the fact that she's not dead.

"*What did you do?*" Dex asks her, a teasing tone to his voice.

He gives the rest of us a wave before jumping down after Lada. Even though I know she survived, it still makes my heart beat erratically to see him follow her down.

Relax. I'm next.

"*Why are we assuming it's Lada's fault?*" I contribute to the conversation, maybe trying to stall.

I'm not a huge fan of how the path down appears to become narrower and narrower, the slide fully enclosed by the stone walls. I'd prefer a sheer drop to the claustrophobic tunnel.

"*I crushed her only friend down here,*" Lada says.

"*I take it back.*"

"*You did what?*" Dex sounds alarmed, and his voice is noticeably raised. But, it may also have to do with the fact that he's sliding at who knows what speed down a tiny, dark tunnel at the moment.

I catch Sin shaking his head. It doesn't speak of real disappointment but rather of minor exasperation. I raise an eyebrow at him, not needing to look past Phoenix to do so because Phoenix already leans casually against the cave wall, totally unbothered by the death drop in his future and Lada's comment.

"She'll explain," Sin says. He walks past Phoenix and me, right up to the edge. "I'm going before you."

I guess he doesn't trust the fact that Dex and Lada seem fine. But, he does trust Phoenix enough to leave me alone with him? Again.

I shrug and gesture toward the drop, giving him my go-ahead. He jumps down, and I watch the slide catch him and take him down as far as my eyes allow me to follow.

It was just a bug, but apparently it meant a lot to her.

And, there's the explanation from Lada.

Sometimes I don't understand how Sin knows what he does since he can't actually read thoughts, but perhaps he knew he'd sense more guilt from Lada if she really had killed something more than a bug.

"Would you like to go first?" Phoenix asks, pushing off the cave wall.

"I might as well get it over with," I say, peering over the edge.

"You say that, but you've been standing at the edge, not making any move to go for some time now."

I look away from said edge just long enough to give him side eye for calling me out on exactly what it is I've been doing.

Maybe it will be fun, like flying, not that I've flown before. I've always thought it looked enjoyable to be on the back of a Kaeli. I'll just imagine the cold, stone slide is a Kaeli and the darkness lit by only an eerie, yellow light is the night sky lit up by funky stars.

I move to jump but Phoenix stops me, holding onto my arm, and my heart skips a beat. Because he startled me. Or, because his hand is warm compared to the cold air that has been blowing across my skin. Or, for some other reason, not having anything to do with what may have almost happened between us outside of these caves and definitely nothing to do with a desire to have his hands on more of me.

Traitorous body. I barely know him, and I can't go feeling feelings for someone just because they said some pretty words about me giving them hope. Except, it's not just that, is it? I felt strongly, even before that, for some crazy reason, that I could trust him.

He's been open about his intentions and actions. I get the sense that all he's hiding from me is personal information about himself, and it only makes me curious to know more. You don't care about finding out about someone if you don't care for them at all.

He lets go the second I turn back around to face him.

"What?" I ask. "Changed your mind? You wanna go first?"

"No," he says, smiling at my eagerness to put this off more. "I just wanted to say thanks."

That's nice. "For what?"

"You broke us away from our fears."

"Well, I did say I wanted to help. But, you actually got us free, reminding us it wasn't real."

"That alone wasn't enough to beat the manifestations."

"It was enough to wake me up *so* I could beat them."

"Alright," he relents. "Then, you're welcome."

I should have just accepted the gratitude while I had the chance. "I'm jumping now," I inform him.

"Okay, bye."

The stone slants right away, so I don't come down too hard on it when I land. I immediately begin sliding. It's like falling into a tube. I hold back a scream as my speed picks up. The yellow veins in the cave walls blur together as I slide down. I resist the urge to reach out and grab for the walls. I might be able to slow my descent that way, but there's barely any room, and I know I would just end up injuring myself. There's also the more than minor fear that creeps in that I might get stuck in the small tube-like tunnel if I slow down.

The luminescent wall forms an image, the veins sharpening into a blade, a sword just like the one from my dream. In a second, it's gone, having fallen behind me, as I continue my descent.

It could've been my imagination. It most likely was my imagination.

At least the stone in this tunnel is smooth. I can't see past my feet because there isn't enough room to lift my head up, but I can now hear voices down below.

The tunnel spits me out. The exit is too close to the floor for me to have time to get my feet back beneath me, so I land on my butt. Hard.

Sin looks down at me and offers me a hand up. A warning about the dismount would have been nice, as well. I take the hand.

We're in a small cavern. Past Sin stands Dex and Lada, who face metal bars that block off the majority of the area. Inside is a female with completely white hair that falls down past her waist. Even in the cave, it has a shimmer. Her back is to us.

"We came here to find you," Lada tells her, but gets no response or even a tell that Styx heard her.

"Why do the Protogenoi have you down here?" Dex asks to no avail.

So, that's who locked her up here.

I hear noise behind me and back away from the entrance to the cavern to allow Phoenix room to enter. As he slides out of the tunnel, I reach out and grab his hand, using the momentum to pull him up to standing before he can hit the ground.

He looks at me surprised and maybe as though he's even considering thanking me again, but I back up and look away before he can attempt it. I love some genuine gratitude, no matter how bad I might be at accepting it. But, this close proximity thing is starting to happen too frequently with him. I'm starting to think I just can't help it.

I fear if I stay close for too long I might become too reluctant to move away, which would be... fine? I glance at him out of the corner of my eye.

Correction. It wouldn't be "fine." I have goals to achieve, like winning Ascension and announcing to all of Havcire that the Protogenoi can be killed. I have to stay focused on those things.

Excuses. That's my own voice whispering at me, but I don't know what she's talking about, so whatever.

"We should let her out."

"What?" Lada asks, turning to face me, as the rest mirror her surprised tone with their expressions.

With everyone's attention now on me, they don't notice Styx turn around to face me also, her eyes pools of mercury.

"If the Protogenoi put her in here, then that's reason enough to set her free."

There's a clanging sound, metal against metal, and then the lock that holds the door to the cage closed simply disappears, as if it whisked itself away.

Styx stares at the door as it swings open slowly.

"I agree," Phoenix says.

"Seriously?" I ask him. "First you can only teleport yourself, then turns out you can teleport other people as long as you're making contact, and now you can teleport anything anywhere without even touching it?"

"Magic, it's crazy," he says.

I shake my head, turning back to the matter at hand, to Styx.

Although, if Phoenix can teleport any object, then why does he even bother to deal with any of the Corporates for resources? He could just poof resources into his lair at any time. Maybe he's simply a glutton for punishment.

Styx. We're focusing on Styx now.

Lada opens the door wider, seemingly inviting Styx to exit, but she stays in place.

"Look," Lada says, no nonsense, holding her arm out to her. She pulls up the sleeve of her white shirt. There, burned into her skin, is Styx's name. "I don't know how it got there, but I thought you might."

Styx looks up from Lada's arm and says calmly, her voice slightly rough from non-use, "I did not do that to you."

Phoenix huffs and walks past me, up to the cage. He swings the barred door wide open so it lies flat against the wall of the cage.

"We didn't think you did," he tells her. "Now, wouldn't you like to get out of your prison?"

Styx's weariness of us vanishes, and she does just what Phoenix suggests. Each step she takes out of the cage and closer to the rest of us seems like a dare, to do what, I don't know. Phoenix has placed himself at the front of our little group, so she walks up to face him.

"Do you know what my power is?" she asks him.

"You're invulnerable," Phoenix answers.

"To what?"

"To other powers." It's Dex who answers this time, and she looks around Phoenix to nod at him.

Styx takes a step back from Phoenix to take us all in. When she focuses on Lada again and looks at her arm, she actually smiles.

"That was smart," she tells her, "and that comes from someone who's spent her immortal life avoiding people because I've found the opposite to be true about them."

"You lack faith," Sin says.

How very Sin. Simple. To the point. Bordering insulting.

Styx's eyes bore into his as her smile becomes crooked.

"But not fight."

She says the words like they are weapons, and their blows land.

I can't help but see the manifestation of Sin's fear, his inability to move. He seems like a fighter to me, at least dedicated to ensuring I don't die at the hands of some assassin. But, he doesn't approve of my actions against the Protogenoi. He doesn't want to bring the fight to them.

"I was hoping to ease you into the reality of your situation," Styx continues, "but Phoenix is impatient."

"The reality of our—?" Phoenix begins questioning, but Styx reaches up and presses her palm to his forehead. His face goes slack, and his thoughts seemingly stall. And then, "—oh shit."

CHAPTER TWENTY

They're coming. This time, instead of trees in my way, it's people. I can't see them until I'm almost right on top of them, and then I have to jump quickly to the side to avoid crashing into them.

I don't have time to stop, but I'm afraid I'm leaving them behind to be victims of those chasing me. Will they come to harm?

I start to recognize those I pass, making me slow my pace despite the threat. Priscilla, my sister from my fourteenth life. Sam, my brother from my twenty-third life. Rachel, my mother from my twenty-fifth life. Face after face of those I thought were lost to me forever.

My legs keep moving like they've been wound up and still have more spin in them, even though I want to stop. The footsteps behind me are louder, but the people I pass begin to thin out, so I push myself to run faster, feeling like I'm tripping over my own feet with each step.

Another person appears directly ahead of me in my path.

I stop.

As I do, my foot hits something that slides heavily across the dirt before coming to a stop at the feet of the other person. She bends down and picks it up. The sword.

Expectantly, she holds it out to me, its blade so clean it looks to be made from mirrors. It reflects my own face back at me, but it's my birth mother's face that has my attention. Her hand holds the sword.

My own hand burns painfully, and I reach for the cool onyx of the blade's hilt. As my fingers wrap around, the burning ceases but the entire world erupts into flames.

My heart continues to beat erratically, but my body is otherwise relaxed, transported to another time and place.

I lie on soft ground, looking up. Flames still fill my vision, but they're no longer all around. They stem from a single source. Above me, a bird is surrounded by the red and orange flames. Its wings release the fire, and the bird twists through the air, stirring the fire in a sort of dance. It passes through the fire it creates, unharmed by the heat.

I come to, awakened out of the dream. Except, I never fell asleep. I stand in the same place I did a moment ago.

I remember.

I'd been standing at the Tree of Life with Phoenix, and then the whole world changed. *Reality* changed.

I'd thought I was a Celestial. I'd killed Chaos, that much was true, but I hadn't even known why. It didn't matter, though. It was simply the only reality I knew, and I didn't question it, didn't reflect back on the flimsy past fabricated for me.

I look around at the others. They're fine... at least I think.

Phoenix looks unaffected despite his initial response to having our true reality revealed. In fact, he already looks to be scheming. Or, puzzling over our current situation, if I want to give his expression a nicer connotation. I, for sure, look puzzled as I stare at him for too long.

Lada stares at her arm, at Styx's name. Her only expression is one of relief. She must have realized what was happening and rushed to find some way to get us out of this situation. She knew that Styx would be immune to any power used against us. It was quick thinking.

I guess her research did us some good. Who knows how long it would've taken us to figure this out without it.

"Why isn't it healing?" Dex asks her, reaching out to gently cradle her marked arm.

"It will now," Lada says, lingering for just a second, before sliding her arm out from Dex's grasp. "I kept it fresh so I'd stay focused."

Dex's own arm drops back to his side. He takes notice when Lada takes another step back, further away from him, and stops just short of allowing a frown to actually form. Lada offers him a soft smile, seemingly in consolation, before turning her attention away from him.

I make a note to myself to question what that's about to Lada later.

Sin stands separate from the rest of us, nearer where we all entered the cavern, like a bodyguard meant always to be present but not seen. He's the one that can read our emotions, but his own are clear on his face. He either doesn't think anyone is paying attention to him or doesn't care if we see the shame written across his features. Still, there's a steeliness that keeps the shame company.

Again, something I don't understand. I can't imagine what he would have to feel shameful about.

"Dabar did this?" I ask Styx, breaking a heavy silence. I figure she must know enough to have gotten herself locked up down here by the Protogenoi. "He created this reality?"

Styx nods her head, her white hair cascading over her shoulders. "Dabar and the rest of the Protogenoi. They all had a part in creating this world. Maze is the reason no one can remember what was before."

"And how they found us," Phoenix adds.

"What do you mean?" Lada asks. "They don't know where we are."

"Not physically, no, but these lives were sculpted for us. Maze was able to locate our minds so that Dabar could shape this reality to suit us specifically as he wanted it to."

See? Puzzling. He was busy puzzling through this all, *not* scheming.

My life— scratch that— My whole world has been manipulated again; and here I am, just having found out the truth about everything yet again, trying to make sense of what is going on in a single person's head. Again. Trying to reassure myself that Phoenix is truly on our side. Because, if he's not, if he's up to some other manipulation, then I have to feel guilty and dumb over the fact that, with my memories gone again, I found myself trusting him, again.

I'd just have to accept that I'm a complete fool, and that simply doesn't sit right with me, so he better not be pulling some trick in this reality or any reality for that matter.

I didn't just trust him, though, did I? I wish my memory would betray me, but I very clearly recall wishing he had me pinned to the ground in a non-friendly and non-enemy-like manner. Maybe I've been mistrusting the wrong person this whole time, and it's me that's the problem here. Because, clearly, I can't trust myself not to fall for him.

"You probably remember now that weird sensation before we were brought into this reality?" Phoenix continues. "Like you were lost in your own mind, not in control?"

Another thing I wish I didn't remember. *Your eyes look like mint.* What a stupid thing to say. I wouldn't say something like that... out loud. Except, I definitely did.

"That was Maze getting into our minds," he explains. "If you want someone dead, what do you do?" Phoenix continues, sounding like he's teaching a class. It's Sin who answers like a good student.

"Make them the most wanted person in the world and offer an award for their assassination."

Now everyone's looking at me, even Styx. Although, she doesn't look as invested as the rest do. Rather, she looks at me merely because it seems like the correct thing to do at the moment, her mercury eyes lazy.

"Why send the whole of Havcire after me, though? Why not just kill me themselves?"

"Why do they want you dead?" Styx asks.

"I assume that really is because I killed Chaos."

Styx raises a round eyebrow, as if she doesn't believe that's motivation enough to want me dead. Personally, I don't think they should want to kill me for any reason.

"Why don't we ask them?" Dex suggests.

"Ask the people who want me dead why they want me dead?"

"Well, we wouldn't need to do it in person. We could send a letter."

"Become pen pals with the Protogenoi?"

"I feel like you're not taking my suggestion seriously."

"You'd be right about that," Sin pitches in.

I try not to laugh, but I do smile at Dex, who shoots me a look of mock offense.

"Phoenix knows," Lada says, in a classic tattle-telling tone. From Phoenix's expression, it would seem he'd like to accuse her of exactly that. "What?" she asks him innocently. "You're only this quiet when you're keeping something from the rest of the group. Not my fault I remember I know you now."

Phoenix rolls his eyes at Lada. "It's just a theory," he relents, "but what if the reason the Protogenoi haven't killed Dawn themselves is because they simply can't. We assumed we trapped them in Havcire with Dawn's barriers around the portals, but what if they've been trapped this whole time in Vest? They're trying to get Havcirians to do their work for them because they can't. And, if Dawn is dead—"

"My barriers come down."

Phoenix nods. "And they can get into Havcire."

Styx brushes past us and toward the only entrance and exit to the cavern, one that I'm fairly certain will be much harder to climb up than it was to fall down. Lada steps in her way before she can make it to Sin, who still stands guarding the front of the cavern.

"Lada," Styx stays in warning, "get out of my way. I have to guard my portal."

Lada doesn't move.

"I know that," she says, "but we have a faster and easier way of getting you out of this prison."

Styx calms, no longer looking at Lada like a mere obstacle in her way. She turns back to face Phoenix, who of course has made himself look comfortable leaning against a rock wall, and actually smiles.

CHAPTER
TWENTY-ONE

Despite it being her first time teleporting, as far as I know, Styx takes it extremely well. Or, maybe she's just glad to be out of the cave and exposed to fresh air again. I was only in there for a short time, and I'm relieved to see the sky again, which is light. We only have one more dark period now before the next Ascension challenge, if we're even still competing.

My whole plan to expose the fact that the Protogenoi can be killed has lost its significance, to say the least. There's no point in starting a rebellion against the Protogenoi when I know that exact war was already fought and won a long time ago. Now, we just need to find some way to reverse what Dabar's done, to get that reality back, with the Council in power. Easy.

Except, even with life returned to how it was, the Protogenoi will be an inevitable threat like they were before, and they're in Vest where they could cause who knows how much destruction before they find a way through to Havcire.

"Wait!" I yell, halting Phoenix before he can teleport Styx away to her portal on the river.

Phoenix backs away as I run up to them, leaving Dex, Lada, and Sin behind me, back by the ditch in the ground that functions as an entrance to Whiro's caves.

"You don't have to go back to the portal," I tell Styx. "The barriers are still up, and we could use your help here planning our next move against the Protogenoi."

I remember now the time I saw Styx through the tile in the Ziggurat. She seemed powerful, harder to move than the boulder she sat on. I'd told Dex, before I knew I wasn't fully human myself, that if I could have the powers of any Celestial, I would choose Styx. She can protect not only herself, but also all those around her with her invulnerability. Maybe the risk wouldn't have to be so great for once if she stuck around.

"You don't need me," is what she says, though, and I have to stop myself from openly disagreeing with her. "If the barriers come down, I need to be ready to fight and defend the portals."

"'If the barriers come down.' You mean if I die."

"You won't," she says, simple.

"But that's what you're preparing for, so how can you really believe that?"

Styx stands her ground, pinning me with a curious look.

"If you knew you were going to die in this fight, would you stop fighting?"

I feel all of a sudden like I'm in one of Gatlin's tests again, at that lever in front of the train tracks, my own body tied down to one of the tracks and some obscure victory hovering over the other.

I've died before, obviously, but it's never been permanent. I made it clear to Gatlin that I didn't like those types of moral dilemmas with only two options.

Phoenix looks on now, even though he'd previously been trying to appear uninterested in our conversation. He's waiting for my answer, same as Styx. Except, he looks to have an opinion on what the correct answer is.

"She will *not* be dying." And there it is.

It comes out with no room for argument, his eyes hard, as he looks at Styx. His hands, though, tremble at his sides before he shoves them in his pockets.

Instead of giving it up, cowering, or reacting in a way I think anyone else would under the heat of that expression, Styx simply smiles.

"Phoenix," I try for a somewhat soothing voice, not something I'm used to, seeing as I'm normally the one most commonly in our group who needs speaking to in a soothing voice. "It's just a hypothetical question. I have died before."

"Only momentarily," Phoenix somehow manages through a still clenched jaw.

He looks about to back off, take a breath, when Styx's follow-up question comes.

"How are you so certain?" she prods.

Finally, he takes a breath, and I do, too, because I don't know what that insane reaction was about. Phoenix doesn't react, at least not in an uncalculated way. Ever. He could still be on edge, as we all are, from Whiro's. Whatever it is, it's over and—

"Because I won't let her, and I'll give up my own life to ensure it doesn't happen."

Phoenix shrugs. Actually shrugs.

He said it so casually.

I stare at him, with what I'm sure are wide, shocked eyes, but he's looking at Styx still, not me, so I can't make out his expression. Styx, however, looks matter-of-fact, like he's just told her the sun is out in the sky, and she's like, "Yeah, I can see that."

I clear my throat, a reminder that I am still standing here, and jab my thumb in Phoenix's direction.

"This egomaniac doesn't mean that," I say.

Phoenix sighs like I'm the exasperating one and finally looks at me.

"I'm finally honest, and you accuse me of lying?"

I open my mouth to say something, but Styx has moved on.

"Some, after an eternity, give up," she continues, her voice raised in a way that signals us both to shut the hell up, saving me from answering both Phoenix and her original question. "They feel they've seen everything, including history repeating itself. I choose to keep fighting."

"Why?"

Styx shrugs, the nonchalant action apparently contagious, but it seems out of place on her sharp shoulders.

"Giving up seems like a boring way to spend the rest of eternity," she answers.

A smile teases the corners of my mouth, and I work to summon as much confidence as possible. I do know that there's little I wouldn't sacrifice to fight for something I believe in. Most everyone still wants me dead, and we don't have a plan to escape this reality, but I want Styx to believe that I believe we all are going to survive and succeed. Because, *we* need to believe it if we're going to have any chance.

"You can guard your portal," I tell her, "but the fight won't be making its way to you."

I back away, signaling to Phoenix that he can take her now.

Styx winks at me, and then they're gone.

"Dex, stop complimenting the Protogenoi," Lada is saying as I join them.

Dex has wandered closer to the walls of the Labyrinth. He looks to be examining them. They appear to be made of cement and oddly resemble more the walls of a rundown Vest building than anything found naturally in Havcire.

"I'm not complimenting them," he says, looking back at Lada. "I'm just realizing that they made the Labyrinth in the Graveyard. That way, anyone lost inside would be locked in with the

Entrapped. Objectively, it's a smart way to make a dangerous place even more dangerous."

"It is wise to acknowledge the strengths of one's enemy," Sin says.

"Thank you, Sun Tzu," Dex says, appreciative.

Sin only looks puzzled. "You know my name is Sin."

Dex's eyebrows shoot up. He looks to Lada, but she's no help, not understanding either.

"I knew him," Phoenix chimes in, walking up from behind me. I hadn't heard him teleport back. "Most Celestials don't get out much."

Dex takes a step closer to the Labyrinth wall. There's a flash, and he's gone.

A portal, the type that leads into the Labyrinth, out of which few find their way.

Without giving it much thought, or really any thought at all, I run at the cement wall, the place where Dex stood a second ago...

"Dawn," Phoenix warns, "don't you—"

...And I'm through. There's a second, as the flash of light surrounds me, that the air around me feels cold, freezing. As my feet hit the dirt ground, the air returns to normal, humid and warm.

I'm relieved to find Dex standing before me. Behind him, as he'd observed from outside the Labyrinth, is one of the trees of the Graveyard.

The trees are at least two times the height of the Labyrinth walls. I can see even from this height that we couldn't possibly just be on the opposite side of the wall I ran at to enter because the Graveyard trees continue on far into the distance in that direction.

"Why'd you follow?" Dex asks.

"To help," I tell him, thinking that much is obvious.

"Did you forget that I'm the one who makes the maps so people can find their way out of this place?"

I did actually kind of forget that. How was I to know if that was a real thing in this fabricated reality, though?

Dex stares at me incredulously, waiting for an answer, and then Phoenix is stepping out of the portal with an aggravated look on his face. Sin and Lada aren't far behind.

"Oh," Dex says, staring at us all, "well now it's a party."

"Who brought the drinks?" Phoenix asks.

"We agreed you'd bring them, Phoenix," Lada says with exaggerated irritation.

"Did no one think I could handle this myself?" Dex asks.

"Of course you can," Lada answers quickly, before Sin can open his mouth.

"You just don't have to," I reassure him.

Dex shakes his head at us.

"You're relieved we're here," Sin points out, in that emotion reading way of his.

"That's just because I like having company that's not the Entrapped," Dex says. "Now, follow me. I do actually know the way out."

CHAPTER TWENTY-TWO

According to Dex, a labyrinth is fundamentally different from a maze. While a maze is made up of various paths, many of which lead to dead ends, a labyrinth is made up of only one path that leads from the outside to the center. The Labyrinth is a labyrinth, which should mean it's fairly easy to find the way out.

"The key to getting out of the Labyrinth," Dex explained, "is getting in."

The reason hardly anyone can ever get out is because the exit is in the center of the Labyrinth. There is no way to get out by navigating your way to the perimeter, which most try to do by climbing up one of the Graveyard trees in order to see which direction the outside is in. The promise of the trees showing the way out is merely another trick, another way to ensure Havcirians remain trapped within.

As long as you are headed out, the Labyrinth will continue on indefinitely.

Dex volunteered to climb up one of the trees in order to find which direction leads further into the Labyrinth. It's not an easy job, considering the tree he chose. The image its outer bark twists to form doesn't make for the best ladder.

Where the top layer of the trunk intermittently weaves open to reveal the smoother layer below, it twists to depict stars. From my count, there are about six stars in the trunk of the tree. Thankfully, though, the stars aren't the only foot and handholds available. Dex also uses the other grooves in the outer bark to pull himself up.

"It's a constellation," Sin says, watching me examine the trunk, plus probably having sensed my curiosity.

I've never asked him if he can control his ability to sense others' emotions but, based on his past behavior, I would guess he cannot.

"Actually," Lada chimes in, "I was just researching it. Well, before all of this mess happened. It's the Tucana constellation."

"As in toucan, the bird?" I ask.

"There's a Phoenix constellation, too," Phoenix says.

I look to Phoenix, who stands against the tree Dex climbs, looking up, perhaps spotting Dex in case he loses his footing. At our answering silence, though, he looks to the rest of us.

"What? There is."

I think Phoenix would love to play a game where the goal was to relate every single conversation back to him, like a spin on the Six Degrees of Kevin Bacon but instead the Six Degrees of Phoenix.

When's a good time to bring up the fact that Phoenix claimed he'd sacrifice his own life to save mine..? Shit. And, why does the thought that it could be true make me just a little panicked? I would murder him if he got himself killed for me.

Now's not the time.

"Anyway," Lada continues, "the constellation was originally named the Turul constellation pre-Vestigium."

Dex jumps down from the tree, the motion unsettling the dead leaves on the ground.

"This way," he says, walking on to my right. "The Turul is the bird in the Hungarian myth that dropped a sword in what is now Budapest, marking it as their homeland," he continues, sounding like an enthusiastic encyclopedia.

We follow Dex down the path of the Labyrinth, the gray cement walls on either side of us. I almost expect to find graffiti upon them. What would it say? "Fuck the Protogenoi." Or, maybe something like, "I've lost my way, and now I'm losing my mind."

What would I write? "The exit is in the center." That would be helpful at least. Actually, that's not a horrible idea.

"I thought you only knew everything about this artificially created world," Lada is saying.

"No, I generally try to learn as much as I can about everything," Dex tells her. "You never know when you're going to need what type of information."

"Why weren't you the one covering the research portion of our job?"

"Because you secretly love burying your beautiful head in books, and I wasn't going to interfere with that."

"I wouldn't have minded some company." I can hear the smile in Lada's voice. "You think I'm beautiful?"

I hide my own smile as Dex answers without hesitation, "You think I'm blind?"

Another needed conversation, one I'd forgotten I already added to the queue. What the hell's up with those two? They've been into each other practically since they met. And yet, Lada is hot and cold, pushing him away the majority of the time.

I leave them to it, whatever it is, and fall back to where Phoenix walks alongside Sin. Odd. I wouldn't have expected them to stick together. Last time I checked, they didn't like each other, in any reality.

They're talking in hushed voices when I approach but fall silent by the time I reach them. Yeah, guys, that's not suspicious at all.

"Can I have paint and a brush?" I ask Phoenix.

"Sure." A can of paint and a brush appear in his hands.

It's red paint. Good, it will stand out. If only I had some white roses to paint, as well.

"Why were you researching the constellations?" Dex asks Lada up ahead.

"I wasn't, not really," she explains. "It was part of my research on the Protogenoi. They designed trials long ago that would allow the winning Protogenoi to be the sole ruler. At the time, they no longer wanted to share the power. Actually, I don't think they ever have wanted to or ever will want to share power, but there was an unforeseen consequence in their creation of the trials. The trials took on a life of their own in order to maintain the balance."

I catch up to Lada and Dex before opening the can of paint. I don't want to fall too far behind them, but I also don't want to tell everyone to hold up so I can do my little art project. I'll be quick. I dip the brush in.

"As bad as all the Protogenoi ruling together was— is for people, at least they have to answer to each other. If one won the trials and became the sole ruler? There would be nothing to stand in their way.

"The Protogenoi found that if any of them were to initiate the trials, then all of them would be compelled to compete, and no one would be allowed to survive but the winner. Because of this, none of them ever declared their start. None were willing to risk their own death."

Finished! Nope. It could use another coat.

"Good idea," Sin says, as he reaches me.

"Thanks."

I raise the brush for the second coat but Phoenix tugs on my arm, pulling me along. The brush drops from my hand. I lunge to catch it but it's gone, disappeared into thin air.

"It's good enough," he says. "Come on."

I frown at him but keep on walking.

He looks over, as if not trusting I'd follow along and needing to check. His face breaks out into a smile, and his lips press together to stop a laugh, which only draws my attention to said mouth.

"What?" I ask, letting anger at myself sound like anger at him because why do I have to be so affected by him when nothing affects him in return?

Except, *something* did finally affect him. He barely kept himself under control with Styx; and, no matter the topic, I've never seen him show such little restraint. Even when he's bothered, he keeps those real emotions in check. So, what was different?

He stops and reaches up to my face, making me freeze, and then his fingers are gently graze my cheekbone, and his thumb...

...taps my nose? Before quickly drawing back. Did he just boop my nose?

It quickly makes sense as he holds his thumb right out in front of me, close enough that I go slightly cross eyed seeing that there's now red paint on the pad of his thumb. I roll my eyes.

"That's what's so amusing? I got some paint on my face?"

"Well, yeah, somehow just right on the tip."

"Is it off now?"

He shakes his head, that smile still on his face. "Nope."

I wipe at my nose with the back of my hand. Look back at him in question. Another head shake.

"You just rubbed it in more."

"Phoenix," I practically whine, in an endearing way, I'm sure. "Teleport it off or something."

He laughs. "I like it. It goes nicely with your resting serious face."

I feel my resting serious face harden, my eyes narrow in challenge. "Fine."

I grab Phoenix's face between my hands. I have to stand up on my toes so we're face to face, nose to nose. I tap the tip of my nose to his, pulling back just enough to see some of the red paint transferred to him and smile, my hands dropping down to his shoulders.

"Now we can match. Since you like it so much."

I go to pull away, but my eyes catch on his. They still hold that flicker of amusement but they pull me in with an intensity behind them. Phoenix's hands find my waist.

"What was it like for you?" I ask, taking a stab in the dark.

"What?" he asks, voice a whisper.

"To be back in a world controlled by them?"

Anger flashes in his eyes, and I know that this is the something that's gotten under his skin. His grip tightens on my waist and I tense, worried his next move will be to push me away. He doesn't.

"You don't think I enjoyed every second of it?" he grinds out.

MOLLY C. GROSS

"Call me crazy, but no, not really. And you're not doing a very good job of convincing me."

"I'm not the one who bottles up their anger."

I go to take a step back in mock offense, but his hands keep me in place. Instead, I settle for raising my own hands in surrender.

"Oh, you got me. I'm just not nearly as in touch with my emotions as you are. Why don't you show me how it's done? Express yourself," I taunt, reaching up to squeeze his cheeks like some annoying, in your space auntie or something.

He smiles bitingly, finally releasing my waist, only to physically detach my hands from his face and wrap my arms around the back of his neck, as if we were about to slow dance.

"Alright, Dawn," he says, voice overly sweet, "or Killer, whatever you prefer."

"Dawn, please."

"Killer," he continues, "I am angry. I am frustrated that I was forced into the same position, where I was basically helpless to help anyone and living a lie, a position that I worked for a long, long time to escape. I am angry that all it took was essentially a single thought for the Protogenoi to take it all away and make all that time I spent escaping that life no longer a reality, as if it meant nothing. All that time meant nothing."

And just like that, the anger takes a back seat. His arms wrap around my waist in a gentle way that makes me melt, and I think

230

that maybe I should take a note from Phoenix's book and get better at expressing myself.

He offers me a real smile, tinged with sadness.

"Sorry, Dawn."

I shake my head, rejecting an apology, because this is real. I'd be willing to beg him to lose his cool with me more often. The whole time I've known him, it's always me leaning on him. I've needed him and been so determined in this life to show that I could be fine without him.

But, maybe, possibly, it doesn't just work one way.

I meet his eyes, letting him see the anger that I may have gotten better at acknowledging and managing but still is always ready to rise, and it surely is incited for him now.

I've never even been physically in the same place as the remaining Protogenoi, but I hate them, how they treat everyone like playthings. They have all that power and all they want to do with it is use it to get more at the expense of those they believe are beneath them.

It's not just Phoenix who's suffering like this. Lada must feel it, too. Not to mention, all the other Celestials and the Incanters who are still being manipulated without their knowledge.

Gatlin.

His desire to help others, conflicting with his fear of offering help to those unworthy. This is why. He was forced under the Protogenoi rule to assist them with whatever they needed, like flooding an entire town of innocent people. I would be wary of those I offered assistance to, also, after living through that.

There must be countless Celestials and Incanters who still live with the trauma of the Protogenoi rule from ages ago. They've had to carry it for so long, and now the Protogenoi have brought them right back into it like they never escaped at all.

"That time did *not* mean nothing," I assure Phoenix. "It happened. If nothing else, I was born between then and now, as were many others who wouldn't have gotten that chance to live and live freely. We're going to stop them again and for good this time."

That sadness burns away before my eyes.

"I promise," I breathe, relieved to see that cocky expression back in place.

"...the flaming sword." Lada's voice reaches me, those two words somehow managing to sound like they were said directly into my ear, despite us having fallen significantly behind.

I pull away from Phoenix, his hands sliding away from my waist, and I almost reach back out but—

I speed to catch up and am at Lada's side in a second.

"The flaming sword?"

The question rips out from me, as if I were sleep-talking.

"It was said that the Turul would declare the winner of the trials by dropping the flaming sword into their hands," Lada continues.

"As in the one that guarded the garden of Eden, that the angel Uriel wielded?" Dex asks, continuing my inquiry for me.

Except, I'm more interested in why it would possibly be showing up repeatedly in a dream of mine.

"That is one of the Vest interpretations. Truly, though, the sword has never belonged to anyone. It was forged by magic alone for and by the trials."

Do I mention how I've been dreaming of this sword ever since we entered this alternate reality? Maybe it's random.

The sword is related to the Protogenoi, and the Protogenoi are the reason we are in this situation. That'd be a really big coincidence.

"How is that possible? For something not even sentient to create something material?" I ask Lada.

"Yin and Yang," Phoenix supplies. "They originated from Chaos, but they were born to prevent it. The power behind the trials, that which took over and created the sword, was Yin and Yang working to ensure that the balance of power remained."

Lada nods in agreement with Phoenix's explanation. So, Yin and Yang are real beings. I shouldn't be surprised. And, oddly enough, like me, come from Chaos.

Perhaps, the sword I've been dreaming about isn't *the* flaming sword. Maybe it's just a sword that happened to catch on fire. Maybe I should just make absolute sure.

"Is the flaming sword actually engulfed in flame?" I ask. "Or is that just an overly colorful name for it?"

Lada looks at me as though I've lost my head. I'm pretty sure of the answer based on that, even without her saying, "It's literal."

One of the Graveyard trees catches my eye. The outer bark of the trunk twists to form into a sword, curls of smoke spiraling out from the blade. The lines of the bark that form the blade's edges shine bright with white light. What I thought were curls of smoke now burn with the red of fire. I can actually feel the heat coming from those flames. I reach out towards it.

"Dawn?"

With Phoenix's voice, the scene before my eyes disappears.

There is no sword depicted on the trunk, no flames, and not even a hint of heat or smoke. Instead, the tree I've reached out towards depicts a conch shell. My arm falls back to my side.

Great. Now I don't even need to be dreaming to see the sword. Correction - the flaming sword. And, it's not even the first time this has happened.

I hadn't thought much of it the first time, because it was only once, but I'd seen the sword depicted on the wall of Whiro's cave. I was hoping I wasn't imagining it that time, that it had actually been engraved into the cave wall. So much for that.

"I've been dreaming of the flaming sword."

CHAPTER TWENTY-THREE

Their footsteps falter at my admission, each coming to a stop even though the Labyrinth isn't somewhere you want to dawdle.

It's eerily quiet here, unlike it used to be when the Graveyard wasn't confined by concrete walls. The breeze that rustled the leaves is absent. Before, the winds sounded eerie, like spirits of the dead whispering to each other, but I imagine even eerie whispers would make good company if one was lost and alone in this place. Any sound at all would help someone feel less hopelessly isolated.

I can imagine how unnerving this complete silence would be as it descends upon our group when they stop walking to stare at me with a mixture of expressions on their faces. Apparently, no one takes my dreams lightly.

Dex, not unusually, looks curious, head tilted as he sorts through who knows how many probabilities. Lada purses her lips, considering my words carefully, not yet having seemed to fully accept them. Sin is the opposite. He looks as though I've just recited another prophecy, which we already have enough of in my opinion, specifically the one that predicted the Protogenoi would rise again.

And Phoenix...

"What kinds of dreams?" he asks, overly suggestive, as he raises both dark brows into the air.

"Dreams where I'm being chased, and the sword seems like the only thing that can save me," I answer seriously, although I have to put in effort to resist the urge to laugh. I know he's just trying to lighten the suddenly tense mood.

"Are you sure?" Lada asks, voicing her skepticism.

"Yes," Sin says, answering for me, even though that one I could have answered. These dreams aren't the type that get foggy over time. I remember them well. I'm just not sure what they mean. "It makes sense," he continues, and he's got me there.

"How so?" I ask.

"Because," Dex says, "you're technically a Protogenoi, as you got your powers directly from Chaos. If the trials happened, you would be required to compete."

"Does that mean the dreams are happening because one of the other Protogenoi is planning on starting the trials? Are they like a warning system?" I ask, trying to play catch-up to their train of thoughts. Except, the train is going off the tracks.

Technically a Protogenoi is repeating on a loop in my head. What is a technicality anyway? Am I also technically human, as well? I have a human body, human DNA from human parents. And yet, it's magic that defines Celestials, Incanters, *and* Protogenoi. Magic is their DNA, and Chaos's magic is my own.

I know I am technically a Protogenoi. Yet, hearing Dex say it makes it sound so simple, and it's not. It can't be. It confuses me.

"Possibly," Sin answers.

Perfect. I've still yet to survive the Ascension Contest, and already one of the Protogenoi is planning to force me into another deadly competition of sorts.

Except, I keep forgetting that winning the Ascension Contest no longer is a priority, unless it could somehow help with destroying this reality and getting us back to our own reality.

If Phoenix or I could win the final challenge and announce to all of Havcire the truth, tell them that Dabar superficially created this reality, would that be enough to destroy it? If his power is sustained by people's belief that the reality he's created is real, then that could work. However, I *don't* know how his power functions. Then again, I'm not the one who was doing all the research on the Protogenoi.

"Lada, if—"

The silence of the Labyrinth erupts into cacophony.

One thing at a time, getting out of this Labyrinth being number one.

Lada's sudden and swift movement is what alerts me first to the threat. She pulls free one of her throwing stars, shaped like the sun, from her knee-high left boot and flings it back in the direction we came from.

Bright light reflects off the throwing star, shining right into the eyes of the Entrapped that comes running around the corner. He flinches away, blinded, and the throwing star thunks into his temple. The light does more damage than the point lodged in his head. There is no killing an Entrapped, but you can slow them down and distract them.

The throwing star disappears from the Entrapped's head and reappears in Lada's palm, courtesy of Phoenix. Unfortunately, it's wet with blood. Lada shakes it off with a less than delighted expression.

"You could have cleaned it," she tells Phoenix.

"My apologies," he says, "next time."

The noise grows. Screams of people at war, reliving forever its horrors.

Five more Entrapped erupt from around the corner.

"Run!" Sin shouts, as he pushes our group forward.

I don't need to be told twice. But, as we turn, it's clear that's not an option. There are more Entrapped coming from our other side. We're surrounded.

Wait. Am I daft?

"Phoenix!" I have to yell over the screams of the Entrapped closing in. "Teleport us out!"

I can't believe we've been wandering this Labyrinth at all when we had Phoenix to get us out the whole time. Talk about thinking inside the box. I genuinely couldn't think outside of the Labyrinth. Apparently, none of us could. Even Phoenix looks surprised, as if wondering also why the idea hadn't occurred to him earlier.

He doesn't waste another second, though, grabbing onto my hand and Sin's. I reach for Lada and Sin for Dex. And—

Nothing happens.

"What's going on?" I ask.

"It's not working! Obviously," Phoenix answers.

"Now is not the time for performance issues, Phoenix!" I shout at him, to which I receive a death stare.

"Everyone climb," he orders, before focusing and turning to face the Entrapped with his bare hands.

Only a minute ago he used his magic to teleport Lada's weapon back to her. What happened? What changed? Because, clearly that's not an option anymore.

It's not like he has his weapon of choice, his spear, stored in his shoes. It wouldn't exactly fit. If he thinks I'm ditching him to face the Entrapped alone, he's got that wrong, and I'm not the only one. Not one of us moves to follow his order.

We stand back to back. Sin, Phoenix, and I facing one direction and Dex and Lada facing the other. I brace myself.

"Imbeciles," I hear Phoenix mutter by my side.

"Takes one to know one," I tell him.

The Entrapped reach us, charging blindly. We're right in their path and, because the Graveyard now has the walls of the Labyrinth blocking us in, there's no place to go to get out of their way. At least, not that we had any time for without leaving someone behind to slow them down like Phoenix had in mind.

An Entrapped runs at me. He pulls a sword plunged in his stomach right out and uses it to swing at me. I duck, no weapon in hand to block the hit, and pull down Lada with me so the blade doesn't hit her either. I release her once we're down, and she places one of her throwing stars in my hand.

From my crouch on the ground, I spin around, staying low, so I end up behind the Entrapped that ran at me and slash the sharp weapon across the backs of his knees. He collapses.

Next to me, Phoenix takes down two Entrapped at the same time by knocking the head of the one closest to him back into the one behind. In one fluid motion, he swipes both their legs out from under them, bringing them to the ground. To keep them there longer, I cut across their achilles tendons as they fall.

Even with the adrenaline coursing through my veins and the threat the Entrapped pose, I grimace at the action.

Still facing the opposite direction, Lada blindly reaches her hand over her shoulder, and I place the throwing star back in her palm, not sparing a glance to spot where she aims with it next.

The Entrapped coming toward us are endless. I throw a few punches to keep them at bay, sometimes aiming lower to bring the male Entrapped to their knees.

I spare a glance at Sin. He's holding up well, pulling an Entrapped into a chokehold. He towers over her, but he uses her as a shield against the other Entrapped until she loses enough air to collapse. As she falls, the arrow that runs straight through her arm, from a war fought long ago, snaps, the arrowhead breaking off.

With my attention drawn, I don't notice the Entrapped coming at me until too late. He holds a long spear, its point already too close to me. I don't have time to duck this time.

Phoenix throws his arm out, blocking the shaft of the spear, knocking it aside as if it were nothing. The spear flies out of the Entrapped's hand, and I hit him to the side of me with an elbow to the face.

How long will it take me to remember I'm not fully human? I was literally just contemplating my existence, and it still managed to slip my mind. I, too, have the natural strength of a Celestial. Technically, I guess, a Protogenoi. If that fact is going to get me involuntarily entered into, and most likely killed in, a trial I'm just now learning about, then I might as well use what I am to save us while I can.

Another Entrapped, this one looking like she's burnt by acid, runs manically at Phoenix and manages to reach him while he's distracted by another. Without a weapon, she merely claws at his face, but her nails are long and sharp enough to act as little individual daggers.

"Enough!" I shout, and push out with my hands.

Gold energy extends out from me, manifested from my own frustration and frantic concern for my friends. The longer we fight this endless fight, the Entrapped continuing to get back up even after being defeated for a first and second time, the greater the chance one of us has of falling and not getting back up.

And, there's no doubt that this is the fault of the Protogenoi. The fact that Phoenix suddenly can't teleport us to safety and that all these Entrapped managed to comes across us. It's not a coincidence.

The energy comes down in a crackling dome around the five of us. The Entrapped reaching for us hit the dome instead. They hiss in pain, but it doesn't stop them from trying to get through. They continue to push anyway.

A couple break through, sparks flying around them as they do. I brace to face them, but they collapse immediately from the effort.

It will keep the majority at bay, at least it will for long enough.

"Now climb!"

I shout the order, and this time no one hesitates.

"This one over here," Dex says, motioning us over to one of the trees with the outer bark shaped into a large spiral that surrounds the entire trunk, creating an almost perfect ladder, if the ladder's rungs were slanted.

We move as one. I have to move the barrier with us so that it remains covering us all, which proves to be a good thing because a moving target is always more difficult to attack. The Entrapped have a harder time getting through, as they can't just continue to attack one specific area, slowly weakening it.

We reach the tree with the spiral, and Lada climbs first. Dex is on his way up after her when one of the Entrapped inside the barrier awakens, recovered from her assault on my barrier. She attacks Sin, a scythe in her hand, but he grabs onto the snath before the blade can make contact and forces the opposite end into her stomach to push her back.

I make a small opening in the barrier around us so she falls through and immediately close it back up. With only the three of us left, none of us move to follow Dex and Lada up the tree. Dex shouts down at us to make our way up.

"Go," I tell Phoenix and Sin. "I have to be last to make sure the barrier holds."

Neither budge. Somehow, I manage to roll my eyes at them even as another Entrapped breaks through and collapses right in front of me.

"I could go, but the barrier will weaken as I do, and you'll be left exposed. Your choice."

"You go," Sin tells Phoenix.

"Remember what we discussed?" Phoenix asks.

"There is no end."

Phoenix nods, shifts his eyes to me for half a second, and then begins climbing.

I've never seen Phoenix give in that easily to anything or anyone. Least of all, Sin.

"Did you guys make a blood pact or something?" I ask Sin, my voice giving away the fact that I am starting to feel the strain of keeping this shield up.

The Entrapped press on every inch of the barrier, not stopping until they pass out, and then there's another one right behind who presses on, taking their place.

He smiles slightly, a rare sight on him.

"Something."

A cold hand clamps around my ankle and yanks. My feet go out from under me.

CHAPTER TWENTY-FOUR

I land on my back, unable to control my fall with my ankle held in a death grip. The air leaves my chest in one harsh breath. I fight to breathe that air back into my chest and ease the pain.

My ankle is released, but hands claw their way up my body, scratching as they go. As the Entrapped reaches my face, Sin grabs onto the back of his neck and flings him into the barrier, which shocks him, rendering him unconscious again.

Sin reaches down, grabs my hand, and pulls me up.

"Thanks," I tell him.

I guess it wasn't a great idea to stand so close to where one of the Entrapped had collapsed. Lesson learned.

"Your turn," Sin says, gesturing to the tree. "I'll be right behind you so don't bother arguing."

"The barrier—" I begin, but a hand reaches down from the tree and yanks me right up off my feet.

I grab for purchase, my feet finding the footholds in the tree, and my other hand reaching up to hold on. Phoenix holds onto my arm like I weigh nothing from his position up on the trunk. I guess he didn't go too far after all.

"Your barrier will hold," he says, with no room for argument. "We all know you're more than capable."

"It weakens the further I am from it," I argue anyway.

"Sure it does, relatively, but you're not fooling anyone. It's still plenty strong because you're insanely strong."

"Aw, thanks," I say, overly sweet, intentionally missing his point.

Yeah, fine. So I wanted everyone to get to safety first. Big deal.

"Come on."

He lets go once I'm sturdily positioned on the tree and continues to climb up. I follow suit. The sooner I move, the sooner Sin can follow the rest of us up.

I don't think I'm a fan of this new pact or whatever between Sin and Phoenix. Phoenix is right. I'm strong, which is exactly why they shouldn't be taking any risk themselves to protect me.

We don't have to climb all the way. At about halfway up the trunk, the Labyrinth walls reach their full height. Dex, Lada, and Phoenix stand atop the six inch wide walls, looking like gymnasts effortlessly balanced on a beam. The distance from the tree to the wall is not far, but it requires a jump.

I look down.

Sin is safely clinging to the tree below me, so I let the energy of the barrier disperse and come back to me. Immediately, my arms strain less to hold my weight and my legs steady.

Shifting my weight fully to my left foot, securely in one of the bark's grooves, I push off from the tree and reach out toward the wall of the Labyrinth. I land smoothly on my feet next to Phoenix, and Sin follows close behind.

The Entrapped below run through easily now without my barrier in the way, blind to our escape to higher ground. From up here, I can see how close we are to the center of the Labyrinth. Unsurprisingly, Dex was leading us in the right direction.

"Guys?" Dex says, and I hope I imagine hearing a quiver in his voice.

I follow his gaze back down to where we came from and find the Entrapped all staring up at us. For once, they're not on the move. They stand perfectly still and don't look nearly as blind to their surroundings as before. Unless, they just have an uncanny ability suddenly to sense exactly where it is that we are. Neither option is desirable.

As if controlled by a hive mind, they start moving simultaneously. Directly for us, right up the walls, not even bothering to climb the trees, which would be easier. They punch the concrete walls, creating their own hand and footholds, the broken concrete falling down around them.

"Give us a break," Lada pleads, tilting her head back to the sky.

"It's the Protogenoi," Phoenix says. "They blocked my teleportation, and now this."

That explains the hive mind. It's no longer the Entrapped seeing out of their blind eyes, but Maze seeing for them. He controls their minds, making them perform like an army. Their target? Us.

"Time to go," Sin says.

Time to test my balancing skills. Balance beam was always my least favorite apparatus. The first Entrapped reaches the top, his hand grabbing onto the edge of the wall. His fingers get stepped on as Sin begins to run, bringing up the end of our group.

I run along the six inch wide wall, keeping my attention straight ahead, ensuring my feet find purchase before pushing myself along. One step after another. Lada runs in front of Phoenix, graceful as always. Ahead of her, Dex leads the way to the center.

I can hear the Entrapped coming after us from behind, but there's no way I can spare a glance back that way without risking my balance. Honestly, I'm not so sure I'd like to look back and stare that threat down right now. Better to focus on where it is that we can escape to.

The center, squared off by the walls of the Labyrinth is now just a few sharp corners away. Scratch that, a couple sharp corners away. The one right ahead of Dex disappears, as if it never existed, leaving a gap in the Labyrinth about five feet wide.

Dex halts abruptly so to not run off the edge, sending Lada running into him. He somehow manages to steady them both while remaining on top of the wall. The rest of us stop quickly, avoiding the domino effect.

I'm thinking I should have forgone with my helpful graffiti message and instead gone with my initial idea. The Protogenoi are truly upping their game, doing everything they can to make life difficult for us. Everything except showing their faces.

They must not be happy about the fact that we've found each other. How do they know, though? They're not omniscient. Are they? Could they know that we've discovered this reality was artificially manifested?

The fact that they're not here to deal with us themselves makes Phoenix's theory seem all the more likely. The Protogenoi aren't here to face us because they're trapped in Vest.

Dex makes the leap over the gap, crossing from one cut-off corner to the other. Lada follows, having recovered from the sudden halt in movement quickly.

I hear Sin grunt, and I turn around to find an Entrapped's barreled into him, or at least tried to. He was met with Sin's fist instead and sent flying from the top of the wall, but more Entrapped follow close behind, running along the wall after us. Apparently, our little pause was enough to give them time to catch up.

Although the wall is only wide enough to allow people to travel along the top of it in a single-file line, the Entrapped rush along, not caring if they push one of their own off as they go, either not caring or not aware enough to realize what it is they're doing.

Either way, there's a whole lot of Humpty Dumpty situations going on.

Phoenix jumps ahead of me, and I rush to follow after, but the stream of Entrapped reaches us, Sin being in their direct path with nowhere to run to until I jump to the other side, and there won't be enough time for him to jump after. They'll get to him.

"Go!" Sin shouts at me over the crazed screams of the Entrapped.

I promised myself I wouldn't do it again, not when I know there's an alternative, but it will help Sin and maybe even them.

There's no more time.

The first Entrapped in the long line of them reaches Sin. Sharp metal claws extend out from rings on her fingers. She pulls back her fisted hand.

Terror. Grief. Anger. The chaos not only seeping from the Entrapped, but overflowing from them. I'd expect nothing else from people who've experienced death and the violence of war without actually being able to die. I pull on it all, taking it away from them.

The red energy flows out of them with such force that their chests yank forward, as if I were sucking out their very souls. I can't help but feel that I am. The Entrapped in front of Sin lowers her fist, no longer having the energy to hold it up. Her trauma is all that powers her at this point. It's all that powers them all.

They fall from the walls, landing on the dirt and leaves below. It's as if they were puppets, their emotions the strings in control of them. Now gone, they crumple.

The energy I stole thrums inside me. I can feel my pulse strongly throughout my body. The ground beneath my feet feels like it's vibrating from the thrum of a bass, but the power is stemming from me, looking for release.

I don't feel the emotions as if they were my own, but that doesn't mean I don't feel them at all. My body feels their effect. My breath comes out shaky from the terror. There's a heaviness at my core, twisting my gut from the grief. And the anger has my hands shaking. But, there are no memories associated with the feelings. I'm on edge with no real motivation.

I jump from one side of the wall to the other, across the gap, and Sin follows, no longer under threat.

"You're stealing my job as the one who steps in and saves everyone," Phoenix says to me, as I land next to him.

There's an emotion of my own. I feel guilt over using the part of my power tainted by the Protogenoi who wanted to destroy everything to control what could be built from the nothing. It's a power that means having to take from others like a thief, and I gave in. But, the scariest part is that I can barely feel that emotion that belongs to me, barely sense myself amid all the energy I've absorbed.

I give into the distraction Phoenix offers, trying to ignore the feeling of pins and needles building throughout my whole body, the feeling that resulted from the supposed saving of us all.

"I thought your job was being the messenger," I say, hating I can't hide the shake in my voice.

"Officially, of course, but only because you're not supposed to shoot the messenger."

Show people not what or who you are but what and who you want them to see you as. If you're seen merely as the messenger, the blame gets placed elsewhere. So does the praise.

"It's here!" Dex shouts from up ahead.

He stands before the squared off center of the Labyrinth, having rounded the next two corners. We run to catch up to him and Lada. The third corner we round is part of the inner square.

Staying atop the wall proves to be difficult. The middle threatens to suck us in like a vacuum. I lean forward to look down, but have to quickly straighten back up to resist the pull.

"That's the way out, isn't it?" I ask Dex over the roar of the wind.

I'm surprised we couldn't hear the noise of the Labyrinth's center from further away. Although, I realize it's possible the screams of the Entrapped drowned it out.

"Ready?" Dex shouts back in answer.

Ready to jump into a tornado that leads who knows where? Dex is sure that it leads out of the Labyrinth. If Dex is sure, then we're getting out of here. So, yes. More than ready.

I let go of the red energy. While I didn't want it or enjoy having it, my knees threaten to collapse as it leaves me fully, like adrenaline abruptly fading, leaving me with an emptiness I didn't have before.

For a weak moment, I want it back, but I resist that irrational desire. The symptoms of the emotions leave me. I might feel like lying down right here, right now, but my breath, heart, and hands steady.

I send the energy out but not back to the Entrapped. They'll be more at peace without it, or at least as at peace as they'll ever get.

I look into the seemingly empty center of the Labyrinth, even the slight tilt of my head forward threatening my balance on the concrete wall.

All right, here we go.

CHAPTER TWENTY-FIVE

It sucks me down, pulling, so much so that my face burns from the cold and my eyelids feel as though they may open wide enough for my eyeballs to fall right on out. It makes me want to never feel even a slight breeze ever again.

In fact, every single thing in existence should just be still always. Earth should stop spinning. Vest, as a whole plane of existence, should chill out, as should Havcire. It should all stop for one second.

And then, rather than pulling me down, I'm being pushed back up. I can't see anything. I can't tell up from down. My feet are suddenly where my head was only a moment before. It was pitch black, but now hints of light seep into my vision. Either I'm making my way back to the surface or I'm heading towards the metaphorical light.

The onslaught of wind stops.

I land on my backside, on thankfully soft ground. It's dark again. The last dark period before the final Ascension challenge has come.

I look around. Phoenix, Dex, Lada, and Sin are scattered around me. It appears we're in the same place we started before Dex walked right into the Labyrinth through the hidden portal and we all followed in after him.

It's spit us out, depositing us right back where we started, as if it hopes we'll forget we ever entered and especially that we managed to escape.

"Please get us out of here before someone wanders right back into the Labyrinth," I tell Phoenix.

He's landed on his feet of course. I wouldn't have even thought it'd be possible to know up from down enough to land on your feet, but Phoenix managed it.

Lada is on the ground, but her one leg is crossed leisurely over the other one as she leans back comfortably.

Sin is crouched on the ground, looking ready to jump up and fight. Actually, he looks a bit posed, like a superhero, which I'm tempted to comment on. However, he most likely wouldn't get any reference I made. Disappointing. Dex would get it.

Dex lies on the ground, not even bothering to lift his head. I'd think he was dead if I didn't see the breath lifting his chest. I'll give him a second.

"Damn booby-trapped world," he mutters.

Phoenix doesn't bother reaching out to us before teleporting.

One second I'm sitting on the grassy ground outside the Labyrinth and the next I'm sitting on cold marble inside...

The Ziggurat?

"What are we doing here?" Sin asks, beating me to the punch.

He's stood up from his crouch. Even Dex has gotten up to look around at our new, yet familiar surroundings. I thought I was done showing up in this place against my will.

"Testing a theory," Phoenix answers.

"The Protogenoi—" I start, but Phoenix effectively silences me with a shush.

Not that shushing me is an effective way to get me to shut up, but it is shocking enough to make me stall. In the silence that follows, I realize just how silent the silence is. There are no guards running to force us back out and no Protogenoi in sight.

We stand in one of the fully white marble hallways, the one that leads down to Max's lab. I can see the large glass doors at the end of the hall.

"The Protogenoi are trapped in Vest, not Havcire," Dex says, voicing the confirmation of said theory.

"Which means they want the barriers around the portals down in order to get into Havcire," Lada adds.

She twirls a piece of golden hair around her finger but the curl doesn't stick, and it falls back down against her shoulder perfectly straight.

"We can't leave Vest vulnerable to them," I say.

Who knows what they've been up to in Vest all this time. The reality Dabar had created completely erased Vest from our minds.

Since Styx helped us, I hadn't fully considered what it would mean for Vest if the Protogenoi were trapped there rather than here.

"We're not going to," Phoenix says. "We're going to let them in."

"Let them in?" Lada asks, sounding skeptical despite her usual support of Phoenix. "Let the Protogenoi into Havcire?"

Phoenix nods. "And then Dawn will declare the start of the trials."

And then I will declare the start of the trials.

"Excuse me?" I say. "The trials that all the Protogenoi must compete in and only one can survive? Actually, I think I won't do that."

I just love how Phoenix speaks with such confidence, as if it is a given that everyone will agree with him. Yes, Phoenix, I will go die in some ancient trial we know next to nothing about, except for the fact that I will die doing it.

"He's right," Lada says, and I face her in shock. Her skepticism lasted a whole second. "We fought them in a war once before, and now they're back again, like none of that ever happened. The trial guarantees that they won't survive." Lada looks to me. "You can be the one that survives."

As much as I'm the enthusiastic leader of Team Dawn no matter what, there are some things that even I have to admit aren't possible, nor can I believe anyone else genuinely would believe that they are possible if I'm here questioning it myself.

"I need everyone to just be real for a second," I cut in. "Every Celestial and Incanter came together to fight against the Protogenoi in the Firstlast War, and the Protogenoi still managed to survive. And yet, you all truly believe that I singlehandedly stand a chance against four of them?"

"You stopped Chaos," Dex says, and I can see that he does in fact believe I am capable of this. That is crazy.

"That was one on one, and my power was a match for hers. And, there was a literal prophecy on my side with that fight. This is different."

"You won't be alone against them," Lada argues. "We'll all be there to help you, right?"

She looks to the rest of our group, staring each of them down. Dex's answer has been made clear enough already. He would think of doing nothing else. Sin stares back at Lada with a look that says he would lay down his life for me. And, unlike with Phoenix, I'm afraid I wholly believe him. I'll have to make sure it doesn't come to that.

"No."

The single word from Phoenix has me feeling smaller than ever before. I look at him in surprise, and he doesn't look remotely apologetic. He also doesn't meet my gaze.

"What do you mean, 'No?'" Lada asks of him, with an anger I've never seen on her before.

"The trials are between the Protogenoi only, and if anyone were to interfere, the Protogenoi receiving that aid would be automatically disqualified. In this case, disqualification is equivalent to death. So, no, you could not help."

If you knew you were going to die in this fight, would you stop fighting?

Lada's always been a good ally, even a good friend. I know about her, though, that she places more importance on doing what she thinks is right than in the well-being of those she cares for. I'm fairly certain she would sacrifice me for the greater good.

I couldn't sacrifice her, or anyone else I care about, including Phoenix, who still hasn't looked at me. Not even for the greater good. But, that's just it. I'm not being asked to put at risk any of *their* lives.

If competing in the trials means I might die, but so will the rest of the Protogenoi but one, one that might be easier to defeat alone, then... I would sacrifice myself. No matter how horrible it makes me, I wouldn't be doing it for the good of the world. The world is always in jeopardy one way or another, but I would do it for the people here.

This is what Styx meant.

I walk up, right in front of Phoenix, so he has no choice but to look at me. Not expecting me right in his face, I catch a lingering hint of fear in his eyes before he masks it in favor of his usual flicker of amusement.

"Ask me."

"I don't have any questions. Except, do you have a preference for what colors you want your cheering squad to wear for the trials?"

"That's not what she meant," I hear Sin say, but I keep my eyes on Phoenix. I'm not letting him off this time.

"Brown," I answer, deadpan. "And, minty green." Phoenix's eyes flash. I move on before he can comment. "But, I didn't actually agree to these trials that you seem to know an odd amount of detail about, more than any other Celestial here."

"Siphoner," Dex chimes in quietly with the correction.

"Are you asking *me* a question?" Phoenix taunts.

"Just ask me," I demand, my frustration building, and gold sparks come with it. I feel them electrify my fingers.

"I think we best—" Sin starts.

"Go," Dex finishes the thought.

"I'd like to see this," Lada says.

"I don't have any questions, Dawn," Phoenix says.

"The more you think you know, the less you do, Phoenix."

I see in my periphery Sin already moving away and Dex pulling Lada along with them.

"I think you should stay," I say, and something about my voice has them doing just that. "You all think I'm the one with the trust issues so let me just do a little recap, yeah?" I ask rhetorically, and yes. That is an accent I hear slipping through.

Irish, if I'm not mistaken. Odd that it's been a while since my nervous habit British accent has made an appearance. I honestly thought it was gone for good. The Irish is new, though. I must be even more riled than I thought. Here's hoping no one else noticed cause I'm trying to make some serious points here.

"Phoenix teleported us here without letting any of us know about his plan to test his theory," I continue. "But, what would have happened if that theory was wrong?"

Phoenix remains impassive. The others don't make a sound.

"We would've been brought directly to the Protogenoi without any warning," I answer my own question. "And now, I'm being volunteered to sacrifice my life in these trials as part of another plan, and I haven't even been *asked* whether or not I'm willing. And *I'm* the one with the trust issues here? I release you from the vow, which everyone encouraged me to do, by the way. But, what we get in return is the same old. You don't even trust me enough to share your plans until I'm already a part of them against my will!"

I am pissed. I am mad that not one of them, Dex, Lada, or Sin, can see that Phoenix is the one who doesn't trust me. I am mad that Phoenix doesn't trust me when I do trust him, and there's absolutely nothing I can do about that fact except commit to it now.

I trust him.

Truth is, he could lie to me all day long, and I'd still trust him. I'm not even ashamed of that fact... anymore. Trust isn't simply rooted in words. It's in actions, and Phoenix has never let me down. He's always been on the same side as me, fighting the same fight. Our values align if nothing else.

Plus, if I've learned anything from this most recent lapse in memory, it's that my gut will tell me to trust him no matter what. So, it's about time I just accept that. All the more reason I am pissed he can't just return the favor and trust me already.

The golden energy retreats back into me, and a sudden calm washes over me.

I just need a break for a moment, to rest for the night. Phoenix has good intentions. I can let this go. I've already made up my mind anyway. His plan is a good one.

"Sin! Get out of her head!" Phoenix orders, his mask of indifference fallen.

The calm shatters, and I realize what's happened.

I turn to Sin.

"I only meant to alleviate some of your distress," he explains.

"It's called anger, Sin, and—"

"She's entitled to it," Phoenix finishes for me.

"Don't go finishing my sentences," I yell, whirling back to him, except it doesn't actually come out as a yell. Despite Sin's power being pulled back, I still can't exactly find it in myself to reach the same level of anger I was at.

Phoenix smiles, holding back a laugh.

I roll my eyes at him, or myself. Or, both and turn to walk away, ready to be done with this conversation. Except, I realize, I've still not gotten my question voiced. He still needs to ask me, and I will die on this hill.

"Dawn is right."

My mouth actually falls open.

"I hold back information because I don't trust people," Phoenix goes on. "I fear what they'll do with the truth," he looks at me, "how they'll react to it."

I've already given him my worst. What could he possibly be holding back from me now that'd be bigger than what he's already revealed to me? He told me I was a Citizen when I'd lived multiple lives believing I had earned my place as a Subject. I was mad at him for what? A day?

That's actually kind of pathetic of me. Our history has made it embarrassingly obvious that nothing he tells me could earn him a ticket out of my life.

But, Phoenix's mouth stays shut after that declaration. Whatever he's still holding onto, despite the admission, it's clear he doesn't plan to share.

I stubbornly keep my mouth shut also, refusing to voice the question. That is, after I've picked my jaw up from the floor.

"It's not about trust," Sin speaks up. "It's about faith."

I groan. "Don't use the dirty F word. You've all been worshipped as gods at some point."

Sin rolls his eyes at me.

"Did you just roll your eyes at me?" I ask, incredulous. "You take a vacation from stoicism to roll your eyes at *me*?"

Dex chokes on a laugh.

"Yes," Sin says, voice completely void of irritation, "that was worthy of an eye roll. Faith isn't owned by religion. You need faith in another person in order to trust them. But, often what manifests as a lack of faith in others is truly a lack of faith in one's self."

"I want to hate you, and at the same time I find it nearly impossible," Phoenix says, sounding genuinely complexed.

"Thank you," Sin responds.

"Anyway," Phoenix goes on, "my point is, it's not Dawn with the trust issues."

"See!" I blurt. "You can all back off now. Bother Phoenix instead." Enough with all the, *Poor Phoenix, give him a chance* stuff from Dex and Lada. From the Celestial's mouth himself, he is to blame.

"Right," Phoenix agrees. "So, you *do* trust me."

"Yes, I thought that—" I realize what I've just admitted. Phoenix's damn smile is a giveaway if it wasn't obvious enough.

Just because I decided to accept it myself didn't mean I wanted to openly share the fact with Phoenix, especially when he's openly sharing the fact that he doesn't return that trust. It's utterly embarrassing.

Trust *isn't* simply rooted in words. But, words are a powerful way to express trust, and it is truly shitty that he clearly doesn't trust me enough to tell me whatever it is he's still keeping from me, which I know is something significant.

I'll settle for what I can get for now.

"You have a question for me," I insist.

Phoenix takes a step back, stands taller, as if bracing himself, taking this surprisingly, yet refreshingly serious.

"Will you initiate the trials against the Protogenoi in order to stop them once and for all?" he finally asks.

"You mean, will I most likely sacrifice my life in these trials to stop the Protogenoi?"

"I won't let you die in the trials," he responds, with an unrealistic amount of conviction because...

"You already said none of you could interfere, so I don't see how that could be true. But, yes. I do agree to the trials."

CHAPTER
TWENTY-SIX

O f course Max keeps blankets and pillows in his lab. I wonder
if he ever goes home at all. I actually don't know if Max has
a family in Havcire, any loved ones that have died and joined him
here. He must.

I set up a makeshift bed under Max's desk, the others getting
comfortable, or as comfortable as possible around the room.

We haven't talked much since I agreed to the trials. Sin tried
to address the whole invading my emotions thing with me, but
I avoided that. I get it. He was just trying to help. No one is the
best conversationalist when they're being driven by anger. Still,
sometimes you just have to let it out for the cathartisism of it all.
Plus, Phoenix needed to see it.

I shouldn't have insisted the rest of them stay, but I'll admit
some of my anger was directed at them, as well, for pressuring me
to trust Phoenix when he's been the one holding things back from
all of us. I wanted them to see that. I'm pretty sure it's blatantly
obvious now.

Phoenix is the one who doesn't trust us. He doesn't trust me, but I do trust him. Whether it's a good thing or not, everyone knows that now. He knows exactly how vulnerable I am to him; and yet, I don't care because I insanely trust him.

It's been an impossibly long day, or maybe an impossibly long multiple days, seeing as it's nearly impossible to keep track of time in this reality. Whatever the case, I'd love to just drop down onto this hard floor and fall fast asleep. But, no matter how tired I am, I know I won't be able to do that until I know what I can expect to wake up to.

"So," I start, ending the silence, which doesn't include Dex's singing, which he's been doing this whole time, "I have to start these trials, but I can't exactly compete, or whatever it is you do in these cryptic trials, against the Protogenoi if they're trapped in a separate world from me, can I?"

"We can wait out the night here, as there are none of Dabar's portals or Void's traps in the Ziggurat, and then Dawn and I will compete in the final Ascension challenge," Phoenix answers, of course, because he's the one with all the answers always, somehow.

"Why do you still need to compete?" Dex asks. "All we need are the portals open again. Why not go straight there now and take the barriers down? Well," he looks to me, "have Dawn take down the barriers."

I bend into a mock bow with a flourish of my hands. I am at everyone's service now.

To be honest, I'm willing to do whatever works.

I won't ever admit to being agreeable, nor could I claim that of myself. But, I'd gotten used to living a life that was my own and *real*. I'm more than ready to find a way to get back to it, even if getting back to it means facing the most ancient, powerful beings practically one on one, with Phoenix somehow impossibly aiding me.

I swear, my frustration with Phoenix could fuel me for multiple more freaky long days. Sleep is for those who don't have a Phoenix in their life.

My point is, I'm open to all suggestions.

Although, the tattoo on my wrist, marking me as one of the competitors of Ascension doesn't look like something that will disappear on its own if I decide to back out of the competition. I don't mind it staying on my skin permanently. It's more the impression it gives that gives me pause, the feeling that Ascension might not be something we can just walk away from even if we wanted. And, it is a *we* because Phoenix bares the same tattoo on his wrist.

"The Protogenoi might not come through if they know it's what we want, but completing the Ascension will give us what we want, while allowing the Protogenoi to believe they've succeeded," Phoenix explains.

"How so?" Lada asks.

"If you couldn't kill Dawn, what would be the only other way to take the barriers down?" Phoenix poses the question to the group.

How casually he speaks of my death.

"To get her to do it willingly," Dex answers.

"Exactly. The Protogenoi haven't done anything to prevent Dawn from competing in Ascension, which means they want her to compete. They will have placed a portal at the end of the challenge. To win the challenge, someone will have to destroy the barrier."

"How can you be so sure that the portals will be at the end of the challenge?" Sin asks, thankfully ever the skeptic.

"Because this whole reality has been designed to bring those barriers down."

Everyone takes a moment to consider Phoenix's answer, probably because it's one of those answers that technically passes as an answer but leaves you with more questions.

Sure, this reality may have been designed to get my barriers down but that doesn't necessarily mean the Ascension challenge will involve destroying the barriers. Logically, I admit it makes sense, but who's to say the Protogenoi are logical? There is plenty of evidence that they are not.

Plus, I've learned many times in my lives that whenever there seems to be one answer for something, it's never the case. There is always more than one possibility, and it's foolish to believe you can see them all. At least, I can never seem to see them all.

"Just imagine you're wrong, though. Then what?" I ask.

"Don't ask me to do the impossible," he says, to which he finally receives the middle finger he has so earned. "Fine," he continues, "Plan B can be to do what you planned to do from the start. If one of us wins, we can announce to all of Havcire the truth about this reality. It might be enough to break it and return things to normal."

"Might," I echo.

"Normal," Dex muses, as though it's the first time he's hearing the word.

Even with things back to "normal," we'd have to take down the barriers and initiate the trial after. In that scenario, the Protogenoi would know we'd wanted the barriers down, something Plan A avoids. Ergo, Phoenix is confident Plan A will work.

"Either way," Phoenix says, "we now have an advantage."

"This whole plan most likely ends in my death one way or another, but please tell me our advantage," I say.

"We want the same thing as the Protogenoi, the portal barriers down. They just don't know it."

The doors to Max's lab open. It's a quiet sound, but one that reverberates throughout the room.

A man walks in, a Ghost if his sluggish, aimless gait is any indication. He looks up, staring blindly at us, and I realize with a start that I'm looking at none other than Max.

I take a step back, a reflex, even though he's already turned away from us and is walking back out of his lab. Part of me will always expect Max to hurry me along to the tub when he lays eyes on me.

Watching him walk slow and heavily is unnerving. It's so different from his usual jumpy and fast walk. It's hard to believe even that the Ghost is the same as the man. It looks more like a doll of Max was poorly animated.

The doors clang shut behind him as he retreats out of the only place he might feel any real connection to anymore.

We were made to think that the Ghosts in this world were people Maze had ripped through subconsciously, leaving nothing of substance behind. With everything else in this world being a lie, I hope that, too, is false.

"Do you hear that?"

Sin's voice makes me jump. Phoenix raises an eyebrow, noting my reaction. Yes, I know, I have to chill. Don't I always.

"No," Dex says, "human ears."

I listen for whatever Sin is referring to, and I do hear something muffled. Lada nods. She hears it, too.

"It's coming from outside," Lada says.

We walk back out, into the hallway, around the corner, toward the front of the Ziggurat and the main entrance. The doors here are pure marble. Heavy, not the type of doors one could easily open without the strength of a Celestial. Once they're moving, though, they glide smoothly across the floor like skates on ice.

271

"Attention Havcirians," the voice is saying.

Dabar.

His voice travels across Zion, and I assume all of Havcire. His face appears in the sky like a projection, something I also assume every single being in Havcire can see, just like the moon in the sky. Except, the moon is much preferable to his too perfect to be real face, with his recognizable bright, purple eyes. That unnatural face forms a smile, which I would have thought his skin was pulled too tightly across his face to manage.

"A special treat is in store for all of you!"

The five of us share glances of concern.

"Have you ever wondered what it takes to be the winner of Ascension?" Dabar goes on. "Well, of course you have. Now is your chance! The final Ascension competitors will be interviewed for all of you to see."

"What type of twisted PR bullshit is this?" I ask no one in particular.

"The type that's a trap," Phoenix offers.

Well, duh. I'm about to respond with as much, but Dex shushes us.

"Find out how they've gotten this far so you can be them next year and have the chance to live in the luxury of the Ziggurat, right alongside us Protogenoi!"

"I'm sold," Lada says, tone as dry as the desert.

She's the one who gets shushed this time. She shoots a glare at Dex, which earns her a deeply apologetic expression but—

"If you don't all shut it, we won't hear when this trap is taking place," Dex argues.

We shut it.

"The final challengers shall assemble as soon as possible at the Protogenoi Fountain in Zion so the interviews can commence. Among the finalists are Morrigan, Eros, Phoenix, Dawn, and Lucifer. We shall—"

"Lucifer completed the first challenge?" Dex asks.

Despite all his shushing, this is the first time I've actually missed something Dabar's said, and it was his fault.

Dex looks between me and Phoenix, eyes questioning and betraying his sudden nerves. I decide not to call him out on his shushing hypocrisy.

"I didn't know," is all I can offer.

"It was too hectic at the end of that challenge to take note of the others up there on the platform with us," Phoenix says. "I thought I may have spotted some familiar faces, but we didn't really hang around, did we?"

Dex shrugs it off. "Yeah, no. Doesn't matter."

Sin's watching Dex carefully. Then again, Sin's always watching at least one of us carefully at all times. I stare at him, trying to will him away from staring at Dex, get him to back off, let him be. But, he apparently can't feel my eyes boring into him.

So what? Dex is avoiding this thing that definitely does matter. We're all allowed to avoid important things every so often. It's healthy to have little tiny compartmentalized boxes.

...And now Sin *is* looking at me, eyebrow raised in judgment.

"It matters that we don't want a Council member dying," Lada chimes in. "We can't get back our reality at the end of this to find ourselves a Council member short, causing instability in Havcire when we most need a united front."

"We'll make sure he survives," Phoenix says.

"Easy. What's one more thing to do while trying to win this thing and beat the Protogenoi? Sure, we'll ensure Lucifer doesn't perish," I say, keeping my voice light. I know I'm resorting to sarcasm. But, at this point, honestly, one more obstacle when our odds are nearly zero doesn't really matter. "I mean, he's killed me a thousand times—"

"Only twenty-five," Phoenix corrects.

"It's called a hyperbole, Phoenix. But, anyway, we'll make sure he lives."

I give everyone a thumbs up.

"Why have these interviews?" Sin asks, everyone moving on, as they should.

"It is odd," Lada says. "They've never done it before." She reconsiders, titling her head. "They've actually never done any of this before, as we all know. But, I mean, even with this false reality

Dabar has us remembering, they never did interviews before—You get what I mean."

"Yes. So, they're trying to draw me out?" I suggest. "Except, why bother? I'll either die in the final challenge or win it. With both scenarios, they get what they want, the barriers around the portals down."

Hm. Now I'm the one talking about my death oh so casually. While I may have accepted that as a possible outcome, it in no way means that it's something I won't be fighting to the very end to try and make sure that it does not turn out that way.

"Maybe they're just getting impatient? And want Dawn dead sooner?" Dex questions.

Phoenix is quiet, clearly thinking through options in his own head, not ready to share.

"If they figured out somehow that we figured out the truth about this reality, could that make them more impatient to kill me?" I ask, posing my question to Phoenix. Because, somehow he seems to have a better understanding of the Protogenoi than the rest of us, and I might as well accept that and use it.

"They don't know," Phoenix says, sure of himself. What else is new? "There is rarely a—"

I've not moved a step and yet...

Everyone's gone, and I can't see a thing. It's pitch black.

I blink rapidly, trying to get my bearings. My feet are still on solid ground. It's concrete.

I *can* see. It's just much darker in here, wherever here is, and my eyes are slow to adjust. But, faster than a pure human's. Everything comes into focus.

I spot Dex. I open my mouth. He's already making his way toward me. No. He's rushing at me.

His hands hit my shoulders hard, and I stumble over something on the floor, falling back into the wall behind me.

"Dex, what the—?"

Pain explodes across my face, warm blood running down into my mouth. My head whips to the side from the force, my body instinctively curving inward to protect myself.

He punched me!

I look up at him, only to be met by a kick to the stomach that brings me to my knees. I gasp for air.

Dex grabs me around the neck, not hard enough to choke, but enough to yank me back up to face him. He gets real close to what I'm convinced must be my now broken nose and...

"You killed my dog."

CHAPTER
TWENTY-SEVEN

I spit blood out of my mouth so I can talk. Except, he's got me pinned by my throat so there isn't much choice when it comes to where I can direct that blood and some hits Dex right in the face. I cringe. His already angry face gets angrier.

I've never seen Dex angry.

"Sorry," I rush out. "What are you talking about, Dex?"

His grip tightens around my throat, and I struggle to get air down.

"Frank, the pug. You killed him!"

That's it.

I knee Dex in the gut. He bends over with a groan, releasing my neck. I reach out. There's a scaffold next to me, a stray metal rod lying on top. I grab it and hold it out in front of me like a sword.

"I would *never* kill a dog!"

The thought of that leaves me aghast. I am actually insulted by the mere suggestion. The idea that Dex could believe I would do such a thing for even a millisecond is downright unacceptable.

It's tarp on the floor that I had tripped on. It covers a lot of the concrete. The walls are unfinished. We're in a building under construction, a Vest building. Except, we can't be in Vest. And, no one teleported me here. So, there's no way I can actually be here.

Not to mention, Dex clearly thinks he's John Wick and that I've killed his dog, Frank, the pug, who was actually my favorite dog at the shelter and has since been adopted by a nice family.

"You killed the wrong man's dog."

Dex charges at me. I dodge, using his own momentum and the metal rod to hit his back and send him falling to the floor.

As I turn around to face him again, to try and talk some sense into him, figure out what is actually going on, he's gone.

I face a familiar hallway of lockers. I'm back at East Olympic High. I've even got a backpack on my back.

Again, a place in Vest and no teleportation to get here. It can't be real, which means it's in my head.

Maze.

I look around the oddly empty hallway. The florescent lights feel even brighter in the absence of people.

Footsteps draw my attention to the end of the hall where Sin rounds the corner. I'm not surprised to find him looking at me as angrily as Dex was a moment ago, but it is surprising to see him dressed casually in jeans and a t-shirt. If I didn't already know something strange was afoot, that would have been a dead giveaway.

He closes the distance between us fast, and I brace myself for another fight. But, he stops a couple feet away and makes no move to attack. He's breathing heavily, and I have to resist the urge to lean forward and inspect him closer when an actual tear runs down his face.

What is happening? If he's not here to try to kill me like Dex was, what is Maze playing at? What's the point of this?

"You broke my heart," Sin accuses.

"I did no such thing," I can't help but blurt.

He's shaking his head at me like a real wounded teenager, and it's so far from the stoic Celestial I'm familiar with. It's like a whole other person is wearing his skin.

"Sin, this is Maze. He's in our heads. This isn't real."

He wipes away that single tear angrily. He walks forward until I'm pressed back against the lockers, his arms caging me in, and I let it happen because his navy eyes are swimming with more unshed tears.

It's not real, but I can feel his sadness brushing off on me, whether he's transferring it to me intentionally or not.

"It's real to me. Do not belittle my feelings."

I'm actually inclined to believe him, but I can't imagine what I could have done to break his heart. Plus, Dex was equally convinced I killed his nonexistent dog so none of this is exactly something I can trust right now, down to my very surroundings.

"We were just at the Ziggurat, Sin. How did we get here? Think about it," I try to reason.

He takes a moment, considering. His eyes land on some spot above my head, truly concentrating, and I think he might be coming around, breaking through whatever Maze has made him think is going on.

He comes to some sort of conclusion and looks back at me. I already know he hasn't snapped out of it by all the emotion he's still drowning in. This isn't him. Sin doesn't drown in emotion, he expertly navigates it.

"You don't love me back."

I push against his chest, but he doesn't budge. A frustrated sigh escapes my mouth.

"You don't love *me!*" I rightfully insist.

"You love him."

What sort of alternate reality does Maze have Sin playing out in his head? Are we part of some fictional love triangle here?

"This isn't real, Sin," I try one more time, urging him to see the truth.

"You love Phoenix, don't you?"

I draw back, feeling that like Dex's punch to my face.

"There is no need for accusations."

If he's going to be a frickin immovable boulder in front of me, then I'll go around. I quickly duck under one of his arms, slipping out to stand behind him.

"If I can't have you, no one can!"

I duck and swing my legs out just in time to stop Sin's lunge at me, bringing him to the floor. He lands hard on his back but jumps up less than a second later.

Sin comes at me, but I get the strong sense that he wouldn't actually hurt me. I'm safe with him. Every tense muscle in my body relaxes, unfazed by his approach. Sin is a protector. He's protected me from one reality to the next. Nothing's different here.

Sin's southpaw punch lands on my face, I swear, breaking my nose for the second time in an extremely short amount of time in the opposite direction. More blood joins the blood that'd started to dry.

I curse, cradling my poor nose.

A blade appears from nowhere in Sin's hands. He draws it back, and I *still* can't convince myself that he means me any harm even though some very internal part of me is screaming to move, defend myself. Live.

The blade comes down, aimed for my chest.

It hits a golden dome of energy surrounding me, and then...

I'm back in the Ziggurat.

I wipe the blood from my face, my breath catching up with me, my body doing its best to heal quickly. My nose cracks back into its rightful place, and I suck in air at the sharp pain, but it fades fast.

Sin almost killed me, and I nearly let him. I'm realizing I have not taken enough time to acknowledge just how deadly his power can be. That can happen when you get used to the idea of your friends not using their power against you.

I'm in the Council Room, I notice with a start. But, not only that, I'm sitting in the center throne, Barnabas's throne.

"Didn't take you long," Lada says, drawing my attention to her as she strolls through the doors at the opposite end of the room.

"Lada." I go to stand up to join her, but I can't.

I'm stuck on the throne.

Red energy flows like veins along Barnabas's solid, gold throne. My own golden energy crackles along my skin and, every so often, the sparks of gold interlock with the red, tying me down.

I try to dispel the golden energy, reel it back in, but nothing works. I'm attached to it, and it is attached to the throne, keeping me anchored down.

"Maze is trying to kill me," I tell Lada, then add, "again. He's messing with our minds, having Dex and Sin—"

I stop, as I see my words are falling on deaf ears. Lada's looking at me like I'm the enemy. This isn't over.

"You're no different. It's in your blood, their magic," Lada goes on, stalking towards me.

The thrones on either side of me disappear, Lucifer's and Minerva's seats just gone. The one I sit on alone remains.

The red seeps into the golden energy coming from me, until its all overrun by red, leaving me sitting on pure red energy. In the space between the bolts of red is charged darkness.

"You're a tyrant, no different from all the other Protogenoi."

"No," I protest.

"No? Look at yourself."

The hair fallen over my shoulders from my struggle to free myself is no longer brown, but a familiar red.

My head shakes. This isn't real. It's not real. It's Maze. And yet, this is definitely harder to dismiss as some ridiculous fiction than what Dex and Sin came at me with.

"I'm not like them," I insist, but it sounds false even to me so I add, "Not yet."

There is no reasoning with her, no more than I could have convinced Dex that I didn't lay a hand on his supposed dog.

Lada steps up onto the dais and raises her hand, two of her throwing stars, shaped like the sun, held between her fingers. She twists her wrist back, readying to throw.

I find my own power ready beneath the surface like it always is and let it out, the gold surpassing the red and knocking Lada back. I tear free from the throne and run, jumping off the dais and heading for the hidden door behind the thrones.

I burst through. I can make out the sounds of her footsteps following after me. I run through the first door on my right and shut it, locking it behind me.

I know this place well enough, having memorized the halls and rooms over the years, like a prisoner secretly planning their escape route, to know that I've ended up in the Ziggurat library. The room is shaped like a cylinder, the single, circular wall filled high with books all around me, with one ladder that swings around to reach them all.

It's not a comfy place, with not a single place to sit. It's also not bright enough to sit down to read, if that were an option. The only sources of light are the continuously burning fires contained within glass along the rims of each bookshelf to illuminate the spines of the books.

Normally, I'd like the darker lighting in here, finding it calming, giving me a feeling of being hidden away. Back when I was a Subject, I knew there was no escaping from beneath the Council's noses. So, the fact that there was nowhere to run to from this room wasn't discomforting. It was simply a nice change of scenery for the few moments I could steal away, to hide in the dark amongst the books. But, under these circumstances...

I back up slowly, hands out in front of me for defense, expecting Lada to attempt to get in after me. But, I no longer hear any sign of her, which actually isn't at all a comfort because there's still one more person Maze has yet to send after me.

CHAPTER TWENTY-EIGHT

An arm locks around my throat, forearm tightening around my trachea. I throw my elbow back, earning a grunt from the impact and enough slack to grab onto that arm with both my hands and flip my attacker over my head onto his back.

Phoenix stares up at me, brow furrowed in determination.

"You know too much," he grits out, sounding like he just passed Bad Guy 101 with flying colors.

He does an excellent job of making those words sound like an outright threat, a heads up that he's going to kill me.

"That's rich, considering how we fight about you telling me nothing."

A dagger appears in Phoenix's grip. With unnatural speed, he's up from the floor. I jump back to evade but end up with a shallow cut across my chest, my shirt ripped and a thin line of blood bleeding through it.

Clearly, Maze is running this show. But, I'm going to see this one through. Maybe I've been just waiting to have this fight. And, if I "know too much," according to these mind games, then...

"What exactly is it that I know?" Maybe I can find out what it is Phoenix is so afraid for me to know.

Phoenix lunges at me again. I release a golden whip of energy, wrapping it around the hilt of the dagger and flinging it from his hand. It clatters to the floor. At least, that's what I hear and see.

The same dagger whips at my face.

Damn illusions.

I dodge, allowing my enhanced reflexes to take over for once, as I reach out and catch the dagger straight from the air, flinging it back at Phoenix, but my wrist twitches at the last second, sending it off course, chickening out of aiming such a shot at him. As if he couldn't easily evade a deadly shot regardless.

This time, he actually lets the dagger clatter to the floor, shooting me a look that mocks the fact that I totally missed. I hold back a groan of frustration, as well as a protest to defend my aim. Instead, I rush him, aiming to punch him right in his smug face.

He blocks me in a way I expect from all the time I've spent training with him and Minerva. So, instead, I go low, sweeping his legs out from under him.

I lean over him, pinning him down, my thighs squeezing his hips.

The dagger's teleported back into his hand. He holds it to my throat. My golden energy whips out, pinning his hands down to either side of us, dagger along with them.

He glares up at me as if this is my fault.

"What you know is what motivates you to kill me," he answers me, in such an expectedly vague manner.

"Wait." I draw back from him, as it hits me what he's said. "Me kill you? I have no such motivations."

"So I must kill you first," he concludes, going on like I said nothing.

"You're trying to kill me so I don't kill you?" I ask, looking for clarification.

A gust of air explodes from seemingly nowhere. Completely disoriented, all I can do is manage to ensure that dagger stays away from me and tighten my legs around Phoenix because I'm no longer on the ground.

His wings spread out around us, and I have to fight the urge to stare in awe. It's only my second time seeing them. I'd nearly forgotten they existed, with their brilliant bronze feathers.

Why so wing shy, Phoenix? More importantly—

Holy. Shit. This library goes up way higher than I thought, and I am too close to the person who wants to currently kill me, seeing as clinging onto him is the only thing keeping me from falling over sixteen feet.

Despite everything, my golden power still restrains his hands, meaning at least the dagger is not at my throat.

"I don't want to kill you," I try convincing him.

Rationality has yet to work, but if the reason he thinks he needs to kill me is because I want to kill him for some truth I found out that I haven't actually found out, then maybe I can reason with him through his own twisted logic.

"Lies."

I push back enough to look at him, trying to convince myself I'm not a deadly distance from the ground. I find only anger there, and my own gets the best of me.

"I'm telling the truth, you untrusting piece of shit!"

Phoenix pushes me hard, and I almost lose my grip around him. I hold on tighter, wrapping my arms around his neck, as well. He may be trying to kill me, but he's also my personal lifebuoy at the moment.

I actually don't think we've ever been physically as close as this, our faces pressed close, my chin digging into his shoulder, my arms practically strangling his neck, my chest flush against his, my whole body flush against his. My legs are so wrapped around his waist that it feels like they could loop back around him a second time.

Actually, I could hang here for a bit, pretend circumstances are different.

I can feel the actual growl of frustration that escapes him rumble through my whole body, and then we're plummeting, his wings tucked tightly in behind us. A scream escapes me.

He's aiming me for the floor. I'll be dead on impact.

I grasp around and find it. I swipe the dagger from Phoenix's grip. He reaches for it back, but I hold it to my own throat.

We pull up so fast, Phoenix righting us moments before I can hit the hard floor, his wings extending out, catching the air. The dagger nicks my throat by my own hand, drawing blood, at the sudden halt in momentum.

The dagger disappears. Phoenix stares at the drop of blood on my throat, then up at me, looking extremely offended.

"What the actual fuck, Dawn? You hurt yourself."

"You were about to splat me on the floor, talking all about killing me because I'd kill you."

I reach up to touch that tiny little cut he's talking about. It's just a tiny little cut. It stings like hell, but is he for real?

Phoenix beats me to it, brushing his own hand briefly across the cut before lowering it back to his side. And, somehow, it no longer stings. It actually tingles pleasantly from his touch, while he hasn't even bothered to stop glaring at me.

"And attempting to kill yourself was your plan?"

"Yeah!" I lose it. "It was the best I could come up with while plummeting. I mean, why would someone who wanted to kill you rather resort to putting a knife to her own throat?"

"I don't know!"

"Exactly!"

Phoenix grimaces and clutches his head. He turns away from me and speeds to the wall, where he braces himself against it and bows his head, looking like he needs the wall's support to hold himself together.

"Phoenix?" I ask, my voice cautious, even though I step toward him again without any hesitation.

"He's still trying to get in," Phoenix manages, his strain evident. "I've got it, just keep—"

His hand closes around my arm, and he pulls me between him and the wall, caging me in with his body.

"Away?" I ask, quickly checking his hands for any suddenly appearing weapons, but they're currently still empty, flattened against the wall above my head.

"Yeah, sorry. Working on it."

His eyes are closed, the battle he's facing inside his head against Maze. It's clearly a strain because he's not only breathing hard from the physical fight we just had. It can't be easy mentally fighting off a Protogenoi one on one in your head. I would have thought it impossible.

I should get out of here. Or, at least pull my power to the surface, be ready.

But, I don't. The comforting crisp smell of the books, mixed with the slight smell of smoke from the fires lighting this place, as well as the scent of fresh snow surrounds me. That last one is all Phoenix, and it is shamefully intoxicating. Plus, I can't stop staring at his muscled chest rising and falling harshly just centimeters from my face. The movement is near hypnotizing.

I trust him. I trust that the things he's not ready to tell me yet won't change that fact, and it won't change how I feel about him at all. Above that, I want this. I've wanted him over and over again, every single time I met him with no memory of knowing him before.

We were thrown into a whole new reality, and I sought him out. I always find him. He's my unfinished business in every single life I've lived. And maybe, if I just give in this once, it could be enough.

"I would never hurt you," Phoenix says.

He's still struggling to gain control, and I'm not even positive he's speaking to me, his eyes shut in concentration.

I answer anyway.

"Only emotionally."

He looks at me then, his ice green eyes piercing through me, even though they betray that his attention remains divided, still putting up a fight against Maze.

"No," he insists. His shoulders lose some of their tension, his eyes focusing, and I know he's finally managed to get Maze fully out of his head. "Not if I can help it."

"Good."

It's all I need to hear.

I reach up and wind my arms around the back of his neck, drawing him down, and I claim his mouth with my own, not bothering to be slow about anything. Neither is he in his response.

His hand is cupping my face a second later, his other hand coming down to grab my waist and push me back up against the wall. I'm yearning for more so quick, butterflies made of chaos fluttering crazily in my stomach at the mere sensation of his hands pressing against me, turning my core molten.

But then he's gone, one too many steps away from me. His hands haven't moved, though, and I find myself shifting in toward him, drawn to the feel of him across the small distance. I brush against him, not even meaning to. A groan escapes him, but he forces more space between us.

"This is a bad idea."

Phoenix's expression is pleading, and I'm not sure whether he wants me to agree and be the one to walk away or insist that he's wrong. I can't do either.

I've embarrassingly thrown myself at him twice now, and I need him to be the one to make this decision.

"Why?" I ask.

"If you knew the truth—"

I cover his mouth with my hand before he can finish that statement and some of his usual self gets through this odd tortured version I've never seen before, as his eyebrow rises up high in judgment of my method of shutting him up.

"I don't want the truth right now, and I really doubt it would change how I feel, let alone make me want to kill you."

His mouth moves under my hand in an attempt at a protest, and I do my best to ignore the feel of his lips on the sensitive skin because I will not be the one making the next move. But, I also won't let him try to tell me what I do or don't want.

"No. And, you know what? Even if it somehow did make me want to kill you, I still don't want to know. I want you. I have for an insanely long time, so if there's even a small part of you that feels the same, then could you—?"

Phoenix presses a kiss to the palm of my hand I have placed against his mouth, and my brain short circuits because never has a simple action caused such a reaction in me. It's as if I can feel that one sensation in every atom of my body, rippling through me, traveling from my palm, down my arm, bursting across my chest, and spreading out to every other limb.

It can't be natural. It feels too targeted, the action specifically designed to have this effect. I'm genuinely about to ask Phoenix how he's done it, but I feel his lips draw into a smile beneath my hand, and I realize there are more important things, like getting my hand out of the way because I'm preventing him from doing the very thing I was waiting for.

I drop my hand, but I don't move. I refuse to be the one to give in.

Phoenix grips me from behind and lifts me up against him. My legs wrap tight around him, though there's no way I'm falling to the ground with the way his hands are pressing me against him. A gasp escapes me, which he captures the sound of with his mouth as it meets mine, and this time it is him closing the distance.

I can't think besides the fact that this feels right, like everything is sliding into place, like I fit here. The fabric of my shirt slips up, and his hand lands on the bare skin of my lower back. His fingers play with the hem of my shirt, going to tug it back down as if on instinct.

We danced at a Regency ball in another life. His fingers briefly landed on my bare back at the top of my dress, but he was quick to shift his hand down so the fabric separated us once again, but not before I felt the effect he had on me.

He was a stranger to me then. He's not now, and we're not in the 1800s either.

I tighten my legs around him, pushing up higher, away from his hand determined to pull my shirt back down over me. When I sink lower, his hand comes up higher beneath my shirt, and he doesn't make any move to pull it down this time.

His teeth drag over my lower lip, drawing on it, teasing me. His mouth finds my neck, and a moan escapes me at the sensation of his mouth kissing, licking, pulling...

"I feel the same." He breathes the words out, his breath hot on my neck.

Before I can look at him to confirm what feeling exactly it is that we're both feeling, he teleports us.

I lose all sense of direction for a second before I find myself on top of Phoenix, in the same room, but now on the floor. His shirt didn't make the short trip, meaning I'm straddling his naked torso.

My shirt's gone next, just disappearing off me.

"Wait," I rush out, holding tight to his belt before his pants can disappear in a similar fashion to our shirts. Phoenix actually takes his hands off me, which is not at all what I meant by my hasty plea. "I want to take them off."

Phoenix smiles, and I focus on the task at hand, ducking my head to hide a smile of my own. Slowly, I undo his belt, sliding the leather band out from the loops inch by inch, my fingers grazing over him.

Phoenix watches me, practically frozen, completely serious now. But, just as the belt comes free and I'm reaching to undo the pant's button, he loses his patience, drawing me back up into his lap as the pants disappear, along with my own.

"Phoenix!" I start to protest, but find myself exactly where I want to be, entirely distracted by him.

He's kissing me again. Everywhere his hands touch my bare skin is overwhelming. My power responds to it, coming up to the surface, as if to be nearer to him, as well. It feels electrifying, and when it meets the surface of my skin where his skin is on mine, it feels like it tries to stretch out to Phoenix, arching me further against him.

I inhale sharply against his mouth as power pours forth from him, meeting my own. As they connect, it feels like it pulls straight from my very center, tugging me even closer to him like a magnet, thrumming between us and within us.

His energy mixes with mine, and it's a pure rush. It's like the chaotic energy I absorb, but this is purer, primordial.

Phoenix reaches between us, a hand teasing the hem of my underwear, but I don't want to take this slow. I've known Phoenix for over twenty-seven lifetimes. He's known every me. The human, the Citizen, the Subject, and whatever it is that I qualify as now. I'm not waiting anymore. It took us actual centuries to get here, and we've no idea what lies ahead.

I push against his chest so his back is back on the floor, but he flips us so he's the one leaning down over me.

I wrap my legs around him, pulling him down closer. I reach up with my hands, but he's faster, pinning them to the floor above my head.

"Dawn," he warns, voice low. "I don't want to rush this, not after so long," he says, echoing the exact opposite of my thoughts.

"Typical. I don't get a say?"

Still restraining my arms, he lowers himself down my body, placing kisses lower and lower and, despite my protests, I arch into him.

He places a kiss on my hip, eyes looking up to meet mine. A red spark passes from his lips to my skin, absorbing into me.

My breath halts.

That can't be possible.

I wasn't trying to steal any energy. Phoenix, a Celestial, shouldn't even have chaotic energy for me to feed on like some parasite. It wasn't my intention. If it wasn't even my intention, and I just did it accidentally—

It feels like everything that was heating inside me cools exponentially. I pull away. Phoenix, visibly confused as to what's happened, reaches out for me, but I've already gotten up.

I open my mouth to offer some explanation, but I feel like I'm about to burst into tears. I don't want Phoenix to think that what just happened would be a reason for me to lose it and cry. It's not that. But, I'm also not going to be able to keep it together.

I have to get out of here, so I turn. And I run.

CHAPTER TWENTY-NINE

I ran to the place I first blindly placed my trust in Phoenix, where I claimed I was going along with his plan just for the promising hope that I'd be reborn for once with my memories, specifically memory of the fact that I hated *him*.

Even then, while I may have hated Phoenix for how I'd believed he'd betrayed me working with Max, I still trusted him enough to put my life in his hands. I seriously was only fooling myself about how I felt about him.

I'm in the hidden armory, appropriately mostly in the dark except for the dim lighting from the copper lanterns hanging from the ceiling.

I look down the seemingly never-ending hallway, filled with weapons of myth. I'm hugging Poseidon's trident like it's a freakin' body pillow.

The door opens, letting in too bright of light. I push the trident away from myself in a panic because that's goddamn embarrassing to be caught like this. It catches on my knees, and I lose my grip on it, sending it clattering to the floor. I cringe away from the high pitched sound.

"No need to use the trident against me. I no longer have the irrational urge to kill you."

The door shuts behind Sin, and I realize I feel both relieved and disappointed at the fact that it's him who's found me in here.

"What a relief."

He lowers himself down to sit beside me on the floor.

"Are you? Relieved?" he asks, voice careful. "Because I could actually feel your distress from the other end of the Ziggurat."

I let out a breath, and if it were anyone else, I'd be embarrassed that it sounds so shaky. I've never felt this unsure in my life. Any of them. I've always had myself to rely on, but now it feels like my own mind and body could betray me at any second.

So, yeah. I'm not surprised Sin was able to track me down. I imagine I'm projecting my emotions more loudly than ever, as if begging for someone to be able to wrangle them because I sure as hell can't.

"I'm taking a minute after all my friends tried their best to kill me," I offer up as an excuse.

Sin shifting beside me is the only indication that this takes him by surprise.

"'All?'" he asks. "Does that include Phoenix?"

Well, that had the exact opposite effect of what I intended. Here we are, focused on Phoenix.

"It includes Lada and Dex, too."

"Phoenix tried to kill you?"

"Yes, Sin. He was mind controlled by Maze just like the rest of you."

What is the issue? I thought Sin was the one who could actually take a hint, very subtle hints at that. And yet, he seems completely oblivious to the fact that I don't want to be discussing this.

"He used his powers against you?"

"Yeah, really gave it his all."

"You survived in a fight against Phoenix?"

That is it.

"I'm here, aren't I? Why is this so hard to wrap your mind around?"

"Did you *win* the fight?"

I spring up onto my knees to fully face Sin and then slap him right across the face. His hand comes up to touch his offended cheek, but his head didn't even move when I hit him. It really couldn't have hurt all that much.

"Ow," he states.

"What's your problem?" I demand.

"Answer the question," he says, in his usual measured voice.

"I—"

I don't know.

I can't count turning the dagger on myself as an actual physical win. It got the job done to get Maze out of his head. It's also not like I was going to bring myself to kill Phoenix in order to win that fight, so I wasn't exactly giving it my all.

Then again, who's to say he was giving it his all? Even before I really got through to him, knowing Phoenix, he was probably already putting up some kind of fight against Maze. He most likely was holding back.

Either way, why does it matter? And, why does it matter so much to Sin whether or not I'm capable of beating Phoenix in a fight? You only need to know you can beat your enemies in a fight.

"Do you know something I don't?" I question.

Sin sighs like I'm the exhausting one and leans back against the wall.

"Don't turn all your suspicions unto me."

"Then don't be cryptic," I argue.

But, it's hard to argue with someone who's always so calm and controlled. I can't force anything out of him. I sit back down, resting back against the wall.

"We both know it's Phoenix you want answers from."

"Yeah," I just agree.

However, there is something Sin can answer for me.

"There is no end," I say, repeating the words I heard him tell Phoenix. "What does it mean?"

Sin gives me nothing, neither a word nor a glance. He stares straight ahead, and it's not even bright enough in here for me to read his expression.

Sin doesn't lie, and he won't. If he's not speaking, it's because the alternative is lying. I've nearly accepted the fact that I'm not going to get any answer when he opens his mouth finally.

"There is no end to the Protogenoi rule without you, Dawn. That's what it means. If we were all to die, as long as you live, there is hope they could be defeated. We promised each other that we'd do whatever it takes to ensure that you remain alive, including risk our own lives."

I swear I can feel my chest cave in and splinter. I've been concerned about Phoenix's and Sin's willingness to sacrifice themselves for me, not fully understanding their motivations, but not wanting them to do such a thing. I foolishly thought it was because they somehow had come to care enough about me to not want me to die.

They're willing to sacrifice because they need me to fight this fight, alone if it comes to that. They need me to bring down the barriers. They need me to declare the trials.

That distinction shouldn't matter to me, but I can't help that it does.

I guess I was right. Phoenix does need me as much as I do him, just not in the same way. He needs me merely for what I can do, whereas I—

The reality of what I just let happen between Phoenix and me, in light of what I now know, hits me hard. I thought things couldn't get much worse. If only someone could have told me about this pact a little sooner.

I'd tell Sin to just leave me here to die, but it's more obvious than ever that he'd be strongly against that suggestion.

Sin rolls his head against the wall to look at me at his side. I raise my eyebrows in a silent question at whatever it is he's debating saying.

"Want my advice?" he asks.

My silence is enough of an answer. I tend to make my protests heard when I have them. And, while we've been sitting in silence since his admission, no doubt my betrayed, somber emotions have been filling the silence. If he wants to try his hand at some advice, he's more than welcome.

"Be honest with Phoenix about how you feel, and it will likely give him the courage to tell you what he's holding back. If he knew there was nothing he could say that would push you away—"

Sin stops talking so abruptly that for a second I think he must not have, that it's just the ringing in my ears that's shut out his voice.

The panic rises up in me so suddenly that it must have been waiting just beyond the surface, waiting for its opportunity to pounce.

I feel Sin's hand on my shoulder, his knees against my legs, as he turns to fully face me. Their weight helps ground me.

My mind had emptied as the panic physically set in, but now Sin's words come back to me, and I realize.

"How long have you known?" I manage to ask.

He doesn't answer right away, still giving me time. He had to have sensed the second he lost me. He had stopped talking because he felt the sudden shift.

"At the Halloween party," he begins, much softer than usual, "I had to make all those people indifferent to you, for Max."

"So you had to watch everything, like a creep," I add, unable to stop myself.

My brain's half on automatic right now, and I can't help what auto-brain resorts to in order to keep me functioning. It's called coping.

"Like it was my job, which it was," Sin continues. "I saw you throw yourself in front of the Oni to save Phoenix."

I nod.

Right. Makes sense.

"But," he goes on, "I really knew the moment I met you in person for the first time. How you feel about him..."

I look at Sin when he hesitates to go on.

He told me once, that with his powers, there's a challenge in knowing what to do with them. It's like that with any power, but there's a lot more gray area when it comes to a power that deals with emotion. It's personal.

The funny thing about emotions is that you can be feeling them and not understand them at the same time, whether that's because you're burying them or because they are simply complex. Sin, however, can do more than just sense emotions, he can make sense of them.

Would he love to go around, telling everyone exactly what they're feeling so they can face it and deal with it? Of course. But, one has to be ready to do such a thing.

I told him it didn't sound much different than being a therapist and joked at the time that he should maybe study up on psychology to better use his power with responsibility.

I know exactly what it is Sin is asking of me now as he hesitates to go on.

Am I ready?

I let myself feel it for the first time without it being suddenly, unexpectedly thrust on me in times like when I get overwhelmed, thinking about how I'm impossibly supposed to keep fighting, and then Phoenix shows up at my side. The doubt doesn't leave me, but I feel capable again. And then, I get scared because I shouldn't need someone like that.

Or, the fact that I think back to my past lives and no matter who was in them, who mattered to me most, it's the moments, however brief they were, that I spent with him that shine the brightest in my memory. I convinced myself for a while that was just because he showed up so often, across all those lives, but that was a lie.

It's the feeling that catches me off guard when he touches me, like I'm in the most danger I've ever been in, and yet exactly where I want to be.

I love Phoenix.

That might make me nauseous just thinking about the truth of it, but I tell Sin as much with the emotions I'm projecting so he knows I'm ready to face it, and he finally finishes his thought.

"...you carry it with you always."

Like the best, heavy ass weight, and I'm fully accepting it. I only wish I could continue to carry it.

"There's no future for us."

The confession leaves me nearly against my will. Except, I know I needed to express it to someone, or I was going to lose my mind... faster than I probably am already doomed to do that.

Sin is clearly taken aback, and that's saying a lot since emotion is especially hard to read on him.

"What are you referring to?" he asks.

"Do you know what Max found out about me after all those years of experimenting?"

Sin just shakes his head.

"I'm more stubborn than the average person. Not exactly surprising." I roll my eyes. "But, I'm so stubborn that I was practically the same person no matter what environment I was born into. I was born one way, and I would let little influence me.

That actually gave me pride, to know that I was immovable in that core way."

A laugh escapes me. Although it's at my own expense, the release of air clears my head a bit, and I take a second before admitting the hardest part.

"That was dumb of me, to think not being able to change was a good thing. I was too caught up in being proud of who I was to realize it meant I'm a slave to my own nature, and now I know that nature includes being a Protogenoi, meaning I'm doomed to turn out like every other Protogenoi that's ever existed."

I see that red spark of energy seep into my skin against my will like it's happening before me at this very moment, the image seared into my brain.

I'm already losing control.

"Dawn, you're not going to turn into them," Sin says, and he sounds like he truly believes that.

"The same magic is in me. It's not something I can easily escape. They all lost themselves to the power eventually. It figures, actually. Everything I've ever had has been taken from me at some point. It's the downside of being given so many lives. You lose them, and you learn to expect that loss."

I shrug, as if I can convince myself I'm okay with what's coming. "Look at me."

I do look at him, and he's the most determined I've ever seen him.

"You can't just give up. There is so much that makes you different from the other Protogenoi, and you don't know—"

He stops himself, looking frustrated at his own words. I want to know what he intended to say, of course I do. I want to question him further, but it's really not the point right now.

He's right about one thing.

"I would never give up. Stubborn, remember?"

Sin rolls his eyes, and I actually smile because I deserve a cookie whenever I get some big reaction like an eye roll out of Sin.

"Then why are you saying this nonsense?" he asks.

"Because, if things don't work out, I don't want anyone close enough to get hurt by me. *That*, I couldn't stand."

I've done a really good job holding back tears up until now. I was so convinced they'd fall the second I left Phoenix but when I made it here, they never came. But now, an embarrassing amount openly stream down my face, like my tear ducts just unfroze.

Sin reaches up to brush them away and leaves his hand there as I admit what I need to say to get him to understand and not push me on this anymore.

"I can't risk pulling him down with me, Sin."

CHAPTER THIRTY

N ow that I'm mental crisis free, for the moment, I take the time to appreciate how Dex went all John Wick on me under Maze's influence. Between that and his reference to Frank the Pug, the boy's got a mind way too occupied by movies.

To be fair, I was the one who named our dog friend at the shelter.

To think that Maze has all this power to get in our heads and mess around in there, but he has to work with what we already know. And, with Dex, that means a lot of good action movies.

My tears finally dried up and, with Sin's support, I made it out of the infinity broom closet doubling as the hidden armory.

I look up at Sin, who's walking with me back to Max's lab, our agreed upon home base in this place, and I can't help myself.

"So... If you can't have me, no one can?"

He doesn't even spare me a glance. But, if he did, he'd see I'm biting my lip to hold back a laugh.

Speaking of movies, has Sin been watching too many erotic thrillers or something?

"I assumed it went without saying that whatever was said under Maze's mind control was not to be taken seriously."

"I don't know. You hurled some actual truths at me while under his control."

"I can assure you Maze took a lot of liberties in his crafting of my motivation."

"Does that mean you're not gonna present me with a better option?" I ask, not letting him off.

Because, one, it's funny, if only Sin would also catch onto the fact that it is funny. And, two, it would be nice to pretend for a second that honest, loyal, good friend Sin could be more than that. What if we really had feelings for each other? Oh, how simple life would be...

Except, of course, for all the other factors that are complicating our lives. But, that one part of it, yes. Simple.

"As if you would take me up on that."

"As if?" I repeat, really upping the level of melodrama in my voice, as if it truly is ridiculous for him to have such doubts about a fantasy where the two of us live happily ever after together.

Come on, Sin.

"Would you, Sin, *please* be my knight in shining armor and sweep me away from all of this?"

"I would happily sweep you far away to safety if we both didn't have very important roles to play here."

...And he still sounds like the no-nonsense duty-bound bodyguard.

"You're no fun," I relent.

He finally actually looks at me and takes notice of the pout on my face.

"I see."

Before I can question what Sin "sees," he's grabbing me by the waist, halting our progress down the hallway and staring deeply into my eyes.

"Dawn," he begins, his tone finally matching my melodrama, and I school my face into an equally overly serious expression. "My heart aches whenever I am near you, knowing that yours has belonged to someone else since long before I ever laid eyes on you. My entire self aches when we are apart, as I yearn to be by your side every moment, despite the torture of my unrequited love. But, I know that pain is preferable to a reality where my path never crossed with yours."

Sin actually smiles and then plants a sweet, fast kiss on my forehead.

"Now, I promptly swoon into your arms."

Sin backs up and holds said arms up. "Proceed."

I laugh, and Sin joins in when I start applauding his performance.

"You know," I say, "while that was all poppycock, I am now determined to find you someone you can genuinely share that hidden passion with."

"Better idea, why don't we prepare for your interview?"

I totally forgot about the interviews, what with all my friends trying to kill me and all. And, the other stuff.

"We don't even know if I'll get to the interview before the inevitable trap springs."

"What if you do?"

"I still don't understand why they're bothering. Clearly, they're impatient to kill me, what with Maze's latest attempts. But, the interviews?"

Sin considers.

"It is possible they're just playing with you."

"Like food?"

"Last I checked, Protogenoi are a lot of things but not cannibals," Phoenix chimes in.

I stop walking so abruptly that Sin continues on without realizing I've stopped. Even Phoenix, who'd been approaching to join us, walks right past my frozen form before realizing I've not gone anywhere.

"I'll go keep a lookout, let you know when the other competitors start arriving at the fountain," Sin informs us, before taking long strides to get away from us.

And I *just* thought of him as a loyal friend. What the hell does he think he's doing, ditching me now?

Awkward doesn't even come close to describing how I feel right now, and awkward is one thing I've never felt before around Phoenix.

I could just claim temporary insanity. Your friends all try to kill you, and the first one that stops in his attempt, your great appreciation for him not killing you turns into lust. That's reasonable. Plus, Phoenix has a legitimate excuse. He was confused after having Maze rummage through his head.

We can definitely move on from this. No problem. Because, the alternative is me outright admitting how I feel, and I wish that the worst thing that could happen in that scenario would be Phoenix saying he didn't feel the same.

I know there was some basic admission of want from both of us, but there's a big difference between that and what I admitted to Sin. I *want* a comfy bed to sleep in for a week. In fact, the mere thought of that is pure bliss. But, that doesn't mean I'd have any feelings of love for that bed.

If that bed tried to kill me, even if it was under mind control, I wouldn't hesitate to tear that bed to shreds. I definitely would not be thinking about sleeping in it as it was threatening to drop me to my death.

This metaphor has definitely gotten away from me.

All I know for sure that Phoenix truly cares about is keeping me alive so that I can stop the Protogenoi, no different than Sin.

Phoenix hasn't made any move to step closer to me, even though he still stands feet away, glued to the spot where he realized I'd fallen behind.

He's got clothes on again. That's about all I can observe about him, seeing as I'm avoiding really looking at him.

"I wanted to—" he finally says.

"Sin and I were talking about what I'm going to say at the interviews," I interrupt.

Avoidance is the name of the game. If I can avoid the subject, I don't have to face the possible negative outcomes. Either he doesn't feel the same way, and that would hurt more than anything. But, it would end there.

Or, he does feel the same, and it still would have to end there because I'm not something he can love. If I don't die at some point in this plan, and that's a big if, then there's a good chance I'll become a danger myself. If so, he'll need to do what's necessary, or at least not get in the way.

"I don't really care what you and Sin were talking about," Phoenix responds, but then reconsiders, his lips lifting up in that arrogant smile I'm very familiar with, "unless it was me."

It's enough for the awkwardness to wash away. My head shaking, I join him at his side.

"That discussion was earlier," I respond, honest, but keep my voice light, as if I'm only kidding.

He looks like he wants to question if I mean it but then gets that mischievous glint in his eye, which has me squirming as if under scrutiny. That look is never good.

He leans back against the marble wall, arms crossed over his chest in that casual, comfortable pose of his, which is even more concerning.

"Actually, let's talk about the interviews."

"Actually, I was telling Sin it's not important, that another attempt on my life will probably happen before we can even get to that part so..."

I lift my arms in an "oh well, what can you do?" sort of way and turn on my heel to keep moving but—

Phoenix steps into my path, and I have to stop suddenly to avoid walking into him.

"All of Havcire will be listening. It'd be your opportunity to announce that this reality was manifested by Dabar. That is what you had initially planned to do when you got the opportunity, wasn't it?"

It pisses me off that I don't know where he's going with this, why he suddenly has such an interest in this topic.

"You know that was my plan before we got our memories back. Since then, we agreed that would be part of Plan B, not Plan A. If I were to make such an announcement now, I'd be giving away to the Protogenoi that we know. It's funny, because I could have sworn you were there when we discussed all of this, weren't you?"

Phoenix slides a finger through the belt loop in my jeans and tugs me closer, running his eyes down my body, assessing with a sudden heat in his gaze, and my breath catches.

"Where'd you get these clothes?" he whispers, as if the answer's a secret for only him to know.

I look down at the clothes in question on myself, if only to hide the obvious reaction I'm having to him. I'm wearing white jeans and a plain white t-shirt, both of which are too big on me, the jeans too long and the t-shirt way oversized in every way. Not to mention, my black bra isn't exactly the right undergarment for this shirt.

Phoenix's finger is still looped through the pants. His thumb brushes the sensitive skin of my stomach just above. It takes all my concentration to pretend it's not affecting me whatsoever. Once I think my expression is passive enough, I look back up at him, and manage to answer the simple question.

"I found them in Minerva's room here."

Phoenix makes some grunt of acknowledgement in response to my answer, before releasing the borrowed jeans, and taking a single step back. And then, the white jeans are gone, replaced by some blue jeans that actually fit. The oversized shirt, however, remains in place.

"Thanks," I mutter, even though he has got to stop making a habit of dressing and undressing me.

"We did all agree to Plan A."

Right, that's what we'd been talking about. I act like my head never strayed from that topic, as well.

"Exactly, and everyone knows you only resort to Plan B if Plan A fails. So, no. I wasn't going to make that announcement."

"But, when we agreed to Plan A, we didn't know this was going to happen."

On "this," I get the feeling he's not talking about the interviews and mentally slap myself in the face for not having picked up on it sooner.

"It doesn't change anything," I insist. "Plan A was good, and we're sticking to it."

"What if something does happen that's too big to ignore?"

"What, we're planning for hypothetical situations now?" I ask, playing dumb.

"Hypotheticals is how you prepare for the unexpected," Phoenix challenges.

I wonder just how unexpected it was for him what happened between us. I mean, how unexpected the announcement of these interviews was, of course, because that's what this is about.

Referring to something such as this as unexpected implies that there was nothing there in the first place, no feelings present on his side, to indicate that this would happen eventually. But, we're talking about the interviews and hypotheticals and whatever so that implication shouldn't hurt.

"We're not ignoring anything. We're moving on," I state, hoping that's the end of that. "With the plan," I add, just to be clear here.

"Adaptation of plans is important," he argues, fraying my last nerve.

I could just walk away.

"So you're saying that you want me to give away our advantage to the Protogenoi?"

"No," he answers quickly. "Of course not."

I roll my eyes and this time do step around him to leave.

"Plan A it is," I tell him, definitively.

"And you're good with that? You're happy with Plan A?"

He asks so sincerely for once that I do have to stop and look back at him. He searches my face for the answer, not willing to wait for whatever I say. Or, maybe trusting whatever he finds on my face more than the words out of my mouth.

No, I'm not fucking happy with this.

"Yeah," I respond, "super happy with Plan A."

"Dawn."

He lets me read the emotion right off his face. There's no indication of how he wishes I'd feel after everything, but his expression is open. It's up to me. If I really don't want to go there, he'll stop pushing it now. It's the perfect opportunity. He'll let it drop, and I never even have to know how he feels or could have felt about this, about me. It can end right here.

I absolutely hate not knowing, but there's no better option. There's nothing else I can do but take this opportunity. I have to put the distance between us before it's too late.

"I'm fine," I answer, convincing myself to let go. "Although, there is something we could do that'd make things better."

I am not sitting around and stewing in my own miserable situation while I wait for these interviews to start, and there's nothing better than finding a problem you know you can solve.

"What?" he asks, eager.

"Go talk to Lada. Help me resolve things between her and Dex."

"You think it'll be that easy?" he asks, even though I can see he's already ready to go. "A little chat with me, and the problem will be fixed between them?"

I shrug, nonchalant.

"Well, I'm going to chat with Dex, as well."

"Oh, then I take it back. This is infallible."

I smile, this side mission already lifting my spirits. Dex and Lada, here we come. I may even be skipping a little as I turn to search for Dex. I can so easily distract myself, and I'm totally self-aware and fine about that.

"That's not Minerva's shirt, by the way. She keeps some of my clothes here for me."

My skip dies.

I spin back around on Phoenix, catching his smug smile, just before he teleports out of there.

I look down at myself. Of course Minerva wouldn't have a plain t-shirt as part of her wardrobe. I picked out Phoenix's shirt when I was searching for clothes to wear in the seconds after running away from him.

And, he intentionally left it on me.

CHAPTER THIRTY-ONE

The sound of water drops plopping down into a body of water echoes throughout these dark, stone tunnels. Blue luminescent light shines from ahead, where I know this path leads to pools of warm water.

A splash of water drops down onto my face from a stalactite, every surface coated in a sheen from humidity. If it weren't for the stairs carved into the floor, I'd find myself slipping the entire descent down from the Ziggurat to its underground tunnels very few know about.

I first found myself here between lives as a Subject, during one of my attempts to make a run for it. It wasn't very uncommon for me to try daring an escape at the beginning. This was when I was still under the illusion that I had a chance of making it away from the most powerful Celestials in Havcire. Funny now to think about, seeing as I had a better chance than we all thought at the time, having dormant magic running through my veins that rivaled that of the Celestials.

There had been one such Celestial missing from my Council meeting that day, and I ran right into him when I stumbled across this location.

I'd reached the dead end, where I spotted the beautiful, luminescent pools. I remember thinking it was the most depressing sight because something about water is freeing. And yet, I knew there was nowhere to go for me but back up and to Max's lab. The water felt like a tease, flowing freely, that light blue color speaking of deep breaths and fresh air.

Lucifer was floating there on his back. His eyes shifted to me lazily, until he registered who it was standing before him, and he straightened up, face intrigued.

I'd been afraid of Lucifer, with his cruel smile and tendency to stab himself on his own throne. It all said to me that this was someone who liked to cause pain, so much so, he'd even draw his own blood to sate that desire. And now, I found myself in a dark place alone with him.

All my determination to escape evaporated, and I collapsed to the ground in front of the shining, blue water. He could drag my body back. But, until he did, I was going to sit right there and stare into the water. Maybe, let my brain just empty of all thought.

But, no. Per usual, my go-to reaction to all things those days came roaring to the surface. Anger. It was better than fear and definitely better than sadness. Anger kept me going, and it was helpful when faced with who I thought was the most frightening Celestial.

Before he could bring me back, I started bombarding him with questions without giving him the chance to answer a single one.

How am I ever going to earn enough points to become a Citizen? Who even is the judge of what makes a "good person?" Are you the judge? Can you tell me who is, so then maybe I can adjust myself based on their totally subjective opinion?

Lucifer came up to rest his forearms on the ground in front of me, still in the water, his legs lightly kicking behind him, like a kid getting swimming lessons for the first time, told to hold onto the edge of the pool and kick. That's what he looked like.

He interrupted my deluge of questions by nonchalantly suggesting, like the suggestion didn't completely rebel against my whole purpose in all my lives: "Maybe you shouldn't bother so much with becoming a Citizen."

"When you've lived as long as I have, thinking of all the days ahead can be so tiresome," he went on. "Want my advice, Dawn?"

I thought that maybe it was the water, the reflection of it moving in his eyes, that made his expression look softer, like he maybe actually cared about just a Subject. This was the Celestial who never bothered to remember the name of my Experimenter.

But, he knew my name.

"Take it one day at a time?" I guessed, half joking and surprised to find myself even close to joking considering the company.

He smiled and not one of those cruel ones. It was soft and real, and I began to question whether the water in here had some sort of drug laced into it or something.

"Too complicated," he answered, like a teacher disappointed in their student. "Just live."

"Just live?"

"Yes."

Just live.

It was so simple and unmeasurably comforting.

Of course, I forgot the advice like I forgot everything else the second I was born again, but there were moments of peace it gave me that I never would have had otherwise.

Lucifer let me stay and sit there for much longer than he needed to, and his cruel smile didn't look so cruel to me after that. I came to realize that, out of all the Council members, he actually sympathized with me most. He understood.

Lucifer can sense every single death that takes place, and I've long since wondered if he doesn't just know it happens but actually feels it and everything that comes with it. Whether it's sadness, anger, acceptance, or even happiness for a life well-lived, I imagine the emotions felt upon death are among the strongest, and Lucifer is the one to guide every soul from Vest to Havcire in the seconds after.

I think it's the ones who can most easily empathize with others that have to do their best to build walls to ensure those emotions don't overtake them. Lucifer's mask of cruelty is that wall, allowing him to at least outwardly not care.

When he could allow me to stay hidden no longer, he leveled me with a serious expression, indicated the pools around us, and asked, "Would you like your next death to be a drowning?"

I shake my head at the memory, an actual smile on my face, before focusing on the important task at hand. I follow the light out into where the area opens up, and the familiar luminescent pools are scattered around.

Dex sits on the ground, his back to me. His legs are submerged in the water up to the knee.

I try to think of some way to make my presence known without startling him but can't for the life of me come up with anything so...

"Boo," I say, in the most unenthusiastic, completely monotone, and unthreatening way.

Still, Dex jumps.

When he turns to me, his face breaks out into a huge smile, the same smile he gives me and any one of us every single time he sees us, like no matter what's going on or how bad things are, our presence alone is worth smiling over. It's sweet, and it's only one of the reasons he deserves everything, including me succeeding at my current task.

"Hey!" he exclaims, sounding slightly offended. "How'd you find me?"

"Were you trying to hide?"

I sit down next to him, keeping my own legs out of the water. Jeans aren't exactly the proper attire for dipping your feet in the pool.

"Not hide, per se. Although, I'm not exactly proud of how I tried to kill you, but that's unrelated to my current location."

"This is his favorite spot, too," I offer up as an explanation, but I only get a confused expression in response.

He's about to question me on it. But, not why I'm here.

"You love Lada, right?" I blurt, because, well...

"I love Lada."

He looks right at me, serious as can be. There's no shrug to belittle the admission. His eyes don't waver a second. He says it unashamedly and sure. And, although I knew it to be true by just seeing how they interact with one another, I'm in awe of how he just said it. I admire him because he made it seem so easy, without detracting from the importance of the statement one bit.

I wish I could do the same.

"Then tell her."

He shakes his head, looking down at the water, the blue light reflecting off his face. He looks lost in his own head, as he thinks through this topic definitely not for the first time.

"It's actually ridiculous if you think about it. She's a god—"

"Celestial," I correct.

He looks up at me with a knowing, sad smile.

"People, our people, who we both grew up around, would worship her as a god. She's a god." End of debate there. "And, not just any. She's the god of *love*. It's crazy to think I'd be good enough for her."

"Ah," I say, like I've figured it all out. "You're suffering from Human Brain."

Dex playfully rolls his eyes at me.

"We're both partially human, arguably you more than me."

"Right! So why are you the one with the issue? If anyone here is going to be plagued by Human Brain it should be me," I argue.

"Maybe you also are, seeing as you made it up."

"Do not call into question what is a real medical infliction. Let me explain—"

"Can't wait."

I clear my throat.

"Human Brain befalls those who grow up human, among humans, and find out later in life that this other world exists. But, they still cling to their smaller world views, despite now knowing for a fact that said world is much bigger. This includes, for example, holding onto the belief that 'gods,'" I air-quote it and all, "are more than simply just an alien group of other people, with different biology and abilities than humans—"

"—whom our most awe-inspiring myths and legends are based on," Dex interrupts.

"You are just as awe-inspiring, Dex," I insist, meaning every word.

"You're blasphemous," he responds, only half kidding.

"Thank you," I tell him. "Look, if anything, *you're* too good for Lada."

Dex opens his mouth to protest.

"I agree."

It's Lada's voice that stops him.

CHAPTER THIRTY-TWO

L ada stands at the entrance to the cave, Phoenix by her side, looking amused.

I shoot off a quick apology to Lada, seeing as I did just indirectly insult her, but then turn my attention elsewhere.

"What the hell, Phoenix? You were supposed to talk to her separately, not invade on my half of the plan," I tell him, indignant.

"This was a plan?" Dex asks.

"I figured this would be more efficient," Phoenix answers me. A smile teases his lips. "I enjoyed hearing about Human Brain. It sounds like a horrible condition."

"Oh my god. How long were you listening?"

Phoenix shakes his head in mock concern, his eyebrows bunching, pulling on that scar of his. He rushes forward, grabs my arm, and drags me up to my feet.

"We have to get you attention immediately. Using such a human expression as, 'Oh my god.' The infection must be spreading."

"You two are horrible at this," Lada butts in. "Are you going to let me and Dex actually talk?"

I hit Phoenix's arm, with a muttered, "You idiot," before pulling him out of the way so Lada can take my place and sit down beside Dex.

Phoenix laughs under his breath, but lets me pull him back to the entrance of the cave. Lada shoots us a look, which tells us to scram. But, neither of us move, both staying to listen in. She rolls her eyes but turns her back on us, leaving us be.

"Did you hear the part where I admitted I love you?" Dex asks.

A short laugh escapes Lada, one that speaks of just how unbelievable she believes that statement to be.

"No, I can't say I did hear that."

"Well, shit. That's embarrassing."

Dex nervously runs a hand through his hair, leaving it sticking up in places.

"Dex, you don't, though."

"Of course I do," he says, sounding so deeply insulted she would question it.

"You might feel that way—"

"That I love you?" he asks, intentionally clarifying, really sticking to it now that it's out there, and I can't help but smile at it.

"Yes, you might feel like that about the fraction of me that you've gotten to know, but it's not the real me. If you knew the truth, you wouldn't feel this way."

If you knew the truth.

My attention snaps to Phoenix, and his gaze falls on me at the same moment, those words sounding all too familiar to the both of us. For a moment, it feels like we're on the same exact wavelength. But, if that were true, then I'd have some way to explain the evident sorrow in his expression.

He winks at me, shooting me a conspiratorial smile, before turning his attention back to the conversation that we definitely should not still be unashamedly listening in on, and maybe we weren't thinking the same thing at all. Maybe he was just feeling super sympathetic to Lada, before convincing himself that this plan of his, *ours*, is going swimmingly and all will be well.

"Who do you think you are? Tell me, and we'll see who's right," Dex challenges.

"Fine," Lada bristles, rising to the challenge of proving she's not worth Dex's love. "I'm the Celestial who believed wholeheartedly that magic corrupted but made the cowardly decision to remain in Havcire after the Firstlast War because I was too afraid to find out who I'd be without my powers."

Dex opens his mouth, but Lada's not done.

"Then, I spent years isolating myself from every other Celestial, as if rejecting them made me better. Really, I was just rejecting myself, and it kept me from doing anything for anyone at all for way too long. So, Dex, that's who I am, no matter how much I try to make up for it now."

Dex grabs Lada's hand in his own, making sure she's looking at him. And yeah, we should leave now. I indicate as much to Phoenix, and he reluctantly agrees with a shrug of his shoulder.

"You're letting your past define you," Dex says.

Phoenix stops.

I go so far as to reach out and pull on his arm to urge him forward, but he's listening to Dex and doesn't budge a damn inch.

"You need to get your head out of your ass and not insult me by claiming I don't know who you are when I'm a very good judge of character," he continues, in his classic, casually profound manner.

This time Lada goes to protest but—

"Hush please. I'm not done."

I can't say I regret Phoenix holding us up. This is some good stuff, and I've not been able to watch TV for what feels like a lifetime.

"You knew there was something wrong with the Subject System, not once, but twice. Without you, Dawn never would have started looking into how unfair it was. *You* were the one to bring it to her attention."

I'd support his claim, seeing as I'm in total agreement. But, not my place.

I turn my attention away from them because it does feel wrong to be watching this closely. That's not to say I stop listening. I just keep my eyes on Phoenix's shoes.

"You fought Chaos with the rest of us, risking your life," Dex goes on. "Without you being the genius that you are, we would still be running around like idiots without our memories in this reality. There's much more, but it doesn't matter because it's not about what you've done. I see every wonderful thing about you. And, you do recognize that you've never once used your powers on me, and I can assure you that I love you. So, do not think that you need your magic to be worthy of such a thing, Lada. You would've made an amazing human, but I'm very grateful you didn't make that decision, as you wouldn't be here with me now."

My eyes are burning. How dare Dex make me want to cry right now. I'm dangerously close to running forward and pulling them both into a big hug.

Phoenix grabs my arm and is the one to pull me away this time, leading us away from the pools and back through the dark tunnels. Right, because that was definitely way past the time to leave.

From one step to the next, I'm suddenly back at the top of the tunnels, the door leading out of them in front of me. Phoenix releases my arm.

"You didn't feel like walking up stairs?"

I can barely see him up here, the only source of light being that which comes from the cracks in the door's perimeter, stemming from the Ziggurat on the other side.

"I didn't want to stick around for what happened next."

"What exactly did you think was gonna happen?"

"That was very romantic of Dex. What do *you* think was about to happen?"

"A PG declaration of love from Lada and evidence our plan was a success."

"Lada is like a sister to me. I'm not risking it."

"*The other competitors have arrived at the Protogenoi Fountain. Time to go,*" Sin says in our heads. "*And, please, get ahold of all your emotions. You are making it increasingly difficult to concentrate.*"

"You don't think he means—?" Phoenix begins.

"*Sorry,*" Dex's unabashed response comes.

I laugh at the pure discomfort on Phoenix's face.

But, my laugh dies real quick when I think about how this means Sin can sense such *emotions* from a distance and about what I was doing with Phoenix not that long ago, and then I'm blushing and back to feeling super awkward considering my current company. It's a good thing it's dark in here.

I go to step around Phoenix, to get out of here and join Sin, as we should be doing. He moves right out of my way, letting me go first.

"Do you think there's any past that is too bad to come back from?" he asks, the question rushing out of him.

I drop my hand, forgetting the door, and turn back to face him. The little bit of light that is getting through, hits his face, showing me that he's serious.

I spent so long trying to make up for a life I thought had earned me my place as a Subject, and my biggest fear was that what I'd done in that life couldn't be redeemed. But, it was more the not knowing that scared me. I knew how much I'd done since that first life and my brain came up with all kinds of horrible crimes I could have committed to justify still being stuck in the system.

There was a part of me that believed it was possible I had done something bad enough that I still deserved to be in the system after all that time and that maybe I'd always deserve it. That wasn't reasonable, though. I am my own worst critic, as are most, and I was blinded by that.

"I might have once said yes," I answer, "but I think it depends on how much time you have to make up for it."

Phoenix nods, and I feel his breath on my cheek as he lets out one of relief. He shifts his weight, and I think he's going to take a step closer to me but he doesn't, just settling back where he started.

"So, if you have all the time in the world?" he asks.

"Then no past is too bad to come back from." And I realize I really do believe that. I open the door, letting in the light, before adding over my shoulder, "Assuming the Protogenoi don't destroy the world tomorrow."

CHAPTER THIRTY-THREE

W e join Sin outside the Ziggurat. Dex and Lada are not yet up here.

"They're taking their time," Sin says, looking not too happy about it.

"The bright side of walking into a trap is they have to wait for you to show up," I point out.

"Speaking of..." Phoenix begins, "I figure Dabar will be broadcasting our interviews, so I've got two outfit options for you."

"Since when do you ask my opinion about what you're going to wear?"

"I'm not talking about me," he says, as if that were obvious.

"So you're suddenly my personal stylist now?"

"It's not anything new. I got you your Havcire Assembly dress, as well."

"Right. I liked that dress. Too bad it got torn apart fighting Chaos."

Phoenix shrugs. "I can get you another. Anyway, I am the guy for supplies around here so you've really got no other option as far as wardrobe goes."

"Okay, points made."

Phoenix smiles, like the idea of playing dress up with me just made his day. The image of him and Lada playing together, her having a blast doing up his hair and him having an equally fun time picking out an outfit for her invades my mind, and I kind of wish I could see it happen in real life, and now I highly doubt the two of them haven't gotten up to something similar before.

"Would you prefer the 'this is a trap, and I'm coming dressed for battle' outfit or the 'I'm ready for my close up but also still ready for battle' outfit?"

I can't help laughing.

"Wow. What a range."

"Well, which one?"

"Ready for my close up," I answer, with little to no thought, but it seems like it has the extra layer of sticking it to the Protogenoi.

In the next second, my clothes are gone and replaced with a new, clean dress.

I look down at myself and take it in because, well...

The whole thing is a vibrant gold. It's the color of my power, or at least the part of my power that Phoenix knows I actually like. The top hugs my skin, the external material velvet. But, it's much thicker than it appears, and I doubt any blade could puncture it. It's armor disguised as a corset.

At my waist, the skirt begins. Normally I'm not a fan of frills, but the layers of this dress flow down like silk. And, the material looks to be made up of gold pieces sharpened to points, as in touch me and you're going to get cut.

Somehow, despite the skirt looking like it's made of metal, when I shift around so it moves around my legs, it only makes a faint chiming sound. It's heavy, but I think I'll manage.

I catch Sin staring.

"I think *I* want that dress," he says.

"It'd be my honor—"

"No," Sin interrupts before Phoenix can finish that thought.

"They are daggers," Phoenix tells me. "Each of them separate and can be used as a weapon if need be."

"You're officially hired as my stylist," I tell him, a huge smile breaking out on my face. "And, it's so convenient! You can just undress and dress me in a second like poof."

I hear the words, and I curse myself. We'd been doing so well, keeping it casual, ignoring the elephant in the room, and I had to word it like that? Phoenix has already got that wicked smile of his taking up residence on his face.

I am supposed to be creating distance and definitely avoiding being the cause of that expression on Phoenix's face, which in turn causes me to react physically in a way I one hundred percent should be avoiding.

"I may have delayed the redressing bit for a second."

Sin shakes his head and removes himself from the situation, choosing to go befriend one of the columns instead.

I test out my dress and yank one of those daggers from the skirt, flipping the blade in my hand so I'm holding the hilt, the point targeted at Phoenix. It sparkles nice and pretty in the moonlight held up against his throat.

"Oh, look. I did need a weapon."

Phoenix holds his hands up in surrender, still smiling.

"You'd really kill me over taking a quick look of admiration?"

"I might nick you for it."

I don't like how he looks so comfortable with me holding a dagger to his neck, as if he knows I'd be more likely to lean in and kiss him than actually hurt him. I especially don't like that a part of me wants more than anything to do the former right now. But, I can squash that part of me because it can't happen between us, no matter how I feel about him or how he feels about me, which I don't want to know because I'm a coward and knowing for sure either way would just make things harder.

So, I roll my eyes and back up, pretending like none of it meant anything to me either. I was also just messing around, something he really excels at, and I can play at, too. I guess.

"I was just kidding," he supplies. "I would never peek. I'm a gentleman."

He takes the dagger from my hand, his fingers brushing my own, sending a rush through me from the point of contact. He kneels down in front of me and finds the spot on the skirt where the dagger had come from.

"They latch pretty easily back in place," he explains, lifting up the blades above the empty space to reveal a magnet. He touches the hilt to it, and it fastens on with a jerk. "Like that."

"Got it, thanks."

He nods, standing back up with a small smile that tugs at my heart.

"Being the stars of this trap is no excuse to take our damn time getting to it," Sin grumbles, drawing our attention over to him.

I do a better job holding in my laugh than Phoenix, though, who gets rewarded with a glare from Sin.

I leave Phoenix's side in favor of the grumpy Sin, seeing as there is something I've been meaning to do. Phoenix is suddenly occupied testing out different outfit options for himself anyway.

Sin stands by that white marble column like he's aspiring to be it, so still and staring out at Zion before him.

"I didn't get the chance to thank you for sticking by me even when you didn't remember who I was," I tell him.

"That's not something you owe me any gratitude for. I was just doing what I thought was right."

"Is that a humble brag?"

"Quite the opposite," he replies, tone completely serious. "I wasn't fighting to save your life, and I wasn't fighting the Protogenoi. I was hiding behind a false sense of justice, simply making sure no one took your life without any trial first to prove your guilt."

"And where's the false justice in that?"

I try to get a look at Sin's expression, but he's still staring ahead. I'd have to insert myself between him and the unseen horizon in order to really look at him, but I get the feeling it's best not to. I'm better off letting him avoid my gaze and just voice what it is that's clearly plaguing him.

"It's playing defense, always responding to injustice rather than fighting to prevent it. It's cowardice hidden behind the gild of justice."

"That's not what you're doing now, though," I offer. "You can't blame yourself for the person you were when we first got put here. You didn't know yourself any better than you knew me."

Sin looks at me, head shaking a dissent, his eyes shining with regret.

"That wasn't some foreign version of myself, Dawn. It's who I was before I lost my brother."

I forget about being a sounding board, letting Sin talk through what he needs to because...

"You had a brother?"

I had no idea.

Sin smiles despite everything and nods.

"A twin, Nannar. I swear he believed he could singlehandedly take down the Protogenoi, even though he was probably the smallest Celestial to ever live," Sin explains, and my heart breaks a little for him at the thought of losing someone who was born at your side.

I also, looking at Sin, find it hard to believe that anyone related to him could possibly be "the smallest Celestial to ever live," and I question how reliable his account of his brother really is. I could imagine Nannar being an inch shorter than Sin and Sin pointing that out every chance he got.

"This was before any talks of rebellion, long before the Firstlast War. He wanted to fight. But, I insisted we keep our heads down, stay safe. He always argued that we couldn't stand by while the Protogenoi ruled without any respect for what was just, but I argued right back that they were the rulers. Therefore, what they said was law, and that determined what was and was not just. I let it justify our lack of action when the truth was I didn't want my twin taking risks that would lead to his fall at the hands of the Protogenoi."

Sin stops, looking away. I reach out to touch his arm to try my best at offering some form of comfort for something that happened an unimaginably long time ago but must still hit him with just as much pain today, as it did when it was a day old. And now, being forced back into a reality where the Protogenoi rule as though nothing ever changed must make the wound even more fresh.

"He died anyway," he says. "When the Firstlast War came, I fought because Nannar was no longer alive to do so, and I've tried to keep up the fight since, even if it's never felt natural to me."

"Sin was one of the best fighters in the war," Phoenix says, of course eavesdropping.

I turn to find him having settled on an outfit, jeans and a t-shirt. The t-shirt has gold writing on it that matches the gold of my dress. It says, "Fuck the Protogenoi." I'd complain he stole my graffiti idea but it wouldn't exactly be fair, seeing as I never shared it with him. Plus, I can't complain about that shirt.

"People told stories about him around campfires to keep morale up. He's a legend," Phoenix goes on.

I look back to Sin, my eyebrows high up on my forehead.

"Why have I never heard about this before?"

"Phoenix is exaggerating."

That wouldn't be surprising, Phoenix exaggerating. I don't believe it in this case, though. But, a legend? Talk of the sixth Protogenoi is the only other time I've heard a Celestial label anything a legend.

Humans have loads of legends. Robin Hood, King Arthur, Atlantis, Headless Horseman, El Dorado, Heaven... Just kidding on the last one. Still...

Celestials don't have legends, *except* for the sixth Protogenoi.

The sixth Protogenoi, too, was used to keep hope alive in the Firstlast War. That's why that legend exists.

Sin's hands cup my arms, pulling my attention solely back to him, willing me already with his eyes to do something he's not yet asked of me.

"I've brought up Nannar because I need you to never let me forget again," he pleads, and I want to promise him that I can of course do that for him.

But, if I know anything, it's that I can't guarantee anything. I could have my memories taken from me again and forget this very moment. How many times is that bound to happen to me, I don't know. It seems like this last time has to have been the last, but I also don't know how much longer I'll stay me and not someone lost to the power in her.

Now is not the time to rehash that point.

"I can't make any promises if people are going to keep stealing my memories."

"You can keep this one," he assures me. "You remind me of Nannar, more fight than anyone else. Just find me whatever happens, and you will be enough of a reminder."

"Okay," I agree, then think of all the times Sin has made it very clear to me that he'd be willing to put his life on the line for my own, including his latest pact with Phoenix. "If you agree not to forget to fight for yourself, too."

Sin draws back.

He nods.

"Agreed."

"Hey, everybody!" Dex says, pushing past us and already heading down the stairs of the Ziggurat, toward the rest of the city.

Lada follows close behind, a beautiful smile on her face. Then again, every expression of hers is unfairly beautiful. But, it is nice to see her happy.

They look back at us expectantly.

"Hurry up," Dex continues, beckoning us forward, as if we haven't all been waiting for him to get going. "We've got a show to get to!"

CHAPTER
THIRTY-FOUR

I can see the fountain, or at least the very top of it, where water flows out of Dabar's outstretched hand and falls down in droplets.

"I like your dress."

"Thank you," Phoenix and I respond to Dex at the same time.

Dex looks Phoenix up and down, taking in his jeans and suggestive t-shirt.

I nearly walk into Lucifer, who speeds in front of us, blocking our path.

Sin takes a protective step in front of me. We brace ourselves, having no idea what the Lucifer of this reality could want, why he's here and not waiting at the fountain like the other competitors.

"This isn't possible," he says, eyes solely on Dex, whose own eyes are wide in shock.

I relax. Never mind. It is obviously clear what's brought him here. Dex has realized, too, taking a step forward from our suddenly tense group.

Lada makes some sound of protest but ultimately lets him go when Lucifer doesn't make a single move. He just watches Dex, confused and searching.

"It won't make sense to you," Dex explains, "but it is possible. It— is."

"No," Lucifer disagrees. It's not a denial but a plea for Dex to make it make sense. "I would remember."

I step out from behind Sin, nudging him back to make sure he lets me.

"You don't have all your memories," I say, ignoring the protests voiced around me at admitting that. "This isn't our original reality."

Lucifer still doesn't look to fully believe me. Of course, why would he take the word of a stranger seriously?

"Excuse me," Lada pipes in, pleasantly, "but what is this about?"

Lucifer doesn't turn from Dex.

"I could sense your power, the power we share, from the fountain. You are my son."

It's a matter of fact statement, devoid of emotion, possibly as a result of still not fully believing his own conclusion.

Lada's mouth actually drops open. I knew, and I still find it shocking to actually hear. Dex himself nods his head in confirmation, but he looks like a deer in headlights, probably never having expected to hear those words ever from Lucifer.

But, Lucifer—

Rushes forward and pulls Dex into a *hug*.

Dex freezes, as if not sure if Lucifer is hugging him or if he's really just concealing an attempt to murder him. But then, he hugs him back, in the way that Dex does everything, with his whole heart. He lets go, melting into it, and Lucifer hugs him even tighter.

My chest tightens and tears threaten my eyes for what feels like the millionth time today.

"What?" Lada practically screams. "Why does no one look surprised? Did everyone know this?"

She looks downright flabbergasted.

Lucifer and Dex pull back from the hug, Dex shooting Lada a slightly guilty look.

"I didn't, but it does make sense," Sin offers Lada.

"I suspected," Phoenix says.

"I was positive."

And that's all it takes for Lada's accusatory gaze to turn on me. Not to mention, the questioning look Dex throws my way.

"Okay, fine," I relent. "Maybe positive is the wrong word, but I was very confident. I mean, look at them."

Everyone does just that, turning their heads in Dex and Lucifer's direction, as if I actually ordered them to do so.

I'm not wrong. Same black hair, lean, muscular build, pale as hell skin, and they've got the same smile. That last one's not visible at the moment.

"Plus," I add, "they've got the same spirit."

"The same spirit?" Lada questions. "That's the most ridiculous thing I have ever heard. Lucifer tortures people for fun. Dex talks to ants."

"I only torture people who deserve it," Lucifer chimes in.

"Ants are intelligent, hard workers," Dex says.

"I also talk to ants," Lucifer says, glancing almost bashfully at Dex.

"See?" I tell Lada.

Dex doesn't look at Lucifer, though. He looks at me.

"Why didn't you say anything?"

"For the same reason no one else did. The truth can get Lucifer in trouble," I answer.

"How? What does that mean?" Lucifer asks.

I open my mouth to explain, but Dex shoots me a look that says he's got this.

"In the reality we're from, relations between Havcirians and humans is forbidden."

"Humans?" Lucifer questions, and I'm taken aback by the fact that, in this reality made by Dabar, people don't even know humans exist.

Of course, if I'd thought about it more, I would have realized. This reality is what it was like before the Firstlast War, before Havcire and Vest split, those who stayed in Vest swearing off magic.

MOLLY C. GROSS

Without the Firstlast War and its fallout, humans never would have come to be.

"People without magic," Dex explains.

"Are you saying your mother was human, then?"

"Yes. I grew up with her to keep it secret, and as long as no one voiced that you were my father, and you never acted in any way to make others suspect, no one had to act on the indiscretion."

"I haven't been a father to you?" Lucifer asks in a way that makes my own heart break for them.

"You haven't acknowledged me my whole life," Dex answers honestly.

Lucifer takes this in, clearly regretting something he has no memory of.

"You were the one to suggest to the rest of the ruling body of Havcire that Dex be brought in to spy on us," Phoenix offers, and my head whips in his direction.

I didn't know that.

"Spy on you? Why was that something that needed to be done?" Lucifer asks.

"Long story," I say. "It's okay. We're all over it."

"I think you wanted a chance to meet him," Phoenix continues.

"I shouldn't have been needing to meet my own son at—" Lucifer stops, looking at Dex. "How old are you?"

"I was sixteen when you met me the first time. Seventeen now. It's really okay. I've always understood. I have a really good mother who raised me."

Lucifer smiles at that.

"I'd like to know her."

"You definitely do, at least biblically," I supply.

"Don't talk like that in front of my son!" Lucifer shouts at me, and I can easily imagine him as the Disney Hercules' version of Hades with his head on fire.

"Oh, Luce," I say, placatingly. "He's heard worse."

"I don't like that nickname," he says, fire going down, but grumpy face intact.

"I know," I tell him, with a smile.

"I'm just realizing I never actually met your mom," Phoenix says, sounding genuinely upset by this fact. "When I first met you, I picked you up at home, but it wasn't really your home because the Council had placed you there to set us up. Your fake mom made me cookies. I really need to get back at you for that."

Dex shakes his head.

"No, you really don't. Dawn just said we were all past that, didn't you?"

"I did," I confirm.

"You tricked a trickster, Dex. I can't just let that go."

"But you're so forgiving, Phoenix," Dex says, trying to remind Phoenix of that elusive factor of his own personality, like that will work.

"That is true," Phoenix agrees, shrugging it off, proud of himself.

Or, it will work. The egomaniac.

"Can we focus again?" Lada asks. "I'm still having a hard time believing these two are related."

"I see it," Sin admits, totally serious.

"Of all the Celestials to have a child, this is the one? Lucifer? Doesn't exactly scream father figure to me," Lada argues.

"He looked after me while I was growing up," I point out.

"I did?"

"Yes, Luce."

"Stop that."

"Okay, Luce."

Before Luce can yell at me or possibly kill me, light shoots up from the Protogenoi Fountain in the near distance, and Dabar's voice surrounds us.

"Welcome Ascension finalists and all those viewing this exciting new event! Like me, I'm sure everyone is eager to learn more about what it takes to become a finalist and specifically what is so special about these finalists."

We share a look and head to close the distance between ourselves and the fountain, to take part in this spectacle and, most likely, trap. We can't put it off any longer. We shouldn't, because this is just a step to the final challenge, after which the real trial will begin, and the Protogenoi will finally, once and for all, be put an end to.

CHAPTER THIRTY-FIVE

"I'm going to swoon," I whisper to Phoenix.

"You're what?"

"Going to swoon."

"I thought you only swooned for me," Sin says.

"Excuse me?" Phoenix questions, sounding seriously vexed.

I glance at a nearby store, that I know Dex and Lada are currently hiding atop. Sin, however, I don't even know in what direction he is, so I can't even shoot him a well-deserved glare. I do know now that he's obviously close enough to use his enhanced hearing to listen in.

We thought it'd be best if they stayed out of sight to keep an eye out for any sign of a trap. Obviously, Maze can sense where we are and that we are together, but it can't hurt to still take precautions. At the very least, their vantage point up on the roofs could give us a heads up if there's any sort of physical attack.

Not to mention, only Ascension competitors got an invitation to this lovely event in person.

"Now you choose to be funny, Sin?" I ask.

"I've always been funny."

"No, you haven't," we all respond to him.

And, apparently, when more than one of us talks telepathically at the same time, it comes across much louder than usual. Fun thing to find out.

"Catch me."

I walk up to Eros, look at him, his perfectly symmetrical, chiseled face, and flowy blonde hair, and...

I swoon. Or, at least, I put on a good show of doing so. Dabar's putting on his own show, interviewing the first competitor.

Phoenix's arms catch me from behind, wrapping beneath my arms to push me back up onto my feet, and I realize I should have asked someone else to catch me from my fake swoon because the most tempting sensation spreads from where his hands land on me. I do my best to suppress a shiver.

I need to get my act together if I'm going to keep Phoenix at a distance, whether he wants that or not, which I don't know one way or another. But, I don't care, and it doesn't matter, all of which would be easier to convince myself of if I didn't take every opportunity I had to be closer to him. That stops now.

After all that, my dramatic swoon and all, I manage to achieve only a hint of a smile from Eros.

Phoenix spins me around to look at him and again his hands are on me, holding tight to my waist, and I don't push him off. He lets go.

It stops *right* now.

"What was that for?"

"Eros looks so sad," I answer, frowning sympathetically.

"And that has to do with you fainting how?"

"Swooning," I correct.

"My bad. What's that have to do with you swooning?"

"You don't remember? You were the one who'd told me Eros was offended that I didn't swoon at the sight of him when I met him the first time."

"And you thought swooning now would lift his spirits?"

My shoulders shrug. Yeah, I did. Or, I hoped. He really does look devastated about something; and while no one in this reality is exactly happy with their life, there's something very poignant about Eros's pain.

"You believe, at this point in the competition, that winning is about who is most motivated?" Dabar asks.

Morrigan, the Celestial known in Vest as a goddess of war and fate, according to Celtic mythology, is the first to fall prey to Dabar's inane questions. I've no idea why he's going through with this at all. If it's a trap, just spring it already. Perhaps he is the type that enjoys playing with his food, as Sin suggested.

He's got Morrigan perched on the side of the fountain, her raven-black hair so long that it falls into the water like spilled oil. Dabar looks down at her, his image projected against the water droplets that fall continuously down from the top center of the fountain.

Although he has her placed below him, Morrigan has a certain energy that, being in her presence, makes her feel like a force of nature. It's like she has her own center of gravity, like she's both holding me near and maintaining the distance between us, so much so that if I tried to approach, that energy around her would keep me back, like a magnet of opposite charge, repelling me.

Dabar, on the other hand, is just a projection. But, I've no doubt that if he were here in person, I would feel significantly more wary of him.

"I do believe, as a rule, that for those who are left standing at the end of a battle, or competition, the fight becomes more about who wants the win the most," Morrigan answers.

"So then, why do you want it? What is your motivation?" Dabar questions.

Why do you care? I want to ask. Why waste this time? Dabar could truly just be bored, waiting for me to die or drop the barriers willingly. He does look interested in this topic, and he definitely, at least, is putting on a show of being interested with his tone.

Morrigan shrugs. Even her shrug doesn't look nonchalant, but a planned move.

"There are no battles being fought right now," she says. "This competition is the only fight worth anything."

Morrigan's dark eyes find my own, the silver flecks in her black irises seeming to swirl, as if communicating something else entirely and, whatever the message, it's for me.

"You can sense who is meant to be victorious in battle. Can you see yet the outcome of the Ascension's final challenge?" Dabar asks, and Morrigan slowly drags her gaze away from me.

But, she offers Dabar no response, not even a secretive smile in answer. Just nothing. I have to admire that hint of defiance.

"*What was that?*" Dex asks.

"*What was what?*" I ask back.

"*That look that competitor just gave you.*"

"*Morrigan,*" I supply.

"*If that's her name.*"

I forget sometimes Dex didn't grow up in this world. With all the numerous, strange facts he knows, it's odd to think it's common knowledge about Havcire and its people that he'd be lacking.

It's still strange to think that I actually did grow up here, at least initially. Even with my memories of just that, it doesn't change the fact that I also remember all the years, the lifetimes, I spent living in Vest as solely human.

Eros is next, taking Morrigan's spot at the base of the fountain.

"*She totally singled you out when Dabar asked her that question.*"

"*She can sense the outcome of battles,*" Lada ponders.

"*I did hear Dabar say that,*" Dex replies. "*That's why I'm wondering if—*"

"If she looked at Dawn because she knows she will win," Lada finishes.

Whether Morrigan knows the outcome of the final challenge or not matters little to me. I'm competing regardless, and I'll get the barriers down by doing so, preferably without dying.

"I think it's more than that," Phoenix adds. *"Morrigan has powerful instincts. She may have sensed not only that Dawn wins this, but that she's fighting for more than just winner of Ascension."*

"You think Morrigan has chosen to support Dawn?" Sin asks.

I look to Morrigan, who now stands to the side of the fountain, watching Eros's interview, her attention trained on Dabar, and her expression shows unbridled hate.

"Yes," Phoenix answers.

Very few actually like the Protogenoi. Except for Hadur, Whiro, and Lamashtu, who have their monopoly on resources and use that to profit off all the other Celestials and the Incanters, everyone else struggles to get by on a daily basis.

But, most are too afraid to stand against them, and all believe that it'd be impossible to do so anyway. They're invincible, as far as everyone is concerned.

Morrigan, however, if she could sense that the Protogenoi are not as untouchable as everyone thinks... Maybe she believes I have a chance against at least one of them. Maybe she wants me to succeed. And, if more Havcirians knew the truth, they, too, would want me to succeed.

That thought almost makes me laugh. It actually feels absurd to be doing something that almost everyone, if they knew, would support. This reality had me running for my life from all these people when we all really want the same thing, and Morrigan might be one of the few who realizes that.

It's not even the first time I've been made out to be a criminal as a result of trying to share the truth. I was made a Subject because I questioned the Subject System. Granted, that time it was Phoenix who painted me as such in order to keep me hidden away in the Subject System while I gained my powers.

Still, these recent months working with the Council rather than against have been the exception in my life. I'm not exactly used to having support.

"Eros," Dabar is saying, "would you share with us your motivation for competing in Ascension?"

"I hoped if I won I could have an alternate reward," Eros says, carefully.

Dabar's eyebrows go up, intrigued, but in a way that makes my defenses rise.

"Something other than being allowed to live in the luxury of the Ziggurat for a year?"

Eros nods his head, clearly afraid to go on, but something strengthens his resolve, hardening his eyes when he looks up to meet Dabar's gaze again.

"My love, Psyche, I lost her to the Labyrinth. I wish for my reward, if I win, to be her release."

"On second thought, I'm sure your swoon really helped," Phoenix says.

I elbow him in the gut.

Dabar smiles. For someone who can craft reality to be whatever he desires, he clearly puts no effort into making that smile appear genuine. At least, it looks brittle as hell to me.

"Eros, of course we would be delighted to provide her release as reward. But, there's no need for you to give up your own reward of living in luxury for the year in the Ziggurat," Dabar says, somehow talking through that smile. "Of course, loved ones are not permitted to join the Ascension winners in the Ziggurat."

Psyche would be released only to spend another year apart from Eros, and who knows what kind of shape she'd be in after being in the Labyrinth for so long? She would need him more than ever, but he'd be essentially imprisoned in the Ziggurat.

"Yes," Eros replies. "Thank you, Dabar."

Still, it's better than leaving her in there, lost.

Eros does appear genuinely grateful, even though I know he's no idiot. He sees what Dabar's doing. It's a fresh form of torture disguised as generosity. When you live in a world with little possibility, though, you'll take what opportunity you can get.

"*Asshole,*" Phoenix comments for our listening pleasure.

His own opinion on Dabar's generous offer.

"Well, I would call that some good motivation for winning. Fighting for love," Dabar goes on in his most TV host voice yet, and I wonder if he and some of the other Protogenoi are passing the time in Vest by watching talk shows. "Thank *you*, Eros."

He nods at Eros in a clear dismissal, and Eros promptly vacates the unofficial hot seat, leaving it ominously empty.

"Now, a special treat," Dabar says. "You all know her name. She has the largest bounty on her head in all of Havcire, and I'd wager she's here exactly for that reason, seeing as Ascension offers its competitors immunity outside of the challenges themselves. Welcome Dawn!"

CHAPTER
THIRTY-SIX

With such an introduction, I expected to be asked questions actually relating to the fact that I do have a bounty on my head, a bounty that Dabar himself and the other Protogenoi placed on my head. But, no.

There are more important questions to raise when it comes to me.

"What is this beautiful dress?" Dabar asks.

Of course the Protogenoi don't want anyone knowing the real reason they want me dead. It was dumb of me to even think Dabar would go there. After all, they've gone through a lot to ensure no one finds out I did kill Chaos, which only begs the question of why they would think it's a good idea to give me an audience in front of all of Havcire now.

Although, the ego, especially when you're as powerful as the Protogenoi are, can be a dangerous thing. Dabar can control reality itself. Why wouldn't he think he could control little ol' me in a simple interview, keep me from saying anything he wouldn't want me to?

But, what am I wearing? Really?

When I just stare up at Dabar like he's lost his head...

"Tell us, who are you wearing?" he prods, and I choke on a laugh, keeping it from escaping.

"You'd have to ask Phoenix. He dressed me."

"Oh!" Dabar exclaims, not even looking down at me anymore but forward, talking directly to the audience we can't see, as if this is something worthy of sharing with everyone. "Is there a romance between two of the competitors?"

"No!"

Oh shit.

That denial sounded way too defensive. I might as well have just declared my love for the guy. I don't dare look in Phoenix's direction. I never thought I'd be gratefully keeping my attention trained on Dabar. It's already concerning Phoenix isn't commenting in my head.

I really should have prepared for this interview, done some media training or something because I'm sucking at this, and I'm only one question in.

"I didn't mean it like that, not literally," I vaguely clarify. "It wasn't like 'Here, step one foot in, another, and then I'll zip it for you.'"

Someone gag me.

"But, there is something going on between the two of you?"

"*No.* "

And there is Phoenix's voice in my head. Short and definitive.

"*Say it calm, normal,*" he goes on.

That settles that.

"No," I answer, calm, even though a part of me hurts from the answer. "I just meant Phoenix has that handy power—"

I can't say that. He keeps the extent of his teleportation ability a secret. Except, I'm not sure if it still is a secret he cares about keeping, seeing as we now know the truth about this world. Although, I'm not positive why he was keeping it a secret in this reality to begin with. Why would Phoenix care about people knowing he can teleport more than just himself?

It could have been simply to better stay off the Protogenoi's radar, as he was going behind their backs, pulling his Robin Hood act and illegally providing Celestials and Incanters with supplies.

He had told that story of the one time he did get Dabar's attention and ended up with his scar from being made human, and that was punishment over his ability to teleport himself only. Clearly, the Protogenoi are not fans of anyone who could come even close to rivaling their power if Dabar had a tantrum over Phoenix being able to escape their little traps by teleporting away.

Now that I think about it, I don't even know if that story of Phoenix's was true. He told it to me before we got our memories back. That was when we didn't have any real memories from before this reality was created. At least, every time I tried to think too much about the past, my mind naturally wandered away. So, how could Phoenix have had such a clear memory?

Anyhow, I just called Phoenix's ability a "handy power." My choice of words is killing me.

"I mean," I try again, aiming for vague, "he's just good at acquiring things. He found this dress."

"You two are in the habit of helping each other? Isn't that strange for two people in competition with each other?"

"Having allies is a well-known technique, at least early in a competition," Phoenix supplies as an answer, but I'm done letting Dabar take the lead here.

"Don't you think people might be more curious about what made you and the other Protogenoi want me killed?" I ask.

So what if Dabar has precautions for this type of thing? What if Maze can just erase whatever I say here from everyone's minds? None of that matters. It's better than the alternative, sitting here and answering questions about my dress and non-existent, or more accurately, one-sided, highly doomed, love life.

"I think the people of Havcire want to know if having an ally in Ascension is beneficial so that they might have a chance of winning next year," Dabar continues, pushing his chosen topic.

"I think they'd be interested to know that the Protogenoi are not as invincible as they think—"

Dabar's booming voice cuts me off.

"What made you decide to ally with each other? Are you—?

"I killed Chaos."

"Sure you did," Dabar says, his condescendingly placating voice pissing me off more than any other response I could have imagined.

It takes me back to every time in every life when I was dismissed without a second thought based off solely how I looked, what people assumed about me. I want to scream at him suddenly. Threaten him. Give away that we have a plan to bring an end to him and all the other Protogenoi, that I will be the one to do it.

But then, I spot Morrigan and Eros.

Despite Dabar brushing off my claim, they are looking at me, a spark of hope in Eros's expression and determination in Morrigan's. They believe me.

If they believe me, then maybe others do, and maybe it can give them something to hold onto until I can make good on this unspoken promise to bring down the rest of the Protogenoi.

"Unfortunately, we have run out of time and must bid adieu to our competitors and wish them luck in the final challenge," Dabar is saying.

Phoenix steps forward.

"You didn't interview me."

"The details for the final competition will be announced at next light," Dabar goes on, not even looking down at Phoenix.

Even just the projection of Dabar looks overly stiff, as he keep his chin high, determined not to spare a glance for Phoenix.

"At least show my outfit to Havcire," Phoenix taunts, indicating his t-shirt with his choice words on it.

I stand from the fountain's ledge, taking my dismissal cue.

"Until then," Dabar says, "an exciting new amendment to an Ascension rule: Anyone who can kill an Ascension competitor will be free to take their place."

What?

I'm not sure if it's my own thought or another's in my head, but I feel the sentiment echoed all around me.

Dabar's image blips away, leaving behind the deceitfully calming trickle of the water fountain.

That rule was all that stood between me and the deadly bounty on my head. Plus, now there's the added benefit that if someone kills me, they get to compete in the final challenge. Even I would take Dabar up on that offer and try to kill me if I were in anyone else's position.

A loud crack sounds, and the ground right beneath Phoenix's feet fissures. I jump toward him, reaching out, catching his arm just as the rest of his body disappears within the now fractured earth.

The weight of him pulls me down. I search for purchase, finding a small groove in the cobblestones to cling to with my fingers but it's too small, and I slip.

I release a lasso of my golden energy, ready to use it as an anchor but—

The world squeezes around me and I'm tumbling through space. I find myself mere feet away from where the crack in the ground opened to swallow Phoenix, still on my stomach and Phoenix's hand still in mine. But, he's now jumping to his feet in front of me, yanking me up with him.

"What are you doing diving head first into chasms?" he asks, irritated.

"Saving you," I insist, irritated by his irritation.

Admittedly, I didn't do much saving, Phoenix teleporting us both away. But, I could have, if given a little more time.

Phoenix's attention catches on something behind me. He pushes me to the side, and I spot a spear flying directly at Phoenix, seeing as I'm no longer in its path.

A spear of my own energy lashes out of me, cutting right through the spear of what appears to be made of wood. It splinters apart upon impact, never reaching Phoenix.

I look to the source of the spear, the reason for the ground opening up. A large, beautiful black wolf leaps up onto the fountain's edge, arctic blue eyes focused now on Lucifer.

Years of study with Minerva and the pieces come together in my mind even though I have never before met this Celestial. Medeina, name chosen after the Lithuanian goddess of forests who was based off of her. She has the ability to control elements of nature and transform into a wolf.

Dabar only just made the announcement, but they're already coming.

We're all in danger. Every competitor has a neon target on their back.

Golden sparks of lightning, shaped like chains, shoot up from the base of the fountain at my command, locking around the wolf's legs before she can pounce at Lucifer. She whips her head to me as she sets out to pull herself free. I brace for her attack, knowing it's just a waste of energy to try and keep reinforcing my makeshift chains to withstand her.

But then, I'm looking at Phoenix's back as he steps out in front of me. I nudge him aside, though it's apparently not hard enough to get his feet to move, so I step up beside him instead.

"Excuse you."

He glances at me quick, keeping his attention on Medeina, who is still fighting against my restraints.

"Excuse *me?*" he asks, tone genuinely confused.

"Yes. What are you doing walking out in front of me?"

"Protecting you."

"*Making my way to you,*" Sin lets us know.

Sin, the other half of the protect Dawn at all costs pact.

"I'm all good," I insist. "Whatever happened to fighting *with* me? You know, at my side, like you normally do, respecting the fact that I can protect myself?"

I actually quite liked that about Phoenix, that he trusted me to fight and treated me like an equal no matter what, even when I was ignorant regarding who I was from one life to the next. But, guess that's done with. Because of this stupid pact.

Perfect. I'll just add that to the list I'm compiling consisting of reasons I should not feel the way I do about him. He's just the jerk who thinks I need someone else to defend me.

Yes, I'm convinced. Feelings totally gone.

"That was before you doubted I'd risk my life for you."

"What?" I ask, wondering seriously where his head is at.

"You called me an egomaniac."

"You are an egomaniac."

"Yes," he willingly agrees, "but what I told Styx was true."

He'd said he would give up his life for my own, and I hadn't known what to make of that. So, yes, I do now recall calling him an egomaniac at the time, but what had happened since between us had overtaken my thoughts, so I hadn't quite remembered that detail of the conversation with Styx.

Plus, then Sin told me the truth about their agreement, and it did make sense of things, why Phoenix would make such a claim. I wrongfully believed for a second he might care about my survival because he cares about me.

I'm a liar. Those feelings are definitely not gone. Still very present and not pleasant.

"I know about your agreement with Sin."

That gets his attention, and he looks so very not happy, whether with me or Sin for telling me I can't be sure.

"That's not why—" he grits out, or tries to, but I don't need any fake explanations right now.

"I don't care," I argue, "I don't want you risking your life for mine."

A growl draws my attention just in time.

I sweep Phoenix's legs out from under him as Medeina leaps at his back, claws extended. I hold my hands out in defense to face her sharp-toothed mouth now coming for my throat.

A pull on my dress drags me down to the ground, Medeina passing harmlessly above my head, as I fall on top of Phoenix. I catch myself before I can actually face plant right into him. He lifts himself up onto his elbows so our faces are nearly touching.

"Hypocrite," he accuses.

"I would have been fine."

"If I can't risk my life for you, you can't risk yours for me."

"I'm just watching your back."

"Do you two have to be told to focus on the fact that someone is presently trying to kill you?" Dex asks.

I go to stand. Phoenix flips me over so he's on top, allowing me to catch a flash of bright, blue eyes as Medeina pounces at us. I throw up a shield of golden energy, repelling Medeina and quite literally guarding Phoenix's back from her claws in doing so.

"Apparently," Lada answers.

It is not my fault this time that Phoenix is on top of me, and I on top of him before that. He pulled *me* down, and he was the one to land us here. I am doing my best to maintain distance, which if I can't manage emotionally, I can at least attempt physically. It is undoubtedly my fault, however, that even under attack, I can't help but react to his proximity.

Phoenix pulls me up with him, not giving me any chance to refuse his help.

I push him back.

"Just stay back," I blurt out before I can think better of it.

"What?" he asks, looking at me like I've lost my mind. "I'm not the one trying to kill you."

"*We have to get somewhere safe before more arrive,*" Sin says.

"*Define safe. Everyone will be looking for them,*" Lada says.

Medeina charges at Lucifer.

Dex gets there first, siphoning Phoenix's power to teleport to Lucifer's side. A blinding light emanates from Dex as he uses Lada's power, momentarily blinding Medeina, along with the rest of us.

"*I know a place,*" Phoenix offers, with no more detail.

Before the light can even clear and the black spots disappear from my vision, a warning shout from Dex fills my head.

"*Incanters!*"

I whip around, searching. There, I spot an Incanter up on the roof nearest to Phoenix, arm pulled back, poised to throw at him some potion.

I reach for the skirt of my dress at the same moment Phoenix does, both of us yanking free one dagger each.

I throw it. It spins hilt over point and embeds itself into the Incanter's wrist, forcing him to release the potion, which burns a hole through the roof he stands on when it breaks upon impact on its surface.

I turn around in time to find that the dagger Phoenix threw found its target, as well, traveling straight through the potion bottle of the Incanter who was targeting me and into his hand. The potion lights his skin on fire, a fire he's frantically trying to put out.

"Call it even?" I offer.

Phoenix shrugs.

"I don't know about that. I provided the dress."

Before I can protest any further or be attacked by any more Havcirians, I'm being pulled through space.

CHAPTER THIRTY-SEVEN

M y eyes open slowly, in no hurry. Breaths still even from sleep, I take in familiar surroundings.

I'm in Phoenix's lair, oddly comfortably lying on the floor, with a pillow beneath my head and a blanket pulled over me. I'm within the squared maze of supplies Phoenix keeps stored in here.

In the empty space beneath the table in front of me, more supplies on top of it, I spot Dex and Lada sleeping on the floor together a few maze rows down from me.

I turn my head to find Lucifer also sleeping, further inside the maze.

The chandelier above is letting off dim, warm light, unlike when I was last here and it was a bright, white light. In fact, everything here - the floor, the pillow, the blanket, the comfortable temperature, despite being surrounded by stone underground, and the lighting is suspiciously calming.

I can't recall how I got here. I remember the telltale signs of teleporting, the shrinking sensation and feel of squeezing between particles themselves. But, I don't remember arriving anywhere, let alone lying down to take a nap. That doesn't seem like something I would do, nor Lucifer, Dex, and Lada.

I think about opening my mouth, whispering for Sin, but I don't. My body feels heavy, my head groggy. Where is Sin? Where is Phoenix?

Hushed voices make it through to my consciousness.

I slowly, with more effort than it should take, make my way toward the voices, essentially army crawling beneath the tables full of supplies toward the curtain that separates this portion of the room from Phoenix's private space, which he refused to let me get a look at back when we were here last and we didn't yet have our memories returned.

I wonder if he'd willingly let me in now.

I lift the white curtain no more than a couple inches off the ground to peer through to the other side and find Sin and Phoenix facing each other.

"You're not exactly doing a good job at hiding it," Sin is saying. He pointedly indicates the painting that takes up the majority of the wall above the bed.

There's a comfy-looking king-sized bed behind here, and we're all out here sleeping on the floor? Which, granted, I had thought only a second ago was insanely comfortable, but that's not the point. None of us even got the chair to sleep in this time.

The painting is what I'd caught only a glimpse of before, of two large wings, one of which is obviously broken.

Phoenix glances at the painting himself, before turning back to Sin, his face a mask of indifference.

"Very few have put that together."

"Enough that you've grounded yourself," Sin answers, raising an eyebrow in skepticism.

Phoenix relents to this point.

"I wasn't in charge of the interior design," he points out. "This is Dabar's reality."

Are they saying Phoenix's wings are a secret? But, I've seen them twice.

Two times.

I realize, considering how long I've known him, that's not a significant amount. I guess I figured that wings aren't that necessary when you're faster than any other Celestial and can teleport to get to wherever you want. At the same time, if I had wings, I would enjoy using them. Everyone wishes they could fly, don't they?

Actually, the two times I did see Phoenix's wings, no one else was around. The first, when Chaos had thrown me through that portal, and he had to dive in after to save me. And then, when he was trying to kill me under Maze's control. In both cases, he didn't have much choice in the matter.

Why keep the wings a secret?

I try to think through it more, what could be their significance. The Celestial tree in the graveyard is marked by wings, despite there being no other Celestial I know of with wings, except for Phoenix.

The performance during the Havcire Assembly showed a Celestial flying against the Protogenoi, leading the charge into battle. So, if that were Phoenix, what difference does it make?

Every train of thought I have fizzles out, my head still groggy.

"At least be honest with her," Sin says, focusing me back on their conversation.

"She'll find out soon enough."

"It will be better if she hears it from you."

"If I tell her any earlier, she'll reject me completely and refuse my help. I need to be able to help her," Phoenix insists, fear in his voice, which makes me yearn to go to him even though I highly suspect I know who "she" is that he's lying to.

"I can feel what you're feeling, so there's no need to lie to me," Sin says, probably sensing in Phoenix the same I could hear from his voice. Difference is, Sin probably can interpret what exactly it is that Phoenix is afraid of.

"I just need a little more time."

"This isn't about you. Dawn needs to know the truth for her own good."

Sin's eyes shift ever so slightly over to me, completely unsurprised to find me awake and listening. He's meeting my eyes when he says, "She needs to know who you really are."

Fatigue crashes into me, my eyes too heavy to keep open.

It's Sin. He's the reason we were all sleeping, and he's also the reason I woke to hear this part of their conversation. He wanted me to hear.

But now, he's forcing feelings of exhaustion back on me, and I can't even think about the implications of what I've heard. I try to cling on, but there's no way.

I use my last bit of energy to shoot Sin a glare because I'm not a damn puppet before once again losing consciousness.

I run through darkness, chancing running straight into whatever lies ahead of me, but I have no choice because I'm being chased.

People appear before me, but only when I'm a couple feet away from them, when they're suddenly lit up from some sort of spotlight coming from above. I have to change course quickly to avoid running full speed into them.

Again, those I pass are familiar faces from my past. And, just like before, I'm leaving them behind.

My legs keep moving like they've been wound up and have yet to fully spin out. The footsteps behind me are louder, but the people I pass begin to thin out, so I push myself to run faster, feeling like I'm tripping over my own feet with each step. I'm overwound.

Another person appears directly ahead of me in my path.

I stop.

As I do, my foot hits something that slides heavily across the dirt before coming to a stop at the feet of the other person. She bends down and picks it up. The sword.

Expectantly, she holds it out to me, its blade so clean it looks to be made from mirrors. It reflects my face back at me, but it's my birth mother's face that has my attention. Her hand holds the sword.

My own hand burns painfully, and I reach for the cool onyx of the blade's hilt. As my fingers wrap around, the burning ceases, but the entire world erupts into flames.

My heart continues to beat erratically, but my body is otherwise relaxed.

I lie on soft ground, looking up. Flames still fill my vision, but they're no longer all around. They stem from a single source. Above me, a bird is surrounded by the red and orange flames. Its wings release the fire, and the bird twists through the air, stirring the fire in a sort of dance. It passes through the fire it creates, unharmed by the heat.

Something warm and wet is on my hand. I look down.

The ground is back beneath my feet, the spotlight shining down on me in the dark. It's blood that coats my hand. My breath halts.

The flaming sword, flames now dead, is in someone's abdomen, blood spilling out of the wound onto me. I've done this. My hand is wrapped around the hilt. I force myself to look up, the rest of me frozen, and I find my mother back before me.

The life goes out of her eyes, her last expression still one of trust, but I'm the one who did this to her. I killed her.

I scream, finally letting out that breath, as she collapses in my arms.

I'm shaking, tears streaming down my face. My throat is raw, but I can't hear my own scream.

That's how I realize it's just another dream, my scream only loud in my head. I come to, the lair coming back into focus, and the shaking stops because it wasn't me but Phoenix. His hands are still gripping my arms from where he was attempting to shake me awake.

"Are you okay?" he asks.

He's pulled me up into a sitting position. My face is wet from tears, but I don't bother wiping them away. My heart is still pounding and my hands are fisted at my sides. My breath comes out sharp and quick, and my head is too heavy.

I know it wasn't real, but I feel like it happened. I can't take it. I've been crying, but I feel like I need to cry more, louder, and scream some more, loud enough to really wake myself up and convince myself that this is what's real and not what I just saw.

Instead, I just let my head fall onto Phoenix's chest. I focus on his breathing, his chest falling up and down and try to match my own to the rhythm. I breathe in the scent of freshly fallen snow.

"I killed her," I manage.

"Killed who?" he asks, softly.

I take a deep breath and exhale the answer.

"My mother."

I can feel Phoenix's voice vibrate through his chest. He lets me stay where I am, one hand on my back. The other comes up to soothingly brush my hair off the back of my neck, letting air caress my too hot skin.

"It was just a dream," he reassures me. "You didn't kill anyone. You're okay. She's okay."

I look up at him. I should lean back, I realize, now that I've gotten a fraction of myself back together. But, I just need a moment. This is an exception. It was a nightmare, and I'm still not fully convinced it wasn't real. I'm in limbo, only half-awake, with everyone else around us asleep. I can stay here, time frozen, in Phoenix's arm for a little longer.

The final challenge can't come right now, at least not while my breath is paced in time with his, and we're stealing time before the rest of the world wakes.

"I found her, but I haven't met her," I admit, not even sure if I let the truth out because I'm ready to share it or because I'm simply desperate to have an excuse to stay where we are. "She's the only one left from my past lives that I haven't contacted."

He says nothing, simply listening, waiting for me to explain if that's what I want. My greatest fear spills out, an admission that

I've carried that fear with me, at least at some level, for much longer than I've wanted to believe.

"I'm afraid meeting her will confirm that I'm nothing like her, that I have more in common with Chaos, the person who killed her. What if I find my mom only to end up being a danger to her?"

The whole truth is I fear I'll be a danger to many more than just my birth mother. What if I'm destined, like all the other Protogenoi, to have my power corrupt me, make me lose my mind, lose everything that defines who I am now?

Sin is convinced I'm a fighter like his brother was, and I have always been extremely stubborn and determined if that's what he means by being a fighter, but if part of being a Protogenoi is losing your very self to your power, then none of that will matter anymore. Everything that I am, which has stayed with me life after life, could be erased by what I am at the very core of my nature.

A Protogenoi.

And now, with that power finally awakened, after all the time I spent living in Vest and my memories returned to me, who knows how much time I have before that part of me takes over?

"Dawn."

Phoenix's hand on my back pulls me tighter against him, as his other hand comes up to cup my face, effectively silencing my spiraling thoughts.

My own hands, unclenched now, land on his thighs, which I somehow hadn't realized are spread out to either side of me. I'm in a cage of Phoenix, and I should mind more. I should get myself together because he is one of the people I am most concerned about hurting if it comes to that.

"When we get out of this reality, we will go to your mother, and you will see that there is no truth to your fears," Phoenix insists. "You are nothing like Chaos, and you won't be just like your birth mother either. You are you."

I want to believe him more than anything. I truly believe he believes in what he said, the conviction in his voice ringing true. I trust him, but what if he's wrong? None of the Protogenoi began as they are now. I could change beyond repair.

Phoenix does know me, probably better than anyone else beside myself. He is right. Who I am now is not just a copy of someone else, and if I can hold onto that, maybe I can avoid the fate of the Protogenoi.

I also know Phoenix, I realize, at least in the ways that matter.

The fog of sleep lifts, along with the too real fear of my dream, and I recall the conversation I overheard between Phoenix and Sin right before Sin forced sleep back on me.

"Who are you?" I ask him.

I see a flash of alarm, then confusion, before his walls go back up and the calm between us shatters.

He moves to back up, his legs lowering, but the movement brings my hands higher up his legs. He stills. I slide my hands an inch higher.

"Dawn," he says, his voice low, a warning. "We should talk about this."

He wants to talk about us, but I can't, and he's wrong. We should talk about *him*.

I lean forward, keeping my hands where they are, and closing the small amount of distance he'd managed to gain between us.

"Who are you?" I ask again.

He opens his mouth, eyes burning in challenge, and I know I'm not going to get my answer.

Natural light suddenly shatters across the room, bouncing from one mirror to another. Another day outside has begun.

I hear a sound of protest at the bright light, realizing someone must be waking up, and I push back from Phoenix, but not before shooting him one of my stubborn looks that promises this isn't over. His response is a cocky smile, which assures me he thinks this will only be addressed again when he finds it necessary.

"The final challenge is here!" Dabar's voice booms, stemming from above ground, echoing off the cave walls all the way down to us.

Phoenix and I share a quick look before jumping to our feet.

"The first to get to the Tree of Life and pick one of its apples will be the winner of Ascension."

My brain works fast now.

"Which is only possible if my barrier comes down," I state.

Phoenix nods. "All roads lead to the Protogenoi."

It's official. He was right. They want the barriers down. They want into Havcire.

CHAPTER THIRTY-EIGHT

"It's best if we don't come," Sin says.

"But what if—?"

"Sin's right," Phoenix interrupts Dex. "You can't interfere with the challenge. It could get us disqualified. Being there will be too much of a temptation."

"We'll still be connected telepathically," I point out.

I, like Dex, am not enthusiastic about splitting up. We've come this far together. But, there's no denying that this is a fight they can't, at least physically, fight with us.

"And you can always teleport us there if you do need us, right?" Lada asks Phoenix, but something about the way she says it makes it seem as though she doubts he will do that. It comes across as a challenge in of itself, daring Phoenix to just try to exclude them and see what happens.

The look Phoenix gives her in response is not at all reassuring.

"We have to go," he states, looking between me and Lucifer.

Lucifer. Between the family drama, the interviews, the all of Havcire targeting us to take our places in Ascension, and Sin's forced sleep, there wasn't much time to speak with him about all of this.

He is, after all, another one of the Ascension competitors, out to win this thing.

"Lucifer, too?" I ask Phoenix, but my focus is still trained on the Celestial in question.

"Luce, too," Lucifer says, cringing at his own use of my nickname for him. "I'm caught up and all Team Dawn winning Ascension. I'll help where I can."

"Sin added him to our mental web," Dex supplies.

"Against my wishes," comes Lucifer's reply in my head.

"Let's go," I say, unwilling to draw this out more than necessary.

The final challenge is not going away. Even if the other competitors get there before I do, they'll never be able to take down my barrier around the tree. I am the only one who can win this. Unless, someone manages to kill me. Either way, that barrier won't come down until I am there.

There's no point in delaying the inevitable and what we need to ensure comes after.

Lada continues to stare down Phoenix, knowing as well as I do, that there's more to why he doesn't want them coming along. Per usual, Phoenix tells the truth but leaves out vital details.

I believe what he said, that he doesn't want to risk them interfering in the challenge and getting us disqualified. However,

I also think that he doesn't want them there when the Protogenoi come through that portal.

Most likely, it's to protect them. I'll take the opportunity to declare the Protogenoi Trials as soon as I lay eyes on them. Similar to Ascension, once declared, the trials will prevent the Protogenoi from killing me on the spot. But, that won't protect anyone else from the Protogenoi. I'll have to ensure Phoenix and Lucifer are clear of the crossfire.

A nod from Phoenix to me and Lucifer is the only warning we get before he's teleporting us away, sentiments ringing through my head from Sin, Lada, and Dex as the world itself deforms around me to allow us transport.

"Good luck," comes from Sin.

"Watch each other's backs or I'll kill you," from Lada.

"Fight like Mulan." Dex's advice.

We stand a football field distance away from the Tree of Life, a game set out before us, except I see nothing but the open field surrounding the tree.

"Predictably, I was prevented from teleporting straight to the base of the tree," Phoenix says. "They want us to participate."

"On second thought, I think I'll hang back and let you two test this out," Lucifer says, as he takes a few steps away, further into the tree cover.

"Afraid of an empty field?" I ask, despite my own cautious glance at said empty field.

"Intelligently afraid of what I cannot see, Dawn."

"Fair."

"I'll go first," Phoenix volunteers. "A reminder that—"

"No," I interrupt, nearly automatically. "I'll go with you."

"Fine," he agrees, easily enough.

"Have fun," Lucifer says, even shooting us a smile.

"I was going to say that although we are working together, we have to put on a show of individually competing," Phoenix goes on.

Lucifer gives him a thumbs up... and takes another step back, again further away from the empty field.

"So, it would look suspicious if we ran onto the field, side by side, at the same time?" I ask, already preparing to take the lead.

"Dawn," Phoenix warns, grabbing onto my arm, "don't you dare."

"I wouldn't," I say, innocently. "We agreed not to recklessly jump into danger, didn't we?"

"I'm not the reckless one here."

"What do you call throwing yourself in front of me and risking your own life, then?"

"A worthwhile risk."

A worthwhile risk because he cares about me even a fraction of the way I care for him, or because without me we don't have a chance of bringing an end to the Protogenoi?

I don't dare voice the question. Although, it's so loud in my own head, I fear he must see it written on my face. I shouldn't be thinking about this anyway.

I rush to cover it up with a smile that almost convinces me that what is coming up is a friendly competition between me and Phoenix and not the life-threatening death trap set up by the Protogenoi that it is.

"There is another way to make it look convincing that we're not working together."

I push Phoenix, hard, onto the field, as if we were fighting, which, I guess, is never too far from the truth. But, because he's still holding onto my arm, like I planned, I'm yanked along with him. The momentum brings us both down.

Together, we enter the final challenge.

Phoenix releases my arm in favor of catching himself. I reach out to do the same, but I never hit the ground.

My hands splash into water, the rest of my body following, water clogging my nose and mouth. I choke it out, looking around to find the field is gone. Phoenix is gone. Clear water surrounds me, a white, marble floor beneath me.

I flip myself around, arms flailing in the water, to search for a surface I can break through to find air. I reach up but my hands hit a glass top to the container I now realize I am within, which is completely filled with water.

The panic rushes in as the pressure builds in my lungs, and I recognize my surroundings. I'm in Max's lab, in the tub. Except, it's sealed above me like it's never been before.

I bang on the glass, the water slowing each hit before it can have any real impact on the glass.

The water's fighting me. The heaviness in my lungs is making my head feel light, unfocused. I'm going to drown, but that's the not the scariest thought circling my brain.

I'm going to be reborn again.

I don't want to start over. I've put in way too much effort to start fresh.

I may find myself currently totally over my head, but I don't want to be forced to just give up. Faced with having a clean slate, I realize how shitty of an option that is.

I may be doomed because of what I've found out I am, but it's still better than losing that knowledge I worked so hard to find.

I don't want to forget the people who matter to me again. The Protogenoi may be manipulating reality itself, but no one is manipulating me anymore. I am free, more than I ever was under the control of Max's experiment.

I'm not going backwards.

I bang the glass hard enough to cause a splintering pain to travel down my arm. A golden spark flickers from my skin.

I am a Protogenoi.

I have to say it to myself. That is the truth I sought and found, and I never did accept it. I thought I was merely confused about what it meant for me to be a Protogenoi, but I never was. I was refusing it.

I've avoided using my power, pushing it down, forgetting even that it's there until I have no choice but to call upon it. But, it *is* there, and me not using it isn't going to change that.

I've been selfish, afraid that if I use my power I'll lose who I am. But, I need this power to give me any real chance at taking down the Protogenoi. I need to risk myself, and that doesn't just mean my life, to do what needs to be done so Havcire and Vest can be free of them.

So, if I'm going to lose my mind regardless, just like all the Protogenoi before me, because of the power that's within me, that *is* me, then I'm going to stop holding back. And, I might as well appreciate the perks of that power, and of what I am, while I'm still me.

I'm powerful. Fuck the consequences.

This time, when I pull back for the punch, I focus on that panic, fear, and recklessness heating my blood, and I wield it. My golden power lights along my arm. When it reaches my fist, it gathers there and explodes out with the impact, shattering not only the glass above me but the entire tub.

The rush of water from the destroyed tub sends me out on a wave. I manage to land on my feet in a crouch and go to stand upright, make my way back somehow to the field but—

"*Don't move,*" Phoenix warns in my head.

I freeze.

"*Can I complete this backflip?*" Dex asks.

"*I'm clearly talking to Dawn,*" Phoenix's answer comes. Then, "*What are you doing backflipping?*"

"*He's performing for me and Sin,*" Lada supplies.

"*He thought it would 'calm our nerves,'*" Sin says, sounding super enthusiastic about that.

"*Is this really what you use this telepathic connection for? Seems the opposite of helpful,*" Lucifer chimes in.

I'm inclined to agree with Lucifer. I look around Max's lab, seeing nothing out of the ordinary, beside, of course, the now broken tub.

"*Why can't I move, Phoenix?*" I ask, nerves making me impatient.

"*It isn't real,*" he explains. "*Maze is controlling what we see, and Dabar is manipulating our actual surroundings, which is littered with traps. It's too dangerous to move blindly. I'm making my way to you.*"

I must still be physically on the field surrounding the Tree of Life. And yet, I can't see a speck of grass. I don't hear the leaves of the trees whistling in the wind. Rather, I hear the usual hum of the machines of Max's lab, and I feel the stale, frigid air of the lab.

I look around again, searching for anything to clue me into the fact that this isn't real. It's like searching a photoshopped picture for any inconsistencies, but I find nothing. I reach out with my hands, feeling for anything around me I can't see, keeping my feet safely, solidly planted where they are. Still, I find nothing.

"Stop moving around," Phoenix bosses.

"How can you tell I'm moving?" I question, simply irritated at his ordering me around. But, then... *"How are you making your way to me? Why is it you can navigate this safely?"*

"I have ways."

The only thing that stops me from giving Phoenix hell right now is the fact that his answer is the most obviously evasive answer I have ever heard him utter. Normally, he's much better at answering without you even realizing he's dodged the question. The fact that he gave such a reply is evidence enough that whatever he is doing to make his way to me right now is taking up enough concentration to distract him from coming up with a more convincing omission.

I'm not willing to put his life at risk to push him further on the matter.

Yeah, I'm a considerate person.

"Can I at least stand?" is all I ask instead.

A moment passes, and I think he's not going to answer, and then a simple, "*Yes*" comes, and I realize he must have been using his "ways" to come to a conclusion for me.

"*Carefully,*" he adds on.

I roll my eyes. What does that even mean? Does he think I'm going to stand so fast that I lose my balance and accidentally take multiple steps off course and end up falling to my death in some invisible trap set by Dabar?

On second thought... fair.

I straighten up, carefully, slowly, enough so that if there were anything above me, my head would barely tap it before I processed it was there.

I let out a small sigh of relief as my knees fully straighten, and I'm no longer crouching, hunched over in fear of some unknown.

The lab disappears.

Everything around me is gone, my whole world descending into darkness, not a thing in sight except for pitch black.

Great. This is much better.

CHAPTER THIRTY-NINE

"**S** *tay still.*"

Phoenix's voice comes to me again in my head, the only thing now that I can sense, as it's not only dark around me but completely still. There is no hint of a breeze nor scent, nothing to indicate the world still exists around me. Even the ground I stand on feels like air.

"*I'm not moving a muscle,*" I insist.

"*Duck!*"

I do, bending my knees and defensively throwing my arms up over my head.

Nothing comes at me, not even a brush of air from nearby movement. I look around as if I can inspect my body for any new injuries.

"*What was that for?*" I question, my voice sounding too high in my own head.

"*Jump!*"

From my crouched position on the ground, the ground I can barely feel, I do as I'm told, quite literally following Phoenix's instructions blindly. I hop up and land back in the same crouched position, keeping low to the ground.

"I swear, Phoenix, if you're fucking with me right now—"

"I'm helping you dodge Eros's arrows. Do not move."

"You keep telling me to move!"

"Don't take a single step more than I tell you to. He's coming to you. Stand up."

I do as I'm told, hating every second, even though I know not complying could mean the death of me. Still...

"For the record, I hate this."

"I know."

If I could only have even a single one of my senses, I could stand a chance on my own. Minerva's training involved blindfolds, where I had to learn to rely on my hearing to locate my attacker, my attacker being Phoenix or Lada of course.

But, this is bad. I can't hear anything other than the voices in my head, and I have to put all my faith in one of those voices. If it were anyone other than Phoenix, I'm positive I would not so easily be jumping when told to jump.

"How is he even targeting me?"

"He can see you. Fighting stance."

I step one foot back, shoulder-width distance, and brace for a fight.

"He can see me but I can't see him?"

"Yes."

"That's so unfair."

"Did you forget the Protogenoi are targeting you?"

"Still unfair."

"Duck now! And uppercut."

I follow Phoenix's instructions in quick succession, feeling no impact when I deliver the punch, but that doesn't mean I didn't hit my target. I don't have any time to question Phoenix on whether I did or not, order after order filling my head.

"Two jabs."

"Hands out. Hit him with your power."

"Drop! "

"Sweep your legs out."

"Slip back."

I do, but I shuffle back at the same time. I thought I couldn't feel the ground beneath my feet before, but now I'm positive, as I find no purchase beneath my right foot and fall backwards into open air.

I inhale in shock, a startled scream strangling in my throat.

A crow's caw pierces the heavy silence around me.

"Dawn!"

I grasp around for purchase, but I still can't feel or see anything.

A hand catches my own, and I reach up to grab onto his arm to find more purchase. I cling to Phoenix like he's my only lifeline, beyond relieved he's finally reached me.

"*What's happened?*" Dex's alarmed question practically screams in our heads.

"*I'm okay,*" I let him know.

"*Keep quiet,*" Phoenix orders, sounding more strict than I've ever heard him. "*I need to concentrate.*"

"*If we were there, we wouldn't have to ask for updates,*" Lada points out.

Phoenix pulls me up the rest of the way back to the ground, which now feels relatively sturdy to me, as in relative to the open air I just accidentally, blindly stepped out into.

I hold onto Phoenix, partly because I want to but more importantly because he's the only solid thing I can apparently feel in this world right now.

"Where is Eros?" I question, focusing on the present threat.

"Morrigan is holding him off. Guess she is supporting you."

"I hate how often you're right."

"You love it."

I slap him away, realization dawning.

"You can't be seen helping me!" I tell him, then lower my voice, which I am glad to discover I can actually hear. "The Protogenoi will know we're up to something."

"It's a little too late. I've been running after you instead of making my way to the Tree of Life this whole time. It's pretty clear I'm on your side."

Fair point.

I feel him nearby, the heat coming off him, so I take step back forward, closer to him. There *is* still a cliff somewhere behind me.

"You should have let me fend for myself then," I protest.

"None of this matters if you die."

Right, because without me there's no Protogenoi to declare the start of the trials, no one to begin a chain of events that could lead to the final end of the Protogenoi.

"Because you need me," I say, voicing those thoughts.

"Because I love you."

I stop breathing. I want to ask if I heard him correctly, but I also can't bring myself to do it.

"No," I go with instead, stating it matter-of-fact although my heart feels like it's jumping around, playing dodgeball with my other organs. "You can't say it like that."

"Dawn—"

I feel his fingers brush against my face, but I move ever so slightly away, my stubbornness winning.

"Now?" I question. "I can't even see your face. It's like you purposefully chose to say that to me at this moment so I wouldn't have any chance of seeing if you actually mean it. Are you trying to mess with me?"

His hand finds my face, and I let him close this time as his thumb brushes against my lips before his lips follow, a feather's touch on mine.

"I love you, Dawn," he says, letting me feel the whispered words on my lips this time.

It feels like he means it.

As much as I trust Phoenix with my life, as much as I do love him, I know him and how good he is at making someone believe a lie. I want to believe it, but it's dangerous either way, whether it's true or not.

"You can't love me," I admit.

It's only going to be more painful when I ultimately lose myself to my power if he loves me. I won't only be losing me but I'll be losing him, and I'd be leaving him behind. *If* he loves me, he'll lose me.

Another cry from the crow has Phoenix drawing back, but his hands hold onto my waist, remaining to keep me anchored in the darkness that still surrounds me.

"I needed to tell you now even if you end up hating me when this is over. I needed you to at least know."

"Why would I—?"

A sudden break in the silence cuts me off. There's chanting around me. It sounds only like noise. I can't make sense of the cacophony.

"*Kiss! Kiss!*"

"*Kiss!*"

The voices in my head, however, those come in clearly, allowing me to interpret the voices outside, as well, which are all shouting the same thing.

"*K. I. S. S. Kiss!*"

"*Sin?*" I ask, wondering if he's lost his mind.

"*It was contagious,*" he responds, innocent.

Hold on—

"Are they talking about us?" I ask Phoenix.

"Yeah, they are."

My head whips around in search of the source of the voices, but I find only darkness.

"Why didn't you tell me there was an audience?"

Life and death situation here, I try to remind myself. Eros trying to kill me. The Protogenoi trying to get everyone and everything to kill me. That is what I should be focused on. Then again, Phoenix is the one who has some unnatural ability to sense when danger is headed my way, and he's currently not speaking up on the matter, so I should be fine. Plus, all I can seem to care about right now is the fact that a whole lot of Havcirians have apparently been bearing witness to me stumbling around blind. Not to mention, the supposed to be private conversation I don't even know what to make of but apparently everyone else does.

It probably doesn't help that Dabar planted it as an idea in everyone's heads during those interviews that something was going on between me and Phoenix.

"There's an audience, on bleachers and everything," Phoenix supplies, too little too late.

"Jerk," I mutter, which might as well be a confession of my love with how little venom I inject in the word.

"*We're here, too!*" Dex adds.

"*It really wasn't worth the headache of keeping them away,*" Phoenix chooses to say telepathically, so they can hear his complaints regarding them.

"*Come on, Dawn,*" Lucifer chimes in, sounding genuinely aggrieved. "*Tell him how you feel. He's clearly been in love with you for forever.*"

My mouth falls open. I quickly slam it shut, remembering that just because I can't see anyone, everyone can apparently see me. My only comfort is that Phoenix can't see either. Thank god, all the gods, or whatever, that he hasn't been able to see me fumbling throughout this.

"Let's get this over with before they throw something else at us," Phoenix says, stalling any response I could have mustered. "Ready?"

I nod, eager to get out of here.

It seems Phoenix doesn't much care to hear what I have to say about his confession. Does he think that because I haven't said it back yet that the answer must be I don't feel the same way, and he's uninterested in me voicing that? Is he so sure that I'm desperately in love with him that he doesn't even need me to confirm it out loud? Does he actually not mean it and therefore doesn't care one way or another how I feel about him? Is he playing some game where he wants the Protogenoi to think for some reason he does have these feelings for me when, in reality, he doesn't?

"Yes," I answer his question, silencing my own internal questions, "but how?"

"I'm going to lead you to the tree."

"Great. I don't understand. Can't you not see anything, also?

"I can sense it, same way I found you," he explains, if you could call that an explanation. I'm about to question him more about it, hoping irrationally he'll finally supply a real answer and one that's quick, but he adds on, "It'll make sense soon."

"That's so annoying," I tell him. "But, fine."

"You're so agreeable."

"There's a cliff nearby, and I can't see a thing."

"So?"

"I'm sorry, is my agreeability not sitting well with you?"

"It unnerves me coming from you."

"Then shut up, and get us out of here so I can go back to questioning your every move."

"Deal, but I'm going to have to trust you."

"What? Did you just say *you're* going to have to trust *me*?"

Is he trying to confuse me? That had to be a mistake. He means I have to trust him. After all, he had said he was going to lead me to the tree.

"Yes," he confirms. "The terrain is too dangerous to navigate, especially blind. The fastest way to do this is for you to make your own path to the tree using your power."

"Okay," I agree, still unsure what that has to do with him trusting me. "Which way is the tree?"

His hand takes my own and tugs me lightly in a direction. "That way."

My fingers naturally curl around to grip his hand. Even that bit of contact has my mind wandering to other things. Phoenix slips his hand back out of mine as quickly as he took hold.

Focus.

"There will still be some obstacles in the way, so you'll have to follow me to know the safest route," he continues explaining.

"Follow you? How? I can't see you. And, wait. You said I'd be making the path. How do I make the path if I'm following you?" I ask, the questions getting ahead of me.

"First, you'll need to use your power to sense me, latch onto my chaotic energy and follow it."

"What are you talking about? You don't have any. Celestials don't have any."

"I do. Try," Phoenix encourages.

This is crazy. My power comes from chaos, and said chaos does not exist naturally in Celestials like it does with humans. To the very core of our being, the matter we are made of and that our world is made of, we are chaotic. But, not Celestials. It's the entire reason I had to become a Subject, to live in Vest, where I could absorb enough power to stand up against my lovely Protogenoi mother.

Despite that, Phoenix sounds sure, and I know better than to question one's own understanding of themself. If he believes there's a drop of chaotic energy for me to latch onto within him, then I will try.

I reach out with my senses, which happens more naturally than ever, as I'm able to devote my full attention to it considering I can't see anything around me. And, thankfully, the noise from the crowd has quieted.

I feel nothing, except for Phoenix's physical presence directly in front of me. Then again, I am hyperaware of that, so I focus on ignoring that, delving deeper.

With a human, I would immediately be able to sense a certain energy vibrating off them. With a Celestial, I know if there's any chance of my sensing chaos it will be within.

A shiver travels through my body, and I resist the urge to shift from the slight twisting feeling that tickles my abdomen and spreads out to the rest of my body, tingling my limbs as if waking up from sleep. The feeling excites my body, while also making me feel like I want to sink into it and stay right there, with whatever the source of it is.

A chaotic emotion, and I am picking it up from Phoenix.

I mentally hit myself on the forehead. Celestials are beings of order, but they still feel emotion. Of course. Emotion is what I pull from most often when I use my own chaotic energy. The fact I didn't recognize that sooner is borderline embarrassing. Then again, human emotions are *loud*. I never have to dig deep to find them like I've now done with Phoenix.

"I feel it," I tell him.

"Second part of your question, you'll be making the path for me. That's where the whole trust thing comes in. I'll take a step off the path, and you'll have to catch me, and on and on, creating the path for both of us as I go."

And... it gets crazier.

"Phoenix, what the hell? You have..." I hesitate, unsure. Is this truly a secret? Can people hear us right now? Can the Protogenoi? "...wings," I finish, settling on whispering. "Why don't you use them so we don't have to play an insane version of trust falls?"

"I'm feather shy," Phoenix answers.

"Bullshit."

If only I could see his face, I might be able to read something, see some reaction to my hushed mention of his secret.

"And," he goes on, "I need to prove to you I mean it."

"Phoenix, this is a bad idea. You can't teleport here. No one will be able to save you if you fall right into a trap."

"You will. You'll catch me," he says, sounding so sure, so confident in me.

"You don't have to do this. I believe you," I insist.

"No. You don't."

"Yeah. I do."

"You believe what?"

"That you lo—"

Damn it. I can't even say it.

"I'll see you on the other side," Phoenix says, and then he's running.

CHAPTER FORTY

I can sense Phoenix because I'm still latched onto his chaotic energy, and I nearly scream when I feel him descend suddenly.

I focus instead, creating a platform of my own golden, chaotic energy beneath his feet to catch him, following the path I sensed he took and jumping on right after him.

The second my feet make contact, the platform becomes visible in the pitch dark that surrounds me, as if reacting to my presence.

Phoenix grabs my arm to steady me a second before he leaps again. I make another platform for him to land on much quicker this time and realize it won't be hard to keep track of him and trace his steps, seeing as whatever emotion it is that I'm picking up from him is drawing me in like a moth to a flame.

He jumps high next, avoiding I don't know what, and I rush to make the next stepping stone before he can drop into whatever trap waits below.

Problem is, I'm not sure I can make that jump, and I definitely can't do it blind. I create a rope from my energy in my hand and whip it up. It catches. I tug to check it's secure.

"I got you," comes Phoenix's confirmation, him being what's anchoring it up above.

I climb, hand over hand on my self-made rope of rippling energy. The benefit of creating my own rope is that the power grips me right back, making it easier for me to maintain my hold as I ascend.

Phoenix reaches down and helps me up the rest of the way onto the platform of my creation, a platform that does not offer much room for the two of us, leaving me standing face to face with him.

"Your rope touched me inappropriately," he says, stubble brushing my cheek.

I roll my eyes.

"You wish."

"Now you're getting it."

And then he's gone, jumping from the platform again, this time down.

"Now!" he shouts.

Within the next second, I create another platform beneath him, my heart skipping a beat at the cue given to me in haste.

A few more last minute cues later, I'm forced to create another platform at an unreachable height, and I decide to try something new.

Rolling my shoulders, I close my eyes, something about the action adding to my ability to concentrate even when already surrounded by nothing but darkness.

I can create anything, I tell myself. Chaos is potential energy, looking for an outlet. I give it one.

Line by line I build up the image in my mind, each line I imagine adding strength to the structure, while remaining light. It's like sketching. I put it all together, shaping them fully and open my eyes, amazed to find sparking, golden wings sprouting from my back, shaped similarly to hummingbird wings.

I smile despite everything. Everyone wishes they could fly. Turns out, I can, when I'm not busy living in denial.

With little more than a thought, the wings move fast, lifting me up, much faster than my self-made rope method.

The noise of the crowd rises as I do, but this time they have a new focus. They're chanting my name.

"So, Havcirians generally go crazy for wings?" I ask Phoenix, as I land beside him.

"Eros has actually stopped fighting Morrigan to stare."

"Are you going to claim you simply don't like attention, and that is why you keep yours a secret?" I ask, poking at that subject again.

"I would never make such an outrageous claim."

"Well, I guess I don't really need you from here. I'll just fly on over myself," I say, taking a step forward, but his hand on my shoulder stops me.

"That's the wrong way," he says, amusement in his voice.

He comes to stand behind me, a hand on either of my shoulders and shifts me around in what I assume is the correct direction.

"But," he goes on, "you are right. You don't need me. It's a straight shot from here. Make a bridge, about thirteen feet long, then jump down. I'll be behind you."

"I could pick you up and fly us over," I offer, arms already out and ready for Phoenix to jump in them.

"As enticing as that sounds, the bridge might be safer, unless that is you've already mastered flying and can guarantee you can fly in a straight, horizontal line to avoid the obstacles Dabar's got placed both above and below us."

With a shrug of my shoulders, I'm back in the dark, the wings I created disappearing. I extend my arms to focus my power straight ahead of me, in the direction Phoenix pointed me in.

"If I knew someone with wings, they could give me flying lessons," I venture. "Too bad I don't."

I imagine a smooth boardwalk, straight across, thirteen feet long like Phoenix had described. The yellow brick road comes to mind, and I suspect that what I am crafting into creation will highly resemble the fabled road from *The Wizard of Oz*.

My first step forward onto the bridge confirms that theory when it shines in the darkness around me upon contact.

I still can't see it, but I know that the Tree of Life lies just ahead, at the end of this bridge. It's where my barrier has remained up this whole time, keeping the Protogenoi out of Havcire, and it could remain there forever, or at least till I die, because no one can outright reverse the power of a Protogenoi, and that is what I am, or at least it is the source of my power.

But, leaving the barrier up is not an option. Even if I could keep avoiding the death traps the Protogenoi set for me, I can't leave Vest vulnerable. And, like Sin said, I won't run from a fight. If I don't face the Protogenoi now, I'm only leaving them to be someone else's problem in the future. So, I reach the end of the bridge, and I step off.

It's a bit of a fall down to the ground but, finally, I can see it. I can see the grass beneath my feet, the sunlight shining down from above. My bridge casts a shadow down on me, drawing my attention back to the direction from which I came.

The open field is so full of deadly obstacles that I can't even see across to the other side where I started. Planks of wood floating in the air, an obstacle course raised high above the ground, offers a way across. But, the planks are set at odd angles, some mere barriers, being completely vertical. Some are not so high up that a fall from their surface would have killed me. But, sharp, metal spikes cover every inch of the ground, a fall meaning impalement.

All in all, it looks like a treacherous jungle gym. If I wasn't here standing, I would find it hard to believe Phoenix managed to help me navigate through that mess.

The quite large audience sits on either side on stadium-like seats, made from the earth itself, like terraces. I can't find Sin, Dex, or Lada in the crowd, but everyone is screaming the same thing now.

"Get the apple!"

You need to retrieve an apple from the Tree of Life to win Ascension. But, that's not what I'm here for.

Phoenix jumps down from my bridge, and I dissolve it, the energy absorbing back through my skin.

I turn my attention to the Tree of Life in front of me and the barrier made from my energy surrounding its trunk with a circumference of over twenty meters, which looks like it was sculpted to consist of overlapping circles and ovals, but I know it wasn't carved by any being. It's natural, every circle interlocked with an oval representing how Vest and Havcire remain connected.

"Get the apple!"

I'm not here to win Ascension. I don't need anything from this tree. I just need to remove the barrier surrounding it, and there's no reason to wait.

I shatter it with a simple thought.

CHAPTER FORTY-ONE

C racks form all across the golden barrier, and it falls apart without a sound.

Startled shouts fill the air, and I look to find that the terraces surrounding the field have disappeared, the ground flattening out once again, the seats for the Havcirians who've come to witness Ascension suddenly gone. They fall.

I spot Dex, levitating, siphoning someone's power. He holds his hands up, stalling the fall of many Havcirians around him.

The field is an empty field again, treacherous obstacle course gone.

My wrist burns. I look down to find the Ascension tattoo disappearing from my skin. The lines of ink flake off and blow away like ashes, leaving my wrist bare.

Ascension's over. It was never about retrieving an apple from the Tree of Life. It was all about my barriers coming down, the portals being reopened.

Phoenix grips my shoulders, and he turns me away from the crowd to look at him. For the first time ever, I see panic in his expression, an urgency. Phoenix doesn't panic. He plans for everything, times everything to a tee. But, I can see it, and it sets my hands trembling.

He glances anxiously at the tree, then back to me.

"You'll never be like them," he insists, the ice in his green eyes biting into mine.

I shake my head, too overwhelmed by his intensity to even begin to understand where he is coming from, what he is referring to.

"Like who?" I ask.

"The Protogenoi," he answers. "Their problem is that they never understood what it was to just live, too focused on power and control from the very start. That could never be you."

My head's still shaking, now in denial. I feel like a bobblehead, unable to stop the action, but it's all I can do. The Protogenoi are coming right now. We don't have time for this.

No matter how much I'm reassured by others that I could be the exception and how much my stubborn self is inclined to believe it's true, no one can make any guarantees.

"You don't know that for sure," I tell him. "I want to believe it, too, but how can I avoid a fate that happened to every single one of them?"

"Because, we are who we choose to be."

He says it like he believes that more than anything, like it's a belief that's motivated him his entire life. For me, it's like a blow right to my chest because I so wish it rang true for me. Like I told

Sin, though, Max more than proved that I have little choice in who I am, nature setting me so solidly down certain paths.

I am who I am. Human, but also Protogenoi.

I blamed Max and others for years for taking away my freedom, manipulating my lives, but I was just as much a slave to my own nature. And, I was fine with that, satisfied with who I was at my core. And then, I learned part of that core was being Protogenoi.

The ground trembles beneath our feet. They're coming.

Phoenix barely acknowledges it, instead holding out a shiny, red apple, which looks like it belongs in a fairytale. An apple from the Tree of Life.

I guess the false task of Ascension was completed after all, and Phoenix won, being the first to take an apple.

An apple from the Tree of Life gives you the truth you are most reluctant to face. He offers it up like a dare, and I take it. I'm about to challenge the most dangerous and powerful beings that exist. If I can't face the damn truth, then what chance do I have?

I bite into it.

I watch the bird, its wings red and orange flames, lazily weaving between the low-hanging branches of the Tree of Life. It takes up my entire world, as I stare up at it from my position on the ground, its movements captivating me, while Phoenix's words tell a story.

He lies next to me, looking a few years older than me, making him around eight years old. I know, like the bird I watch, his appearance is an illusion. He's told me his real age, which I can barely wrap my head around being so old. But, he's explained to me before that he likes appearing near my age when he's with me so he doesn't have to look down at me. I think he means literally, but he did also tell me that when he crafts an illusion of his younger self, his mental age adjusts as well.

"The five Protogenoi ruled with no care for those below them, as they had an unimaginable amount of power," Phoenix begins a story I've heard many times, but one that I still enjoy listening to when he tells it. "Dabar could control reality itself. Maze controlled minds. Magister mastered time, how to move it and how to see it, the past, present, and future. Void was the only being who could cause absolute destruction, the type of death where no life could possibly exist after. Lastly, Chaos had power over anything that did not fall under the others, anything lacking order. There was a legend of a sixth—"

"A sixth Protogenoi?" I ask, turning my head to look at him, this part of the story different.

He doesn't turn to face me, but his mouth lifts slightly in a smile before going on.

"A sixth Protogenoi," he confirms, "rumored to have power over all physical matter."

I listen, my attention fully captured. I've never before heard of a sixth Protogenoi.

"He began as the Protogenoi's secret, sent to live amongst the Celestials and Incanters to spy on them and report back if there were ever talk of rebellion. Over time, the other Protogenoi suspected him of sympathizing too much with the Celestials and Incanters, those 'below him.' Dabar thought that if the sixth Protogenoi could see what it was really like to be one of them, to be so powerless, then he'd leave behind his false sympathies. So, Dabar, for seven light phases and seven dark phases, made the sixth Protogenoi a reality where he no longer had his power over physical matter. He was as good as human, in a time before humans even existed."

My eyes widen, and I'm unable to stop myself from interrupting.

"He was the first human ever?" I ask.

For some time, Phoenix doesn't respond, and I think maybe I hurt his feelings by talking during his story.

"I guess you could see it like that," he says, and I realize he was actually just thinking over the answer in his silence.

I smile, thinking about how the first ever human, even if it was just for a short time, came from one of the most powerful beings in the world... according to this story.

"Dabar's plan backfired," Phoenix goes on. "The sixth Protogenoi grew to respect the Celestials and Incanters more after that, recognizing their true strength, as it takes great power to live a life worth living when you're not born with that power at your fingertips. When talk of rebellion began, not only did he not report it to the other

Protogenoi, but he supported it. When the war started, he fought against the other Protogenoi."

"What was his name?" I ask, hearing the tone Phoenix takes on when he's concluded a story. Except, like many times before, I want more information.

"According to legend?"

"No," I deadpan really well, something I learned from Phoenix, "in real life."

I roll my eyes. Of course according to legend! He already told me the story was just a story.

"The Protogenoi called him Nephil after the day he spent human, as it means to fall, and they saw becoming human as something less than. But," he pauses, turning to look at me now, pulling his own mind back to reality, "We are who we choose to be."

The story Phoenix told me of how he got his scar. It mirrors the legend too closely. A punishment from Dabar, according to Phoenix, for being able to escape the Protogenoi's traps with his teleportation. But, according to the legend, a punishment for sympathizing with Celestials and Incanters.

He could find his way, blind, through the Ascension challenge. He could *sense* where I was. He could *sense* where the traps were.

The sixth Protogenoi has control over physical matter. The sixth Protogenoi could find his way blindly through an obstacle course by sensing the matter that composed it.

His wings. If the sixth Protogenoi was known to have wings, he would want to keep them hidden to keep his identity hidden.

We are who we choose to be. He chose his own name, rejected the one given to him. He chose a new identity, to be a Celestial.

The big secret he still held, that he was sure would be the last straw, that I'd never see him the same way.

An apple from the Tree of Life doesn't reveal what you don't know, but the truth you are most reluctant to face.

I knew everything I needed to know to put it together; and yet, I didn't.

We are who we choose to be.

Not all the Protogenoi succumbed to their power. One chose a different path.

I spit out the piece of apple. With the magic gone, it's turned bitter in my mouth, and I open my eyes to find the rest of the apple in my hand has turned black.

Phoenix no longer stands right in front of me, but a considerable distance away, eyes trained on the Tree of Life.

From the huge trunk, through the low hanging branches of the wide canopy, the four Protogenoi step out. The tree itself is a shimmering portal now, allowing them access. Void,

Maze, Magister, and Dabar, whose attention immediately falls on Phoenix, a cruel smile lighting his unnaturally sharp face.

"Congratulations on your win, Nephil."

Though I knew, and the Tree of Life itself forced me recognize it, the name still settles in my stomach like a boulder.

Phoenix is Nephil, the sixth Protogenoi.

CHAPTER FORTY-TWO

I step forward to do as planned, declare the trials, even though no one seems to have any interest in me anymore now that I've done my part and lowered the barrier blocking the portal.

I barely feel the ground beneath my feet. I think people are talking. I think the crowd is running from their now destroyed seats. But, my mind is numb, on autopilot, but autopilot has stalled, as well. My broken autopilot is releasing a hum that vibrates through my brain, trying to restart but failing.

Someone steps up from behind me in my peripheral. I have enough survival instincts still functioning to take a defensive step away and raise my guard, but then I realize it's Lucifer. He doesn't look at me, just stands at my side, and I find it gives me more relief than I ever could have expected.

I just have to speak. I get so far as opening my mouth but—

Phoenix is the sixth Protogenoi.

The simple, logical conclusions calculate. If I declare these trials, he will be required to take part in them, and only one Protogenoi can come out alive. I'm one. He's one.

I said I'd risk my own life to stop the Protogenoi, but how could he expect I'd agree to this? He wanted me to know. He handed me the apple. I don't understand—

"I declare the Protogenoi—"

Phoenix's voice breaks through the ringing numbness of my head, the shock of what he's saying enough to snap me back to the present.

"Think about this," Dabar interrupts, hastily. "Is that really what you want?"

He was going to declare the Protogenoi Trials himself, something, I realize, he knew he could do without me all along, as he is a Protogenoi. He didn't need me, but he did need me to take down the barriers to let the other Protogenoi through.

He used me. He was always using me, but I at least thought I was aware of how I was being used, that I had agreed to everything. Somehow, this hurts more than finding out that he's been keeping from me, the whole time I've known him, who he truly is.

He's done with me now. In fact, neither Phoenix nor any of the other Protogenoi even spare me a look. I guess Phoenix had the same interest in me as they did, and it only extended as far as getting those barriers down so they could get through to Havcire.

I may have Protogenoi power flowing through my veins, but they don't see me as such. I was just a means to an end, whether they got there through my death or me willingly taking down the barriers, they couldn't have cared less.

As if sensing my thoughts, Dabar glances my way but just as quickly looks away. He waves his hand in a dismissive gesture, a cue, but for what, I don't know.

But then, Void turns to face me and simply looks up. I see the shadows from the large hood draped over his face begin to lift, and then I'm staring at Lucifer's back as he falls to the ground before me, my gaze falling right along with him, my knees giving out, bringing the rest of me down with him as I realize what's happened. What he's done. What Dabar so casually, uncaringly ordered done without a single word.

I pull Lucifer into my lap. His familiar brown eyes stare up at me, but they might as well be foreign because I have never before seen them rimmed with tears.

No Protogenoi power can be directly reversed. Void's stare means instant, permanent death. At least, that's what I thought, but Lucifer still breathes as the color drains from his every feature.

My vision is blurry. I'm afraid to take my eyes off him for even a second, but I look to Phoenix, despite everything, for something. Help.

I see it now, how he fits in with the others, with that arrogance he's always worn proudly. Lucifer, practically family, lies dying in my arms, but he doesn't spare him even a glance, as if it's all insignificant, below him.

He rolls his eyes at the Protogenoi.

"Of course this is what I want," he answers them.

To declare the trials. That's all he cares about.

Even though their intended target was me, the Protogenoi don't spare us a glance either.

"Why?" I ask Lucifer, a tear escaping as I look back down at him. It falls on his face, and I wipe it away as quick as possible. "Why would you—?"

"I remember, Dawn."

His voice is strangled, weak. And yet, I'm the one who can't speak.

"Minerva, genius she is, figured it all out. She brought Styx to me to make me remember," he explains.

Lucifer's literally fading before my eyes, his skin near translucent. I hold him tighter. My head shakes.

"You can't die. You're Council. We need you. When this is over, we need you. I need you. Dex—"

I choke on a sob.

Lucifer's face crumbles at the mention of Dex.

"Tell him I only regret not having more time with him."

"We can get you to an Incanter, heal you. You'll survive. Maybe—"

"Raising you was the best choice we made."

He's gone. No final exhale. No body left. My arms are suddenly empty, and I kneel on the ground alone.

He sacrificed himself for me. I was so focused on Phoenix and Sin's stupid agreement, insisting they didn't risk their lives for mine, and I let Lucifer jump right in front of me.

"What's happening?" Dex asks.

I forget he can speak in my head, and I look up, expecting to find him before me voicing the question. But, it's the Protogenoi who stand there.

They don't care. I'm disposable now that I've played my role. Lucifer was disposable to them. It's my first time seeing them in person, but they might as well be the statues I looked up at from the pool of the fountain. When their faces do show emotion, it feels programmed, one dimensional.

I also can't sense a single bit of chaos off them. They're empty.

Maze's eyes dart around. Though he doesn't actually seem to see a single thing around us, a smile lifts his lips in amusement at something. He reminds me of a clown, except his hair and everything else about his appearance is immaculate.

My breath quickens when I look at Void, but not in fear. The hood of his dark cape is pulled over his head, hiding the majority of his face, which is shrouded back in shadow, all light dying before it can touch him. I'm feeling homicidal, not suicidal, so I don't keep my attention on him for long.

Magister stares right at me, but her eyes are glazed over, and I'm positive she can't actually see me. While Maze looks like a clown come from a circus, Magister looks like a marionette who's fighting to hold herself up out of sheer force of will. Her shoulders droop, but her chin lifts her head up high, as if to counterbalance.

"*Teleport us back to you, Phoenix,*" Sin orders.

I notice the now emptied out surrounding area. Everyone has fled. No Sin, Dex, or Lada in sight.

"*I thought he had teleported you here,*" I manage to reply.

"*He sent us back the moment the Protogenoi arrived.*"

"The Protogenoi have abused their power for too long," Phoenix continues, "including against me, keeping me under your boot, forcing me to pretend to be a Celestial so you could use me to spy. I'm done. I'll be the only remaining Protogenoi when this is over."

Something sparks in Dabar's unnatural purple eyes. Pure hatred.

I slowly get back to my feet, my knees shaking beneath me, but I manage to stay upright.

I search the others' faces for any hint toward how they feel about Phoenix but have no luck. They were the first beings to exist, as hard as that is to wrap my mind around. They were together from the beginning, and the only read I can get on them from this reunion is Dabar's extreme dislike for Phoenix. But...

Chaos had recognized him, when she was possessing Minerva's body. She'd said, "I remember you" and looked at him with such familiarity. I couldn't imagine then why she would have reacted that way, so I brushed it off, thinking I'd imagined it.

She hadn't said anything more, but he was their spy after all, and maybe she figured he was still keeping up the act. But, I should have seen it.

Her only reaction to him was amusement. Maybe I'm misinterpreting, but it seems Dabar's hate for Phoenix is personal.

"I'm going to kill him," Lada chimes in. *"I knew he was up to something."*

"So you've finally worked up the courage to face us, to take your revenge one on one rather than hiding behind a war you orchestrated behind the scenes, using Celestials and Incanters to fight for you?" Dabar baits Phoenix.

"It's not safe here," I tell them.

I feel like a fly on the wall. Less than. They don't even care to swat me, but that doesn't mean that they couldn't turn their attention back to me at any point and easily accomplish that.

"Which is exactly why we should be there with you," Dex argues.

But, it doesn't matter. The person who can teleport them isn't coming to the phone right now.

"War?" Phoenix asks, overkilling it at playing dumb. "I don't know what you're talking about. I don't remember any war."

"He's too busy talking to his kin," I say, and I swear Phoenix grimaces.

Lucifer just died right in front of him, and he showed no reaction from what I observed. He didn't even look at him. He can't have just reacted to anything he heard me say.

"*To who?*" Dex asks.

It hits me that, in this new reality made by Dabar, he placed Phoenix right back in the same position he'd been in before the Firstlast War. Phoenix must have believed at the start that he was a spy for his fellow Protogenoi.

And still, he was going behind their backs to help the Celestials and Incanters, providing them resources for free that they otherwise would have had to risk their lives, or more, for.

I can't imagine what that must have been like for him when we got our memories back, to realize that he'd fallen into the same exact role he'd been stuck in all those centuries ago. No, not fallen, but manipulated back into it by Dabar. And, I do have some sense of how that made him feel.

He was angry, and he let me see it. He couldn't stand that a mere thought from Dabar trapped him back in a place he worked so hard to free himself from. Of course, I hadn't known the details before when he'd confessed that. Now I do.

"*Phoenix is the sixth Protogenoi,*" I blurt.

A stunned silence follows but I realize, at least for one of them, this is no surprise, and I direct my next thought at him.

"*But you already knew that.*"

This is what Sin was trying to convince Phoenix to tell me. He saw the image of the wings in the lair, apparently a symbol few know represents the sixth Protogenoi, Sin being one of those few and maybe the only one to put it fully together who Phoenix is.

After he found out Maze sent Phoenix after me, his insistence that I tell him who won the fight when it came down to me and Phoenix... He not only knew, but he knew what it meant for us both to be Protogenoi, that we'd end up here.

I don't even need Sin's confirmation, and I don't get it. I can only imagine he has two others to explain himself to at the moment.

"Is that true?" Dabar asks of Maze, without even sparing him a glance.

"No," Maze supplies, eyes still wandering everywhere, landing nowhere. "He remembers."

Phoenix is corrupt just like the other Protogenoi. He said he wants to be the only remaining Protogenoi. It makes the most sense. It is the most simple answer, that Phoenix did this all to have the power for himself. He lied to me about who he was and his true motivations. He never needed me to declare the trials, only open the portal so he could declare the trials and win them.

The simplest explanation is most often the correct one. Except, if I know anything about Phoenix without a doubt, it's that he is a talented liar. He knows how to make a lie sound like the simplest explanation, how to tell the lie that others will be most likely to take at face value. It's when he gives you the truth that things sound most convoluted. So, the simple admission that he's no different from the other Protogenoi and has done this for revenge against them and for power...

I don't believe it.

"How did you get your memory back?" Dabar asks, frustration coating his voice.

I believe the story he told me under this tree when he had nothing to prove to me, when I didn't even know he was telling me his own story. Regardless of everything else, I believe he truly cares for the Celestials and Incanters, for everyone. It's for them, not himself.

He just watched Lucifer *die*.

But, he didn't, did he? He refused to look. He refused to show he cared. He's telling the Protogenoi his motivations for wanting to begin these trials for a reason. He wants them to believe it. Showing a care for Lucifer would detract from that goal.

He wants to win these trials so he can stop the other Protogenoi and protect everyone else. Everyone except me. I'll be forced to fight against him in those very trials.

Still, even if I believe I'm right about his motivations, he just let Lucifer die. Dabar is to blame. Void is to blame, but how could Phoenix act like he didn't even care? Even if it's just an act, to act that cold, to not come to Lucifer's side— But, I can't think like that right now. I have to figure this out.

"What does it matter how?" Void asks, voice so deep that I swear I can feel the bass of it rumbling up through the ground. He moves to pull his hood back. "Let's finally end him."

Magister's arm shoots out, stopping him, even though her eyes are still cloudy, seemingly unseeing. She shakes her head, slowly, in warning.

Void shakes her off but makes no further attempts to remove his hood.

"It doesn't matter how," Phoenix answers Void, despite the question clearly not having been directed at him, "because no matter how many new realities Dabar creates, there'll be a new way I can outsmart him in each and every one."

Dabar's face looks like it's about to crack from anger. He whips to face Void.

"Do it."

Void yanks his hood back without any hesitation.

He looks to Phoenix.

My power explodes around me.

CHAPTER FORTY-THREE

A wall of golden electricity stands between Phoenix and me and the Protogenoi. Void looks right at Phoenix, but Phoenix still stands, alive. A Protogenoi's power may not be able to be reversed, but my golden energy is holding up against it.

There is a hint of surprise in each of their expressions. I'm the one they used and were ready to discard of so easily, and I'm fighting back, holding my own. I am one of them, regardless of what they think or what I want.

I feel Void's power. It wants to consume my own, pulling on it, rather than trying to break through. It wants to take everything from me and more.

So, I pull on everything I have. Every particle of my physical being that serves its own purpose but, at its core, contains chaotic, potential energy. Every single atom that my body contains, that makes me, is a source of power.

Sensing the chaos in everything that I am, ironically, for the first time in a long time, I am wholly convinced of my humanity.

My emotions are another source. Betrayal at being lied to again. Fear for the same person who lied to me. My anger. My grief. My doubt. My resolve.

I will fight to the death against the other Protogenoi. Against Phoenix.

Pain at that thought only adds to my power. Because, no matter what, I do love him. I still do. The sixth Protogenoi. He is proof there is another possible future for me that doesn't involve submitting to power above all else and losing my very self in the process.

He's tricked me again to finally get his chance to kill the other Protogenoi. Not a day ago, I actually believed he'd risk his life for my own, but he was only trying to get me this far. Now, I realize he's willing to take my life himself if it means accomplishing what he's strived for since before I was even born.

Before I was even born.

How could I possibly think I stand a chance against them? I don't have the strength. I have a drop of a Protogenoi's power, but I am just human. I've lived a fraction of the time the other Protogenoi have.

I can feel Void's power, and it is pure destruction. He'll take every ounce of my power and blink it into nothing, and then he'll just as easily do the same to me.

Void's looking at me. My power flickers, but the wall holds. For now.

A hand grabs my chin, forcing me to look away from Void's gaze, shimmering from behind my wall. Although it's my own wall of energy I look through, it only makes him look more formidable, otherworldly.

Phoenix stands before me.

"Don't let him in," he insists.

"I'm trying," I insist right back, indicating my extended arms from which the golden wall stems from.

"Not that. Having any negative thoughts?"

"Lucifer just died in case you didn't notice!" Damn it. Tears threaten again. I focus on my anger instead. "You betrayed me. Again. Five Protogenoi, including you, are planning to kill me, and I'm weak. Of course I'm having negative thoughts!"

I'm not strong enough. My wall is going to fall. Void will be able to destroy me with one look.

"That's Maze," Phoenix says, not missing a beat. "Keep him out of your head."

I let out a growl of frustration, knowing for sure at least that feeling is real and mine, and I latch onto the other source of power I can to fortify my wall. I pull on it for the first time without any hesitation because it is *my* power now, not Chaos's, and there is at least one Protogenoi who successfully fought his nature. If he managed, I sure as hell can.

I am a Protogenoi, but it will not define me.

Red joins the gold around me. I take it from Phoenix, feeling and understanding the meaning of it this time as I absorb the power.

Humans are naturally chaotic, not Incanters, not Celestials, and definitely not Protogenoi. But, there is one emotion chaotic enough to steal even from a Protogenoi if they are capable of feeling it, and Phoenix, despite everything, feels it.

He was telling the truth. He loves me.

As I stare back at him, the red and gold energy mixing together to solidify the wall guarding us against the other Protogenoi, I can see it in those glacier green eyes.

He loves me, but he will kill me.

To permanently end the reign of the Protogenoi, he will do anything. I vowed to Styx that I would risk my own life to see their end. The vow wasn't necessary, though, because I have never run away from a fight. Where that will leave Phoenix and I, I don't know, but I'm not backing down now.

"I declare the Protogenoi Trials, with full acknowledgment of the risk, for the chance to be sole ruler," I say the words that Sin drilled into my head so I'd be ready for this.

I shout them to ensure the four on the other side of my protective wall of energy hear, but they echo inside me, and I am sure they do the same for the others.

I let go, absorbing the power back into me, returning what isn't mine back to Phoenix.

We all face each other, no barrier left between us, but the others make no move to attack. It's official.

We all must abide by the trials.

Acknowledgements

Thank you to my parents, always the first readers of whatever I write and my greatest supporters.

To my friends and family, thank you for your help in making life enjoyable when I'm not absorbed in a fantasy world, for the support and motivation.

Vic Gonzalez, thank you, once again, for creating such beautiful cover art and making sense of my nonsensical ideas.

Thank you to the readers! It was a joy to write this book and continue the story for these characters, and I hope you experience just as much joy reading it. I love sharing this world, and the people that exist in it, with all of you. Together, we make it real.

About the Author

Molly C. Gross grew up in Boca Raton, Florida and then decided to switch coasts and move to another equally warm place, Los Angeles. Molly studied criminal justice, psychology, and creative writing in undergrad, before going on to get her masters in screenwriting. When not boxing, dancing, watching TV, or reading, she's writing in one form or another, incorporating her love for fantasy, psychology, and mystery.

www.ingramcontent.com/pod-product-compliance
Lightning Source LLC
Chambersburg PA
CBHW020006120726
47903CB00004B/1153